MAYHEM, MURDER AND MARIJUANA

The Los Angeles Marijuana War

ARIK KAPLAN

ISBN: 978-1-54391-765-9 (print)
ISBN: 978-1-54391-766-6 (ebook)

PREFACE

In 2011, the author aggressively started purchasing legal medical marijuana dispensaries in Los Angeles County. This series is divided into three distinct books dealing with various facets of the MMJ industry. The first book deals with my initial investments in dispensaries, and the antagonistic confrontations with illegal growers and dishonest dealers.

Due to the legal uncertainties of the marijuana industry and the tremendous profitability, the business is prey to individuals looking to make a quick buck in any deceitful manner possible. In 2013, the California marijuana industry was divided between legal dispensaries, and an enormous illegal market dominated by street thugs. Although the story is jam-packed with factual violent events, this doesn't mean the MMJ industry is inherently violent. The violence tends to be merely associated with the illegal fringe elements.

Although this is a work of fiction, the story is based on actual events. Rumors of my writing this novel have circulated in the southern California cannabis industry. I have received death threats from illegal MMJ cultivators, and consequently I have decided it's best to use a pseudonym rather than disclose my identity.

I want to thank Carissa Bluestone, Vice President of Kirkus Editorial, for her excellent work editing my manuscript.

CHAPTER 1

Davao, Philippines and Los Angeles, CA

Not far from the city of Davao, on the southern Philippine island of Mindanao, is a sprawling, impoverished village where squatters have built shacks on every parcel of neglected land. Leaky tin roofs and warped plywood walls provided sparse shelter for large families and, often, a few chickens. The annual monsoon season, starting in late June, brings calamity: flooding, collapsing shacks, and death.

Mindanao is the second largest island of the country's 7,100 islands, and home to the Moro National Liberation Front (MNLF)--an Islamist terrorist group. A negotiated peace was imposed on Davao after a decade of internecine warfare. The structure of the peace was the MNLF agreed to eschew attacking the city, and the Davao Mayor acquiesced not to send his cold-blooded anti-terrorism corps into the countryside-the stronghold of the MNLF.

It's here where Pacifico Bing de Asis got his very humble start. Bing's parents were already among the few lucky ones in the village—they had consistent work on an American naval base south of Davao—but their fortunes increased precipitously with Bing's arrival, thanks to an ingenious ploy ICE officers call the Virgin Maria

Reenactment. When Bing's mother was five months pregnant with him, her husband sent her to "visit relatives" in Monterey, California, on a hard-to-obtain tourist visa. A month prior to the flight, despite the pernicious effect on the embryo, she ate only one small meal per day. Under a loose-fitting blouse, she corseted her minuscule baby bump to hide her pregnancy from the US immigration officers at San Francisco International Airport. This cunning move helped her achieve American citizenship for her child. She gave birth to baby Bing while on "vacation"—at the Monterey Peninsula Hospital.

Bing and his mother did return to the village near Davao, where the family lived on and off until Bing was fourteen. Then his parents applied for, and passed, a US immigration interview. Soon the entire clan was granted a Family Immigration Visa from the American Embassy in Manila. The three de Asises departed Davao for Reseda, California, where they shared one room in an aunt's house.

The family settled in to California life. Bing's father worked as a clerk, and his mother was a companion for an elderly lady in Sherman Oaks. But eternally embarrassed by his hard-working parents, who couldn't shed their thick Cebuano accents, Bing would tell all his friends that his father was a CPA, and his mother was both a registered nurse and a medical doctor.

Bing envied the Jewish kids at Manchester High School, whose parents owned large and expensive homes with swimming pools south of Ventura Boulevard in Sherman Oaks and Encino. One morning while walking to school, Bing revealed a secret to his best friend, Morrison Guzman, otherwise known as M. "I'm converting to Judaism."

M was one-half Irish on his mother's side and one-half Mexican from his now missing father. M's mom had married a champion Mexican surfer one night after drinking too many tequila shots at the Gato Taco bar and restaurant, a tourist trap for American visitors looking to get drunk and laid in Ensenada. That didn't mean he was open-minded about cross-cultural matters.

M said, "A *Jew*? What the fuck? You're Catholic like me. I never go to church, but I sure as hell wouldn't be a . . . *Jew*. Why the hell do you want to be a fucking Jew?"

"Look at our friends," Bing said. "All the poor kids are Latino. All the rich kids live south of Ventura and are Jewish. Shit. My new motto is 'Be a Jew and be rich.'"

The two knuckleheads continued to debate the pros and cons of being a Jew as they walked to school. Though they ignored what should have been Bing's paramount concern—that conversion would mean getting his inconsequential Schwanzstucker clipped.

Los Angeles schools range from commendable to atrocious. Elite students generating near-perfect SAT scores generally attend Harvard-Westlake School on Coldwater Canyon Boulevard. Athletes like John Elway made the San Fernando Valley a hotbed for future football stars. The Crossroads School for the Arts & Sciences in Santa Monica produces the musicians that head to the East Coast conservatories and the actors who attend New York University's Tisch School of the Arts. Manchester High School produced . . . a 60 percent dropout rate for Hispanic boys.

The teachers at Manchester High excelled at one thing: cognitive dissonance. Aware that their teachers were blind to the drug dealings at the school, Bing and M followed the Manchester High tradition of dealing marijuana (and harder drugs) on and off campus. Bing also liked to smoke weed before and after classes, though M never smoked "the product"— he only worked diligently to sell it.

The budding entrepreneurs mocked the few serious students and ignored their homework assignments. The two boys felt like they were in on a little secret—that there was indeed a future without attending college, or even most of high school. Regardless, they both managed to graduate, and then had an easy transition into the real world—they just expanded their drug trade.

A few years after graduating high school, each boy concluded he was best at selling marijuana and at establishing relationships with dispensaries, dealers, or other buyers. And they were both correct. M was sleazy handsome, simpleminded but charming, and sold his weed to giggly bud-tenders at valley dispensaries either for cash, or at a higher price if on consignment for seven days.

It took Bing about eighteen months to recognize that he would be perceptibly better off working unaided by his high school friend. In the course of time, Bing negotiated an amicable division of their joint business dealings. M had no idea Bing had already been selling scads of marijuana across state lines with new east coast partners for at least two years. Apparently Morrison would remain friends with the devil if it helped him make money, and no reconciliation was necessary because the two boys coequally yearned for independence to strike out their own.

Despite his charms, M struggled for years to make ends meet, though that didn't stop him from eventually marrying a Persian-born woman named Nonie, eight years his senior. They had two daughters. The oldest was named Athena and later came LadyBrianna. Having more fun than money, they called the girls M&M's, for their Mexican and Muslim heritage.

The core development in Bing's life transpired about four years after graduating Manchester High. The occurrence was a conversation he had while sitting at a bar in Toluca Lake. It thoroughly altered his business.

Bing recounted this to M one night during an enchilada dinner. "This Israeli bar owner had spent a tremendous amount of money to make his bar resemble some hot location he liked on Third Street. Somewhere, I think, between Fairfax and La Cienega. It was called El . . . El . . . something in Mexican."

M raised an eyebrow at the reference to a new language (Mexican?!), but didn't bother correcting his friend.

"Anyway, this Israeli dude," Bing continued, "well, this dude is whining about not having customers, and he's losing tons of money. Next he looks right at me, and says he would pay a lot of money to someone who has the right contacts. Man, this dude needs women in his joint to attract clients."

"Yeah," M said, "So what happened, dude?"

"Simple," Bing said. "I asked him what he would pay me if I filled the bar with chicks. Shit. All I had to do was look in my client book and select the top-twenty skanky babes who bought weed from me? Right?"

So, Bing became a card-carrying pimp, utilizing his extensive contacts to fill bars and nightclubs with either out-of-control teenagers or his certifiable red-light women. He became a favorite of the local club owners since he could fill any location with a few phone calls. Eventually, he met a number of important Hollywood executives who frequented the same clubs. They then happily attended the parties Bing threw in his leased home in Studio City, which was not far from NBC, Universal Studios, and about five hundred adult film studios in the Valley.

Bing's house was on a narrow street that became jam-packed with cars during his parties. Not surprisingly, he soon received an eviction warning from his landlord for noise complaints—and for the vodka bottles and condoms strewn the length of the block.

Shortly after the hand-delivered warning was served, screams echoed through the hills near Bing's home. Two dead bodies, from overdoses, were discovered in one of Bing's spare bedrooms by a Sony exec and his "companion" for the evening, a fifteen-year-old Oakwood High School student. That fracas combined with the destruction of the walls in the living room, where Bing and his imbecilic roommates played handball, allowed the landlord to legally and swiftly evict Bing. This barely fazed him, though. Business was so good, that he and his roommates rented a mansion in the Nichols Canyon area of the Hollywood Hills—and paid an unheard of nine months' security deposit. Star Maps described the house as the former residence of Kevin Costner. Bing deemed this prominent residence perfect for his lifestyle, and sufficiently large to accommodate his business operations.

Independence from M allowed Bing to succeed despite, or because of, Bing's quirky personality. Bing continued to make it big. His new East Coast partners permitted him the good fortune to distribute grass grown in the San Fernando Valley to clients in downtown Atlanta and its suburbs. He quickly set his sights on more Southern cities—customers there would pay double the price for weed from Southern California.

Apparently Bing was unconcerned about the 'Controlled Substances Act' governing the illegal manufacture and distribution of controlled substances; interstate trafficking and selling of marijuana violates federal law. Also, not reporting sales is a gigantic legal risk if the IRS investigated Bing's business. San Quentin is the closest thing to a debtors prison in California.

Life was good for the boy from the slums of Davao. And he hadn't even converted to Judaism.

* * *

Los Angeles weather is like an obituary; the local newspapers always had something positive to say about it. It was late spring in Beverly Hills with blossoms budding on deciduous trees, and awe struck tourists reading Star Maps to locate estates of past and current hot Hollywood legends — a staple of life in the hills was blue vans cruising the area with tourists pointing at dubious celebrity sightings.

Four miles south from the glitz of Rodeo Drive is Culver City, where middle-class housing tracts are shoehorned between large expanses of modern industrial buildings, strip malls, and film studios.

It was in one of these industrial areas that Jamal Holloway sat in his Ford Explorer, peering at a row of trucks in a warehouse parking lot. *I like everything I see. It's goin' down just like I planned*, he thought as he put down his binoculars. He took a long drag off one of the five joints he had rolled the night before, and then handed the doobie to his laconic cousin, Lamond, who was slouched in the passenger seat. In the back seat was another cousin, sixteen-year-old Jamarqua, or Jam.

Their grandfather was an African Methodist Episcopal Church preacher from Cullowhee, North Carolina. Gramps Holloway instilled the spirit and comfort of the Lord of the New Testament into all the Holloway children, grandchildren and great grandchildren. There had been heated family debates between Gramps and Jamal's father, Muhammad Holloway, over religion. They never settled their dispute.

Sprinting across Higuera Street was Jamal's eleven-year-old neighbor, LouRawls Johnson. When he reached Jamal's window, he looked up at him proudly and said, "I did exactly as you told me. I put those things right under the cars just like you said. No one saw me. I killed it, man, like you told me to."

Jamal liked the kid's attitude, and as promised, he put a crisp twenty-dollar bill in his outstretched hand. This was a bargain compared to the $49.95 Jamal had spent on each of the five tracking devices LouRawls had just placed under the five trucks across the street. It was all money well spent, though, and would help Jamal keep track of the trucks once they left the warehouse in case the predators lost sight of their prey on congested Los Angeles streets.

"The lord is about to deliver the goods into my hands. My grubby hands," Jamal said sardonically, while he continued to patiently observe the loading platform across the street. His gang members looked a little grumpy, standing there in the bitter-cold morning air that was blowing east from the beach at Playa del Rey. Jamal had been hard at work for the past few weeks scouting this location and constantly revising his plans. He was on a mission—one fueled by his personal resentment for his former employer, Bing de Asis, or "de Ass" as everyone called Bing behind his back.

Lamond and Jam—and several other cousins—were members of Jamal's newly formed gang, the Black Death Squad (BDS). Jam had picked out the name. Jamal's initial plans for BDS was to prey upon illegal marijuana growers. Despite the obvious obstacles—most grow houses had security cameras, barbed wire on top of tall fencing, and heavily armed security guards—Jamal decided they were perfect targets for BDS. With all the security features protecting a grow house, they might not seem like a golden target. However, employees lived in an interminable mental fog due to continuously smoking joints at the cultivation site. This predicament preordained that security was porous, especially entering and exiting a grow site.

Although all members of Jamal's newly formed gang were athletic; they all had to look up, not figuratively, to Jamal. Weeks ago, when he'd assembled his crew at his mother's house, he'd said, "Who the hell are these idiots going to call when we hit them? They ain't callin' no po-lice. Puh-leese. No way. I can guarantee that, my man. The po-lice ain't gonna be our problem.

"We're going to specialize in one thing and only one thing. Every damn grower I know spends half the day smokin' his own weed, and getting fuckin' high." Jamal knew these facts intimately since he was a failed grower, and smoked weed from the moment his eyes opened until he went to bed.

"Shit! No way, man. Are you crazy? That is suicide," said his cousin, DeTracy Holloway. "Those dudes got more guns, rifles, and

Uzis to protect them than that famous fort. What the shit. Yeah, it's called Fort Knott. Yeah."

Staring DeTracy down, Jamal said, "You dumb-ass tweaker. It's Fort Knox, not Knott's Berry Farm, fool."

Jamal was the only one in the group who had spent any time in college or read books. After high school, he stayed home and attended Mt. San Antonio Community College. Then he received a basketball scholarship for his remaining two years of eligibility at Fresno State. The college was located in the central valley, which was once called the nation's breadbasket.

DeTracy always was a thorn in Jamal's side, but since he and the others were cousins, Jamal decided to share the wealth within his family. And the wealth was sometimes called Purple Dream, Big Buddha Cheese, or Acapulco Gold—Jamal's favorite.

"Now fuckin' listen. I need you to listen to what I'm saying," said Jamal. "We are gonna get something better than gold. We robbing the fuckin' dopers and dealers, and I'll tell you all how."

Now even the distant cousins listened up. Jamal continued, "To tell the truth, when that fuckup Bing fired me, well it was, man . . . it turned out to be the best day of my life." Sounding like a stoner Dale Carnegie, Jamal concluded, "Good things can happen to you, man, if you . . . look at it the right way.

"Bing lost a damn good grower in me. But I learned from working for that little turd how his whole operation works. He talks too much. He tells all of them ho's he has around his little Filipino prick exactly how he works. Bing's just a plain-ass dumb little fuck.

"So I know where his grow sites is. I know who works there, and I know their shifts. And I know that bastard security guard in the Culver City warehouse is cleaning windows and floors most of the time rather than watchin' the monitors. This ain't gonna be no piece of cake, believe you me. But robbin' fuckin' marijuana growers is our ticket to money, money, money."

It was at that moment that Jamal's mother returned home from her nursing shift at Kaiser Hospital. Jamal and his cousins instantly transformed from the coarse hoodlums they were becoming, to all sweetness and "yes, ma'ams."

When Mrs. Holloway went to her room to have her bath, business recommenced. "And this is just the beginning of my plans," Jamal said. "We'll branch out from Los Angeles. We'll hire my friends to copy our operation." Thinking of all the ex-jocks he played with during his brief stint at Fresno State, he said, "Shit. I know people from here to Tallahassee. Yeah. We're goin' to do okay, boys."

DeTracy laughed and added, "Right. We going to be the Mickey D's of grass."

Staring at his dumb-ass cousin, Jamal said, "You are finally right. Our next step is to locate more grow sites. We can't rob every fuckin' grow. So what we do is walk right up to the grower when the security gate opens. We say 'Listen here. See how easy it would be to pop you. We tell them they is on our turf, and to pay up for protection or get busted. They pay blood money or we burn the place down. Blood money or they become blood soup. Fire, take me to burn, boys. Yeah, we are now extortionists. Robbing these rich-ass growers is like taking candy from my sister's baby. Green-colored candy that is."

And they all smiled, unaware of the meaning of the word extortion, but the use made it sound like there was money in there someplace.

"Fuckin' Bing gonna find out real quick like who his friends are," said Jamal. "He'll regret firing me. And now we all is gonna share the wealth. This deal is gonna fix all my problems." Imitating his beloved grandmother, Jamal said, "Lawdy me!"

All the cousins raised their beers, laughed, and repeated grandma's favorite expression, "Lawdy me!"

Up to this point, Jamal's chief achievement was assembling a pliable and averring group of relatives that wouldn't challenge his authority. He could dictate the details of his plans and if his cousins wanted to profit as BDS members, they had better adhere to the letter of his scheme.

Now, weeks later, Jamal's informant confided that Bing was in Las Vegas, and it was the perfect time for BDS to spring into action.

CHAPTER 2

Los Angeles, CA and Las Vegas, NV

De Asis spent more time schmoozing up any blond under 23 years old, without a visible malignancy, then his intended reason to be in Vegas — negotiating with east coast dealers who wanted to affiliate with his growing nationwide supply chain network.

Definitely not a workaholic, the Holy Grail for Bing and his cohorts was being perpetually high and having fun: in the pool, in bed with a new women in tow every few hours, gambling at the roulette table whacked on cocaine, and perpetually high smoking a reefer in his two-story rental named the Julius Caesar suite.

Vapes allowed him to smoke marijuana unnoticed in the casino and restaurants. Insanely smoking grass each and every minute of the day generated constant all-out stoner cravings for any munchies readily accessible.

One of the many inclusive perks for guests paying $1,500.00 per day for a suite was a partitioned 'high rollers' line at restaurants and show rooms. A chain with thick red velvet kept the riffraff out, allowing Bing's group to bypass lengthy lines of ravenous diners. Brutally indiscriminate, Bing joined thousands of lowbrow tourists who frequented the 'All day buffet for $49.95' at most Harrah's Hotels. Gluttons could eat flavorless food endlessly at ten hotel locations, and gain one or two pounds per hour.

To placate his latest blonde girlfriend back in LA, Bing had named his burgeoning vape busines Master Doobie, or MD. As CEO of Master Doobie, Bing wanted to act the part of an executive, and like all bosses, he delegated everything but the fun. The supervision of the warehouse was gifted on his roommate underling, Rex Mueller.

Rex was six three, with a long thin nose that he'd broken a few times in high school fights. He was only twenty-eight years old, but was already combing his yellow hair forward to cover his acutely receding hairline. He wore glasses, too, and even worse, he never smiled because of a formidable overbite that had earned him the nickname T-Rex.

As was Rex's habit, he arrived at the Culver City site an hour late. The eight workers, originally from El Salvador, knew from past experiences how to load the trucks with their valuable cargo. The grass was placed in plastic Ziploc baggies and piled into gym bags placed inside wooden crates. Outsiders might think this was a legitimate business: the men were dressed in blue uniforms with baseball caps sporting the company's *MD* logo. In front of the loading dock were five twelve-foot-long yellow trucks stamped with the Penske logo—even though Bing owned the trucks. Every trick in the book was employed to throw off the cops. Each truck had only a single driver and no security guard. Bing had decided Pinkerton-style guards were an unnecessary cost. "Hell," he'd told Rex, "We've never been hit. The best approach is to lay low, and be cool. Stay cool, man."

The sun was now sparkling as Rex stepped out of his blue BMW, holding a coffee cup in one hand. He yelled to the men on the loading dock. "Hey! I stopped at Dunkin' Donuts if you dudes

want some." He waved an apple fritter in his other hand to empha-
size his words.

* * *

Across the street, DeTracy leaned into Jamal's window and asked,
"Why ain't we hittin' the trucks now? They just sittin' there. They
doin' nothin'. Shit, man. It's easy pickin's."

Jamal sighed. "You is fuckin' hopeless. Do you know why I'm
the boss here? Cause I'm smarter than you. You dumbass. Here's
why we is not robbing the fuckin' trucks as they're sitting still. This
location is supposedly secret. Nobody's supposed to know it's a grow
house. Now we gonna rob them trucks elsewhere so that bitch Bing
don't know we watchin' them all the time. Besides, they have around
two hundred lights in that building. Probably cost Bing more than a
cool million dollars to build that joint. He's staying right here in our
backyard. I've got plans. Lots of plans."

Jamal had instructed each BDS member on exactly which
truck to follow, and on how to lay low and when to strike. Without
taking his eyes off the building, he said to Jam, "They almost packed
up. Gonna take off any minute. Make sure they all ready." Jam got out
and walked down a line of cars behind Jamal, giving instructions to
the other BDSers.

"Get in your car, dumb-ass!" Jamal snarled at DeTracy. DeTracy
scrambled away as Jam climbed back into the Explorer. Jamal started
the engine as the first yellow truck left the warehouse. Jamal took
off in his Explorer with a laconic cousin riding shotgun. Lamond
Holloway recently moved from North Carolina with his girlfriend
who supported the couple working the night shift at Fatburger on
south Figueroa.

* * *

After departing the warehouse, Bing's drivers avoided the freeways and headed to various skateboard shops owned by Mark Ware, one of Bing's partners. Ware was a notorious wild man at Bing's parties who rented his own apartment in Doheny Towers in Beverly Hills.

Ware's business was the perfect front. The partnership had been born at one of Bing's parties, when Ware had boasted about distributing coke to dealers in the Midwest in skateboard boxes shipped via friendly FedEx drivers. One-tenth of his deliveries were true skateboard sales. The remaining nine-tenths was cocaine. Bing and Ware, smashed out of their minds on the house party drug of the night, endlessly and loudly discussed the merits of a "joint" venture—a pun they found endlessly funny.

Understandably, the El Salvadoran workers we're deeply suspicious of power, and hated police and authorities. Consequently each man drove carefully and slowly to their destinations, which wasn't out of the ordinary for them as they spent evening's slowly cruising Whittier Boulevard in east LA looking for caliente Latina's.

The first truck stuffed with marijuana reached its destination. The driver went through an alley behind the store. He backed the truck into a designated parking spot in the rear of Ocean Blue Skateboard shop on Colorado Boulevard in Eagle Rock. The largest employer in Eagle Rock was Occidental College. The most famous Oxy student was our 44th president, Barack Obama.

Jamal followed the truck and parked in the Norm's restaurant parking lot adjacent to Ocean Blue. Lamond was ready to move on the driver. Lamond was a giant at six ten, and didn't seemed worried about intimidating a lone driver who was barely five feet tall. But when he started to open the door, Jamal firmly extended his right arm across Lamond's chest, and held his left index finger to his mouth.

"Wait a sec, man. Make sure no one is coming out to help."

The truck driver knocked on the back door of the closed shop. No one answered. He knocked harder and harder on the steel door, skinning a knuckle. He pushed the defective door buzzer over and over. He waved at the security camera. He called out a name they couldn't hear out a few times, then made a short and similarly frantic cellphone call. The call was to T-Rex who had difficulty understanding the man's heavily accented words.

"Shit. Are you kidding me?" Said T-Rex. With his other phone, Rex called the shop with the same dismal result.

Even with an inconsequential, walnut-sized brain, T-Rex realized the urgent importance of the situation. He said, "Give me a minute to call Mark, and I'll call you right back. He must have a spare key tucked away somewhere. Whatever you do, don't move. Hear me? Don't move." The driver thought, 'This is why I'm starting to get gray hair in my twenties'.

The line went dead, and the man thought, 'Yeah. Like where will I go with this shipment?' The thought of taking the truck to Bakersfield where he had friends crossed his mind. But Vargas knew marijuana gangsters were no different then coke or heroin gangsters. You don't mess with their sacred product if you wanted your family back in San Salvador to live another day.

Jamal and Lamond watched the driver pace back and forth like a sentry in the Queen's Guard at Buckingham Palace.

Lamond said, "Something's up."

"Yeah, something's up all right, and I know exactly what the fuck it is. These dumb shits don't have no one to open the friggin' door. That's what's up, Lamond."

Abandoning his original plan, Jamal touched the ignition button on the SUV. He swung out from Norm's and backed up adjacent to the truck.

"Follow my lead," he told Lamond. Stepping away from the truck, the two men approached the driver. Jamal smiled larger than life. A smile even larger then when he dunked, in a summer league game at Pauley Pavilion, over Dennis Rodman.

He said, "Listen here, my man. We is the cal-va-ry here to save your sorry ass. You can call me the Texas damn Rangers. I got a phone call that you all needed help getting into the shop."

The driver extended his right hand, balled up to fist-bump Jamal. Jamal caught the driver's fist in the palm of his huge right hand. He squeezed it tight, and in his best mixed-martial fighting stance, propelled the man to the ground. Lamond kicked the driver several times in his ribs. Then Jamal picked up the man's head in his free left hand, and without hesitation smashed his skull into the asphalt with all his might. In Jamal's jargon, "The man is no more. He's joined the dust-to-dust congregation and is singing away. Shit man. Now he can sing spirituals with the Blind Boys of Alabama. In Spanish of course."

Jamal and Lamond stepped over the blood oozing from the driver's skull. The two men opened both rear doors, and stared at the wooden crates stacked to the truck's ceiling. Jamal thought he heard faint movement inside the shop.

"Quick, Lamond. You take the truck. Follow me. Let's get going, man."

Jamal slid into the Explorer. Lamond already had the truck started. He followed a little bit too close as Jamal drove side streets to the Pasadena Freeway, but otherwise, the first of five heists went off smoother than planned. Unless you count the first death as a complication.

Overnight, BDS was a force to be reckoned with.

Never cautious or discreet, pompous Bing was in Vegas fucking, overeating, and consummating new distribution deals while his profits were now destined to a house southeast of the Mt. Wilson Observatory.

Bing and his boys were minus one hard-working Salvadoran, and one ton of marijuana valued at $5,000,000.00 was AWOL. Eventually Bing had to emerge from his marijuana high, and would check his voice mail. He couldn't conceal for long the information from five dangerous distributors in Atlanta. He would need anesthesia to numb the pain in his ears at the time he told them that their product wouldn't be arriving in spite of his endless claims concerning timely monthly deliveries.

No, definitely not good. Bing's Vegas ebullience would soon change to torment.

CHAPTER 3

11AM, June, 2013
Las Vegas, Nevada

While the BDS was smashing skulls, eight drug dealers were arriving in Las Vegas for their first meeting with Bing de Asis. It was unseasonably hot even for the Mojave desert, about 118 degrees, and the tarmac at McCarron Airport was softening like a melting Hershey's chocolate bar. All flights were delayed or rerouted—extreme heat creates changes in the atmosphere making it more difficult for planes to land and take off.

Introduced by a shyster intermediary—Bing's criminal attorney—the eight men needed to "feel him out," and determine if he could supply them with "sufficient product" for their significant base of smokers. "Sufficient product" was their euphemism for tons of grade-A grass. They all had specific concerns, but primarily, they just wanted to gamble and sample the quality of Bing's product.

Bing's current blonde girlfriend, who he kept in LA so he could have uninhibited fun and games, had made a 10 p.m. reservation for the group at the Prime Steakhouse in the Bellagio Hotel.

* * *

The only dealer who drove to Vegas was from the Philly area, twenty-six-year-old Cary Sweetzer. He was overwhelmed by Sin City, especially compared to his customary gambling spot, Atlantic City. Las Vegas was vast, opulent, and filled with Asian junkets. Macau, Atlantic City, Nassau, or Monte Carlo—it didn't matter. There was no gambling scene anywhere on earth that could match the kaleidoscopic neon lights of the Vegas Strip.

Under the cloudless desert sky, Cary intended to gamble night and day. He desperately needed to break the casino bank. It was his only remaining chance to survive in the cannabis business. With the gambling winnings he could buy Bing's weed and pay back his moneylenders, who were charging a 20 percent vig per month. Hitting the jackpot was Cary's only hope. Every recent drug deal he had arranged had gone sour. Twice he was robbed at gunpoint during large-scale deals. Another time, after smoking three joints with a client, he forgot to collect the money owed by the South Philly pusher.

Cary's oldest and best friend, Kenny Lutz, from his hometown of Hunting Park in economically depressed North Philly, joined him for the drive west. They drove the 2,400 miles in two long days. Neither man could afford an airline ticket or even a room at Motel 6.

Luckily, Bing had set them up with a suite at Caesar's Palace. Cary got plenty of stares as he strolled into the shallow end of the swimming pool. He was excessively muscular from the noxious use of performance-enhancing drugs. He was six one with a ruby-red crewcut. And he was tattooed everywhere on his body somewhat like the "Illustrated Man" in Ray Bradbury's novel. He desperately wanted to maneuver to the deep end of the pool, near the diving board, to flirt with a gorgeous woman with one visible tattoo. Clinging to the travertine coping of the pool, and inching forward was not a macho option—the problem was, Sweetzer couldn't swim.

Cary concluded his feeble attempt to hook up with the woman in the pool. Sweetzer rarely talked in a calm tone. Unhinged that he hadn't secured a woman, he yelled for the toga-clad server, and said, "Bring me and my boy each two more of those drinks." The server had recommended a Mai Tai for the two men originally from Steelton, Pennsylvania, an unfamiliar drink to both men. They downed the drinks quickly. *Tastes like adult Kool Aid*, Cary thought. The rum buzz kicked in, and they were off to the casino.

In advance of their dinner reservation, Bing was supposed to meet with Cary at the Caesar's buffet around noon to discuss their potential arrangement. In Caesar's cavernous casino, Cary rushed past a line of elderly women. At the buffet entrance, he looked for a tall, good-looking Asian man wearing a brown hat. Anyway, that was how Bing described himself on an earlier call.

Bumping into an old codger waiting in line, Cary continued his futile search. Everywhere he looked, all Cary could see were more seniors, more toga-clad servers, and everywhere young boys and girls in shorts. Furious, Cary called Bing's room. No answer.

"Fuck this shit," Cary said. Then he realized Lutz was missing. He saw him waiting for a long line of Keno-playing women to pass. Cary back-tracked and said, "You got to keep up with me, Klutz." Cary had always been protective of Kenny, telling people that Klutz (Cary's contraction of Ken Lutz) wasn't dumb, he had ADHD and dyslexia. Cary felt beneficent telling any person who would listen to him, how he cared for and looked after Kenny. Cary couldn't pronounce *dyslexia*, so he would say Kenny's brain wasn't wired right. But Klutz didn't have either affliction. He was plainly dumb as dirt. His mother, descended from a French Catholic family in a small village in the Auvergne, raised him in a strict household. She constantly berated him to be polite and nice to everyone unlike his best friend,

Cary. As an adult, each and every time Klutz introduced himself to a stranger, he resembled a proper little school boy who was reading out loud a greeting according to his mother's direct exhortation.

Bing de Asis snorted mucho quantities of cocaine, drank incessantly and smoked so much weed he couldn't smell trouble if his pants were on fire. He ignored phone calls, and didn't make the scheduled meeting with Cary at the Caesar's buffet around noon to commence discussion about their potential arrangement. Bing figured he'd have fun first, and meet Cary later. Furious, Cary called Bing's room. No answer. Bing was in his room, ignoring all calls since he arrived in Vegas. His full attention at the moment was given to a blond from Goodnight, Texas, whom he ruthlessly threw on the king size bed under a mirrored ceiling, next to an indoor hot tub. Like a Hollywood stereotype of a blond, at a young age she discovered the benefits of being a dumb gorgeous blond in the Texas panhandle.

"I left a message for that mo-ron Bing," Cary said, fuming. "I'm going to gamble. You do what you want. You can come with me or go off and eat by yourself. I don't give a damn." When Kenny followed him, Cary said to himself, "I knew the big Klutz would follow me. Just like my good little puppy dog."

Since Cary rarely read, he was unaware of the recent interview given to the *Las Vegas Mercury* by the president of the Nevada Gaming Association. The man said, "I'm unequivocally embarrassed that we still have slot machines in our casinos. The return to slot players is simply too low. They are an anachronism . . . What person in their right mind would throw money away playing slots?"

Cary viewed slots differently. He'd paid $99.99 for a DVD that touted a revolutionary, foolproof system than even Kenny could understand. After three full hours of implementing this foolproof system, Cary was down $500 on the credit line extended by Caesar's based on Bing's voucher.

"Kenny, don't let anyone touch this machine. I'll be back in a sec. Understand?" Cary said. Even simple Lutz thought, *Waiting for a slot machine miracle is no good way to live.*

Down one-half of his credit line, Cary felt like a fool. "What am I doing here?" he whined. Walking past the Memory Lane Lounge, Cary listened briefly to a tall, thin man impersonating Catskills' comedians. Doing his best copy of a fossilized comedian, Henny Youngman, to a near-empty room, he said, "It's not true married men live longer than single men. It only seems longer. Take my wife. Please." No one looked up from their drinks, no one laughed, no one applauded.

Cary groaned. It appeared his only success that day would be burning his pale, freckled skin.

* * *

Rudy Peralta was one of five bodyguards surrounding Frankie Tapia. Tapia was one of the Gang of Eight dealers waiting to meet Bing. Tapia ran drugs from Nuevo Laredo, Mexico, north through Laredo where his mules spread out in godforsaken Texas desert. They went northwest to El Paso and then to the American southwest. Others went north on Highway 35 leading to San Antonio, then drop off more product in Austin for Longhorn students, and eventually to Dallas. His territory was large, rich with a growing population. Peralta was young and devotedly loyal to his boss. Rudy never dreamt he would earn so much money for doing what came naturally, fighting and killing.

While Cary had been at the buffet searching for Bing, Tapia and his men occupied two tables for brunch at 'Cafe Americano'. Rudy followed Frankie's lead and ordered a Bloody Marisco to drink, and a tall stack of buttermilk pancakes with whipped butter. Rudy's speech was slurred after a fight he had a week ago beating a deadbeat dealer to death. The dealer whacked Rudy with a pipe across his jaw before Rudy beat him senseless.

With his sore jaw, Rudy tried not to talk, and sipped the Bloody Marisco through a straw. When the food was placed in front of Tapia's men, Rudy noticed the whipped butter which appeared to be the easiest food to eat with his tender jaw. Frankie nudged the man next to him, and pointed his right index finger at Rudy. Rudy picked up his spoon, before sampling the pancakes. He took a moderate amount of butter, and feasted upon what he thought was vanilla ice cream. He quickly picked up his napkin, spit the butter into the napkin while Tapia couldn't stop laughing at the man that had never been to an IHOP or Denny's for breakfast.

* * *

After a trip to the men's room, Cary felt renewed, like a metamorphosis was occurring—perhaps urinating cleared some space in Cary's brain. He hurried back to his personal slot and said, "Kenny, do you feel crazy lucky?" Without waiting for a response, he said, "Kenny, let's attack this baby." He commenced hour number four standing at the "Wheel of Fortune Wild Red Sevens" $1 progressive slot machine. A large, brightly colored jackpot meter above the slot machine advertised a current value of $1,499,900. Kenny occupied himself by diligently keeping an eye on the jackpot value, as it increased every time Cary plunked two more $1 tokens into the machine. Kenny was easily entertained.

Thirty minutes later, the slot machine rang up three red sevens. Bells rang, drums rolled, coins clinked down the opening, and a photo of Wheel of Fortune's Vanna White appeared on the monitor. Cary's former apoplectic rage dissipated instantaneously, and

Kenny's jaw appeared to drop to the carpet. Both men were momentarily in shock.

Several female sailors from Devon, England, drinking margarita's in oversized 24-ounce tacky souvenir glasses were passing Cary when the slot machine rang up three red sevens. Bells were still ringing when one of the English woman said, "Blimey. That's whizo". Another chipped in, "Truly first rate mate."

Spinning around and around, Cary waved to the crowd assembling behind him like an obnoxious celebrity. Holding his hands clinched together above his head as though he had just defeated Muhammad Ali, he yelled, "I'm not fucking poor anymore!" The room seemed to spin faster and faster like a dervish had control of the earth's axis.

Within seconds, what seemed like hundreds of well-wishers cheered and patted Cary on the back. Kenny squeezed his shoulder, and the first of three prostitutes propositioned him.

Lightheadedness forced Cary to sit on a stool. A security guard escorted a cashier to his slot. Looking at Klutz, Cary said, "Kenny, my magic money tree is alive. It does exist. Magic money tree."

The security guard motioned for Cary to follow the cashier to the office. The cashier said, "Various forms need to be completed prior to giving you your check for $1,500,003." Cary suddenly felt exhausted. "Whew, all this is happening so fast," he said.

Then he realized what she had described. He said, "Shit. I don't want no check. I want crisp hundred-dollar bills with my homeboy's face on it. Philly's own Benji Franklin. Yeah, all hundreds. How many hundreds will I get?" Cary was already plotting to avoid taxes, and how to spend the money.

As Cary left the cashier's office, he looked out over the immense casino. The cashier was getting perverse enjoyment listening to Cary blither. Part of the myriad of paperwork to be filled out was Internal Revenue Service Form W-2G and 5754 for reporting Cary's slot winning's. She thought, "No way Cary. No way are you avoiding paying your fair share of Uncle Sam taxes." She cursed her state for not taking any portion of his money in taxes. Cary would soon be stunned at losing 28% of his fortune to the government, or in his case, a tax lien.

His face turned towards the elevator bank, and waved for Klutz to join him. He was so used to being without money that the bulge in his nest egg inspired a brainwave. Entering the elevator, Cary said, "Kenny, here's what we're going to do. Bing has to be on our floor in one of the other suites. I'll start knocking on doors and yelling for Bing. You go to the other end of the floor and knock on every door and yell Bing." Cary realized *he needed to meet Bing and purchase his weed before he spent all his winnings.*

With his customary blank gaze, Kenny nodded in agreement. Five minutes later, Cary's impulsive strategy accomplished his goal when Bing irritably answered the door wrapped in a towel. After Cary explained his plight of being saddled with more than a million dollars, and Bing's negative expression markedly altered. The libertine directed his Texas blonde to stay in the bedroom. Bing's attention was momentarily arrested measuring up Cary, and reckoning he had a new client.

* * *

Ignoring another phone call, for the umpteenth time, metrosexual Bing said, "I don't give a piss about what's happening in LA. At this moment I'm fucking Bobby Sue. I love how you Texans have two-first names." He stared at the Goodnight blond, and remembered all the girls in Davao with two names — Maria Elena, Maria Rosa, Maria BuenaFlora. Ah. He remembered how Flora-dora did every dirty deed he requested on the promise of taking her to the states as his teenage bride — fat chance.

Business types generally went to the Convention Center to attend business meetings in Las Vegas. Not Bing, even though there was a bi-annual Marijuana Conference at the Rio Hotel. The Bellagio Hotel was only three hundred yards south of Caesar's, across Flamingo Road. Nevertheless, Bing and Cary climbed into a limousine for the ride. "Appearance is everything," Bing said.

The two men were twenty minutes late for dinner, which Bing described as "fashionable" but was really just "pompous." Bing was a cultivator of sycophants, and he relished being the big boss unaware how much time Steve Jobs or Jeff Bezos put in to make Apple or Amazon dominant. Bing preferred flattery to hard work, and believed all the adulating words from his minions. Bing's exotic business was like Bing, absolutely sui generis.

High overhead in the Bellagio lobby, they ignored the thousands of magnificent hand-blown glass blossoms hanging from the ceiling, designed by Fulbright Scholar Dale Chihuly. Chihuly was the equivalent of Murano's Venini glass factory meets Las Vegas.

There was something clownish about tiny Bing and hulking Cary, known in Philly circles for bungling deals, trying to navigate through the labyrinthine casino. While attempting to locate the restaurant, Bing noticed a slot machine with an Asian theme titled *Big Red Lantern*. Bing said, "The Asian design on that slot reminds me of my home in Davao. About 90 percent of my country is Catholic."

"What the hell do you mean your country, dude?" Cary said. "Aren't you a fucking Americano?"

"I have dual citizenship," Bing explained. "I was born in California, and moved back to the Philippines. Later my parents moved to Thailand to work on another American military base. And now I live here in the states. The best pussy and best food is Thai."

"Yeah," said Cary. "I've heard of the Flip-uh-pines. And I've been to a Thai restaurant. Good stuff. Fragrant Taiwan is the name of the restaurant in Philly. Yeah. A bit too spicy for my tastes, but I like Thai food."

Bing couldn't be bothered to correct someone so distinctively stupid. He did his best to ignore the buffoon as they reached the entrance to Prime.

Trying to look important, Cary pushed past a group of men ogling the hostess. Trying to strike up a conversation with the Vietnamese-French woman wearing a name tag, Boa, he said, "Reservation for eight people under the name *de Asses*."

More the professional than any of the men, including *de Asses*, the hostess didn't bat an eyelash at Cary's bungle. "Please follow Sheila. Your other diners are already seated, and Sheila will escort you to your table. Enjoy your dinner at Prime."

Bing followed Sheila. Cary continued to blatantly stare at the hostess' well-endowed brown breasts, and wanted her 'de Asses'. He said, "Listen. I just won a few million dollars over at Caesar's. How about you and me getting together after you've finished your shift. I'd love to promenade you around Caesar's and get to know you better."

She wasn't snobbish, but this uncouth slob had as much chance of getting in her pants as Wrong Way Corrigan landing in Long Beach. Curtly she answered, "Mr. Kerkorian is very strict that employees cannot date customers. Sorry," and she turned to call the next party.

"Thanks for nothing," Cary said as he stomped off to find his new good buddy, Bing. He thought, "Fuck her. Fuck Kirk Orion. Fuck everyone. Shit I'm a millionaire, and I'm going to win more slot money tonight. Fuck that bitch."

Of course, he could not stop thinking about her.

Approaching the table, Cary saw six white guys, one Hispanic guy, and one black guy. "Shit," he mumbled. "I told Bing no fucking niggers. They've robbed me every time I deal with those fuckers. They're good to party with but never do business with 'em." But he nodded and sat down.

The sommelier swanned over. "And what are we drinking tonight?"

If a blind tasting were held that night, Bing wouldn't be capable of discerning the disparity between an illustrious 1990 *La Tache* or *Gallo Hearty Burgundy*.

Without consultation, Bing said, "Cristal, my man. Cristal for all my friends." The crystal clear fact was Cristal had become a grossly overpriced, though majestic cuvee, after it became the hip-hop and rappers choice for Champagne. With hundreds of people in Prime, the table that habitually attracted loathsome attention belonged to de Asis. They were the loudest in a loud restaurant, and they were the most uncouth employing crude language and scatology in a city renown for lowbrows. They were straight out of Pieter Bruegel the Elder's engraving of the Seven Deadly Sins.

A busboy standing near their table didn't respond to Cary's incessant hand waving. Finally he bellowed, "Hey". The busboy and half the restaurant looked at him. Cary was wiggling his right hand to motion the busboy forward.

"May I help you sir?" The busboy asked.

"Listen dude," said Cary. "You know that great looking chick at the door?"

"You mean Elliott Ness?"

"What the hell do you mean, Elliott Ness?" Cary said. The busboy said, "We call her Elliott Ness because she is 'Untouchable'. She belongs to one of the most prominent gamblers in Vegas, Wayne Rady. He's the brains behind the computer gambling syndicate that takes down tens of millions each year betting against the sports books. He also owns five golf courses here. No one touches her if they value their life." His response made Cary's evening rotten, and was an unintended effective way to emasculate Cary.

* * *

The tall, thick black man Cary was eyeing suspiciously was Marvin Mason. He was the antithesis of Bing. He had a shaved head and a ferocious Fu Manchu. He had been educated at the London School of Economics, and even Cary had to admit he was a classy guy. He wore a custom pink jean jacket over a pink t-shirt, and sported a large diamond earring in his left ear.

Looking at Bing, Mason said, "My business has been modest because I can't get consistent quality."

Cary interrupted. "Man, you look familiar. Where are you from?"

"I live in Atlanta. As an undergrad, I played football at Clemson. Maybe you saw me in the Peach Bowl. I was MVP," said Mason.

Mason quickly redirected the conversation away from Cary to Bing. "My customers range from pro athletes that I represent as their agent to small-time, street-corner punks. What they all have in common is a thirst for the Big 3: Kandy Skunk, Alien OG, and Lemon Kush."

Bing nodded, well aware that Atlanta smokers wanted citrusy hues of yellow and orange in their smokes.

Cary interjected. "Yeah, Bing. I need Purple Urkle, some Grandaddy Purple, and mucho Purple Orangutan for my Philly boys."

Bing barely acknowledged Cary and turned toward Colin Cooper, Jr., another formidable figure. A former world-class pole vaulter at Syracuse, Cooper was six two and fit as a fiddle at age sixty. The Scottish-born man, who had been an executive at the Imperial Bank of Scotland, had true poise—a combination of age, education, and experience. Cooper's first thought as Bing had made introductions had been, *How can I work with this runt of a man who resembles a very ugly turd. He reminds me of a despot from a banana republic.*

Cooper abstained from smoking weed or drinking alcohol, but he was rapidly learning the marijuana business. He had already made a major investment in an MMJ greenhouse with a major California dispensary owner: a $15-million investment in a 125,000-square-foot greenhouse cultivation facility to be built in Gomez, California, just north of Gilroy—the garlic capital of the world. That area would soon reek from garlic and cannabis.

Cooper, too, was becoming aware that the preferred strains were as multicolored as a fall day in the Hudson River Valley. Looking down on these men, Cooper had neither east coast contacts nor an interest in working with any of these people he deemed inferior. His resentment was based on the fact that he felt he was a better quality person than these specimens of street toughs. He controlled his inward antipathy because he was there to learn, not make relationships.

Colin hated wasting time with these 'types of people,' more accustomed to a worldly circle of Wall Street investment bankers and Arab oil sheiks. This group was grating on him. Petulantly gazing at the table of prehensile banal neanderthals, he remembered he was there to listen, to learn, and perhaps make a few worthwhile contacts despite his current tedium.

Coopers multi-million dollar bet was varied, he already duped Bing of his interest in partnering. And now exposed to Bing's concept, he had no difficulty adopting Bing's plans, utilizing his own production in Gomez. His partner, formerly head of Wealth Management at Morgan Stanley, stressed they must be the innovators for the industry with Madison Avenue professional marketing and branding appealing to the tactile senses of MMJ smoking creatures. Incontestably used car dealers were honorable Boy Scouts in comparison to back-stabbing predatory drug dealers.

Next to Cooper was Andy Graber, a former designer of aeronautical equipment turned cannabis distributor to Huntsville's space techies. A myth circulating among sophisticates was that the American South was "backwards," but Huntsville, Alabama, is known as "The Rocket City" for its legions of defense contractors working on US government space missions. In the city, the HudsonAlpha Institute for Biotechnology is part of the 4,000-acre Cummings Research Park. Intelligent researchers and PhDs also require "relaxation," and for those electrical engineers who didn't regularly get drug tested at work, cannabis was a favorite way to kick back.

Due to Graber's education and space background, he spent many days working long hours in Houston, for NASA, at the Johnson Space Center. In Houston, he met and smoked grass with Benny Dufau on four separate occasions at Graber's motel room. Dufau wisely decided to replicate Graber's cannabis distribution network in South Texas. Personally, Benny Dufau preferred a six-pack to smoking a joint. The man was about forty with curly dark hair and a trim moustache. Infatuated with his blue 2012 Porsche 911 Carrera S, Dufau branded his business Carrera Cannabis.

Dufau's influence extended 400 miles east, where he had a younger step-brother, Billy Bob Mobley. Billy Bob lived in Biloxi, Mississippi, and had a low-paying job as a maintenance man at one of the twenty-four-hour gambling joints. Consider Biloxi a mini-Las Vegas—where Southerners could ignore their serious, pressing issues, and be frivolous gambling at Jimmy Buffet's Margaritaville Hotel, the Hard Rock, or Harrah's Gulf Coast. The gambling mecca was the perfect place for Mobley's transformation into a successful dealer. Graber, Dufau, and Mobley all required dependable marijuana supplies for their hungry base of customers.

Neighboring Dufau and Mobley at the table was the Florida dealer, Sundog Sweeney. He was having his regular cannabis shipments from the Caribbean Islands cut off by the Coast Guard. He desperately needed more grass to sell. Sundog mentioned to Bing's attorney, "I don't want none of that outdoor shit grown in Humboldt and Mendocino. They use pesticides, and all sorts of bad shit. Plus that crap is only available once a year around August or September. Once-a-year harvest just won't do. I can sell cheap weed, just remember the key for me is that I need consistent supplies of product."

Lastly, there was Frankie Tapia. His territory was large, rich with a growing population. His five bodyguards sat conspicuously behind him at a nearby table.

Bing stared around the table. "Now that we're sitting down together, you should know I only own three grow sites. But I party with every major grower alive. Everyone knows me in LA 'cause no one moves their weed as fast and for as much money as me."

Cooper looked at Mason and raised his eyebrows. Both knew the score; Bing was grossly exaggerating his reach.

But Bing gulped some champagne and pressed on. "I only drink good wine. Now I want to tell you how we are going to work together. FedEx drivers will pick up my weed and take it to a location in Arizona for the first drop. Next a UPS truck will take it to Dallas for another drop. Remember, these trucks stop at weigh stations so when we make drops, we add boxes weighing the same amount to fool 'em." Bing wisely decided not to proceed with other geographical descriptions until all connections were more secured — with cash.

He had their attention now, so he explained his method of filling the skateboard boxes with grass or hash, and how the payoffs for the $20-per-hour UPS and FedEx truck drivers were cash bonuses generous enough to ensure they kept their mouths shut.

Cary, who had managed to stay quiet for a whole ten minutes, said, "Mr. Cooper, you just look kinda out of it. Like, man, you're not enjoying yourself. I'm going to call you Grumpy if you don't change your fucked-up mood and start drinking with us." Cooper smiled tightly at Cary, and Bing quickly got back to business.

For an industry shrouded in secrecy, these negotiations were directly from the Alice-in-Wonderland School of Economics: consignment pricing options, merits of flower versus oil and vapors, haggling down to the gram on price. The two established businessmen, Mason and Cooper, discussed the anticipated internal rates of return and the high free cash flow.

With the dealing done and the champagne still flowing, the group of eight elaborately recounted their personal stories. A few told of how they evaded police detection, and, more importantly, the Feds. Doubting the veracity of some of the tall tales, Mason said, "In the ghetto, when I see a group of suburban-looking white boys walking from their truck carrying air-conditioning units, lights, and ballasts into a building, well, I know what's going on in there." Everyone, even the clueless Cary, laughed at that.

Bing sat back, enormously self-satisfied. His dream was coming true. From the Midwest to the East Coast, these men covered the areas essential for him to be one of the nation's top dope distributors.

The group talked straight about marijuana, not like politicians beating around the bush. These men who were strangers three hours ago, now were members of a new aristocracy. Unnoticed by those studying at Harvard Business School, these marijuana entrepreneurs had thin start-up costs, and profit margins rivaling Silicon Valley.

At 1 a.m., Bing thought it was time to leave the steakhouse. Everyone seemed to have had enough discussion, champagne, and food. He suggested meeting at a club in the Hard Rock Hotel, and said, "Let's sin tonight, boys."

All Bing could think was, *And this is only the beginning.*

CHAPTER 4

Las Vegas and Beverly Hills
June, 2013

⟨⟨ ☾ ☽ ⟩⟩

I n the immediate aftermath of Bing's successes with the Gang of
Eight, and blond Bobby Sue, Bing waited patiently as Cary drove
his shimmering new yellow Corvette, with two-bucket seats to the
entrance of Caesar's Palace. Klutz loaded the suitcases in the trunk,
and then got in the taxi line for the airport. The extreme heat was
still bedeviling flights, and Cary had convinced Bing to ride with
him to Los Angeles. Cary had suffered through enough biting-cold
Philly winters, and with his newfound wealth, he decided he and
Klutz would permanently "live big" in Los Angeles. With only two
seats in the Corvette, they left Kenny to wait for a flight at McCarran,
whenever a seat was available on an eventual flight. Big-hearted Cary
even paid for Klutz's flight.

Sweetzer had spent hours during the day of June 18th and the
early morning of the 19th pouring coins into another progressive
slot machine. His $1,500,000.00 was now minus $92,000.00 for the
Corvette, $650,000.00 in slot losses, and $150.00 for Klutz's airline ticket.

Sipping an iced coffee, reclined in the passenger seat, Bing finally felt ready to turn on his phone. He stared dumbly at the 211 messages, and instead called blond Tiffany at his house.

"Where the hell have you been?" said Tiffany.

"Wow. What a greeting," said Bing. "What feather is up your cute ass?" She hung up on him, which he took as a sign to stop looking at his phone. Cary pulled out a joint from his shirt pocket, and they lit up for the four-hour drive.

Just as he exhaled, Bing received a text from Tiffany: *You've been fucking robbed, you idiot.*

He called her back, his heart pounding. "Are you kidding me? Right? This is a bad joke, right? You're pissed at me 'cause I left you home when I'm in Vegas, right? Tell me, bitch. This is a joke. This isn't funny!"

"No joke. I've been calling your cell and hotel phone for days. You have one driver dead. Four in the hospital. All the grass shipment is gone. This is not a joke."

She'd seen Bing mad many times before. Automatically she ran to her dresser and threw her clothes in two of Bing's suitcases. She wasn't waiting to see him when he returned. She and Bing were history.

Bing's mind was moving in slow motion with the impact of the dollars involved. The grass was consigned to him by growers to move east. He owed money to every major grower around LA. He owed millions. The growers didn't care if he was robbed. The debt was his. He needed help fast. Shaking, Bing texted his old buddy, Morrison: *Be at my house in 4 hours. Emergency!*

His innate cunning mind had imploded like a bad physics experiment.

* * *

Adam Copland was late, had not called his wife, and now he was hell-bent on getting home. Granted all of the these hot water issues would be problematic for an average Joe, but were even more so for this fellow acknowledged to be anal-compulsive pertaining to punctuality and everything else under the sun. Gabriela had arranged a sleepover for their daughter at a friend's house so that the two adults could enjoy a rare romantic evening together.

Despite his current stress over his tardiness, Copland was an exceedingly happy thirty-five-year-old man, who drove his diavolo red Aston Martin convertible absurdly fast as he headed north of Sunset Boulevard on Benedict Canyon.

So many American cities have a specific image or stereotype: Seattle is grunge hipsters and coffee. Manhattan's upscale restaurants are perennially reviewed in Zagat as gourmet heaven. San Francisco is LGBT friendly. Detroit is known for the least attractive women in the country. For many people in Beverly Hills and Bel Air, image is everything. And for Angelenos, image means sex and cars.

The truism in Los Angeles was when men became very successful and wealthy — those men that were reported on in Forbes or publicized in Variety — turned 40-years old, they had to decide between a mistress younger then their children or a red convertible. Both wealthy and successful, not to mention enamored with his family, Copland selected a convertible over a mistress.

As a result of investing, usually with other people's money, and establishing a policy of holding and never selling his Los Angeles area real estate, Copland had became a well-to-do man at a young age. Then again, anyone moderately bright was a millionaire if they owned LA property, at least a paper millionaire. It was just that Copland was always slightly different and kept purchasing investment properties until his firm—Diablo Capital—became one of the largest landlords in the city with an extensive rolodex of high profile investors.

In addition to his real estate holdings, Copland owned four legal MMJ dispensaries in Los Angeles County; in contrast to Bing who owned illegal cultivation sites. The 'PRE-ICO Proposition D' compliant dispensary in Van Nuys was his first MMJ endeavor. During the past few years Adam had been spending an inordinate amount of time in Colorado investigating the network of legal dispensaries and marijuana cultivation sites in the state where recreational grass was already sanctioned. Adam anticipated a post-Volstead era eventually for marijuana in the most populous county within the most populous state. Copland was jumping from the high dive directly into the depths of a pool containing more marijuana smokers than anywhere else on earth—the ten million people who populated Los Angeles County.

He took his time to learn more and more about the operational side of the most profitable business venture outside of Silicon Valley. The dispensary was a veritable cash cow, and he owned it privately—without any partners. The dispensary had to generate ten times more cash flow than the property it sat on, which one of his investment groups owned.

A strikingly handsome man, Copland was husky, though at five foot nine inches, he was an inch shorter than Gabriela. He had straight light-brown hair that naturally bleached blond every year in the summer sun. He had a high forehead, and a powerful chiseled jaw that offset his prominent aquiline nose. His piercing green eyes with brown speckles (his wife preferred to call them gold speckles) would always stare directly at the person talking, making anyone bluffing or feigning knowledge of the topic being discussed uncomfortable.

It was almost 8 p.m. on that Sunday evening as the Aston clung to the sharp turns off Sunset into Beverly Hills. Whizzing past

Jacaranda trees, which bordered most houses on lower Benedict, Copland was uncharacteristically oblivious that they had just begun to bloom with purple-blue flowers. The glutinous flowers kept the gardeners cursing as they blanketed yards, and uninvitingly scattered over the street.

He slowed down ever so briefly to pick up a call from his mentor, Irving Green, who had been ringing Adam's cellphone incessantly.

"Where have you been? I've been calling for hours." Green was closer to Copland than Green was to his two sons who were the type of boys who bullied kids at Beverly Hills High. 40% of the student body at BH High was immigrants that spoke Farsi as their primary language. The boys were from Green's third marriage to a woman 30 years younger than his first wife.

"You know I don't answer my phone when I'm in a meeting, and I had that five o'clock investor appointment at Il Fornaio. Jeez. I didn't realize it's already eight o'clock."

"Well, Adam . . . how did your meeting go, boychick?" Green was prominent in the Forbes 400 for the past three decades, and Irving wasn't accustomed to waiting, or being ignored.

"I just completed the presentation to my new investors," he said.

"And . . ."

"I raised $12.5 million from the 'foreclosure kings' for our new deal." Known to his friends as AC, he was roused that extraordinary summer evening. Conforming with the legions of Los Angeles drivers talking on their cell phone to clients about business, or sending text messages to a mistress about a rendezvous; Copland routinely talked with investors while driving.

"Really?" Green said. "That's absolutely fantastic. Excellent!" Green and Copland were co-General Partners in numerous investments. Copland desperately needed the funds for the purchase of a new strip mall located in the South Bay that he already had in escrow with a $400,000 nonrefundable deposit after having waived contingencies. Banks considered his financial statement 24-karat, but Copland was like a farmer—land rich and cash poor as he kept acquiring more and more income properties. Green was land rich and cash rich. He once told Adam, "If I don't have $25 million cash in the bank, I'm uncomfortable."

"After anteing up the money, they invited me to the new Wolfgang Puck restaurant in the Beverly Wilshire, which I declined. I'm so exhausted all I want is a quiet evening. Maybe listen to Duke Ellington's 'Mood Indigo' and have dinner at home. Celebrate with Gabriela."

Green laughed. "I know you two. It's whoopee-schtuppy time. That's my boy. Ah, to be young and virile with your gorgeous wife. Well, have fun. Lots of fun. I'll be home with Ardith." And he let out a loud sigh at the mention of his jabbering wife.

They hung up in time for Copland to barely slow down for the left turn onto Cielo Drive. He zoomed past famous sites, like the place where Sharon Tate was murdered, and only-in-LA signs, like "Coyote Alert!" The only person Adam had passed that night was a morbidly obese older woman named Myrna struggling with her Rottweiler named Zeus. Zeus was infamous in the immediate neighborhood for attacking other dogs, and biting people walking them. You needed more than your own fingers and toes to count how often the dog escaped when Myrna's Spanish speaking maid, intentionally or not, didn't securely close the gate. Her sloppiness allowed Zeus to prowl the neighborhood searching for feral Santa Monica Mountain animals, or unconfined pets, not unlike a piranha among soon to be shredded minnows. Myrna would state, "Oh. Somehow dear Zeus escaped." She was the unctuous sort that doesn't have the words 'I'm sorry' or an apology in her vocabulary.

Finally, he turned right on Vue Soleil Drive. As he approached his house, he noticed the security gate was open. He drove smoothly up the long driveway lined with Italian Cypress to the four-car garage. He grabbed a large paper bag from the passenger seat and headed toward the house.

Inhaling the sweet-smelling Eucalyptus trees surrounding the garage, he ignored the jillion-dollar panorama afforded of the LA basin from the well-lit mountaintop retreat.

It was early evening, and the only sound in the canyon was that of a captured cat crying, trumpeting his pain, and being consumed while it was still breathing by a well-fed coyote. It didn't look like one of its scrawny desert relatives whose subsistence was tenuously dictated by sparse desolate fauna. No, these coyotes regularly dined on house pets whose owners went out of their way to buy pet food without grain in the mixture, but were too obtuse to bring their beloved animals inside at nightfall. Careless canyon residents had made the area 'Coyote Paradise'.

He headed around the back past the swimming pool. The walkway was lined with James Galway double-flower rose bushes climbing white wood trellis' that hid an ugly cinder block retaining wall. He reached the master bedroom in the rear of the house. The weather was sufficiently warm to generate a strong aroma from the night blooming jasmine strategically placed under the bedroom windows. Past the house was an herb garden containing mint, basil overflowing in five containers, Serrano chilis, cilantro, and numerous rosemary bushes.

He surreptitiously opened one of the French doors, and slithered into the bedroom. He smiled at Gabriela's clothes placed neatly on the bed—as he had anticipated, she was showering.

Without dispute, prior to their marriage, Gabriela was keenly aware of her man's reputation for excessive playfulness. Complicating his congenital devilment was her tendency to be jumpy — like when she was a child at the Roxy Theatre in Hershey, Pennsylvania watching Bambi in the fire scene — at any of his monkeying around.

Once going overboard teasing her, she loudly stated, "Somewhere along the way your mental development was stunted. You are simply a child in a man's body. You just never-ever matured. What's wrong with you?"

An imbecile would have recognized that he went too far, that he had pushed her wrong button. But he had to say, "You wanted me. Now play with me," which was his stock answer, and it was true.

Rapidly stripping off his clothes and throwing them on the floor, he donned a newly purchased black balaclava that had three holes in the face portion for seeing and breathing. The cold weather material irritated his skin, but it was integral for his gag. Next he pulled a black Ruger SR9 out of the paper bag, and moved towards his target in the shower.

The clear glass shower door was foggy from the warm water. Still Adam could make out her figure. Instead of proceeding with his plan, he stared at the body that long ago had wowed him over. He had no idea how much time elapsed. Ogling his naked spouse had aroused him, and allowed sufficient time for his wife to rinse out the shampoo.

Noticing a shadow, Gabriela opened the now opaque door, and said, "You're not a very competent criminal." Adam was standing naked wearing only his goofy ski mask. He was as incompetent a criminal hiding in a balaclava as Lord Raglan directing the disastrous 'Charge of the Light Brigade' at the Battle of Balaclava.

His quasi voyeur minute had created a huge erection that he decided to use sooner than later. He threw her a towel. As she started to dry her body Adam decided to shoot his Ruger. A feeble steam of water hit Gabriela's towel.

"Well, I know your other pistol has a bit more oomph in it," and staring at his naked body, she continued, "You big schmegegge. Come here and kiss me already."

He stopped when his emergency ringtone sounded. Conflicted, he retreated to the bedroom and picked up the phone from the pocket of his discarded pants. His security chief had texted him: *We've been ROBBED!!! FUCKING ROBBED! Get here now. ROBBERY!!*

He yelled at top of his lungs, "Fuck. Shit. Fuck!"

Naked and disappointed, Gabriela said, "Another damn problem?"

Looking forlorn, he said, "The dispensary has been robbed. I love you, but I've got to go."

Back in the car and driving north on Benedict, he yelled, "Robbery? What the hell is going on? Why do I pay all these security guards only to get robbed!"

His thoughts were bouncing around like pinballs, and his dream of a perfect evening with Gabriela was evaporating.

"What a screwed-up life I live," he kept repeating. "What a screwed-up life I live." He owned palatial homes in Beverly Hills and Malibu. He was married to a former fashion model. They had a gorgeous and healthy daughter. Adam's annual income rivaled small developing countries. He had more money than he ever could imagine.

He was flat out wrong — he wasn't living hell on earth. He was living a dream life, and he had a life that would be envied by 99% of the world's population. And he knew it. There were always bumps in the road to success.

Or to quote the great dramatist Pierre Corneille, "To win without risk is to triumph without glory."

CHAPTER 5

Sunday 9:30pm - Van Nuys
The Devil's Playground and Health Center

《《ℭ ℭ》》

Glancing left when he reached Mulholland, AC turned west and in a split second arrived at Beverly Glen. He continued driving too fast in the next canyon bound for the San Fernando Valley. Adam was the caricature of Evelyn Waugh's warning that he "did everything at deleterious speed." With the convertible top still down, he felt the beginning of a dry warm Santa Ana wind, also known as 'devil winds'; funneled into the area from the Cajon Pass.

At the corner of Ventura Boulevard and Beverly Glen, Copland's face transformed from hostility and now appeared deeply dejected. Crossing Ventura, Beverly Glen became Van Nuys Boulevard and the area morphed from high-end single-family homes to upscale retail. Driving further north and going beneath the Ventura Freeway overpass, the quality of the retail firms significantly declined. Taco shops serving questionable meat, car washes, tawdry pawnbrokers, and cheap fast food chains occupied storefronts as Adam approached his shopping mall at the corner of Van Nuys and Ojai Street.

A humongous Samoan man around six five with a swelling paunch waved as soon as Adam pulled up. Waiting for the man to remove an orange traffic cone, Adam noticed the guard's biceps were larger than most professional football players. The man personified the stereotype of a security guard — a former agile lineman on the Carson High School football squad with an upright rigid posture, and a menacing face ready to frighten even Maori warriors dancing to the haka war cry. He pointed Adam to a parking space in the singularly unimpressive commercial center.

Looking down at Adam as he turned off the 12-cylinder engine with an eight-speed automatic transmission, "Are you Adam Coleman? Nick described you and your great wheels. He's waiting for you in the conference room."

Wrong name. And they didn't have a conference room. But Adam ignored the mistakes and dashed to the front of the dispensary. Another security guard opened an innocuous glass front door, allowing Adam to enter a metal cage with a second door made of reinforced steel. Serious security was now in full play.

During business hours a standing security guard, adjacent to the seated receptionist, inspected all individuals who sought admittance. The gated cage door was propped open as the building swarmed with guards wearing "Phantom Security Services" patches on their company-issued shirts.

Another Samoan guard allowed Adam to pass through a large waiting area with two red couches and eight chairs. During business hours, a pretty but bland receptionist verified State of California issued Medical Marijuana (MMJ) ID cards. Regrettably yet realistically, a splinter was sufficient reason for rapacious MMJ doctors to issue a written certification.

Nicholas Petriv, the general manager of Copland's Phantom Security Services, met Adam halfway down the hall. Shaking Nick's hand, Adam said, "A damn robbery. What did they get, Nick?"

Copland had amassed slightly more than $500 million of income producing properties since graduating college. Vertical integration inured profit to Diablo Capital in numerous creative methods: as the General Partner of Limited Partnership syndications owning real estate, AC received a hefty 35% of the profits after a sale. He also earned a 5% Property Management fee. In addition, he generated a 1% fee of the total annual revenues collected as an Asset Management Fee. The fee was a catchall phrase that was obfuscated in every offering prospectus with legal mumbo jumbo, but the comprehensive term earned Adam a cool additional $1,000,000.00 net income every year.

Leaning against the door jamb with his right palm pressed against the painted wood, Nick calmly stated, "Nothing. Absolutely *nada*. The jerky kid sneaked into the store as the cleaning man was putting trash in the dumpster. The old man always uses his bucket as a doorstop. The kid sneaked in and hid in the storage area unaware that the camera system we installed is monitored 24/7 at our headquarters."

"Where's the thief?"

"He's handcuffed, and one of my boys has a 12-gauge shotgun directed right at his pointy little head."

Numerous ideas raced through Adam's mind. How did this man know the exact time to sprint through the open back door? How did he know where to hide? He was glad that only he and Nick knew about the bolstered security system with laser tracking of movement. Also, AC had told Nick a hundred times to get rid of the shotguns since they were illegal in a licensed dispensary and could get him closed down.

Nick was loyal, annoyingly blunt, tenacious, and hard working. Unfortunately he was also the epitome of a loose cannon — always reasoning that he had the best answers to any question, and more argumentative than a politician with poor polling numbers. Every person he met detested him.

Scratching his right temple, Adam preferred time to think but there was no time to think. Although normally congenial, if a person lied or stole from him, Adam had an uncontrollably violent temper. Having experienced a few intemperate incidents that later embarrassed him, AC learned to consistently wait 24 hours before responding to an acrimonious situation. This allowed him time to fully think out the ramifications, how to respond rationally, and to 'cool down' allowing him to be pragmatic. Well, at least he was aware he had a volatile temper, which is the first step in controlling it; or worse case with AC's personality, modifying it.

The shop had closed at 8pm, per city Ordinance 2006-0032, and would reopen Monday at 10am. The shop was open 365 days per year for the legally allowable 10 hours per day, and usually did enhanced sales on holidays.

"Nick, how did this kid know our routine? He had to have inside help, right? Isn't that normally the case with robberies? For a few dollars, some schmuck endangers his job to share in the loot?"

Nick said, "Yeah, I agree. What do you propose? How about me and the boys loosen him up a bit?" Then he gave his annoying "hehe" sound, which he uttered whenever he thought he was clever.

"Let's play good cop bad cop like in the movies. You go back and knock him on his noggin a few times, and I'll step in looking shocked and astonished at how you're treating him."

Nick didn't say a word and headed to the kitchen where the kid was detained.

"All right, kid," Adam heard Nick say in a sick tone. "Let's get this ballgame going."

Although Adam didn't care about the kid, he instinctively cringed as the kid screamed in pain. He decided to take a walk and wandered into the Bud Room. He gazed at the counters brimming with marijuana flowers, each strain pegged to a crazy bizarre name like Golden Goat, Lamb's Bread, Gorilla Glue, and Alaskan Thunder Fuck.

Side by side the spacious allocation for Indica and Sativa strains was a small area dedicated to CBD products. UCLA and other research hospitals were experimenting to test the medicinal benefits of using cannabinoid therapies against placebos. Researchers had already proven the beneficial aspects of CBD to counter medical ailments when the psychoactive element THC was expunged or minimized. The resulting flower was absolutely nonhallucinatory.

In addition, CNBC documented the efficacy of Charlotte's Web high-cannabidiol (CBD) and low-tetrahydrocannabinol (THC) strain. Cannabis life-saving attributes minimized epilepsy, Parkinson's and other diseases associated with seizures.

The Bud Room was divided between flower counters where a prominent sign pushed the daily special, 'Today only $35.00 for an 1/8 of Sour Diesel'. Other counters displayed edibles where the THC laced candies and gummy bears were favorites. Vapes were the hottest item and seemed to become more popular by the day. Pint-sized marijuana 'baby' plants, to be grown at home, were also for sale.

An expert on what attracted men; Gabriela had fitted the female bud-tenders with Devil-issued too-tight fitting white t-shirts with black bras, if the women wore bras. Around 80% of the dispensary sales were to men. To produce generous tips the women flirted with the male clients, and made certain their breasts were exposed copying the pose and artificial sweet talk of newswomen on the local TV stations. Though they spent countless hours bickering, gossiping and back stabbing one another, they all agreed that the baby marijuana plants regularly died by amateur-growers with black thumbs and due to negligence.

The edibles counter gave Adam an idea. He went back to the kitchen turned Inquisition court. Adam feigned shock at how his personal Torquemada was treating the kid. Blood oozed from the teen's mouth. His black t-shirt was ripped exposing the outline of a tattoo that needed to be completed. He now appeared so frightened that Adam was surprised the kid's shoulder-length curly black hair had not been straightened out of fear like in a cartoon.

Adam snapped, "Nick! I need to talk to you outside. Now!" And Adam left the kitchen in a huff.

An animated Nick said, "Wow. This is the most fun I've had since I worked security at the Playboy Mansion. And that was . . ."

Before he could say another word, Adam held his right index finger to his mouth indicating silence. "Follow me," he said.

Pointing to the small refrigerator behind the counter, Adam asked, "Do we have any of that THC-infused tea?"

Nick reached into the fridge and grabbed a Hi-Light brand tea with his big paw, placed the bottle on the glass counter, and said, "What gives?"

"Grab a few glasses and pour the tea into one glass and some Snapple into the other glasses for us," Adam directed. Faced with an unusual situation, a situation he had never experienced, Adam decided on a counter-intuitive approach to the robber. Adam picked up the glass with marijuana-infused tea and kept telling himself in his customary OCD fashion, 'It's in my left hand. It's in my left hand. Remember it's in my left hand'. In his right hand was the glass with Snapple for him to drink.

Faced now with three hostile adults in the room, the kid blurted out, "Call the police. I want the police here. Now!"

Nick snapped, "You're supposed to ask for your lawyer, you numbskull," and whacked the kid on the back of his head.

"Stop it now," yelled Adam.

Adam pushed the glass of tea to the kid. Copland sat down and lifted his glass of Snapple. He said, "Drink up if you're thirsty, kid, because today is your lucky day."

Wiping his sweaty, grimy hands on his jeans, the kid gulped the tea as though it was water.

Moving in close to him, Adam inspected him like he scrutinized everything and everybody. Adam realized the kid was only fourteen or fifteen and petrified. "Do you want more cold drink?" Adam asked. The kid was too nervous to look up or answer, and Adam continued, "Do you know why I said this is your lucky day?" Not expecting an answer, Adam said, "Did you notice that Green Cross outside?"

The teen gulped the glass of tea lickety-split. He let out a thunderous burp. "Yeah, man. I saw it. I ain't blind, you know."

"That's a start," he said. "Now what's your name, and then I'll explain the green cross to you."

The teen said, "Gonzalez. My name is Bozo Gonzalez. Before you ask, yeah, my loco mom liked watching old television shows, and her favorite show was some clown named Bozo. Now I have to live with this fucked-up name."

Adam calmly said, "That green cross, besides indicating we're a Medical Marijuana Dispensary, is a sign we approach health in an alternative manner. I can call the police, and sure, you'll be arrested. I don't think you want that, do you?"

At this point, the cannabinoids in the tea were acting like a dimmer switch on Bozo. Slowing down brain cell connections, which were unfortunately sluggish congenitally. He shook his head so violently Adam expected to hear rattling.

To soften the kid more, Adam said, "The saddest thing imaginable for me is to see a young man in your situation. It's totally unnecessary. We are concerned here with people, the environment, and doing the right thing. Social justice is our quest. The right thing here is for us to talk this out in twenty-first-century terms. After all, Bozo, we're good guys here. We're not uncivilized yokels here. Right?

"Do you know what the word 'chutzpah' means?" Not expecting an explanation, he continued in a louder, more aggressive tone, "It means nerve. And kid, you had some nerve robbing me." He gritted his teeth, and hissed, "Robbing me, you little schmuck."

Nick lightly kicked Adam's chair to remind him to play the role they agreed he would play, and not let his emotions surface.

Adam resumed his pretense, smiled broadly showing his pearly white teeth, and renewed his milder tone. He said, "Your night has been a disaster so far. You are either going to be arrested, or worse, one of these men is going to break your knees."

The kid was now flying sky-high, having consumed a full bottle of THC-infused tea instead of the prescribed portion of 1/8 of the bottle. He seemed unconcerned about the barefaced threat. Adam knew it was time to strike.

"Listen, Bozo. You seem like a nice kid, and I don't want you to get into trouble or have a police record. I want you to tell me the truth. I don't believe you figured out this robbery scheme yourself. Did you have someone help you? Maybe someone here? Did one of my employees help you? Who do know at the dispensary? Who planned this robbery?"

Before Bozo could decide if he was going to answer the questions, Adam rose, and said, "Make your decision carefully. You've already lost enough blood."

Nick opened the door for Adam, and followed him back to the Bud Room.

"For all our occasional petty bickering, we do pretty well working together," Nick grudgingly stated. "And I think your psychological ploy was great. You're not really leaving, though, are you? The fun and action is just beginning."

Adam said, "Yes, I did not my best Sergeant Joe Friday imitation. Now he needs the fear of Nick in him, not my pussy footing. Call me when he gives up his partner. I could stay an hour for when he decides to talk, but I need a few hours of sleep. I'm exhausted. And he will talk, one way or the other."

Nick appeared to be salivating and let a laugh that Satan would have been proud of. He said, "Give him a few hours with me, and Bozo will change his attitude pronto and spill the beans."

As Adam left, he heard Nick singing the "Mr. Rogers" theme song.

"It's a beautiful day in this neighborhood,

A beautiful day for a neighbor,

Would you be mine? Could you be mine?

I have always wanted to have a neighbor just like you to fuck up."

CHAPTER 6

Van Nuys, CA

Walking out of the dispensary, Devil's Playground resembled a fusion between a funky 60's head shop and a hip H&M store. Copland viewed the other businesses in the center and smirked that the city father's would definitely deem his hodgepodge activities as inappropriate. More important than city council members not being into his tacky ventures, his high-priced Century City lawyers had accumulated all necessary city and county permits, zoning approval and corporate by-laws to insure that these firms were all legit.

Clear-cut seediness he readily acknowledged. Nevertheless his firms were so successful that without hesitation they gave the appearance of being the proverbial Money Tree printing dollar bills. The young Copland was not congenitally predisposed to 'sin' industries. Unambiguously he was amenable to any straightforward and fast path out of poverty as long as it didn't hurt other people. Hell, he would invest in bat guano futures if he could and it was profitable.

Voracious eclectic reading, rather than formal education, facilitated AC's dismantling of the puritanical values indoctrinated by his parents and Horace Mann's Prussian-genus schoolteachers. Same old stuff memorization doesn't engender creativity. In consequence, Adam singularly instilled his own all-encompassing iconoclastic-contrarian temperament by independently reading Nietzsche, H.L. Mencken, Bertrand Russell, and Mario Vargas Llosa, over and over. It didn't hurt spending inspired long evenings quaffing fine wines from Bordeaux with his charming English drinking buddy, Christopher Hitchens. Borne out by studying human frailties and history, he invested his own funds in what sophisticated unctuous people considered crude and vulgar business opportunities.

Having listened for years to the public rantings of bombastic clergyman and other members of the morality police castigate liquor consumption, drugs and women dancing the 'hootchy koo'; Adam decided his investors would do nicely with the prohibitively high rents paid by questionable tenants whose existence would be nullified if Carrie Nation types prevailed. As vacancies occurred in his retail centers, or when AC paid failing firms to vacate their leased premises, he filled the empty areas with every disreputable business imaginable as long as they were extraordinarily profitable and paid the rent punctually.

Proudly scanning his L-shaped property just past the witching hour, the 100% leased site now accommodated a large liquor store whose primary business was selling discounted premium wines by the case on the internet, a massage parlor featuring 'Acupressure,' a strip joint that employed a doublespeak title describing itself as a 'Gentleman's Club' as though they were an offshoot of the Bohemian Club. Finally he did a double take at his premier cash cow — the Devil's Playground and Health Center.

There was no doubt that these four Copland owned businesses were equal to a thrill ride for adults while providing the Copland family financial peace of mind distinct from the passive investors in Bernie Madoff's ruinous scam including Steven Spielberg, Sandy Koufax and Kevin Bacon.

Within Copland's consciousness, in spite of his inordinate success, was a constant feeling of insecurity. Most of his friends had attended an Ivy League school or the equivalent such as Stanford or UC Berkeley. They all had advanced degrees; and belonged to some club that, although it didn't truly interest him, made him feel like an outsider.

So to give the appearance that he was a member of the upper crust of Westside society, and in defiance against his better financial acumen, he accepted Irving Green's solicitation and invested in West Wilshire Bank at its inception. At Irving's behest, Adam was elected to the Board of Directors of the Bank, which soon led to joining the Board of Trustees of Edge-Hill Psychiatric Hospital and various charities. Although West Wilshire Bank was a horrible investment decision, his unmistakable rationale for the choice was to say 'Au Revoir" to his plebian heritage, or in Gabriela's words, "good riddance to bad rubbish."

It turned out that the ulterior motivation was money well spent. The investment and concomitant directorships yielded untold relationships with the cream of Los Angeles society that more than compensated for the substandard bank return. With Adam's admittance, this parvenu couple now made the scene at yawn-producing nouveau riche functions. After all the cocktail parties she attended in Manhattan during her modeling days, and all the 4pm pitchers of martini's, Gabriela could give a damn about society types. On the other hand, they did make benign fodder for her overt caustic slights. Also, she took for granted Adam's deceptively simple stratagem for rendezvousing with the city's elite, or called the 1% by those who were envious and rapaciously covetous.

Once the couple was admitted to this prestigious 'haute monde', or purchased admittance in Copland's case, he realized this situation was akin to repeating Ali Baba's phrase 'Open Sesame' as more doors opened to deep-pocket investors for his real estate acquisitions.

Among his new acquaintances were five men who were thick as thieves. They always invested together, golfed together, vacationed together, played bridge together, and unbeknownst to one another, occasionally screwed one another wives. Each man had made a substantial fortune joining forces and thereby monopolizing the county's foreclosure market. Coincidentally they called themselves the 'Forty Thieves'.

Auspiciously for Copland and his cohorts, this found formula for success was replicated in three additional locations; plus with the 40 thieves backing he would soon add another sleaze mill. Adam learned long ago not to be concerned that his hugely profitable firms lacked esteem or prominence. Rather he relished the benefits that these were not only highly profitable, but with the exception of the Internet wine sales, were primarily cash ventures. As a sin entrepreneur, the ventures afforded an incredible life style for the young man and his family. He proceeded with the philosophy that the numbskulls at the IRS didn't know where to begin looking for his cash, gold and Bitcoin due to the myriad of his interlaced firms. Plus if he saved annually $15,000,000.00 here or there in cash dealings, he was ecstatic to pay an occasional $200,000.00 or $300,000.00 after an audit. Wealthy yes, and precociously rich in experience.

Sophisticates that mocked sleaze did frequent his brazen businesses, only they went through the back door hidden from public view, not the front entrance used by the hoi polloi.

Outside under the alabaster crescent moon, fatigue finally overpowered Adam's robust stamina. His only desire was to drive home, cuddle next to Gabriela, who he was certain was sound asleep.

Pausing from thinking about and rationalizing about his wickedly profitable firms, AC suddenly realized he had a bellyache and how hungry he was. The bevy of extra guards had gone home. He got in his car, drove a few yards to the exit on Van Nuys, and anticipated an empty Boulevard. Instead an endless progression of low-riding cruisers queued up with their candy-colored or metallic painted cars. He was stopped flat by laid-back goofs that he knew were flying high; so he hoped at least they were smoking Devil's Playground ganja.

Waiting for these slow-driving slow-thinking motorists to allow him to turn on to Van Nuys Boulevard hardened his unhappiness. He finally barged between to two cars moving at a snails-pace. Driving south he was too drunk with exhaustion to notice two young girls flashing the enervated man in the snazzy car. Twenty minutes later he pulled into his garage under a now rayless moon.

A slight flare-up from the network of thousands of neurons at the base of his cortex emerged as he walked to and opened the front door. He asked himself, "How did I get here?" Immediate fear engulfed him when he understood he was so tired that he couldn't remember any aspects of the drive home. He didn't like not being in control. His OCD protective aegis had dissolved, and that wouldn't do for a man who depended on his wits to survive.

Walking slowly past the living room filled with south and east Asian artifacts, he went through a long hallway plastered with second tier California Impressionist paintings from circa 1900. Another of Gabriela's unique terms was the living room was the LR. Adam entered the master bedroom and feasted his eyes on the woman he called 'Sex Ball' sleeping supine. Her bedside lamp was on and the latest Jonathan Kellerman mystery novel was lying on her stomach.

Removing his clothes, he methodically placed the shirt and suit on hangers, and threw his socks and undies in the hamper. Careful not to wake Gabriela, Adam slid into bed and wrapped his arms around her like a comforting duvet. His movement disrupted her sound sleep, and she mumbled, "Umm. Dinner's ready."

Adam held back laughing, and fell fast asleep with his left arm wrapped around Gabriela. His head shared her pillow; too exhausted to care he was in a puddle of melted moisturizer that she had applied on her face hours ago.

* * *

Five hours later, the early morning June fog lifted. Adam was out of bed and within sight of the kitchen where the fragrant aroma of French press coffee brewing wafted through the front of the house. The bodum was filled with the caffeine he desperately yearned for when his cellphone rang. It was Nick, asking where he was.

Momentarily forgetful about last night's robbery, he said, "It's 6am". Then his disagreeableness lifted like the morning fog and he vividly recalled the robbery.

He asked, "What happened after I left? Was I correct about an employee touting the kid on how to rob us? Come on. Was it an inside job? Who ultimately is to blame if my guess is correct?" Adam's proclivity was for his left arm to quiver as though he had Parkinson's when he was excited or nervous, and he was agitated.

Nick was many things, and prominently he was a master manipulator. Uncharacteristically patient, he didn't interrupt. He enjoyed letting his epigrammatically articulate boss ramble, and he imagined the confused look on Adam's face. "It's all right," Nick assured him. "I've got all the facts. Want to have coffee and a bagel at Peet's and discuss last night?"

Gabriela appeared at the kitchen door with two frisky dogs that had chased squirrels prior to their diurnal defecation. She couldn't allow the dogs outside without supervision for two reasons: coyotes would enjoy the boys (as she called the dogs) as dim sum, and the older dog had an obnoxious habit of eating his feces if left alone.

Husband and wife being fun-damently eccentric, agreed to name their two Maltese's after favorite Mediterranean sheep cheeses, Feta and Ricotta, which were appropriate names for the pure white pooches.

While the boys attacked Adam's legs, Gabriela stood stalwartly silent, listening to Adam say, "7:30 ok? Let's meet at Solly's Deli in the Gelson's center on Van Nuys."

"So what's happening now?" She asked.

"Last night's wild ride is starting again," Adam answered. "Though Nick is overly suspicous, he wisely didn't want to talk on the phone. I'm meeting him in an hour for an update on just what happened."

She muzzled her despondency, and said, "Well, if the kid spilled the beans. What are you going to do to him?"

"Good question," and Adam left her hanging as he didn't have an answer, yet.

Gabriela tried to be indifferent; instead she retained her distinctive sense of humor for a minute. She mustered the courage to tease, "Well, your dinner and my kitty cat will be waiting again tonight if that interests you in any way, shape or form."

Eventually her stone cold face crumbled as she reacted in the manner how she always reacted to a problem, or when confronted with anxiety — she started to cry and cry until the house seemed to reverberate with her sorrow.

Seeing her drop to the kitchen floor, Adam rushed to her side but was second to her rescue as the dogs sympathetically commenced licking her on the face, or any part of her body that was accessible. Once again her plans to spend the day with Adam had gone kaput. She felt like the floor beneath her was dropping, and after being awake less than 30 minutes, she was listless.

Adam assumed the herculean task of comforting her nervous mania caused by his impending departure. He briefly considered a Valium as the answer to her exaggerated reaction. Personally detesting opioids even when he was in pain, however the very real fear of her addictive personality quashed that palliative.

"Listen baby. You know how much I love you," Adam said and she looked at him with the mascara she had applied this morning running over her face. "I have to settle this issue. You know that. I promise to be home early. We'll pop the cork on a 1990 Krug and I'll party with my sweetie. If I'm late again, well." He stopped talking and tried to come up with an exaggeration to make his point, and said, "Well, you can pull a Lorena Bobbit on me. Okay?"

Gabriela sighed. From the moment they met and he started spending all of his free time with her, she abandoned any pretense of Manhattan-like refinement. Extraordinary for a sophisticate, she even developed a soft spot for his propensity for puerile demented humor.

She said, "Hug me really tight. You are a crazy man. But you're my crazy man forever." After a few minutes, she said, "The sooner you get dressed, the sooner you get home," and kissed him as though she was preparing for tonight.

* * *

When Nick returned from the restroom, he dropped into the seat next to his boss. A waitress, with dyed-black hair, held a tray with their order of two bagels, cream cheese, and two hot mocha coffees. Nick said, "I'm breaking my Atkins Diet," and distributed the food and utensils.

"Gabriela told me a funny story about Dr. Atkins," Adam said. "Seems Dr. Atkins is a serial entrepreneur. When she was a model in Manhattan, she and her girl friends got their black beauties from the one and only Dr. Atkins, now of Miami Diet fame."

"Speed is dangerous stuff," Nick said. "I know. Why was she speeding?"

"Models have to stay thin," Adam said. "And the speed pills killed her appetite."

"Dangerous stuff," Nick reiterated. "Switching the subject. Well, last night was interesting, to say the least". Talking with his mouth packed with bagel, he said, "I followed your instructions. Stood Bozo up and sandwiched the kid between Petey and myself. We bounced him between us a few times. He remained quiet. I told Pete, no matter what he says, bounce him 100 times. To relieve the boredom, we punched him each time he bounced over to us. Changes occurred with about the fifteenth punch when I also kicked him in the balls. That kid was actually fairly tough."

Unaccustomed to violence, Adam wanted to skip the details, and said, "Did Bozo have a partner?"

"Apparently you wrote the manual when it comes to reading people," Nick said. "The luck of the draw was when I kicked him. By then he was more than willing to give up his partner. Turns out that one of our employees, Isabella Rojas, is his aunt. She was the driving force in this botched robbery. Her mother kicked Isabella out of her apartment and Isabella's living at a friend's place, and dumpster diving for food. She has no moolah. Flat broke. Spent all her money on drugs."

Together they said, "What a shame."

Quietly Adam asked, "What do we do now?" The question was more figurative, rather than literally asking Nick a question.

Nick pushed the check to Adam. "You pay the bill. Leave Isabella to me," said Nick, and he was gone faster than a world-class Jamaican sprinter.

Adam felt preposterous leaving the Isabella problem with Nick. Then he thought. 'How much worse can the situation get? In one way or another Nick will clear up the issue'. Adam had a headache, and it wasn't getting better.

* * *

Nichols Canyon, Sunday 10PM

Morrison Guzman was accustomed to Bing living in large houses, but the estate in Nichols Canyon was immense. He parked on the street and walked up a steep driveway to a six-car garage. To the left of the garage was a walkway leading to the front door shaded by tall California Pepper trees. Not that M would know a pepper tree from a cactus—all he knew was money.

Par for the course, the door was unlocked. It looked like an opulent frat house, with a few pieces of furniture dotted around the living room, three dried-out ficus trees, and overturned beer cans everywhere.

Nothing new here, thought M. He climbed the circular staircase to the master bedroom where Bing conducted business. Appearing to be bed-ridden, Bing was sucking on a red lollipop, and wrapped tight in a down comforter with the air-conditioner blasting.

Seeing his old high school buddy, Bing said, "This summer is starting off wrong. Somebody fucked me."

Bing tossed M a lollipop. He started to open it but instead placed it on the counter. It was the fashionable opioid of the moment—fentanyl in a lollipop.

"What the hell are you blasting the a/c if you're cold?" M asked, gesturing at the comforter.

Bing's eyelids appeared weighted down, and he laughed. "Back in the Philippines, my friends and I would go to homes of our rich friend's, wrap ourselves in their parents' comforters and turn the air-conditioning up all the way. We all fantasized about living in the cold United States. We all had relatives already living here. They told us how cold it gets in New York in winter. So we played New York, New York with comforters and the air-conditioning."

'Really bizarre,' thought Morrison. Being geographically deficient, "So your Filipino," said Morrison.

"You've known me for ten years,' Bing said. "You didn't know I'm a Flip?"

"What the hell is a Flip?" Said Cary, walking in from the hallway.

"Flip is what Filipinos call ourselves," Bing said. "Like blacks calling each other niggers."

"Truly weird," said Cary as he sauntered in, constant vape pen in hand. He stood, looked at M. "Who's this guy?"

"That's my buddy M, short for Morrison," Bing said.

"Morrison?" said Cary. "Like Jim Morrison?"

"Yeah," said Morrison. "Except it's my first name. My mom was addicted to the Doors and named me after Jim Morrison."

Bing sighed loudly, victim card on the table. "Bro. I've been robbed. Five different locations. They took millions. Millions, man. I'm dead meat if we can't figure out who did this to me and get my grass back."

"I know," said M. "I feel for you. The news is all over town."

"Shit. I'm a desperate man. Any thoughts? Any suggestions?" Morrison had warned Bing that selling weed grown by the Peckerwoods and other street gangs was trouble. And he knew that to collect a debt for a consignment of marijuana, the Krazy Ass Mexican (KAMs) or Peckerwood gangs wouldn't hire an attorney to file a lawsuit in superior court. No way, Jose. The KAMs and the Peckerwoods collected their debts by the barrel of a sawed-off, 12-gauge shotgun.

Apparently even a dimwit has an epiphany once every ten or twenty years, because after a moment of deep thought, M said, "I got it. There's this dude I sell grass to. Adam Copland. He has a slew of dispensaries and some grows. Here's the kicker. He owns on the sly a private security company that has private guards for MMJ dispensaries. Why don't I put you two together? Maybe he can do some snooping around and find out who stole your shit."

Continuously pacing around the room, Cary said, "Sounds like a plan, bro," and continued inhaling.

Bing didn't answer. Thanks to the effects of the fentanyl mixed with coke and grass, he had crashed in the middle of one of Morrison's few intelligent thoughts. A doctor had warned the 37-year old man that his flamboyant lifestyle was perniciously toxic to his health. Bing never said no to a new Blonde, or to drinking, or to nonstop partying. Outwardly still a young man; apparently Bing had the heart and respiratory system of a 70-year old man.

CHAPTER 7

Winnetka, CA
Monday 8AM

From the broken door of the shed in M's backyard, two men carried empty bags of fertilizer and a burnt-out, thousand-watt HPS lamp. The shed contained ten grow lights with eight marijuana plants under each lamp. M had never parked in his garage. Instead he hammered plywood connected to insulation to the walls, and used it to grow baby plants in, virtually without aroma escaping from the garage. After four weeks of growth, M transferred the babies grown in the garage to the backyard shed for another eight weeks until maturity.

A virtuoso distributor of grass, he was an absolutely dreadful grower. M was disappointed that he was incompetent, and had never attained the marijuana industry norm of 1.5 to 2 pounds of cannabis per grow light. He failed to recognize that growing marijuana is an agricultural business, and to obtain high-quality weed required utmost cleanliness combined with constant attention. His garage and grow shed had ponds of scummy water scattered in different spots, and spider mites regularly devoured his plants. His backyard grow never yielded more than a pathetic 1/2-pound per light.

Still the work did provide him around $60,000 net per year, tax-free. It was a matter he misrepresented on his IRS Form 1099 as income from an IT consulting firm. The bottomless pit of avarice blinded Morrison to the fact that a raid by the LA City Safe Streets Task Force on his home would also bring Child Protective Services to latch on to his M&M daughters.

Guzman is the Peter Principle incarnate. Unhappy with merely dealing grass, he constantly attempted to raise money from his extensive dealer contacts to start a large-scale grow. Luckily for his contacts, he failed to raise sufficient funds or locate a building owner that would lease to him. Otherwise his investors would have lost their entire investment.

M and another high school buddy, Ricardo, tossed the trash in garbage cans, and drove to Starbucks for their daily buttery croissant and coffee. Ricardo stormed his way to the only empty table before it was lost while Morrison used his debit card to pay for their breakfast. As usual his checking account was overdrawn, and he paid cash.

He filled Ricardo in on his plan to put Bing and Copland together. "Bing's freaking out. I've got this feeling if I have Bing meet Copland that I'll make money in some way. What goes around, comes around. I don't know how, but somehow I'll benefit. You know that Chinese saying about Yun and Yang. Well we have Bing and Adam." M screwed as many young bud tenders as he screwed up Chinese proverbs.

Ricardo was tossing down his croissant, and could only nod his head in agreement. After chewing loudly, he laughed and said, "Yo, Bing's famous for his hissy fits. What a crybaby. How can you stand him, M?"

"Jesus Christ. The man is out a ton of weed. Literally, a ton of weed. The Peckerwoods are gonna slice off his balls. Give the bastard a break."

M called Copland's Century City office. He heard the phone ring, and a receptionist said, "Diablo Capital. How may I direct your call?"

"Hi," said M. "Adam Copland, please. My name is Morrison Guzman."

"Hello, this is Adam," AC said.

"Morrison Guzman here," said M. "I met you a few times at your shop on Van Nuys Boulevard."

"Of course," said AC. "I know who you are. The bud tenders have nothing but good things to say about you. What can I do for you?" In fact, one of the bud tenders who was perpetually pregnant, would swoon every time Morrison appeared at the dispensary.

"Great," said M, happy and somewhat surprised. "A close friend of mine has gotten into a mess. An incredible mess. It's best not to talk on the phone."

"I have a meeting at ten in Beverly Hills. Want to meet around noon for lunch?"

Morrison jumped at the opportunity, and said, "Let's meet at Pink's Hot Dog stand on La Brea."

"No," said Adam. "That won't do. I'm a vegetarian. How about Nate 'n Al's on Beverly Drive, just south of little Santa Monica?"

"You're on," said M and the phone went silent.

Feeling like a real gangsta, M went back for a second croissant.

* * *

Standing up, putting on his jacket, AC left his office. He said to his secretary, "Marina, I've got a meeting at 10 and another at noon. Probably won't be back till late."

The Russian woman was nearly 6' tall with an attractive but vapid face. She had huge natural breasts, and was too thin—to a fault.

When it came to Adam, she was always in a playful mood. She said, "Maybe we have drink tonight. No?" She hiked her skirt up which wasn't fair to a normal man without AC's forbearance.

"No, Marina del Rey. Not tonight," Adam said. Adam thought, *'You're gorgeous, but not any night'*.

"Why you always call me Marina del Rey?" Asked Marina. "You know my name is Marina Nazarovych Bubka."

"It's just a joke," Adam said. "A play on words. Listen. When I stop teasing people that's the time to worry. I tease people I like."

That was the opening she was waiting for, and said, "Ah. So you do like me. I knew it. I can make you very happy man. You …"

Adam dashed off, and said, "Got to run. See you." Once walking in Century City, Adam and his lawyer commented on the extent of attractive women in Los Angeles. Adam had said, "Yea, they might have great bodies. But very few have a beautiful face like my wife. That is without paying $40,000.00 to Dr. Leaf over on Camden Drive." His lawyer replied, "Yup. If one is going to fool around, better be ready to pay the alimony train. It's just not worth the trouble." And that summarized their mutual belief on infidelity.

* * *

On Highway 15, outside Baker, Jamal Holloway pulled his Explorer to the right lane to exit at Kelbaker Road. Pulling up at Alien Jerky, he placed his joint in the ashtray, and said, "Jamarqua, wait till you taste this jerky, little dude."

Jamal was training the younger Holloway to be his main man. Someone he could rely on, dissimilar to the bungling DeTracy. Jamal wasn't going to blunder using the wrong man as his backup.

Jamal had made this trip every other week since robbing Bing, conducting himself in the following order: First, he placed his stolen grass in five large coolers so the product wouldn't be damaged under the intense summer sun in the desert. Second, he drove from Altadena to Las Vegas, and always stopped at Alien Jerky in Baker. Third, he dropped off his stolen marijuana with numerous dealers in Las Vegas. Unlike Cary Sweetzer, Jamal always got paid. True to his 6'10" stature, Jamal had to consume at least 5,000 calories a day just to maintain his weight. His cousin Jamarqua was accustomed to southern food, not southern Indian cuisine. Entering India Palace on Twain, south of the Vegas strip, Jamal was mobbed by the staff that was delighted to see their old customer. They knew him as a charming aficionado of their spice-laden food, and knew nothing of his killer instinct. Fourth, he drove Interstate 93 through Kingman and Wikieup to still more marijuana dealers in Arizona. A few dealers from Flagstaff and Tucson joined him in central Phoenix with local dealers for his "*pot*-luck." The strategy of offering free samples always worked.

Lastly, he took his time returning to LA. The two men would share a motel room with twin beds, always staying at a motel where the daily charge included a complimentary breakfast. Jamal's giant frame needed his hourly food injection more than a diabetic. He would get his haircut, tip the maids, stroll gift stores, and buy his mother a gift. He did everything to blend in as just another tourist enjoying the desert. If the speed limit was 65, Jamal drove 62 The last thing Holloway wanted was to be a black man unnecessarily pulled over with his retirement funds in the back seat.

Banks are required to alert the IRS of a deposit of $10,000 or more in cash. So Jamal buried the cash in waterproof bags under his pit bull's doghouse. He dug a hole next to the doghouse. Then tunneled under the house, and plopped his blood money—no one was going to fool with that dog or his cash.

* * *

Parked across the street from Bing's house, Morrison said, "Ricardo. We need to wake Bing up and get him to this meeting. That *idiota* is probably still hung over from last night." They didn't meet anyone on the grounds or as they opened the unlocked door.

"Shit, man," said Ricardo. "What an easy place to rob. How much weed does this wuss keep in the house?"

"Don't even go there," said Morrison. They shot up the stairs, ignoring the women sleeping on the living room couch, contentedly unaware of them. Wrapped in his comforter with the air conditioner blasting, Bing was asleep next to his favorite new blonde. A thick pond of vomit lay next to him.

"Jesus, that stinks," said Ricardo. "This dude parties way too much." The two men spent the next hour cleaning him up, while the blonde slept on and Bing's Vietnamese pot-bellied pig roamed the room.

* * *

At noon, Adam walked past and nodded to Frank, a man begging on the pavement in front of the deli. Three men—one nearly as disheveled as Frank—approached him. The handsome one introduced himself as M, and Adam now understood the bud tenders' rave reviews. M introduced the disheveled man as Bing. Occasionally, Adam took an instant dislike to a person. Today, as he watched Bing hand Frank a dollar, that person was Bing.

As they entered the deli, Adam said, "Happens to be that Frank, the fellow sitting on the sidewalk, does incredibly well. At the end of every day he comes into the deli, after his begging stint, and cashes in around three hundred in change. He has a family and isn't destitute." Bing looked at Adam sideways, and Adam felt a wave of satisfaction, knowing he had just thoroughly pissed off Bing.

Evelyn, Adam's favorite waitress for her jet-black hair, handed them menus and pointed to his usual table. "Let's order first and then tell me why you wanted to meet," said Adam.

After ordering, as they waited for their food, Bing recounted his weed robbery. His suspicions of AC persisted, and although he had weed debts to two deadly gangs, he didn't betray his inordinate veracious fear of the Peckerwoods nor the KAM's in front of Copland.

Carefully modeling his behavior and questioning to copy his mentors thinking that was 'less said is better'. Adam could tell Bing wasn't telling him the whole story, but he said, "Well boys, how can I help?" Irving Green had taught him the benefits of appearing diffident in the face of danger, or even in the remote possibility of Charlize Theron propositioning him.

M said, "I've heard you're also a banker. Can you lend Bing money? He's good for it cause of his incredible marijuana biz." Bing's life and business were in jeopardy, but Morrison summoned up the fortitude to put up a deceptive façade.

Deliberately stalling, Adam called over Evelyn and ordered a New York-style cheesecake for the table. Just as he could see M start to shift around uncomfortably, he answered. "Banks are federally insured, and are prohibited by the FDIC from making loans to MMJ-related firms. But there are other approaches contingent upon your cash flow and credit."

"Credit?" Bing chuckled. "Banks would die laughing looking at my credit. I owe money everywhere." Bing would not let anyone help with his books beyond telling whatever blonde was around that there was $100,000 cash in his safe—usually left wide open. Consequently, stoned most of the day, the week, and the month, he persistently overlooked paying bills on time, and no one else stayed around long enough to care.

"Shit, Bing," said Morrison. "Tell him the truth already. I put you two together so Mr. Copland can help you."

Bing seemed to relent—after all, relenting gave him an opportunity to brag about his wealth. "Look, man. I appreciate your help. Here's the scoop. I owe some very dangerous people around $3 million. I make a lot of money. Probably around $150,000 a month. All cash. But I can't pay $3 million at one time. Also, I need a lot of my money to run my business. That's the straight situation." He also shared the specific details of his grow locations, his vape business, and his distribution network.

Adam straightened up, and considered the preposterous loan request. In addition to their bank ownership, Irving Green was CEO and sole shareholder of the largest Second Trust Deed lender in the nation. For the past twenty years, Green had maintained a $200 million line of credit at Union Bank. High-yield loans that banks wouldn't consider was his specialty, as long as the jerk/borrower paid the usurious interest rate.

Adam pondered Bing further. *What interest rate would Green want for this chancy loan to this desperate and careless dealer who owed scads of money to treacherous men?* Adam assumed—correctly—that Bing was mathematically deficient. "Here's what I can do. First off, you need to show good faith and pay these men $300,000 up front. I'll lend you the money at 15 percent interest per month. That means every month I'll ante up $300,000 for you to pay your debt off in ten months. If you agree to my terms, I'll have my attorney draft a Loan Agreement specifying that from the revenues of your firm you will repay me monthly on a five-year amortization. What you don't pay accrues and compounds interest. Also, you need to personally guarantee the loan."

Bing, of course, readily agreed to the terms. He clearly hadn't done the math. Adam would be paying out $300,000 per month to reimburse the Peckerwoods and KAMs, which sounded like a great deal. But all the while Bing would incur $390,000 in monthly debt, which Adam would collect—ruthlessly.

Bing said thank you the one way he knew how. "Adam, do you dig boys or girls?" He paused and looked the straight-shooter over. "You're so straight arrow, it's probably only girls. Any time you want to party with me and my boys, just let me know. I'll get you laid by any Playmate you want. Just tell me her name or I'll pick one for you. And she's yours for the night, baby."

Ignoring Bing's proposition to fuck a bimbo, Adam said, "Just pay the debt, and we'll all be happy. I need your contact information. I assume this will be a cash payment. One of my men will pay the gangs directly. Also, they will pick up your monthly payment on the tenth of each month. There is no grace period. Don't pay, and I take over your business." The giant cheesecake arrived just as Adam said *business*. The choreography delighted him.

While Adam ate his dessert, Bing spiraled into bigger and weirder lies, claiming that he had attended UC Berkeley, majoring in business. Adam could tell that Bing knew more about beer pong than Internal Rates of Return or a Net Present Value formula. This man had never had a business plan. He had never dickered with a bank or lender. Bing never took business seriously, and he had just entered the Financial War Zone.

For the first time in years, it was a brunette instead of a blonde who had just screwed Bing.

CHAPTER 8

Nate 'n Al's Deli, Beverly Hills

◖◖ⵜ ⵙ◗◗

As Ricardo walked the still-shaky Bing past still-begging Frank, M asked Adam to hang back for a minute.

"I want to talk privately," said M.

"I know," Adam answered. "Let's walk to my car and talk. You have to understand that 90% of our time is wasted. So let's walk and chew gum at the same time." Another Copland epigram—walk and chew gum. The quip threw Morrison for a loop, he didn't understand the play on words but he didn't complain. Before Morrison could broach the subject that he wanted to discuss, Adam was standing and waved goodbye to the staff. As they headed toward the parking garage, Adam looked M up and down and said, "You have lots of tattoos. Any studs or piercings?"

"No," said Morrison. "Tattoos are permanent. They are a commitment. You can get rid of studs. Not my style."

The valet had Adam's red Aston Martin parked between a silver Bentley and a black Lamborghini. They were at the front of the structure for the sake of auto hierarchy. It was Beverly Hills, and parking location and appearance connoted power.

"Listen," Morrison said. "I want to thank you for meeting Bing. I know he can be weird. Or let's say, well, a little difficult and different. But he's a really good guy. And Bing knows a lot of important people. These guys are executives at Sony and Warner Records. Plus tons of entertainers. Bing told me they are dying to invest in an MMJ grow. Here's my thought: The three of us sit down again. We have Bing raise the money from these record execs. You bring credibility to the group and can find us a building to grow in. And I'll be the grower."

Adam seemed mildly interested. Of course, he couldn't know what a horrific grower Morrison was, and that Bing would sell St. Peter down the river to make a buck.

M continued, "I'm talking about raising millions from the heads of record companies. You could meet the guys at Bing's. You do your business thing, and I'm telling you the deal would be a slam dunk."

"We just completed a fairly risky deal for me," Adam said. "Let me think about this proposal, and I'll get back to you in a few days."

He gestured to the Aston, and they both got in. Adam backed his car out of the space, and dropped a twenty-dollar bill in the attendant's waiting hand. As they reached the exit emptying onto Beverly Drive, M said, "You can drop me off here. My car is just down the block."

Had Adam looked in his rear-view mirror, he would have glimpsed the very non-Beverly Hills sight of a heavily tattooed man nearly skipping down the block in excitement.

* * *

Everyone who knew Bing, knew he didn't lock his doors. Just an old habit from Davao, he told people. But that Monday, prior to leaving the house for the meeting at the deli, Bing had listened to Cary's suggestion and hit the security code for the home-monitoring system. They might have bedrooms adjacent to one another, but that didn't mean T-Rex and Bing coordinated schedules or meetings.

Sometimes when Rex was unavailable for a marijuana drop-off, he would tell an old client or another dealer where he left the marijuana hidden in his bedroom. On June 10 at 1 p.m., an operator at Frontline Security Systems noticed the alarm ringing at 2626 Nichols Canyon Circle. Reacting in proper Frontline protocol, she dispatched the closest Frontline Security car to speed to the address, and next notified the LAPD to respond to the scene of the suspected robbery.

Twenty minutes later, a police helicopter circled the residence as a Frontline guard car pulled up. The guard waited fifteen minutes, during which time a man left the house with a bag filled with exactly one pound of weed measured out by T-Rex. The guard detained the buyer until a black and white police car with two cops arrived. The cops handcuffed the weed purchaser, placed him in the rear of their cruiser, and called for assistance. They had a free and legal path to enter the house after confiscating one pound of marijuana—far in excess of the legal limit of possessing 28.5 grams.

Each year there are more bank robberies in Italy (approximately 3,000) than in the rest of Europe combined. Each year in the USA, police arrest more people for marijuana use than for all violent crimes combined.

The Frontline security guard and the two cops entered through the unlocked front door, just like anyone else could conceivably do. The guard plugged the correct numbers on the keypad to stop the siren blasting, and the two young cops freely roamed Bing's residence. After searching Bing's bedroom, one cop yelled, "Come here quick." Inside Bing's sauna, which was never used or turned on, the cop found more than four garbage bags filled with freshly picked and properly dried cannabis.

"Jeez. Did we hit the motherlode or what? This jerk is one major player. Can't wait until he gets home."

"Let's move our car off the cul-de-sac, so we don't frighten the occupant, or dealer, that is, away. Soon as he drives up the driveway, we pop the asshole."

The two cops waited behind a gardener's truck on the main boulevard while a backup unit picked up the buyer of the pound and transported him to the West Hollywood Sheriff's department.

In their few short years in the LAPD, these two cops had never been handed such a simple and shut case. Within thirty minutes, Cary and Bing drove up in Cary's garish yellow Corvette. The two men stepped out of the car, and were smoking a joint when the two cops popped them. "Hands up, motherfuckers!"

The two stoned men were searched and handcuffed, seven other cars arrived with sufficient policemen to search LAX. The two lucky cops bestowed Bing and Cary as a gift to the West Hollywood Sheriff's department, where they joined Rex's buyer.

* * *

Bing's one call was to M. "You need to do me a solid. First, call our lawyer. Don't take any of that 'he's busy' shit from his secretary. Second, you need to get one of your PRE-ICO dispensary owners to sign a letter that I'm a part-owner of the dispensary. I remember long ago our attorney told me that letter would get me out of trouble. Got it? I need a letter ASAP. Understand? Pronto, man."

Morrison's tone was the most serious Bing had ever heard. "Shit. What the fuck. You know, any owner is going to want a lot of money to risk the letter you're asking for." An owner could lose a PRE-ICO license worth millions if their perfidy was detected. M would have to convince one owner to accept $50,000 for the risk.

"Fuck the money," said Bing. "Get me out of here as soon as possible. Talk to that prick Copland we just met. Just get me out of here. Now!"

Bing was well aware that a felony conviction would prohibit him from ever owning a legal dispensary or a grow site. And a city-sanctioned extraction business for his planned legal edibles business was essential for his expansion plans. He was already negotiating with Palm Springs and Paradise Hills dispensary owners to lease their license for extraction. This felony would kill all negotiations.

The West Hollywood jail is located one hundred yards north of the Pacific Design Center, or maliciously called The Blue Whale for its slick blue glass skin and its mammoth 1,200,000 square foot of design show rooms. A nondescript masonry building housed the jail, which resembled a medieval fortification that anticipated an attack from plundering Visigoths. Brick walls surrounded a two-story brick structure. Not one window faced the street; accordingly there was nothing fragile that could break.

In West Hollywood, the barbarians were already inside this brick fortress, behind bars. Furious at T-Rex, Bing looked around his cell. The inmates were what every college admission officer's sought — ethnic equality and diversification. He saw a hefty black man about 6'1" wearing a ring on each finger, and dressed as a woman. Bing considered ladyboys back in the Philippines; Filipino's were much more adroit at cross-dressing, and notably more feminine with their slight physique.

An older Caucasian man with shocking white hair, who was probably around 65, was whimpering. His name was Phil Peterson, a West Hollywood florist. Peterson was arrested for solicitation in the bathroom at the metro bus station due east of the WeHo jail. The harebrained horny hoary man solicited within 200 feet of the Sheriffs station.

With one exception, everyone in the waiting cell bored Bing. His face turned to a handsome Hispanic man, and he fixed his gaze on the man. He swore that he knew the man, but couldn't place him. At that moment the man stood up, smiled, and began to walk towards Bing. That's when it clicked. Bing jumped up, and said, "Rodrigo. I haven't seen you in ages. I didn't recognize you."

Rodrigo pointed to his head, and said, "Red hair and blue eyes." Bing stared at Rod's eyes and took note of the blue contacts. For some unknown reason, the gospel truth was Bing hated red hair. He would never date a redhead; and that he neglected them was possibly a fabulous contrivance for women with red hair. Bing asked, "What the fuck's with your red hair, dude?"

"I always like a change in life bro. Life should be like your parties. A new woman all the time. Keeps things interesting," Rod said. "Plus my Latina girls like red heads. Bing, you ever had a Latina?"

"The trouble with Latina's," Bing announced, "Is that they weigh too much. If I see a cute Latina one day, the next month she's fat. Beside, I only date blonds."

"You don't get it. You don't understand my culture," said Rodrigo. "What you call fat," and Rod expanded his arms as though hugging a sizable woman, and said, "Man, there is just more to hug with a big momma." And they both laughed. The men then discussed their predicaments, ignored Cary, and decided to work together selling low quality weed coming south from Humboldt in Rodrigo's home town of Montebello.

Fortunately for Bing, within two hours of his incarceration, a huge bail bondsman, sent by Bing's attorney, provided the proper paperwork for the secured appearance bond (surety bond) and Bing and Cary were freed. Bing's second thought was to call M to find out the status of that damned letter. His first thought was to kill T-Rex.

* * *

Weaving through traffic, Adam dialed Irving Green as he sped home. In a tone ubiquitous to executive secretaries, the harried woman answered Green's private line, and said, "Mr. Green's office. How may I help you?"

"Hi Dorothy," Adam said. "It's Adam. Is he available?"

Her boundless resentment crumbled aware that AC was her boss's favorite person on earth, and she had learned to mildly enjoy him. Plus her recently divorced daughter thought he was gorgeous. Dorothy said, "My daughter said to say Hi. Hold on for Mr. Green."

"What's up kiddo?" said Green.

"How's your available credit line at Union Bank?"

"What am I, chopped liver? You don't even say hello to Uncle Irv before asking about money."

"Sorry. I'm trying to get home early to make up for ruining last night with Gabriela. Very poor manners. I'm truly sorry."

"So," Green said, "NU?" He regularly used the Yiddish word *Nu* instead of saying, "What's up?"

"I need a commitment for $3 million. This is the deal. I've got a desperate putz willing to pay out $300,000 monthly. I just sand-bagged this schmuck for 15 percent interest per month. We get 390 a month for our 300 outlay. He'll never be able to pay off the loan. The security is his profitable marijuana business. Granted it's risky, but I like the return."

"Fine with me, as long as you like the deal and can operate his business, if necessary," said Green. "I'm in." A $3 million deal was that simple when implicit trust was involved.

"Good," said Adam. "I already committed us to the deal."

Green laughed and said, "I can just imagine your smiling 'punim.' I'm well aware you pulled one off. Be careful. Don't get too cocky . . . Dot's buzzing me. My next appointment is early. Gotta run. Let's have lunch soon. Bye."

A moment later, Green thought about the $3 million loan, 'Adam is one clever maven marrying our financial abilities with this debtors marketing and distribution network'. Green was an enthusiastic supporter of Copland, second only to Gabriela. Adam unconditionally reciprocated Green's positive attitude.

Continuing north on Beverly Drive, Copland recalled being schooled by Green over a questionable transaction when they first met. Green had said, "We don't do things like that here, kid." It was an initial learning session that Adam never repeated. Admittedly they both had questionable business dealings that walked a fine legal line and more than once crossed moral boundaries. Nevertheless, Green insisted on strict, though ersatz, parameters that he constructed. AC readily acquiesced to Green's Rule #1—he who had the gelt, made the rules.

Hubris would never be AC's dilemma. The two men understood each other like an old married couple. Over the years together they learned how the other person would react before a question was even asked.

Passing Sunset Boulevard and the pink stucco Beverly Hills Hotel, Adam turned left on Lexington and right on Benedict. Not shocking for LA traffic, the canyon was already clogged due to a fender bender. Glancing ahead, he realized he wasn't going anywhere fast. He automatically recalled today's noon meeting, and pondered, *Just maybe, I'm being overconfident. Bing's loan is riskier than most loans—and in a business constantly disrupted due to legality and innovation.*

Finally turning left on Cielo, Adam had to slow down as an approaching black Volvo station wagon slowed with numerous arms waving from every window. "Ciao, Mr. Copland," said his Italian maid, Marissa, originally from Bologna.

Rebeccah yelled, "Daddy!" Adam motioned for her to stay in the car. He parked in a red zone, and scooted across Cielo. He stopped a foot short of his daughter, and said, "Marissa. Who is that Bella Donna in the back seat?"

"Stop it, Daddy," Becky said. "It's me, silly Daddy." An impatient driver honked and Adam was ready to kill.

"Looks dangerous with these *pazzo* drivers," Marissa said. "Mrs. C asked me to take Becky home to play with my children tonight. I made a *delizioso* Asian Tah-Foo with spicy vegetable dinner for you. With all the children at my home, no Cass-E-No for me this weekend."

Adam kissed Becky and waved goodbye. He knew Tah-Foo was Marisa's pronunciation of Tofu, but Cass-E-No was a new one. Her speech was a long-standing joke at the Copland home. Different syllable inflections gave entirely new meanings to standard words. Then again she spoke four languages to Adam's three.

A lazy coyote was resting unnoticed by Adam under a thick bush on the hillside as Adam parked in the garage. Getting out of the car, it hit him. Cass-E-No was casino with her distinctive syllable emphasis.

Under a patio umbrella, Gabriela was sitting in a chaise reading the *Times*. "Hi, baby," Adam said. "I saw our cutie with Marissa."

She didn't smile, her hair was ruffled, and she appeared ready to do battle.

He pulled up a chair and sat next to her. He asked, "What in the world is wrong, sweetie?"

She slapped the Metro section of the newspaper on his thigh. He was ready to explode but instead picked up the paper.

Body found in Pacoima refrigerator ID'd as 25-year-old Van Nuys woman.

The body found inside an unplugged refrigerator in the backyard of a San Fernando Valley home that was doubling as a marijuana growhouse has been identified as a 25-year-old woman from Van Nuys.

"Isabella Rojas was probably in the fridge for days," said homicide Det. Richard Williams of the Los Angeles Police Department. It appeared that Rojas had been killed sometime in the last few days then stuffed inside the fridge, he said.

Officers were called to the home in the 8000 block of Lynwood Street about 4:30 a.m. Monday by a neighbor, who had received an anonymous call that there was a body on the lot, Williams said.

While checking the house, police found more than 200 marijuana plants and equipment for a grow operation, he said. There have been no arrests, but detectives believe they've identified the people who ran the operation and are looking into whether they are responsible for the body in the fridge.

Pretending to be shocked, Adam was careful not to smile at what had to be Nick's handiwork. Neat job—put her away and distract the police with an illegal grow operation.

Gabriela glared at him and said, "What the hell is going on? I recognize her name. Isabella worked for you. Has this something to do with the robbery at your dispensary the other night?"

As a child Adam had developed an ability to lie effectively. He wasn't sociopathic; he knew the truth but sometimes found a lie was easier, or wouldn't hurt someone. He tried never to lie to Gabriela, but hell, this wasn't the end of the world. He needed to flat-out lie for the first time to his wife.

Leaning forward, Adam calmly picked up her glass of Chardonnay. "Isabella did work for me. But she had nothing to do with the robbery. And apparently she was involved with an outside grow. Well, I guess there must have been a terrible dispute. It's that straightforward. Nothing to do with me." Lying to evade the truth regarding Nick killing Isabella reminded him of Vince Lombardi's saying, 'Winning isn't everything. It's the only thing'.

She knew her man was lying. She was thirty years old, and as a teenage model in Manhattan had a boyfriend directly related to a Mafia Don. Like all dazzling models in her little world, these women dated powerful men whose ethics were questionable. Personally she detested violence, but seemed to have a parallax view of ethics when it involved a person she cared about.

Gabriela eyed him suspiciously, and Adam took a big swig of wine to soothe his mind for deceiving the most important person in his life. She took the glass back, placed it on a small table, and stared off into the distance with her brow furrowed.

A movie buff for older cinema, Adam saw in her face a fusion of Faye Dunaway's sculpted facial features and Mary Tyler Moore's exuberant smile. . Gabriela looked the part of a model, or a dancer, or actress, or newscaster. Fortunately she had the IQ of a bookish academic rather than a monotonous model who only read Vogue or Cosmopolitan.

Graduating high school at 16, she had skipped a grade in grammar school, and went from 8th grade to 10th grade in high school. She accepted an academic scholarship to Bennington inasmuch as they didn't offer dance scholarships. Approximately 5'10" and weighing around, at most, 125 pounds, she had brown hair with bangs that forever veiled a portion of her eyebrows. She had an elongated elegant neck, and garden-variety breasts that were still firm and perky after childbirth. It was her nipples that excited Adam. He proclaimed, "They're the largest nips on earth." A detail she claimed no one else had ever noticed or stated which Adam found difficult to believe. Her divine body was the embodiment of Da Vinci's Golden Ratio. She was his vision of Botticelli's timeless Venus, though svelte.

Finally, she said, "I'm glad you weren't involved in this dirty business." And then she added the kicker, "Just don't lie to me next time."

For every moment of Adam's life, his victories seemed short-lived. He believed history showed an incommensurate aura of hopelessness always counterbalanced all triumphs. He had always found Gabriela to be a uniquely fascinating and the most extraordinarily devoted person imaginable. Now that she had detected his damn lie, without elaboration she gave an unambiguous warning—just don't ever lie to me again.

CHAPTER 9

Beverly Hills, CA
4AM Tuesday, June 11, 2013

Beyond a shadow of a doubt, it was one of the most exciting evenings of Adam's life. Following Marissa's Tah-Foo dinner, the Coplands finished off a forty-five-year-old Chateau d'Yquem and smoked a joint. After making up, their torrid sex was as loud as the cannon fusillade during the 1812 Overture at the Independence Day celebration at the Hollywood Bowl. In reality, thirty-five-year-old Adam didn't need the joint to induce arousal, but Gabriela treasured his "stoner boner" in her for what seemed like an eternity.

Alarm clocks were a novelty for Adam. His circadian rhythms routinely awakened him at 3 a.m. Lying in bed, staring at Gabriela, the words "dazed and confused" entered his mind. Smoking marijuana distracted him from Bing and other superfluous matters. Instantly the term "illegal" sobered his enthusiasm for Bing's loan. Adam owned legal MMJ firms. Bing's profitability was substantial with patently illegal grows and soon an illegal edibles firm. And Copland wasn't even aware of the interstate trafficking.

Marijuana was classified as a Schedule I drug by the feds—the same as heroin and LSD. The federal government considered marijuana more dangerous than prescription opioids like OxyContin and Vicodin, and that was Adam's concern. Adam was more than a bit hungover from the Riesling they drank during dinner, the Sauterne after dinner, and the joint smoked in bed. Half sleeping and half awake, he imagined the *Federales* busting in the doors at Bing's grow. Laughing out loud, he heard Bing say, "Show me your badges."

The G-man said, "Badges? We don't need no stinkin' badges!" And with that, Adam was awake and quickly dressed in a t-shirt, gym shorts, and sneakers.

While shaving, Adam's resignation increased as he realized he might be in Hollyweird, but this wasn't a movie, and Bing wasn't John Huston. Instead of being Sierra Madre gold miners, he and Irv were on the line for $3 million.

As he walked past the bed, Gabriela asked, "Where are you going so early?"

"I'm going for a walk. I have to think something out," he said. She was sound asleep before he finished his sentence.

Inhaling the refreshing morning air, he took off on his morning jaunt. He kept the classical music on KUSC low to focus on Bing. Without slowing down to look at a doe and her two fawns, he commenced his analysis. The deal he structured with de Asis was classic Green and Copland: wickedly clever. But he pondered was it perhaps just too clever? His conundrum was hard money lenders took awful risks obtaining outsized gains. He wondered, 'Was this the right risk?'

Adam's morning walk was the time to play devil's advocate with himself. Straight out it became apparent to him. The true reason for his angst was downright simple: it was whom he was dealing with. On the surface, Bing appeared incredibly unreliable. Then he recalled Green's paradigm for lending: "When one lends to lower-quality credit risks, we more than compensate by higher interest rates and foreclosure opportunities. Also remember, I don't buy pride-of-ownership real estate, I buy pariahs with turnaround options for significant upside." It was this implicit conviction that assured Adam that he wasn't being reckless. Risky loans and speculative commercial enterprises were his professional calling cards.

Adam stopped worrying and thought about sharks that can smell blood in the water. That was the Green-Copland partnership. They were real estate sharks that had no compunction about turning on their own if a default occurred. It wasn't a pleasant fact; they fed on society's carrion. Dealing with a ditz like Bing was perplexing. But thinking it over, Adam now relaxed, somewhat.

At the thirty-minute mark of his walk, Adam chose to return home by retracing his steps at an even faster pace. Finally relaxing, he took deep breaths in the manner taught by Gabriela's yoga instructor. At that very instant he noticed two doves dancing in the air as graceful as ballerinas from the American Ballet Theatre that performed annually at the Shrine Auditorium. Their cloacal kissing amused him, and reminded him of last night in their bedroom. Living with Gabriela was a veritable dream come true. She was beautiful, hot, intelligent, animated, passionate, sexy, and staunchly devoted. He had everything in life he wanted, and was willing to die for her. Without excess sentiment, their life together was inalienable; and Adam felt both sorrow and distaste for other men who inexplicably chose to live life saddled to obese, noncaring, envious, self-centered women. He stuck out his tongue and said, "Yuck," at the yawn-producing thought.

* * *

Ricardo and Morrison worked their backyard grow early to avoid neighbors taking a gander, and to avoid conflicts with their primary business—cannabis distribution. At 5 a.m., Morrison texted

Copland: *Are you available to meet today? Bing has 5 investors ready. How's 4pm?*

Adam stared at the text on his phone. *That's one fast turnaround on the investor promise. This is quite a gesture of goodwill from these fellows. Maybe I'm wrong about these two characters. Or is this random and merely good luck?* He responded that 4 p.m. was fine, and walked to the patio with coffee, an old calculator, a legal pad, and a pen. Two lively dogs followed him. The coffee was too hot to swallow.

Sitting under a redwood pergola covered with pale blue wisteria, he relaxed, looking toward the infinity pool and to its east where, on the hillside, a royal purple Bougainvillea vine spread luxuriously soaking up the sunshine. The proposed meeting had been set up so quickly that no arrangements for partnership allocations had been proposed, negotiated, or agreed upon.

The sportier dog, Feta, chased a lizard into a one-inch space between the concrete base and the patio's wood floor. For minutes Feta stared at the location where he last saw the lizard, while the lucky lizard disappeared through the other side of the patio. Adam laughed, thinking about one of Gabriela's numerous mottoes for their family, "When you're cute, you don't need to be bright." Apparently this also applied to the dogs, as Feta remained glued to that location, staring and occasionally barking for another twenty minutes.

Having filled the morning with exercise, coffee, and a dog diversion equal to Animal Planet, it was time to plan for the 4 p.m. meeting and be prepared to outmaneuver these two simpletons. A lack of an outline or an agenda made planning more difficult, but a lightning bolt opened his eyes to the desired direction. He thought about the known facts: 1) They wanted an alliance. 2) The strategic point M mistakenly divulged was their shortcoming in his industry—they needed an industrial building to lease to grow marijuana. 3) He deemed the best approach was to enhance Bing's successful business so Bing could endeavor to pay back the $3 million loan.

The dogs started barking, jumping, and licking the glass panes in the door. It was their official announcement that Gabriela was in view. The door opened and she kissed Adam and reached for the boys.

"I'm still dead-tired. You wore me out last night." Dramatically, she placed the back of her hand on forehead. "Last night was breathtaking." Then laying it on too thick, she continued, "I've never met a man like you . . . Did it work? How about bringing me a cup of coffee?"

His wife's humor and radiant smile fired up his senses. He said, "I'll get you coffee." And imitating Eddie Cantor's wisecrack from a very old movie, he said, "I'll clean the dishes. I'll scrub the floors. I'll take care of the kids. If you need more kids, I'll take care of that."

A minute later, savoring her coffee, she noticed him scribbling away and said, "Whatcha working on? Some big deal? Maybe our next vacation?"

"Do you know what a Potemkin village is?"

She shook her head.

"If I recall my Russian history class correctly, Potemkin was a governor of a province, I don't recall which and it doesn't matter. More important, he was one of many lovers of Catherine the Great and an adviser. As she traveled around Russia, he built a fake portable village to impress and deceive the Czarina that rural Russia was prospering under her rule. Remember the fake Rock Ridge town in *Blazing Saddles*? They built the city solely to deceive Slim Pickens and his bandidos. Imagine that this fake village truly happened in Russia."

She giggled and said, "So are you Mongo or Hedley LaMarr? I know that I'm Lili von Shtupp. Do you want me to feed you another schnitzengruben? And last night, schatze, it is twue what they say about the way you people are . . . you are gifted."

Half laughing, Adam said, "Well, Lili. My Potemkin village is going to bamboozle the men at my four o'clock meeting." She glared at him, and he responded, "Nothing bad. Believe me. I came up with a concept, and I'm simply going to outmaneuver them. That's all! In fact, this concept could become a major real estate play for Irv and me."

Thirty minutes later, Adam went to his home office, picked up his briefcase, and placed his laptop into another case. He wore a celadon Armani linen suit with a light-beige T-shirt. He detested wearing a tie. He stepped onto the patio, kissed Gabriela, and said, "I'll call you during the day. I'll be home around six or seven." Looking at the two dogs, he said, "You're in charge Ricotta. Bye, boys."

* * *

The San Fernando Valley was filled with bedroom communities where housing prices were one-half the cost versus west Los Angeles. Adam drove north, opposite the nonstop traffic on the San Diego Freeway, or as the locals call it, the 405 parking lot. The Santa Monica Mountains blocked the cool ocean breeze from reaching the valley, and his destination in Woodland Hills was constantly ten degrees warmer than Beverly Hills. Thirty minutes later and after finishing another cup of coffee, he reached his location on Topanga Canyon Boulevard, near Warner Center. The shopping center was clearly a Diablo Capital property, replicating the Van Nuys retail center tenants, with the addition of a drive-through coffee kiosk and a restaurant, neither owned by Adam or Green.

High above the center was a signboard announcing the tenancy. The most prominent name was "Adam 'n' Eve Healthy Garden PRE-ICO." A large green cross was next to the business name indicating, for illiterates—and there were more than you would want to believe—that cannabis was sold here. Notably, the strip club and massage parlor were not mentioned on the signage in this unmistakably upscale neighborhood. In spite of the moneyed demographics, this didn't prevent the bold and flamboyant dancing ladies to generate more in tips than in lower-middle class Van Nuys, thirteen miles east.

At 10:12 a.m., five people waited in line to enter the dispensary. Blackout curtains reduced intense sunlight in the dispensary, but undoubtedly they were more for protection. Phantom Security Guards could see out; potential troublemakers could not see in. Every Copland dispensary was originally built-out to replicate the Van Nuys location.

Adam skirted the column of waiting patients, and a security guard opened the glass door. The two men walked through the metal cage and the guard held the heavy metal door open. Inside, lights illuminated the glass wall reception area where a cute twenty-something woman sat at her desk. Most of her day was spent inputting patient identification information into a canned software system designed specifically for the marijuana industry. In the reception area were twelve people, each one waiting for a person to vacate from the bud room. The manager strictly obeyed the fire code maximum of twenty-two people in the bud room. The waiting patients ignored the magazines and cannabis literature. The store's appearance most closely resembled a polished Apple store except for the aroma of marijuana wafting through the air.

Instead of purchasing sufficient weed for a week or a month, these early morning customers, interestingly, arrived every day and purchased just enough grass for the day. Did they come daily due to insufficient funds for larger purchases? Or was their daily purchase an opportunity to flirt with the bud tenders? Or was this their equivalent of a daily fix? Who knew?

The guard sitting adjacent to the receptionist, who stared at her legs more than the customers, buzzed Adam through the locked solid steel door to the bud room.

A third security guard led him down the corridor, past the bud tenders, past the office and lunch room, to an attached industrial building. The building walls were eighteen feet tall, and the ceiling was R40 insulated. The buildings total usable space was approximately 20,000 square feet. He paid his partnership that owned the retail center a rental rate of $2.00 per square foot for the grow space, and $4.00 per square foot for the 2,500 square feet of dispensary space.

Adam didn't need a Conditional Use Permit to grow grass there. In Los Angeles County, Proposition D compliant dispensaries could grow marijuana contiguous to their locations legally. Unfortunately, the ordinance was absurdly drafted. City council members were oblivious to the fact that very few retail spaces on major Los Angeles arterials had sufficient rental space required for cultivation. The one and only cultivation contingency was the quantity of plants was regulated and dependent on the number of dispensary patients. "Adam 'n' Eve" averaged more than four hundred patients per day, and had a total patient census in excess of 6,000. Consequently, Adam could grow all the marijuana he wanted to in that huge building under its four hundred grow lights.

A series of cultivation, or flower, rooms measured 24 feet by 28 feet. Each room contained twelve 4' by 8' flood trays with six Gavita 1000 watt lamps over each table with a ballast. Eight marijuana plants were under each light, and a CO_2 tank was set at 1200 pounds per square inch. Each tray had a wall fan mounted to circulate air, and a 180-pint dehumidifier was in the center of the room to mitigate mold and fungus.

As a result of Copland's knowledge of real estate and owning industrial buildings, he instructed the general contractor to build out the interior using refrigerator walls. These were the same variety of walls used in frozen meat lockers to maintain a steady temperature. Thirteen of the latest high-tech, German, ten-ton central air-conditioning systems had been anchored on the roof. Maintaining a cool environment in the valley, where scorching summer temperatures approaching 120 degrees were commonplace, was essential. There were numerous electric panels; all were 3-phase/480 volt high output power. The lot was defended with twelve-foot-high fencing topped with barbed wire, and security lights sufficient to light the Rose Bowl.

Each room had plants ranging from one foot to six feet, depending on their maturity. Also, on the door of each room was a calendar designating dates for fertilizer, trimming, and harvesting. Water was automated through a drip system.

Adam came to a work area where five women were clipping the largest buds from the harvested plants, and then placed the rest of the plant into a $25,000 trim tumbling machine. Men were carrying plants from the "Mother Room" used to slice healthy cuttings from mother plants to be placed in one-inch cubes in the "Veg" room where the babies were grown.

His new grower, Angelo, was at work teaching workers how to transplant germinated clones into their permanent pots for the eight- to nine-week cycle. During this cycle, he would determine when to prune the plants, and when the plants were ready to move from the vegetative stage to the flower stage. Patience was the key. Then voila, nine weeks later, it was harvest time.

The past year the facility had harvested 6,000 pounds of flower that sold for $2,400 per pound. In addition, 100 pounds of shatter/wax was produced from the plants trim, and sold for $4,600 per pound. Total revenue for this division was $14 million.

Adam adhered to a strict division of expenses for each department to constantly and proficiently scrutinize profitability. The buyer of the entire product was located 100 yards in front of the cultivation building—the "Adam 'n' Eve Healthy Garden PRE-ICO." The dispensary paid the going wholesale, or street, price to the cultivation unit for the marijuana, and doubled their purchase price to the retail public. Consequently, an additional $14 million in flower revenues was generated from the dispensary, which did not include the sale of CBD, vapes, and edibles. In the propaganda morality movie, *Reefer Madness*, marijuana was portrayed as leading high school students to addiction, and then straight to hell. Marijuana wasn't hell for Copland, it was financial paradise; and the substantial profit allowed him to build a wine cellar housing more than 5,000 bottles on Vue Soleil.

Adam saw a worker he knew, and said, "Jimmy. Bring me a baggy of our new strain. I don't remember its name. Then tell Angelo to meet me in the accounting office. Thanks."

Jimmy was one of about sixty full-time individuals working in the grow. He said, "It's called Purple People Eater. Angelo is a true wizard. This is a cross between Bubba Kush and Granddaddy Purple. You'll find this strain is way-out, a real heavy-hitter. Plenty of THC in this strain. Better stay at home when you smoke this. Don't drive, or if you need to go out, better call Uber." Jimmy trotted off to find Angelo and relay the message.

The accounting office was off limits to all except Phyllis Boston, the branch bookkeeper. Phyllis was territorial about her work for two reasons. First, with state and federal auditors forever monitoring MMJ ventures, it was essential to maintain spotlessly accurate books and records. Equally important for her self-imposed and defined boundaries were Boston's personal habits. She was super obese, or she had entered the twilight zone beyond morbid obesity, and ate continuously in her office. Phyllis treasured potato chips, and other salty junk, in the manner Adam esteemed a 1959 Chateau Mouton-Rothschild.

Boston flared up if any employee caught her eating, so she kept her door locked. If all the accounts in the office were accurate, and the office gossip was correct this one time, Phyllis seemed to get some bizarre gustatory gratification from shoving as many chips as humanly possible into her mouth.

To avoid Boston fireworks—not the type at the Hatch Shell by the Charles River—Adam knocked on her door. Phyllis yelled, "It's unlicked. I mean, unlocked."

Opening the door, Adam said, "Good morning, Phyllis."

"It's all yours," she answered. Phyllis grabbed an oversized 7-11 plastic cup from her desk and left the office.

Angelo joined Adam minutes later. Adam started the meeting by saying, "I'm extremely happy with your first ninety days on the job. The yields are up. The place is cleaner than ever. And our employees seem happy, too."

"Thanks," answered Angelo. "I appreciate you acknowledging all the hard work. You laid out everything correctly when you built the grow. Your Denver consultants were right on. It's just your last grower was lazy and sloppy. I like to think of a grow like a clean room in a university lab. Mold and fungus grow in dirty conditions, and this place was filthy. Sorry to say so, Mr. Copland, but it was dirty."

"When I bought the dispensary," Adam said. "There was this empty industrial space in the back of the retail center. To everyone else it was an albatross. No one wanted to rent space behind a dispensary. I saw an opportunity. And my hunch has paid off handsomely. That's how I want you to approach my business. I own it, but to be innovative, I need your input. There'll be a bonus every time you develop a new strain that is a top seller. And you, of course, remember I promised to review your employment after three months. Well, I never hide my true thoughts just for negotiating purposes. Rather, if you make more money, then I make more money. You're actually exceeding my expectations, and I'm raising your monthly salary from $12,000 a month to $15,000. Is that okay? And please remember that this is an unusual situation. Normally, I only give personnel reviews once a year. I simply own too many businesses to review thousands of employees more frequently. My policy is be happy with your wages when I hire you, and after one year everyone gets a bump in pay."

"Wow," was Angelo's answer. "I'm impressed that I didn't have to remind you of your promise to review my performance. And the new amount is absolutely fantastic." His last employer cheated him out of every bonus he had been promised.

"I'll notify Phyllis to make the changes retroactive to your ninety-first day of employment," Adam said. They spent the next few hours discussing other improvements to implement, and replicating the changes at the other three dispensaries. LA County law clearly prohibited individuals from owning more than one PRE-ICO dispensary. Adam circumvented the law by putting the ownership title in partnerships he controlled without being the general partner.

Angelo Mendoza's father worked for more than twelve hours a day in the vineyards in Sonoma County. As a kid, Angelo helped his father and learned to love the dynamics involved in agriculture. Hiring a graduate from the UC Davis School of Agriculture was already paying off. Adam didn't know Angelo had minored in Viticulture and Enology. That fact alone would have clinched the job interview five months ago. The young man was professional, and knew the ins and outs of growing grass after spending three years growing weed in Humboldt at illegal cultivation sites.

CHAPTER 10

Woodland Hills, and 2626 Nichols Canyon Circle

((☾ ☽))

Copland and Mendoza spent the day discussing additional requirements to enhance the harvest yield from two pounds per light to their mutual desired goal of three or more pounds per light. Adam decided a profit participation plan would encourage Angelo even though he seemed self-motivated due to his fascination with growing, and appreciation of the medical benefits of marijuana. His mother had Parkinson's disease. Consuming CBD gummy bears mitigated her spasms, her tremors diminished, she slept better, and it definitely gave her a healthier appetite.

Adam said, "Every time you have a harvest over two pounds, you'll receive a bonus. It'll be calculated in this manner: For every quarter pound over two pounds, you will receive a bonus of $25,000. Reach three pounds per light, and your bonus is $100,000 per annum. With bonus and salary, you'll be earning around a quarter million a year."

Angelo remained silent; he was flabbergasted since he had never received a raise or bonus from the Humboldt growers without kicking up a dust storm. And even then, the acknowledged bonus was never disbursed.

By contrast, Adam memorialized all agreements to avoid confrontation over any possible misunderstandings. That way, he avoided disagreements, and he maintained the original intention of his promise. Previous to this discussion, Adam had run spreadsheets with the potential augmented profitability for the dispensary—he would earn an extra million for every quarter pound Angelo increased the harvest. With five harvests a year, if Angelo eventually hit three pounds per light, that would be about double the current net of $14 million, since the expense outlay for increasing the yield, projected by Angelo, was de minimis. Primarily, he proposed a different formulation of nutrients, and a radically preternatural pruning technique to obtain three pounds per light. Adam was always innovating, and was amenable to Angelo's suggested changes as long as they obtained the potential miraculous improvement, or close to it.

On a related subject, Adam asked, "Angelo, have you heard of either Morrison Guzman or Bing . . ." And he realized he didn't know Bing's last name.

Angelo said, "You know I only moved down here six months ago. I know a number of growers, but I'm not really part of the community yet."

Adam's opinions were dogmatic and occasionally traditionalistic. Although he was the reputed "King of Marijuana" in the preeminent MMJ market on earth, he detested hackneyed terms like "community." *There is a gay community, a Jewish community, a vegetarian community, a senior community. Why not have a left-handed community if the term is now so plebian.* Enduring a personal history of losing friends over political or societal discussions had taught him to keep his thoughts private, and not alienate people.

He said, "They're not growers, they're both distributors. Or dealers. Whatever is the correct term?"

"Just be careful," Angelo advised. "Dealers are not the most ethical group of people, in general. They're a pretty shifty group of people. Normally they don't have much money, and are middleman between growers and eventual buyers. The grower usually trusts a dealer he knows well, and consigns the grass to him. It's not uncommon for the dealer to call the grower for approval when haggling over pricing with a buyer. Just be careful."

Adam nodded, and said, "That's a pretty good summary of these characters." He realized Angelo had an excellent grip and insight into this "community." Also, Angelo was intelligent and delightful to work with. Two rarities in this industry filled with avaricious miscreants. Thanks to unrealistic anachronistic Federal marijuana laws, historically the industry in California was dominated by the Mexican Cartel, street-wise thugs, and various ethnic gangs.

A green cross on a dispensary was not the fictitious symbol of compassion and caring promulgated by the MMJ lobby, rather it truly denoted an industry with astonishingly high profit margins that would be condemned by politicians if the products sold were fossil fuels or a new, high-priced pharmaceutical breakthrough. Cumulatively, these MMJ entrepreneurs made used car salesmen appear to be ethical paragons.

After Angelo headed out, Adam closed and locked the door. He dialed his attorney, prepared as always to pay his exorbitant hourly rate. The receptionist at the law office had strict orders from the firm's senior partner to immediately locate Thomas Beard if Copland called.

As usual, Adam was connected quickly and Beard said, "Ah, my favorite property shark. How are you Adam?" After perfunctory pleasantries, Copland explained he needed a new Limited Liability Corporation formed, and answered Beard's question regarding the specifics of and the intent of the LLC.

Adam said, "Check with the secretary of state if the name 'High Powered Industrial Properties' is available." A paralegal made the confirmation while they continued their conversation.

"What's the primary business of this company?" asked Beard.

"I'm going to acquire industrial buildings ranging from 10,000 square feet up to around 100,000 square feet. Marijuana growers often make tons of money but have lousy credit ratings since they rarely pay taxes—it's an all cash business."

"Oh, my gosh, no. Absolutely not, Adam," said Beard, his voice rising. "You don't want to go down this road. Believe me—"

"Listen," Adam said. "I've given this a lot of consideration. I contacted a former DEA agent now in private practice, and he said the DEA never goes after a landlord. They want the grower. Here's my rationale. Just like the Volstead Act was eventually repealed, and prohibition ended, California will eventually legalize recreational marijuana just like Colorado. And I'll be on the cutting edge of legalization. I intend to purchase upwards of $250 to $500 million worth of buildings. Down the road they could be converted to a REIT, and I could go public. Plus here's the real score. Downtown Los Angeles is filled with old unoccupied garment buildings selling for a song. You know the schmatta business has gone offshore, to China or Mexico. I can literally walk into these deals with little down, clean up the structure, upgrade the electric panel, and charge rents triple to quadruple the current market rate. With Irv's and my credit ratings, we can probably finance 100 percent of the purchase price plus the renovations. That explains why I'm doing this, and why you aren't talking me out of it. Capishe?"

They spent quite a bit of time going over more salient information, and Beard effectively ran up unnecessary billable hours.

Next, Adam called his print shop and emailed the copy of the brochure he wanted printed for the new firm. The first page had a stock photo of an industrial building, and the narrative read:

High Powered Industrial Properties (HPIP) is Los Angeles's top landlord for industrial medical marijuana cultivation buildings.

HPIP specializes in real estate with high power specifically suited for secure indoor cultivation of legal medical marijuana.

HPIP purchases, renovates, designs and manages secure warehouse space for professional cultivators.

The second page of the foldout brochure had a photo of another attractive building that would not be for rent to MJJ growers, but it looked good. The narrative read:

High Powered Industrial Properties is Southern California's best landlord for industrial medical marijuana cultivation buildings. We specialize in real estate with high power uses, specifically suited for secure indoor cultivation of medical marijuana.

The third page didn't have a photo, and the narrative about tenancy read:

For Tenants:

HPIP is Los Angeles's leading owner of buildings designed specifically for medical marijuana cultivation. Our tenants range in size from 10,000 to over 100,000 square feet. We are the trusted source for secure, discreet, and well-suited properties for legal indoor marijuana cultivation in Los Angeles County. Our tenants are some of the most successful and respected marijuana cultivators in the industry. HPIP supplies the real estate and improvements for cultivation. We do not supply any equipment, and we do not provide space for dispensary activities.

HPIP leases only to professional medical marijuana cultivators who have proven experience with indoor cultivation. We require current copies of all legal filings and agreements with dispensaries or patients. All our tenants sign standard lease agreements and do not have any pertinent outstanding legal issues. HPIP rental rates are determined by the location and the size of the property. We do not partner with our tenants, share-crop, or charge a percentage based on harvest yield.

HPIP believes that legal medical marijuana cultivation is a legitimate business, and we treat our tenants like professionals.

A licensed general contractor or electrician must do all improvements and construction. We inspect all construction to insure that it meets or exceeds local building codes. It is important to us that our tenants provide safe spaces for their employees to work and also maintain a secure facility.

If you are interested in leasing a space, please contact us at info@highpoweredip.com.

Later in the day, Adam signed checks Boston had prepared and reviewed financial statements she printed out. They worked carefully together to make certain the financials were ready for his CPA's review. He saw a few minor errors that needed to be cleaned up, but as usual, Boston was on top of her work.

* * *

On the Ventura Freeway at 3:45 p.m., traffic moving east to Bing's house stopped only twice. Exiting at Laurel Canyon, within minutes Adam was in the hills shaded by mature capacious trees. Unfortunately the magnificent oak trees were being attacked by bark-eating beetles, and slowly dying, or being chopped down by City landscape crews.

Adam reached the location of Gabriela's rental house — the house she lived in when they first met which made him smile remembering the many nights they initially spent together.

Turning left on Mulholland, Adam realized this area of LA was Eden-like for urbanites. Lush vegetation, feral animals, and steep hillsides offering spectacular city and valley views. And to prove his point that this was a wonderful location, an exotic looking woman emerged from behind a fence, in her bikini, to water her front yard. Yes, New York and Hollyweird attracted the most attractive people in the country seeking to attain their vainglorious ambitions; aspiring stars moved to Los Angeles with pipe dreams of making it big in Hollyweird. Most never achieved an accomplishment greater than being a waiter, clothing salesman, or maybe a porno star. The older they became, more often than not, they were still thoughtless of their predicament. It would take a mental earthquake of 7.75 magnitude to shatter their failed fantasies and make them realize they would flounder forever.

Nichols Canyon Road twisted and turned repeatedly, definitely a challenging neighborhood for student drivers. Two miles south, he turned right, and arrived at 2626 Nichols Canyon Circle. It was a quiet cul-de-sac, except for Bing's endless string of raucous parties. Adam decided the most accurate description of Bing's residence was *dramatic*. The two-story Monterey-style house covered two lots including a pool, and tennis court. There were numerous citrus trees scattered on the grounds, and a breathtaking view of the city. This was truly a refuge. Nevertheless Adam wondered, *How did this clown with so many discernible faults afford such opulence.*

Walking up the driveway, Adam noticed Morrison standing by the pool, staring. Two uninhibited women were sunbathing topless. Unmistakably they were only fifteen or sixteen years old. "Check them out," Morrison said without greeting Adam. Instinctively Adam looked away, uncertain if his actions were *morality based, congenital shyness, or prudently incorruptible with respect to his wife.*

Tearing himself away from viewing the contemporary Nereid's in the pool, Guzman led Adam through the open garage to an unlocked door, leading to the kitchen where Bing's latest manifestation of a blonde archetype was arranging food for the meeting.

"Ashley. What's cookin'?" Morrison asked.

"Hi, M. I've got Bing's favorite foods for everyone to snack on," she said. "Fresh OJ, Arizona tea, Spam with American cheese sandwiches, and Bing's favorite dessert, Ube cake from Red Ribbon Bakery. Bing's upstairs. I'll get one of the twins to help bring the food upstairs."

Looking at Adam as they walked upstairs, M said, "Could you ever imagine? It's a fucking dream. Gorgeous twins. Those girls at the pool were twins. This is like being at Hef's pad."

He overlooked any recollection of his wife Nonie and their M&M daughters for the brief thrill Bing could arrange for him. Bing's strategy was historically accurate. He would arrange a tryst with these hypnotizing attractive nymphs for any person that he endeavored to impress. Even bright men usually and as a rule, forgot that women with mind-blowing good looks, or girls in this case, were rarely worth the trouble.

Crowded together on his Cal king-size bed were two men and Bing. Cary stood up, and said, "I've heard of you dude. Bing told me about that deal at that deli. This is my bro, Kenny Lutz."

Following his mother's prescribed manner to properly greet strangers, Klutz rose, extended his right hand, and said, "Hello, sir." Socially awkward, Kenny looked at the floor when he talked. Consistently Klutz was a man of two words, or less.

Bing nodded, but didn't say a word to the man he needed a $3 million loan from. The curtains in the room were pulled back and light filled the area. Standing motionless, Adam took in his surroundings. His private exclamation was *who the hell conducts business in the bedroom?*

Never one to waste time, Adam said, "We never discussed how the cannabis growing partnership split would be divided, between the three of us, the general partners. Also, what percentage the investors would receive." He waited for a response.

Finally Morrison said, "Let's divide our shares equally. Each partner gets one-third of 60 percent. We get 60 percent and give the investors 40 percent. Sound okay?"

No one knew, not even Bing, that M was stretched out financially. His autobiography would include a chapter on his State of California and Federal tax liens and that he was unable to pay his credit card debt. Morrison was drooling over the prospect of a monthly grower's salary as much as he slobbered over the topless twins.

Adam said, "I had a slightly different take on this." He was interrupted when Ashley appeared at the door with a tray of food she had prepared, followed by the twins. Each twin wore a water-soaked T-shirt and bikini bottom. Klutz was noticeably unnerved. His petrification enhanced when Chastity, the other twin was named Dolce, bent over exposing her youthfully firm tiny breasts. "Here's your milk and sandwich," she said.

Dolce distributed sandwiches to all. Adam accepted the orange juice and declined the pork byproduct sandwich.

Bing laughed and said, "I send cases of Spam to my relatives in Davao. Manila is the Spam capital of the world. If you look at the two countries that colonized the Philippines, Spain and America, just take the first two letters from each country and it spells Spam— SP from Spain and AM from America."

Adam was fond of anecdotes, and refrained from didactically correcting Bing that the first two letters in the United States of America was UN for United. That would make Spam Spun, and Bing had spun a good tale. After all, Adam now found out that General MacArthur and Spam saved the Philippines from the Japanese in World War II.

Filipino's had such an obsession with SPAM that a restaurant called 'SPAM JAM Café' had opened in a Manila Megamall. SPAM Jam's menu featured SPAM nuggets, SPAM Spaghetti, SPAM Burgers, and SPAM Musubi. SPAM Musubi is made with a "sushi-style" slice of SPAM that is sandwiched in seaweed and rice.

Dolce delivered a plate of Ube cake, plopped it on the table next to Adam. "Try it," she said. "Ube is a purple sweet potato." She smiled, and taunted him, saying, "It's really tasty good. Sweet like me. I like putting ice cream and Southern Comfort on it."

The truth was Bing instructed her to flirt with Adam, suck him into Bing's House of Horrors, and destroy his marriage. Bending over, she tried to kiss him on his ear but he pulled away. She stroked his arm like Gabriela did. Only Dolce's stroke didn't generate Gabriela-like goose bumps on him like when his wife touched his arm with her long nails. Dolce said sotto voce, "I'll be waiting in the bedroom down the hall. The bed will be hot with you and me in it, baby." She would need to wait an eternity before she would see AC in bed with her, and it still wouldn't occur.

Adam looked at the statuesque girl. Light brown hair with blonde streaks, breasts no larger than a ping pong ball; the gorgeous teen could be a runway model if she wasn't stupidly addicted to drugs and Bing. Adam stood up, and said, "Let's make this perfectly clear. I'm married. Happily married. You're not going to wreck my marriage. Please, don't touch me like that again, ever. Do you understand me?"

She stomped off, but the beautiful young girl's attitude was that she could change Adam's mindset. Beyond any doubt, her narcissism led her astray, and she certainly didn't comprehend Adam's fidelity. Adam fiercely disagreed with one of his favorite philosophers aphorism on fornication when Montaigne described "sexual love as no other than a tickling delight of emptying one's vessels." If that was sex, Jean Rostand was correct asking "how do we compare to the forty days and nights that a toad copulates with his mate, without pausing an instant to take a break?"

Adam changed the subject, and said, "I believe I've solved the issue of how to equitably arrange the investment. I don't believe you're aware of my real estate background. I don't mean to brag, but I'm on the board of directors of a bank. I've syndicated more than $500 million in real estate investments. I've informed you of this so that you grasp my suggestions aren't from some wild-eyed novice. Here's how I recommend doing this deal. I own many industrial buildings throughout LA. I'll lease one of my buildings to a partnership that Morrison and Bing control. You two grow and sell the grass. I'll help with the presentation to your investors." He picked up his briefcase. He pulled out two spreadsheets and distributed them to M and Bing. "I've run the numbers on leasing you a 10,000-square-foot building that I own in the Valley. It's on a month-to-month tenancy, and already has heavy power in it. The current tenant can be out in thirty days. I own four grows currently, with more than twelve hundred lights, so I have a fair handle on cannabis income and expense projections."

M and Bing didn't understand the spreadsheet. They focused on his statement that they would be the only partners. What Bing didn't realize was Adam charged his current tenant $.50 per square foot, and the new rate to the marijuana growers was scheduled to be $2 per square foot. Adam would earn an extra $15,000 per month over the $5,000 base rent, and not participate in an illegal grow. It was a widespread myth that the DEA penalized, or confiscated, grow buildings. Perhaps there was confiscation if the grower was also the building owner, but rarely or ever was there confiscation from a distinctly independent ownership. In reality, Bing and M would need to spend around $1 million in tenant improvements, and the TI remained with Adam's building, increasing the valuation.

The doorbell rang, and Bing laughed. "Somebody actually rang the bell instead of just walking in."

M walked over to Adam and softly said, "Don't mention that you are only the landlord. You being a businessman and all gives us credibility, that is if you're a partner."

"Can't do that, Morrison," Adam said. "If you start off lying to investors, it will all go downhill from there. I'll help you, but I won't lie." M's posture drooped but he didn't argue further.

Ashley led a group of men into the room, and Bing introduced his four angel investors. They were all executives at local studios with surplus millions to invest in grow sites. Pleasantries were exchanged while Adam studied the four men. Before he could commence his MMJ investment spiel, the three women returned with more food.

While Adam described the proposed approach for their marijuana cultivation scheme, he studied the men's appearances. He wore Armani; these men wore Levi jeans, $20,000 watches, white t-shirts, and comfortable shoes. Their status in the entertainment industry was established by their indifference to clothing. The film executive's attire of choice was this expensive-casual look, just as pinstripe suits used to be the sole domain of bankers.

Adam went over the terms of the partnership, and the first man to speak up was Kelly Kawasaki. "Let me see if I understand this correctly," said Kawasaki, an executive at Relativity Studios. "The construction will take three to six months depending on permits and all. A year from completion, if I invest a million, your numbers indicate I'll get between $500,000 to $1 million back. That's a great variance, but a phenomenal return. Why the discrepancy?"

Adam explained the exogenous variables associated with growing—harvest yields, mold problems, and pricing depending on marijuana quality.

"The conservative number is a 50 percent return," Bing added.

Adam thought, *Conservative is the most overused trite term in financial modeling. Even rats learn, but not Bing, probably repeating inane quotes he heard on CNBC.*

Tommy Owings, an executive at Warner Records, said, "I'm leaving on tour with a client next week. When do you need the funds?"

"Yesterday," Bing said. "Make a commitment, and I'll save your share."

That was about all there was to the discussion. Film executives were notorious for reckless decisions, and each agreed to kick in to fund the first grow at one of Copland's buildings: Kelly Kawasaki, $250,000; Bryn McCarthy, $250,000; Carl Rabbit Sarkis, $225,000; Tommy Owings, $100,000.

Last, and to Adam's surprise, the grotesque Cary Sweetzer ponied up $175,000 (which left him $25,000 from his original slot winnings). It was agreed that Sweetzer's funds would be used as a deposit to secure Adam's building in Pacoima, and the initial required hydro supplies. Copland didn't offer any free rent, and Bing and M weren't well versed with real estate negotiations to ask for it.

The lease would require a security deposit of $20,000 and commensurate amounts for first and last month's rent, or $60,000.

Bing and M took it for granted that the men's promise was solid gold. Adam said, "My attorney will draft a binding Commitment Letter, which I'll email to M." Looking at the future Pacoima grower, he added, "Please get all the signatures, as soon as possible."

M nodded. Judging from the handshakes, everyone deemed it a successful meeting, and Bing suggest a celebratory dinner at the latest hip restaurant on Melrose Place, just east of La Cienega at 9 p.m.

Walking out of the Bedroom from Hell, Adam indifferently said, "Thanks, but I can't make it." And he was gone with greyhound swiftness, successfully avoiding the amorous Dolce.

As he drove away from Nichols Canyon, Adam contemplated the afternoon session, and his first foray into marijuana cultivation leasing. He felt like an Egyptian plover who had just given the Nile crocodile a good teeth cleaning. He prayed the relationship would remain symbiotic like the plover and the croc and that he could fly out of the croc's mouth unharmed.

CHAPTER 11

Los Angeles, CA
6PM, June, 2013

《⊙ ⊙》

The Hollywood investing herd had absorbed Adam's MMJ investment spiel, concluded positively, and decided to follow their modern-day Caligula in funding a cultivation site managed by the Bing-Morrison partnership. Essentially, Adam had raised $1,000,000.00 for Bing's marijuana grow through his experience and lucid presentation. It was agreed that Adam's 10,000 square foot building in Pacoima, in the northeast San Fernando Valley, off the Reagan Freeway, would be the first leased location.

As Adam Copland was leaving, an unmarked police car, a dark Ford Crown Victoria, was pulling into Bing's driveway. Unmarked Los Angeles Police Department cars announced themselves with various 'tells' — spotlights on the driver's side and heavily tinted windows. The big black box cars didn't deceive anyone. Adam had escaped the audacious teen, Dolce, and decided not to wait around and see what the LAPD was doing at Bing's.

The amount of luck accruing to Bing that day would have pleased the greatest gamblers on earth, or a soothsayer. Though an unannounced visit from the LAPD was rarely a thing to celebrate, this time it afforded Bing a bit of undeserved luck. Because also poised on Nichols Canyon Road, a hundred yards from Bing's residence, was a large black sedan containing three massive, angry men. The men had intended to swoop down on Bing once his guests had left, and teach little "de Ass" a lesson concerning repaying his debts to growers. The serendipitous arrival of an unmarked LAPD car was clearly more trouble than "de Ass" was worth. The men wrongly assumed "de Ass" saw the waiting car on Nichols and contacted the police. Often life is simpler than people presuppose, and consequently those with a paranoid style complicate life with counterfactual assumptions.

The two policemen were members of a joint LAPD-DEA-FBI task force to eliminate gangs and narcotics in Los Angeles County. Auspiciously for Bing, these men were there to do business.

Their bimonthly trip to meet Bing was another de Asis alliance. They knew it was unnecessary to knock on the front door or ring the bell. The pair entered the unsecured house and went straight to the master bedroom. Bing was now alone, occupied with his favorite hobby, painting. He had a six-foot-by-four-foot canvas with a half-painted copy of a hundred-dollar bill. It was his conception of art vis-a-vis Warhol's Campbell tomato soup can.

"Ready for business?" The first cop, Richard Wilcox, asked.

Bing looked up, surprised, and then happy. He put down his brush and said, "What's on the menu today, my good friends?"

The second cop, Whitney Blake, was carrying four large garbage bags. He opened one bag, and said, "Give it a good smell."

Hired to 'Protect and Serve,' these two officers weren't strangers to Bing or his felonious business. The phrase 'questionable moral character' was a laughable understatement regarding Wilcox and Blake. Bing didn't need a narrative from the policemen about where the weed originated. The cops and Bing had conducted a thriving confiscated cannabis business for the past few years. These two LAPD detectives were as dirty as the Los Angeles air.

Blake said, "We measured it out. All the strains were mixed together. Still it's primo goods."

Scrutinizing the contents of the bags, Bing said, "Smells good. But you know mixing strains always reduces prices." Bing couldn't do the math in his head and wrote on a piece of paper: 25 gallons of weed times 4, or 100 gallons. Then he grabbed his conversion chart, indicating a gallon mason jar should hold around 3 ounces of weed. Therefore, 100 gallons of marijuana times 3 = 300 ounces or a total of 20 pounds.

"I'll give you twenty thousand," Bing answered. There was no bickering. The cops would each put another $10,000 in cash into their safety deposit boxes. If Bing ever picked up a newspaper, he might have read the byline, "Driver busted with 8 bags of Marijuana."

Wilcox and Blake were equal opportunity distributors of marijuana they had confiscated from dealers. They were concerned about Bing's blatantly sloppy habits and felt involving other buyers for their contraband was prudent. Their knowledge from fifteen years in the Devonshire Gang and Narcotics division was that hubris, testosterone, and the madness associated with success made once invisible dealers conspicuous. Bing's perpetual blundering made him an open target for theft from tweakers, or worse, a bust that would send him to prison.

Last year, more than 600,000 individuals were incarcerated for possession of marijuana. In his house, Bing stored pounds of grass, had a 1-liter CO_2 extraction machine for making pure THC oil for vapes, and had thousands of vape vials ready to be filled. Also, he currently kept $150,000 cash, now secured in a safe in a padlocked bedroom used solely for storage. If Bing had a falling out with these policemen or any dealers in his network, landing in prison might be preferable to the lethal results of a shootout in the confines of his house. Bing should consider himself lucky it hadn't happened yet. But it would.

Wilcox and Blake held the same prima facie awareness of Bing that everyone that knew him professed; his marijuana business outcome would be very different if he attended to his business rather than round-the-clock partying. When the occasion called for serious strategic deliberations, both policemen knew you could count on Bing doing something ludicrous. That was his nature. Like the trite cliché that a leopard can't change their spots, people can try to change, but at most, perhaps, accomplish minor behavioral modifications. Ultimately, the brain is hardwired tantamount to a computer, and individuals can try, but can't overcome their providence. If given an opportunity to replay their life, they would repeat the same mistakes. Granted the mistakes are in inconceivable variations that we can't imagine, or anticipate, but still they are on the original theme.

Blake asked where the head was and disappeared for a few minutes. Wilcox said, "There's a man we've been watching. We know he's moving vapes, 'cause we have the illegal vape manufacturer under surveillance. Can you move somebody else's vapes?"

"Easy sale. Nothing to it," Bing said. "Get me the vapes. I'll put my Master Doobie label on them, and they're as good as gone. And you know my word is good as gold. And I always make sure everyone gets paid."

And he continued naming his attributes, doubling down on stupidity. Seen in the light that men, in general, will believe anything that promises them financial gain, maybe the cops believed him. Proving he was arrogant and the Filipino version of PT Barnum.

Blake returned and said, "Did you tell him the story about what happened last week in Burbank?" Wilcox shook his head. Blake said, "This man, Frank something, goes into a dispensary and identifies himself as a police officer. He tells the security guard and the shops manager that they're selling illegal vape products. He states that he would have to confiscate them. Meanwhile the security guard doesn't believe him and calls the Burbank PD. They arrested him, and charged him with felony criminal impersonation of a police officer and misdemeanor petty larceny. You believe the nerve of this guy?"

Bing did believe it and would remember it for later use. Diogenes would be looking forever for an honest man in Bing's house, and would be wasting his time.

* * *

Adam called home, got the voicemail, and said, "I've got one appointment left. I'll see my two beautiful girls soon." Three years ago in the Cedars-Sinai delivery room, Adam was ecstatic that Gabriela gave birth to a daughter. Rebeccah was a mini-Gabriela. Her delicate features would have been dreadful on a boy. Too dainty and tender. A great look on a female, perhaps all right on a baby boy; but would be a markedly effeminate look on a boy.

Edging west on congested Sunset Boulevard, Adam turned toward his Lanewood apartment building, located one block north of Sunset and just west of Hollywood High School. Fred Lyon, his general contractor, and partner in Diavolo Construction Partners LLC, waited for him at the building. The words "reliable contractor" were an oxymoron for every contractor Adam had engaged except Lyon. Business partners, friends, and Fred and Adam jointly owned a brewpub in Pasadena's Old Town.

Values were everything to Copland. A traditional code of conduct might seem incongruous and questionable for the Los Angeles King of Marijuana. Values such as— dependability, trust and credibility, respectfulness, honest communication, and above all, loyalty were the accepted norm in Adam's concept of the world.

He attempted to maintain his life with the virile vision these words connoted, successful most of the time.

Marijuana was going legit throughout the nation, and that fact necessitated an industry in flux. It was inevitable, outside of a few insignificant locations in remnants the old Bible belt, located in the evangelical Protestant southeast, that businessmen (whose greatest enjoyment in life was wearing a Brooks Brothers suit) would soon monopolize marijuana dispensaries and cultivation. A catch-as-catch can approach no longer sufficed for MMJ entrepreneurs; and despite the advertising indoctrination about MMJ humanitarianism by MMJ lobbyists; this most certainly was a business, a multi-billion dollar business.

Copland was certain that Wall Street financiers and Silicon Valley techies would, very soon, inundate the marijuana marketplace with inordinate amounts of funding for cannabis projects ranging from canned software to cannabis home delivery services. As a consequence, in a few years he anticipated depressed MMJ prices due to an oversupply from too much planting. Adam didn't have a crystal ball; he based Colorado's experience as his example that plainly marijuana cultivation was agriculture. And despite skyrocketing marijuana consumption, the laws of supply and demand that dictated prices on the Chicago Mercantile Exchange, also governed marijuana pricing.

Historians and economists had extensive studies on speculative bubbles. The tulip mania in the Netherlands is described in great detail in Charles MacKay's wonderful book 'Extraordinary Popular Delusions and the Madness of Crowds'. One of MacKay's examples is the delirious Dutch speculator who insanely traded a single tulip bulb for 5 acres of land in Holland. Recently we witnessed the 1999 dot-com stock bubble when eager crazed investors were willing to pay absurd valuations for unprofitable Internet firms claiming, 'But this time it's different'. Nobel Prize laureate and Yale economist, Robert Shiller, coined the now popular term, 'Irrational Exuberance' to characterize this recurring phenomenon.

Accordingly Copland prepared for an eventual glut of marijuana production, probably arriving around 2020 in California. To prepare for this economic inevitability, AC planned to execute MMJ permutations in the following manner: Designate branding of Adam 'n Eve Healthy Garden products (or a distinctly new brand name), competitive pricing analogous to Costco or Wal-Mart, lowering costs of production, and most essential, implementing Angelo's hypothesis how to increase the harvest to 3 pounds per light.

In addition, AC believed marijuana taxes would eventually outstrip alcohol taxation for state revenues. MMJ wasn't the evil portrayed; it was a much safer alternative than a six-pack.

Lyon was one of those competent individuals Adam depended on. A true believer in Euripides maxim that, "One loyal friend is worth ten thousand relatives," Adam was always fast with a witty and cutting retort if someone insulted a friend. Copland preferred selecting friends as family, always calling them his 'Chosen Family' rather than be foundered to his bloodsucking blood relatives whom he couldn't't abide for more than 60 seconds.

Admittedly Adam's atypical and antiquated attitude appeared acutely alien amongst Angeleno's. He not only appreciated loyalty but also cared deeply regarding the well-being and happiness of his few cherished friends. This protective aura was incalculable for his mentor, Irving Green. And don't even get started concerning his patriarchal vigilance over his wife and 3-year old daughter. Both females appreciated his affection, but even the little girl was dog-tired of his zealousness

Copland arrived at a first-class building with third-rate tenants. Adam and Green had purchased the 79-unit Lanewood from a plastic surgeon who defaulted on the first and second trust deeds.

The exterior of the building was stucco and redbrick hardboard paneling. The property was two years old, with a flat Mansard roof. There were two dramatically tall glass doors at the entrance of the two-story building. The former incompetent property manager was the surgeon's brother, who filled the complex with deplorable tenants: Hollywood prostitutes, pimps, and drug dealers. The only desirable tenants were a number of students who attended Los Angeles Film School, less than a mile east of the building. They didn't seem to mind the drug deals in front of the building, or the johns traipsing through the building to their call girl appointments. Their favorite hooker in the building was Gloria, a diminutive, voluptuous black woman who wore a long blonde wig when she was with clients, or walking Sunset Boulevard.

The buzz among Los Angeles doctors was concerning the defaulting physician's audacity and greed after he butchered Michael Jackson's face. Jackson's long-established plastic surgeon, Roger Harrison, had refused a request that he believed would make the 'King of Pop' resemble Jocelyn Wildenstein, who had so many surgeries she was called, and resembled, the 'Catwoman'.

Interestingly, Dr. Harrison's great-great grandfather was William Harrison, the 9th President of the United States and was one of the first signers of the Declaration of Independence. Dr. Harrison's great-grand father was president Benjamin Harrison, who was the 23rd president of the United States.

Fred Lyon was installing a Bose speaker system that Adam had requested. Adam vividly recalled a vacation in Peru where a Lima shopping mall owner blasted classical music throughout his center to rid the area of teenagers who hung out bothering shoppers. The kids liked skateboarding and pilfering from shops, but abhorred Vivaldi or Bach or Beethoven. Copland's plan was to replicate the classical music blasting at ear-splitting decibels each time the new property manager noticed a drug deal, or Gloria meeting a trick, in front of the building. Hopefully, aggressive evictions would rid the building of deplorables.

Uncommon for property owners, Adam had convinced Green to give Lyon 2.5 percent ownership in the building—Green agreed that it was advantageous to maintain a reliable contractor who had a stake in the quality of the renovations needed. Lyon put to memory Green's statement, "You make money when there is blood in the streets. Buy property like the Rothschild's and you can't go wrong. It's not when you sell the building that you make money, it's the timing when you buy." At Green's age, and his success, he was prone to homilies.

Adam and Lyon spent thirty minutes checking out the work accomplished, and another ten minutes on Fred's Lanewood plans for the next two weeks.

In the middle of rush hour, Adam called home again, and left another message. He said, "I hope all is well. Haven't been able to reach you. Call me back and confirm you two can meet me at Da Pasquale Trattoria for an early dinner. Bye. Love you."

The five-mile drive lasted more than thirty minutes. Adam drove south on La Brea, west on Santa Monica Boulevard through Boys Town, left on Bedford and into the parking lot on little Santa Monica Boulevard.

Already seated at their favorite casual Italian restaurant, Gabriela was sipping a glass of super Tuscan while Rebeccah amused character actor Henry Silva and his wife at the next table. They were regulars at Pasquale's as were the Coplands.

Having to choose between story telling and her father, Becky gingerly mastered getting off the full-size chair and ran to Adam. They never dined without Adam first telling a joke or story. Tonight's story sent Gabriela exploding with laughter while Becky asked, "What's a posse?"

A courteous waitress brought a glass of water to the table, believing Gabriela was choking. Another waiter approached, smiled, and asked, "The usual?" The usual was a large platter of vegetarian antipasto that they shared, a cheese pizza for Becky, Spaghetti Aglio e Olio with extra garlic for Gabriela, and Penne all' Arrabbiata for Adam.

Adam noticed Gabriela looked tense, and asked, "Something wrong, babe?"

She picked a newspaper out of her open purse, and placed it on the table.

Before looking down, Adam thought, *Oh no. Not another Times story about Isabella Rojas.*

Instead, he saw:

8 OC teens reportedly ate THC-laced gummy bears and became ill, police say. (Reuters)

Police in Costa Mesa reported that 8 teenagers became ill and had to be hospitalized after they consumed gummy bears reportedly laced with THC, a substance associated with and found in marijuana.

Orange County Police said they are investigating the incident after they received a call asking for medical assistance, according to KTTV. When police arrived at the home, they found a 15-year-old teen outside the residence.

"The male told Deputy Leff that he had ingested an unknown type drug and was ill and wanted to go to the emergency room," a press release from the Orange County Sheriff's Office stated.

The young man said his friends, who were at a house nearby, also consumed the drug.

Police were able to locate the home where they discovered the other male and female teenagers, aged between 14 to 18 years old.

"All complained of rapid heart rate, pain in their legs and blurred vision; several were suffering from hallucinations," police said.

Police were able to determine that the gummy bears were in fact laced with THC, also known as tetrahydrocannabinol, a substance found in marijuana.

The teenagers were transported to hospitals and police are investigating where the gummy bears came from and if criminal charges will be implemented.

"Terrible. Absolutely disgusting," said Adam. "Why are you showing this to me?"

She said, "I'm glad for all you do to provide us with everything we need. We don't want for anything. I appreciate your hard work. I know you sleep five hours a night, and work three times that amount during the day. But this business. Marijuana. It's never bothered me until recently. Now with all these terrible newspaper articles. Honestly, I'm panicky that something will go wrong. Very wrong. And I'm worried about losing you."

"Let me explain something to you," said Adam. "Newspapers are a business. Sensationalism sells. Don't forget that I have my real estate business, the bank, which might be profitable very soon, the healthcare firms, and my mortgage lending. Nothing has the explosive growth possibilities compared to weed. If I were brilliant, we'd be living off Sand Hill Road in Silicon Valley, and I'd be a venture capitalist. But I'm not brilliant. I just work hard. And grass is the future."

"You are a talented businessman," she said. "Can't you focus on something else? Anything but marijuana."

The waiter served the food. They waited until he was finished to rekindle the conversation. Adam could barely eat his pasta. He said, "What you said is giving me a massive headache. I'm planning incredible transformations for my MMJ business. I'd bet, surefire, that my little o' business will be worth a billion dollars or more in five years." He declined telling her that he recently put in an offer to purchase three dispensaries in Phoenix. Grimacing, he scratched his chin, leaned back in his chair, and didn't know what more to say.

"Well," she said. "Honestly, I'm worried about your safety. And I'm worried what would happen to your business if you're sued due to kids getting a hold of THC candies like in this article."

He watched her tapping the newspaper with her long, slender fingers. He adored every part of her body. Her fingernail beds were elongated and almond shaped, and perfect. That was what drove him nutty as a Texas fruitcake. Every part of her body was beautiful. Perfection. And that was why he discussed buying his daughter a metal chastity belt like the one they saw in the San Gimignano Torture Museum in Tuscany. Someday soon, she too would be perfect like her mommy, and he wasn't prepared for her dating. Nope. He wondered if little Jewish girls could be cloistered in a convent?

Finally he said, "What I've accomplished is no small feat. What do you want me to do? I'm only thirty-five."

Between bites of pasta, she said, "Focus on your other deals. Buy a whatever. Go back to school. Get your doctorate and teach. How much is this marijuana business even worth?"

He ignored her question. "My MMJ biz is what drives me. It motivates me from the time I wake up in the morning until I go to sleep. I know my marijuana business is going to be huge."

"It's weird," Adam said. "I check my stock portfolio value daily. No make that hourly. I can tell you how much Bitcoin we own. I've never stopped to contemplate the current value of the 4 dispensaries. Give me a sec, OK?"

His gaze was fixed at the kitchen, though not aware of the chef yelling, "The Ossobuco and lamb chops are ready. Pronto!" He scratched the back of his neck with his left index and middle fingers. "Wow. You made me think about our Bitcoin value. I started buying it around $3.00 a coin in 2009. It's now at $135.00. Not bad." In 2017, Bitcoin would hit a new high of $11,000.

"Yes," she said, starting to get testy. "But exactly how much is this marijuana business worth *now*?"

"Yeah, sorry," Adam said. "First you have to assume a license alone is worth a million or two. Next, you would use a multiplier versus the gross or net income. Thirdly, I have a grow attached to each dispensary which doubles the income, thus doubling the value." He continued thinking, and said, "The four dispensaries with the contiguous cultivation sites must be . . ." He further hesitated, and finally said, "Well, I probably net around, give or take, $50 million a year. Depending on the valuation multiplier, the value of the business is probably between $250 to $500 million. That's a huge discrepancy, but valuing marijuana is different than valuing an industrial building." He paused as a chocolate bomba was placed on the table with three spoons.

All three Coplands were bananas for chocolate. This bomba had chocolate ice cream with caramel, surrounded by peanut butter gelato, chunks of dark chocolate covered in a frozen chocolate glaze, and decorated with peanut butter drizzle.

"You mean you could sell this damn business for $250 million and never have to see these people that you never stop complaining about?" She cocked her head to the right and stared at him.

"Yes," he said, "I could." And he used his knife to cut into the frozen bomba.

Although it was a warm evening, it was, unmistakably, going to be a long, cold ride home.

CHAPTER 12

Beverly Hills, CA
June, 2013

During the previous night, after the trattoria, Gabriela read a book, and consciously avoided conversation with Adam. Their mutual silence was a far cry from their declaration while living together, just prior to marriage, that "they wouldn't be like Adam's parents. They would discuss problems, and hopefully ameliorate whatever was wrong." That solemn oath was never go to bed mad, unlike Adam's parents who never talked after a heated discussion. Adam's attitude toward Gabriela was "She's everything in the world I want," and they agreed to never act like a pair of brainless blockheads by not talking.

Growing up, Adam was haunted when an uncomfortable stringent silence was forced on the Copland household after his parents had one of their frequent yelling fits; the speechlessness could last days or weeks. Ill at ease in such an environment, Adam had the brains to read incalculable psychology books to overcome the paradigm he learned from his parents of punishing one's spouse by "ignoring the problem."

Educated at one of the ubiquitous California State universities, he was a man shaped into a smooth and successful entrepreneur originating from a coarse lower class background. Cal State wasn't Stanford or Princeton. Recruiters for Wall Street firms or the State Department never stepped foot on a Cal State campus.

Still, Adam was proud that he was first in his family to attend college. He worked nights and weekends at the New Peking restaurant to pay for his tuition and books. He lived at home, and never affiliated with a fraternity, although he spent many nights in a sorority house with his girlfriend. He declined suggestions by his college counselor to attend law school or consider being a CPA. He knew exactly what he wanted. He knew the way to attain the level of success he desired was by being an entrepreneur. He also adamantly knew he would never work for anyone but a character he liked: Adam Copland. After graduation, Adam could intentionally discard most of what he learned in school, and his education commenced.

Adam's unmistakable morning habits included his walk, a cool down swim, shower, shave once every third day, and make coffee. Carrying his laptop and the Wall Street Journal outside, the dogs followed, each holding a toy in their mouths. It was still too dark to read the paper. High above a redtail hawk floated, held up by a soft breeze, searching for breakfast.

Adam flicked his computer on and searched his emails. He had pointed out to Morrison to use email rather than text messages, and there was one email from him that read, "I listened. No texting. Bing has another investor ready to meet u. Name is Harlan Gordon. Available for coffee or lunch? Very Respectively, Morrison Guzman."

Shaking his head, Adam wondered, *What is "Very Respectively?"* His peripheral vision told him someone was to his left. Gabriela was staring through the panes of the door. Even though she was the one who ignored him last night, he felt guilt-ridden, absolutely Janus-faced for breaking their time-honored promise to talk problems through. The shroud of his parents' approach to arguing made him shudder.

He rose from the lounge, dropped to his knees, and knee-walked to the closed door. Opening the door, he looked up, and in his worse French accent, said, "I'm your humble servant. Please forgive me for last night." Standing up, he said, "I'm really sorry. We aren't always going to agree on everything. But last night stunk. We're in love, and we're supposed to talk things out."

She threw her arms around his shoulders, and kissed his neck, which always frightened him that she would give him an unpresentable hickey. She swept her long fingernails on his back creating goose bumps. No matter how long they lived together, her touch created the same tingling sensation it did the first time she touched him. She said, "Please get me coffee and then tell me why you were shaking your head a second ago."

"*Je suis votre serviteur*," he continued to joke using his pathetically limited knowledge of French from college, and went to the kitchen. Every Wednesday and Sunday was what Adam anointed "Special Coffee Day." He poured espresso over ice cubes and doused the Arabica coffee with Kahlua. Today, he poured a sizable amount of Kahlua into two tall glasses to compensate for last night. He poured almost, but not quite, as much Kahlua as espresso.

After placing the glass with slightly more Kahlua next to Gabriela, he said, "Those characters I met last week have another investor. Remember me mentioning Harlan Gordon?"

She shook her head, and said, "Sorry. No. The problem is when I haven't met someone, I don't always remember names or the connections."

"I've met Gordon," Adam said. "When I did consulting work for the Katz firm, Gordon was an associate. He wasn't doing well. Instead of firing accountants, Katz gives them a few young actors they don't think will make it big, and suggests they start their own business management firm."

"Just what is a business manager? Exactly?" asked Gabriela.

"A CPA," Adam answered. "Nothing but a glorified CPA. Usually their client becomes immensely successful and wealthy, and the CPA starts calling himself or herself a business manager. A business manager makes investment suggestions. Ha. Maintains their savings and checking account records, and pays bills. Any and everything to do with a client's bookkeeping summarizes their service. Obviously, I don't think highly of the competence of most of these pencil pushers."

"That came through loud and clear," said Gabriela.

Adam said, "I remember reading that Gordon stole more than $7 million from his clients. I thought he was in prison. Guess I'll learn the facts of the story if I meet him. Or at least his version."

"You are going to meet with this Gordon character?" Gabriela asked.

"Sure," said Adam. "I'll be entertained if nothing else."

* * *

Morrison was at Bing's house at 11 a.m. Bing was still dressed in his pajamas. M was serving as the conduit on the sale of five pounds of weed, grown at a friend's Northridge house, to Bing. Bing said, "Remember in school how we cheated on tests?"

M said, "Did you ever see my crappy grades? I never cheated on tests."

"Oh, that must have been me with my homeboy Gustavo. We got cute Suzy to help us, and we paid her by giving her a joint. Then we all smoked it together, and fucked her. What a great life we had at Manchester."

"Judging from this house," M said, "your life is slightly better now."

"Yo, bro," Bing said. "You don't get what I'm saying. Smoking joints, fucking little high school girls, partying every Friday and Saturday night, cruising Van Nuys Boulevard with all the low riders. That was some easy life."

"Except for cruising Van Nuys," M said. "That sounds like your life now."

And they couldn't stop laughing until Bing said, "I can't get over our luck. We meet this Adam dude. And he doesn't want to be part of our grow. He only wants to be the friggin' landlord. He's the dumbest asshole this side of Kenny Lutz."

"That reminds me," said M. "I dropped off the lease for Pacoima at your attorney's office. Did you talk to him?"

"Yeah, yeah," said Bing. "He'll take care of it. So whose grass is this?"

"H and W," answered Morrison. "Primo as always."

"What's new with them?" Bing asked.

"Just growin' and partying," said Morrison. "That's their life. Sounds good to me."

H and W were a two-man show. They leased three houses in the north Valley, stole electricity, and earned a reputation for growing great grass. H was Henry Hartwell, the son of William Hartwell, owner of one of the largest framing companies in California. Hartwell constantly collided with the State of California over the employee and independent contractor status of his workers. The state wanted him to collect payroll taxes from his workers, and had slapped a tax lien of $9.4 million on his business and homes. Without the tax lien, William still would not have funded Henry's marijuana business. Father and son hated each other. William was now married to his fifth wife, and she was the same age as Henry.

W of H and M was for Will Marks. Will was originally from Coeur d'Alene, Idaho. A friendly guy and dedicated grower, he kept to himself, and Morrison had heard rumors he was wanted for homicide, gun running, and was certain that he sold meth.

* * *

Gary Prager, Copland's accountant, felt absurd. Instead of doling out tax advice, he was acting as the conductor of meetings for his latest client, the Scottish Banker, Colin Cooper, Jr. The financier was currently on trial in Scotland for conspiracy to commit fraud. He had been Chief Executive Officer of Imperial Bank of Scotland's Private Equity Group, and Chairman of Investment Management for the oil-rich Gulf countries based in Doha.

He singlehandedly arranged the $4 billion investment in Imperial Bank made by the ruling families of two Gulf countries through their multi-billion dollar sovereign wealth funds. London gossip rags estimated, at his suggestion, that in 2010 Cooper made somewhere between $50 million and $90 million, making him reputedly the highest paid banker in the history of Europe.

Cooper owned houses in Laguna Beach, Anse Soleil Beach in the Seychelles, and St. Tropez, on the French Rivera. He obviously enjoyed sand, sunshine, and girls in skimpy bikinis. His recent purchase of a penthouse apartment on the 163rd floor in the Burj Khalifa skyscraper in Dubai was just in case he was found guilty in Scotland. The accusations from the Serious Fraud Office, at the trial in Edinburgh, could send him away for twenty years.

The *Wall Street Journal* already convicted him in a front-page article claiming that Cooper and his associates set up a company co-owned by Cooper and numerous former board members of Morgan Stanley. The new firm, Gaul Financial and Commodities,

LLC, had zero employees, products or clients. The article stressed that Gaul had pretax profits in excess of $500 million from assets such as mortgage securities issued by South Africa and Chile, and Russian Treasury notes, on which it paid Scottish taxes of $150 million.

According to an article in *Forbes* magazine, "Thanks to elaborate structure and cash flows, both Cooper and his partners were able to take credit for a full payment of the tax, meaning the $150 million could be claimed twice. The report suggested that Gaul was one of at least thirteen structures involving US banks set up by Cooper. Cooper declined comment."

One of the meetings Cooper had requested was with Adam Copland. Bewildered, Prager rung Adam.

"Good morning, Adam," said Prager. "It's Gary Prager. How are you and Gabriela?"

Adam said, "We're fine. What's up?"

"I have a new client, Colin Cooper. Ever hear of him?" Prager asked.

"No. Should I know him?" asked Adam.

"Colin's worth more than $500 million," said the CPA. "I thought your paths might have crossed. Cooper is our latest VIP client, and he asked to meet you."

"Why in the world does he want to meet me?" Said Adam.

"I'm uncomfortable discussing certain issues on the phone," said Prager. "Can I give you his number and you call him?"

"No," said Adam. "Have him call me." And Adam hung up, and Googled Cooper.

* * *

Reading the descriptions of Cooper, Adam wanted to vomit. Throughout all his years in business, he had trusted his instincts for judging people. *I don't trust this character without even meeting him. No, he's definitely not my kind of businessperson. Too slick for me. He'd just as soon slice my throat for filthy lucre as . . .* and he stopped day-dreaming when his cell rang again.

The call was from Nick Petriv, who didn't bother with hellos. "We've got trouble here."

"I'm listening."

"There's a short, longhaired man here who claims he has an appointment with you," said Nick.

Adam made a face and said, "I'm at my Century City head-quarters today with appointments on this side of the hills. I don't have any Valley appointments. What's his name?"

"His name is Doobie," Nick said. "And it's just as I thought. He's lying. He's a small-time grass distributor. Everyone wants to meet the boss like you have nothing better to do. I'll refer him to the manager. He can take it or leave it. Personally, I smell trouble. I think he would be a pain to deal with."

Laughing, Adam said, "Tell him I'm sorry. But I have a very urgent call from my plumber. There is a huge problem in my toilet, and it's more important than meeting anyone so stupid to voluntarily call himself Doobie. Thanks, but no thank you."

Nick made his laughing sound, "Eh Eh Eh. Take care. Let's have lunch soon. OK?"

"Sounds good," Adam said without much enthusiasm.

* * *

Downtown Los Angeles

The Gegamian brothers, Arat and Zakaria, hung out in the least desirable parts of Downtown LA. This area was bordered by four crisscrossing freeways. It was almost like civilized society created this area, and said, "Keep your dirty little secret of drug-infested poverty within these four corners. Far removed from my safe hometown." Aside from the pervasive decay and crime, everything was old and rundown. The streets east of the Civic Center, between Main Street and San Pedro Street, were crumbling and had potholes. Day or night, it didn't matter, the traffic in the area always seemed congested.

Numerous buildings and small strip malls east of downtown had been vacant for more than a decade—abandoned and boarded up. According to the LAPD, this despised part of the greater Los Angeles Metro area was relatively safe during daylight when druggies were sleeping it off. Safety in the locale was another story after 10 p.m. It was best to keep your doors locked after midnight. That's when tweakers would come out to do their Christmas shopping in June, or whatever month of year it was. The Gegamian boys and other tweakers kept stealing and stealing to pay for their ugly synthetic habit.

The Gegamian Brotherhood (or G-brothers) was an offshoot of Armenian Pride, the largest Armenian street gang in Los Angeles with hundreds of members. Arat Gegamian could have written a book called *Ten Alternatives to Wasting Your Time in College*. The books Table of Contents would have included a chapter on each potential alternative income source, including: drug trafficking, murder, assault, fraud, identity theft, illegal gambling, kidnapping, racketeering, robbery, and extortion.

South of downtown, south of the 10 Freeway, is the garment district, or known in the trade as "the schmatta business." For the past twenty years, most major schmatta firms had moved their manufacturing offshore to China, or followed GUESS Jeans to Mexico. The once thriving area now had a scattering of Korean and Chinese sewing contractors, and an abundance of unoccupied industrial buildings. The residential neighborhoods that were formerly African American, now were occupied with recent Latin American arrivals.

Middle-class black families had departed the crime-infested area in the 1980s for safe affordable housing in what was called the Inland Empire—San Bernardino and Riverside counties. That primarily left the elderly, or the most impoverished blacks residing south of the Santa Monica Freeway—those who couldn't escape to a better life.

Both Gegamian brothers were balding, had excessively hairy muscular bodies, and their arms and shoulders were tattooed with Armenian symbols. The G-brothers found it too boring to reconnoiter buildings to rob, so they had Arat's girlfriend, Natalie, cruise the area east of USC, near Jefferson and Broadway for possible hits. Arat's instructions were straightforward: "Real garment contractors have Hispanic or Asian employees. Look for young Caucasians driving flashy cars. They don't belong in the area. Landlords there are greedy and desperate for money. They now rent out their buildings to marijuana growers. That's our target to hit." Arat rightly assumed a female would be less conspicuous in the area than a brassy gangbanger.

Years ago, Natalie Demirjian met Arat Gegamian at Christ Armenian High School in Los Feliz. He was immediately smitten with her, and called her his turd cutter—he appreciated large asses. Since she was not beautiful, bright, or appealing, Natalie decided that "Arat the Tweaker" would have to do.

To avoid the monotony inherent in her scouting mission, Natalie's friend, Yeva Hagopian, accompanied her on the hours-long scouting mission. Tired of driving, Natalie and Yeva parked on Broadway in front of a fire hydrant and lit up. Yeva gestured to two white men exiting a clean white BMW. A security fence was automatically closing. The mistake the two men made was not placing a canvas tarpaulin over the gate. Every move they made could be viewed from the street. Natalie said, "Look at the roof. Too many air-conditioning units for a garment building this size."

Yeva smiled. She knew the payoff for successfully scouting was their choice of gold baubles at the Gegamians' father's jewelry shop in the Glendale Galleria. The next tell the scouts noticed was the enormous new stand-alone electric transformer in the parking lot. Again, too much power for a 7,500-square-foot garment building.

"This is it," announced Natalie. "Arat is going to be so happy, that is whenever he wakes up today. You know, Arat and I'll never have a child. All he does is sleep all day. He wakes up around nine at night. Gets fucked up on all his drugs, and . . ." She turned to Yeva and looked extremely serious. "Don't you dare repeat what I'm telling you. Arat and I never have sex anymore. All he does is his drugs, gambles, and robs. What a way to live. Living back in Yerevan might be better than this." She shook her head.

Their scouting expedition was now complete. Hungry, they sped north to Beverly at Rampart for a Tommy's double cheese-burger, a side of chili cheese fries, and a cola. They enjoyed the All-American diet of excessive fat, salt, and sugar.

Late that night, after the G-brothers woke up, Natalie explained the location to the brothers and showed them photos of the building and the surrounding area. Planning the robbery didn't require any magical tools or incantations. Arat simply directed the women to go back tomorrow. They should wait across the street from the grow site, and were instructed to take notes on the following: how many people worked at the site, their hours, any noticeable guards, is there a camera system, barbed wire, a dog? Natalie had done this so many times, she had created a laundry list to check off every item.

Although enthusiastic that a new grow was attainable, the brothers were never in a rush to rob. Arat preferred taking his time and analyzing all the possible options. The problem at the moment was this building was on turf ruled by a Hispanic gang. Arat got along with blacks, Russians, and Israelis. But Hispanic gangs were a problem. The Gegamian Brotherhood was constantly in territorial disputes with them—alliances were impossible to form. He said, "Zakaria, you know those bastards are going to find out that we hit a building in their territory."

Zakaria was more basic than his older brother, and had a simple response: "Fuck 'em."

The Gegamian Brotherhood had one thing in common with every other small tweaker gang—they started out with relatives that they could trust. Related by blood or marriage, they could be called "tweaker thieves-in-law."

Four days later, assured that they were well positioned for a quick hit-and-run heist, two cars filled with G-brothers left their dirty space in a vacant building. Zakaria followed in their twenty-two-foot truck. The stench of urine and garbage filled the air as they drove south on Main Street. At that hour, the street was busy with a few lot lizards wasting their time trying to sell their bodies to penniless vagrants. Cardboard box homes lined the street as they passed 5th Street, two blocks from the Los Angeles Mission.

Arat had to keep the loud cheering of the excited zombie tweakers to a minimum so as not to attract unwanted suspicion. As whacked-out as the G-brothers constantly behaved, before a robbery, Arat would sit with his brother, smoke a cigar, and drink Armenian ArArAt-label brandy. Together, they carefully staged the approach for each stage of the heist.

For the Broadway break-in, Arat had his cousin, who sold real estate in the Glendale-La Crescenta area, run a property search on the ownership of the building. The title search indicated the three brothers from Northridge owned the industrial building, plus five houses in Porter Ranch.

Arat sent Zakaria to eyeball the Valley houses, and the report was what he anticipated. The Valley houses were wired to steal electricity. For further verification of the obvious, Zak inspected the trashcans. They were filled with packaging for light bulbs, fertilizer, and auxiliary marijuana cultivation supplies. Smart growers pack up their trash and haul it to the dump. They were definitely below-the-radar growers. The three brothers owned well-located homes. Each owned more cars and trucks than they could use. Two brothers were single, and partied nightly in Hollywood or downtown. The youngest brother recently married a former porno star that went by the stage name Jasmine St. John. Jazzy was all of 5'1", and was proud of her absurdly huge silicone implants. Due to photos disseminated over the Internet, she consistently embarrassed her prim-and-proper family back in Cartagena, Columbia.

Following their careful review, the G-brothers knew the industrial building owned by these unsullied Valley boys were the perfect target. Over the years of being a tweaker-robber's companion, Natalie had skillfully learned to prepare summaries that were irreproachably accurate. She knew that these growers never employed fewer than five workers at that site, all trusted men from Honduras. Every night one of the Hondurans slept in the building armed with one gun. The key fact was he worked all day, and slept in the building at night. Sleeping isn't guarding. Otherwise, there was no security guard, no cameras, no vicious dog, no barbed wire.

The G-brothers watched silently as their man, Farhad, wearing a backpack, climbed on top of a large closed trashcan. He carefully moved right to the drainpipe, and shimmied up the gutter pipe to the roof.

Every secure site has at least one vulnerability. Old industrial buildings often had glass skylights. Street-level windows were normally covered with iron bars to prevent a break-in. Entering through the ceiling was considered improbable, and the skylights rarely had bars. Why waste money in a garment building? Fortuitously for the G-brothers, this building didn't have iron bars on the skylights.

Farhad never hurried. Entering through the roof was a difficult task. His predecessor worked so quickly that he died falling through a skylight, landing on top of the shattered glass.

Farhad delicately pried open the dormer. Next he pulled a rope from his backpack, and secured it tightly to the air condenser. The interior was well lit by LED lights, and directly below appeared to be a safe drop spot. Except for a Spanish-language radio station playing music softly, the building was quiet. Nothing stirred below. Feeling satisfied with his progress, Farhad carefully descended to the floor. Noiselessly he approached the Honduran.

Sticking a small-caliber gun to the sleeping man's head, Farhad pushed the sleeping man on his shoulder and said, "Wake up."

The man couldn't believe it was morning and said, "Leave me alone, Juan."

"Shit, man. Juan is in your home fucking your pretty wife."

The tired man turned over, rubbed his eyes with his fingertips, and opened his eyes. He said, "*Que es esto?*"

"No Spanish," Farhad said. "Speak English. Now get up slowly. Remember to move slowly. Show me your hands."

On that warm summer evening, the man only had a sheet covering him. He slept naked, and his useless gun was on a table about five feet away.

"Dammit, man," said Farhad. "Cover up. I don't want to see your ugly body. Now stand up."

After he was dressed, Farhad shoved the man forward. He stumbled once approaching the door. He opened the door, and Zak raised his flashlight and struck him. The man fell, unconscious.

Arat said, "You couldn't wait till he was further inside? Now you drag him inside and tie him up. You sit with him to make sure he's quiet." Before allowing Zak to move him, Arat searched the man's pocket, and found the building keys. He walked over and grabbed the gun on the table plus a gate opener. Arat threw the keys to a pudgy man and handed him the gate opener. "Tell them to move the cars inside, and back the truck up to the loading dock. The lights are to the left of the door. Turn them on."

There was an abundance of unopened boxes. Replenishment of supplies in a cannabis grow was constant, and these supplies would soon be used. All the supplies were placed in a corner of the building, and had been purchased at Green Thumb hydro store. Arat directed the men to load the boxes on the truck. Next he had them cut the hundred or more grow lights throughout the building and load them on the truck. He knew they would sell quickly on eBay or Craigslist.

Of the nine G-brothers working that night, seven worked to load all the items onto the truck. Two men had experience working in growhouses, and Arat directed them to chop down all the cannabis plants that were within two or three weeks of harvest. They wrapped their "harvest" with Velcro rope ties, and neatly placed them in a pile to be carried to the truck.

One of the G-brothers, Armin Petrosyan, loudly called out, "Arat, come over here." Pointing to a little cart on four wheels that looked like a small woodchopper, Armin said, "This is a real find. You know what this is? This is an automatic leaf trimmer. Must cost around $15,000. It makes trimming so much faster and easier. It does almost all of the work. This is great. I'll roll it over to the loading dock for the boys to put it on the truck."

Never satisfied, Arat said, "See if you can find the guarantee for the trimmer. It should be around here someplace."

Now with their latest free gift, the G-brothers could quickly prepare their take for sale. Six or seven days after the plants dried, Armin and his crew would cut off all the large buds. Then they would place the rest of the plant in the automatic leaf trimmer. The cannabis would tumble in the trimmer and come out ready to sell after drying—or ready to smoke.

Tweakers intrinsically moved at the speed of light—the only benefit of their addiction. Still their brainless consciousness caused them to return to locations of items they had already moved, and stare dumbfounded at the empty space.

When the G-brothers had loaded every last piece of booty into their trucks, Arat told Farhad, "Now paint our marker." Farhad reached for his pack on the ground and lifted out a can of black spray paint. He sprayed the Gegamian Brotherhood symbol on a wall— the Los Angeles City Hall building gripped in Arat's hand, with "G Brothers" printed below City Hall. The building Superman used to jump over now was Gegamian property.

Time was an overriding factor in a heist. Do it quick. Do it quietly. And split. The G-brothers left the Honduran worker tied up.

With his usual theatrics, Zak announced to an empty warehouse, "Men you did a good job. We've finished our work here."

Arat pushed him out the door and looked around the building one last time. Satisfied, he said, "Time to move on, boys."

CHAPTER 13

Bel Air, CA
June, 2013

Morrison had emailed Adam the meeting time and the address of Harlan Gordon's residence in lower Bel Air, a few miles from where Nancy Reagan still lived. Apparently Gordon, who valued his life, had good reason not to leave his house these days and deferred meeting in public. Parking on Copa de Oro Road, Adam walked down the shady street with mild resignation. Meeting Bing and Gordon right now, and anticipating a call from the Scottish scofflaw banker, Copland was starting to understand Gabriela's concerns.

Assembled in front of a roach coach were gardeners and a number of construction workers. Peering at the physical laborers, Adam realized, 'America's obesity epidemic hit the working class, not his upper class. His friends joined health clubs, jogged, and paid mightily for liposuction. These working stiffs sweated on the job, ate calorie-laden foods to have the energy necessary to cut trees, build houses, and repair every thing that people like Adam had no idea how to fix. These days no one repaired appliances. No, nowadays it was cheaper to toss the item and buy a new one'. He realized, 'These men were throwbacks to another age. These overlooked men, disparaged by elites, did backbreaking work unlike pajama boy Bing'.

Leaning against the pole holding the intercom system were M and Bing. Adam heard Bing say, "We're here to see Harlan." After departing the Katz firm, Harlan Gordon had been the only non-CPA partner at the accounting of Knuth & Strunck, LLC. His role at Knuth was rainmaking. He didn't use scientific algorithms or data mining. No, he had been a streetwise kid and never changed. The tough man from Asbury Park rolled up his sleeves and went to old friends, walked from building to building in industrial areas, and tapped his Jersey street relationships. Similar to Jews, many Italians Americanized their distinctive names. Masciarelli became Gordon, and the stigma of New Jersey and an Italian cognomen evaporated. Gordon became the guru of accounting rainmakers, and was responsible for 70 percent of the Knuth firm's revenue. He went from anonymity to accounting stardom, and life in the LA fast lane tasted good.

A tough voice answered, "I'll buzz you in. Use the side gate, just to the right of the driveway gate." Adam joined the two men passing through the six-foot-high gate. On the other side, they were patted down by a muscular security guard.

The air smelled of grease coming from buzz saws. Workers were cutting down old gnarled oak trees, clearing every bush and tree that obstructed the view from Gordon's house to the street. His security firm demanded that every possible hindrance for a clear view—a euphemism for a clear shot—be eliminated.

At the open door, a young, brown-skinned woman was waiting and directed the men to Harlan, who was sitting on the patio. Seeing Harlan was jolting for Adam. Gordon had aged a lot—nervous aging—since their last meeting five years ago.

Harlan ignored Bing and M and said, "Adam, it's been a long time, amigo. You've garnered quite a reputation over the last five years. How's Irv?"

"Good to see you, Harlan," Adam said. "Irving is well. Busy as always." Adam didn't like small talk, and always cut to the chase. "What's your interest in MMJ?"

Harlan Gordon rambled for five minutes, explaining the financial and legal imbroglio he was in. He implied, though did not state definitively, that he had been granted some sort of immunity for divulging record payola information to the IRS and the FBI. He was an East Coast character and didn't complain when he commented on spending months in LA County jail negotiating with the Feds. Harlan said, "I liked being in the jail. That is, I didn't actually like being in jail, but I liked the people there. The inmates knew they were assholes. Crooks, murderers, pimps, drug dealers filled the joint. They had no pretensions about being someone else. They knew they were scum. The assholes out here, in LA, know they're assholes but try acting like saints or constantly putting on airs to hide the plain-ass fact that they is vermin."

He looked at Bing and M and said, "No offense, boys." The shallow thinking of Bing and M didn't allow for offense. Harlan had aptly described their friends and associates, and they had no reason to be provoked.

Next they discussed Adam leasing a building to Bing and M; their conversation about MMJ investing sounded no different than that of a bunch of old bankers in suits smoking cigars.

Harlan waxed philosophic and said, "The typical old person simply knows more because these *alte kockers* have read more books, seen more real life experiences, than you two kids. These old guys ain't necessarily smarter, they have street smarts. That's all."

Before Bing could interrupt, Harlan said, "No way I'm investing with just you's two, and with Adam here as the landlord. I've got a few million to test your ability to bring home the bacon. But I'll only invest if Copland is a General Partner. I want his experience. Not you kids."

Bing and M were the same age as Adam, but Harlan considered them to be child-men, grown men with adolescent minds.

Adam said, "Harlan, your trust in me is gratifying. But I'm not growing with other people. I'm starting up, in essence, an incubator. These first few buildings will test my MMJ leasing concept. I'll eventually turn it into a public REIT, down the road in maybe 2020. Sorry, I'm simply not growing with other people. Morrison told me he had an ownership interest in a PRE-ICO, which might protect you in case of a bust." Adam knew it wouldn't protect them, but that was the story M was selling to suckers. Patently false. If the police detected an illegal grow, they didn't care about your paperwork. They would rip up the plants, tear down the lights, and do as much harm as humanly possible. And realistically, there were no legal repercussions for the LAPD. No lawyer was going to waste time suing the police over an illegal grow.

"Are you taking in investors? What's the return on your MMJ real estate?" Harlan asked.

"It's obviously a riskier investment than simply buying an apartment house," Adam said. "I haven't finished writing up the pitch deck yet, but the cash flow will probably be in the 30 percent area. Per annum, of course."

"Jesus, boys," Harlan said. "Fuck grass—30 percent return is three to four times what I get in the stock market. Find these two fine fellows a building, and I'll put up the cash for the building."

Bing started to protest. This time Adam interrupted him, and said, "I could do that, but I have another thought. How much are you going to invest? The two million you mentioned?"

"With you," Harlan said, "whatever you need. You, hmm, know I have various funding sources besides my own money."

Looking at an unhappy Bing and a disconsolate M, Copland said, "Here's how I propose putting this deal together. Harlan invests a million with me to buy a building. He also invests a million with you two to fund the grow. He gets the safety of a real estate investment, and the high yield from your grow. Everyone wins."

Harlan said, "Sounds possible, AC. Find the building, and count me in." He stuck out his hand to shake to seal the deal—a Jersey commitment.

Bing wasn't happy. He brooded, and said, "What type of name is AC? Sounds like an air-conditioning repair man." He took out his vape and laughed at his own comment. "Air Conditioner. Yeah, let's call you the air-conditioner man."

Adam glowered at Bing, and M, as he had had to do since he and Bing were in high school, stepped in and tried to lighten the mood. "The deal proposed sounds good for everyone."

But Bing never apologized; he always attacked. Bing laughed and said, "Yo. I like the name Air-Conditioning Man. It's like now. I know you're fuming mad. I see you. I can read your face, man. But you stay cool like an air conditioner. You are the Air-Conditioning Man." And he continued laughing.

Adam noticed Harlan's discomfort, but wasn't going to back away from this little schmuck who wanted $3 million from him. Gabriela was right. Dealing with Bing was more trouble than leasing a few buildings was worth.

Physically it wouldn't be a battle. Pudgy doper Bing against Copland, who had mastered Krav Maga from a former Mossad agent. The Israel Defense Forces invented Krav Maga, which consists of various techniques; combining judo, boxing, wrestling, and aaikido. It's known for its focus on expediency and relentless and merciless attacks on knees and elbows, rendering an opponent incapacitated, usually crippled for life. It is for defensive purposes, and purely for street fighting. And Adam wasn't one to back off. He had two approaches to problems: First, he always tried humor. Then if humor didn't work, he would be a lowdown good-for-nothing motherfucker; both came natural to him.

In his best imitation of Sean Connery's Bond, Adam said, "I'm not an air-conditioning man. The name is Copland. Adam Copland." Looking at Harlan, he said, "I'd like a medium dry martini, lemon peel. Shaken, not stirred. Don't make me repeat. Shaken, not stirred." Everyone but one short, squat man laughed.

Bing was a fool, authentically out of step with the events unfolding. He said, "You'll always be Air-Conditioning Boy to me."

He was the only one laughing. Still Adam kept his cool. He innocently said, "By the way. I need two items back from you fellows. First, Bing, I need the loan documents signed and returned or I can't fund the $3 million loan. Next, Morrison and Bing, I need the deposit, and the signed lease for the Pacoima building back by this Friday. I have been advertising another building in the City of San Fernando. I've been inundated with potential tenants ready to deposit a year's rent to get an MMJ-friendly landlord. Seems we're somewhat of an anomaly out there being most landlords are inhibited leasing to an MMJ grow. They get cold feet fast."

"Shit," said Bing. "Why don't you also lease me the San Fernando building?"

"Before we discuss anything," Adam said. "You need to step up and give me back the documents I mentioned and the deposit." If he was truly vindictive, which he could be, he would have said, "Or negotiate it out with the Peckerwoods."

Harlan thought, *'$3 million loan. MMJ building lease. And this schlemiel is belittling AC. He better not underestimate Copland as an enemy. I've heard of foolish people that battled him and most lost; becoming financial corpses'.* With Nick Petriv involved, they didn't know that some apparently became bona fide corpses.

Harlan walked the three men to the door. He took Bing aside, and said, "Listen, kiddo. It's obvious you have some issue with Adam. My advice, for what its worth, is don't mess with him. He's a good Joe, and can help you. He's the proverbial elephant in the room."

Bing glared at the ground. Harlan continued, "On another subject, I can't leave the house these days. How about you bringing some friendly women over here? I'll throw a pool party and introduce you to more high rollers. You just bring the cunts."

Bing looked up and smiled. Nothing more was said, or needed to be.

* * *

In his Century City headquarters, Adam employed people from enough countries to populate a small United Nations. Every Friday one person brought a platter indigenous to their country to feed the staff in his office.

This Friday it was Copland's secretary's turn to feed the office. The joke that spread among the employees was Marina del Rey would bring a meal consisting of a new recipe, hash-brown cocaine.

Earlier that week, when Copland was out of the office, Marina closed her eyes while pretending to type on her computer. Eventually the good-looking woman placed her head on the desk, snoring after too much vodka and cocaine the prior evening at the Sky Bar in the Mondrian Hotel on Sunset. For now, Marina was a head-turning hot number with a heart of stone. She only wanted 'older boyfriends, also known as chumps, to buy her gifts'. At the rate she was going, with her screwing around, excessive alcohol and unstoppable drug habits, she would probably die before the age of forty.

Since Marina had never boiled water for tea, she purchased a Russian salad from Yasha's Market and Deli made with mayonnaise, and similar to a potato salad containing pickles, hard-boiled eggs, boiled carrots, boiled potatoes, meat, and peas. The salad was old world, with none of the requests to be 'free' of some item declared taboo as dictated by the latest pseudoscience diet fad. Food fads held a sanctified cultural level in Los Angeles similar to that of sacred cows in New Delhi.

* * *

At 4 p.m., Morrison arrived at Bing's house. There were no topless teens in the pool, but the front door was unlocked. Upstairs, Bing was lying in bed staring at the ceiling. Cary was asleep on the floor, and Klutz was playing a video game. M said, "How's my bud?"

Bing was nonplussed seeing M arrive uninvited, and shrugged. M said, "We've been friends a long time. I've been through some tough times, and I've never asked you for anything. Nothing. Nada. When you want to screw my fees down for selling grass you can't move, have I ever complained?"

Bing shook his head, too bored to talk.

Morrison plopped papers on Bing's bed and continued. "But I'm begging you to sign Copland's documents, and put up the Pacoima deposit. Cary already gave you the cash. What are you waiting for, dude?"

Bing said, "Yo, you're right on. Leave the papers here. My attorney told me it's a standard industrial lease, and I could go ahead and sign it. I'll take care of it."

"When?" asked M. "His deadline is today."

"No worries," said Bing. "I promise I'll take care of it." M sighed, aware nothing would happen soon. He sat down on the bed, and joined Bing smoking a doobie.

* * *

At 5 p.m., Michael Scarlatti called Adam. Copland had promised Scarlatti that if Bing and M had not signed the lease, and the deposit was not delivered to his office by 5, the Pacoima building was his to lease. Scarlatti said, "I've signed your lease, and I've got $60,000 cash ready for you. When can we meet?"

Adam said, "First, I actually declare all my income, so a check is preferable. Next, I'm heading home in minutes. The building is yours, you have my word. I don't work on Saturday. Let's meet Sunday or Monday, 9 a.m. Your choice."

"Sunday 9 a.m. You know Sweet Lady Jane Bakery on Melrose? See you then."

The challenge for an entrepreneur, with varied enterprises, is keeping track of one's pursuits. As a sole owner, he had to know every position in the firm, how to accomplish every job, and who was a valuable employee, and who wasted time.

Adam had learned that sincere compliments and an occasional generous bonus generated ongoing veracious comments about his staff from division chiefs and whistleblowing employees. Unfortunately for Adam, most employees claimed they urgently needed to talk to the boss. They occasionally talked about items pertinent to his business. By and large, they mostly wasted his time describing their mundane personal lives, and most information he received was more gossip than fact.

Copland wasn't blind to Marina del Rey's shortcomings, but her beauty was a facade every CEO prefers for his executive office. He ignored most of her silliness until it became deleterious to his effectiveness.

AC walked down the hall as staff happily prepared to go home. Men and women were cheerfully kibitzing in Spanish about their weekend plans. Once Adam had mentioned to Gabriela that he should learn Spanish since ninety percent of his staff was from Central American countries: El Salvador, Guatemala, Honduras and Panama. From that point, Gabriela changed their origin to Middle American instead of Central American. In Gabriela's imaginative vocabulary, AC called it Gabriela-ese, she inventively declared these immigrants from countries south of Mexico as Middle Americans. Linguistically, as many people—Gabriela and Rebeccah—spoke Gabriela-ese as Esperanto.

As numerous critics of long-legged, too skinny Marina confronted Adam with facts depicting her deep flaws, even Adam decided it was time to wish her 'Hasta la bye-byes'.

He had one key point in firing employees. He was adamant that the firing occurs when he was out of the office, and his HR manager fire the person. He abhorred the crying and whining that unfailingly occurred during a termination.

Priscilla Buchanan, the perfect HR manager, initially harrumphed at the Marina del Rey announcement, convinced the firing was long past due. She then sighed in relief that Marina del Rey would be in Adam's words, "Hasta la bye-byes."

"Give her two months severance," he said, and was gone before he finished the sentence.

* * *

The last shipment of Bing's pungent weed had been certified at Ganja Testing and Laboratory Services in San Diego. Ganja Labs sent a courier to pick up a small amount of cannabis that was tested in their lab, which was as clean as any Salk Institute lab. Bing and other cannabis distributors and growers counted on these labs to determine the level of THC and CBD in their flower. The lab also certified that the cannabis was free of mold, spider mites, and pesticides.

All prior cannabis shipments had been sent to his Atlanta contacts by long-distance freight haulers. Worried about the condition of the cannabis during the hot summer transport, Bing called a meeting to discuss implementing a new, more expensive system to protect the precious cargo. Joining him were Mark Ware and T-Rex.

"Morrison told me about these things called refrigerated sea containers. They say Costco on the side," Bing said, once again slightly off the mark. Through the game of Telephone that was any conversation between Bing and M, *Cosco* (the acronym for China Ocean Shipping Company) had become *Costco*. "And M said we have our choice of container size. They are twenty or forty feet long. Plenty big for our use. Before we buy one, just so you know, they're used as coolers to bring frozen food from Asia to the states."

Bing was certain Morrison was being facetious when he'd told him, "The best part about these sea containers is that they are called 'reefers' in the container industry," so Bing didn't repeat this accurate and coincidental nomenclature.

Ware agreed right away. "It would be insane not to use these containers. Definitely. Good business decision, Bingo."

The other concurrence between the cannabis industry and the shipping industry was in the lighting field. The giant Dutch technology firm, Phillips N.V. manufactured the LED lights used to light the refrigerated sea containers. Exhibiting corporate agility, in 2013, Phillips was also the parent company of Gavita Grow Lights—the largest horticultural lighting company in the world—and the favorite grow lights for marijuana cultivation. Curiously it all appeared to coalesce from Amsterdam. Eventually Phillips sold Gavita to Scott's Miracle Gro.

The reefer's journey would start at the Culver City warehouse. Several trusted men would load the container with two crates of

Master Doobie Vapes, odor-resistant bags chock full of Bing's Kandy Skunk, Alien OG, and Lemon Kush cannabis placed in bins surrounded by glass jars filled with honey—all to be sold in Atlanta. After packing the truck with Bing's valuable cannabis, to throw off inspectors, the warehouse workers would also add boxes of T-shirts and skateboards from Mark Ware's shop.

Otherwise, the drivers would follow the usual routine. Safely make the delivery and earn a sum greater than their FedEx or UPS salary.

Bing's biggest fear was never the DEA, FBI, or the truck inspection stops. He rightfully feared that a greedy trucker would tell a gangster or a friend about the shipment and a "third party" would hijack the cargo. Mark Ware wasn't brighter than Bing, but he was a more astute and conscientious businessman. Ware convinced the partners to add a "Buffalo Bill" Cody riding shotgun to guard against a piggish driver. An armed guard would be more than capable of warding off hostile forces. Or worse case, they better think twice before attacking an armed shipment, if he toted a coach gun straight out of the Pony Express. The contemporary Wyatt Earp would keep Bing's truck drivers on a straight and narrow path.

CHAPTER 14

Benedict Canyon
5:50PM Friday, June 21, 2013

I t was Friday at 5:50pm. The short drive from Century City on Santa Monica Boulevard to Merv Griffin Way between the Beverly Hilton and the old Robinson's building was jammed, not uncommon on Friday evening. North of Wilshire, Griffin Way changed names to Whittier Drive, which took Adam to Lexington to Benedict.

As soon as he turned on to Benedict, he tried to relax, but lamentably reflected on Bing and Morrison. He thought, 'I need to stay away from these characters. One reason they are so lackadaisical is they have 'no skin in the game''. They were using other people's money, which he also did, but they didn't do it responsibly.

Once on Benedict, as usual, Adam drove his Aston Martin fast heading north. Then again, Copland did everything fast. As a boy, he was the fastest sprinter in his school. As a student, he was customarily the fastest completing a test (consistently making a careless error or two due to his pace). And later as a businessman, he was habitually a contrarian and a fast study.

Unambiguously he thrived at being the fastest and first at all of his endeavors; not counting one blatant exception — not being fast at foreplay and intercourse with the wife whom he loved and adored. Yet even when it came to Gabriela, he was 'fast' at their initial meeting critically observing every detail about her strikingly sculpted facial features, gorgeous long legs, and her tart Manhattan tongue.

While driving he remembered their second night together. After finishing off countless glasses of a favorite Prosecco at a causal restaurant, he finally got up the gumption to be openly flirtatious while still gentlemanly. It was fitting that an inveterate ingénue required copious sparkling wine to stimulate his ability to articulate his ardor whereby the fire between his legs occurred automatically, merely holding her hand.

Growling almost as well as Roy Orbison in the song, "Pretty Woman," he then said, "I can't take my eyes off your long legs". Shaking his head and gritting his teeth, he continued, then like a schoolboy, he said, "You're simply gorgeous. Absolutely gorgeous". His face was flush from the vino, but more likely his rosy cheeks were produced by their tete-a-tete.

Turning her head diffidently away from Adam, she nonchalantly gazed around the dining room. Slowly responding in her throaty voice, she answered, "Yes. My legs go from my hips all the way down to the ground." They were polar opposites and it worked perfectly.

If Gabriela had any doubts about his intentions before dinner, there wasn't any room remaining for suspicion after his bluntly honest comment. Wisely he didn't state how proud he was walking with his eye-catching woman; and he noticed how all the straight men in the restaurant gawked at his date while a few of the gay men made goo-goo eyes at him.

While they were dating and before they became an item for the local gossip rag, he regularly commented, like an admiring adolescent, about one part of her body or another. He knew it. She knew it. It was pure and simple for anyone watching and listening. He was infatuated. Although he knew she was some kind of a hoity-toity fashion model, if he had ever taken the time to look at an au courant fashion magazine, he would have seen her legs donning nylon stockings and plastered in provocative layouts more befitting Playboy or Hustler.

* * *

Adam announced he was home, saying, "Where are my girls?" His arrival was like electric shock therapy to Rebecca. Her normally high energy level now focused solely on, as she liked to call him, silly-daddy. Two dogs were first to reach him. They were followed by two Copland girls, with wide as life smiles, running down the hallway to his waiting wide-open arms. His daughter's first words, every time she saw Adam, were, "Let's play."

Instead Adam swept her in his arms, kissed his wife, and said, "Nap time. See you in 15 or 20 minutes." Lying in bed together, not at all tired, Rebeccah giggled, and constantly touched his eyelashes trying to keep him awake even though he desperately wanted some shuteye. Adam's ability to function while sleeping only five hours per night was to take a brief nap once or twice a day for about fifteen minutes.

Suddenly Becky was running down the hall to her mother's side. She said, "Why is daddy yelling in his sleep?"

"Daddy has nightmares. Just like you do sometimes," she explained. "You know how I close your closet so you don't see figures? Well, daddy's closet must be open and he's having a nightmare seeing figures. Let's leave him alone. We'll wake him in twenty minutes for a glass of wine before dinner. Help me set the table, sweetheart." She picked Becky up, and said, "You're my little angel. Aren't you?"

* * *

"Listen Bing," said the oil wildcatter from the affluent Highland Park district of Dallas. "I've go this damn yacht ready to leave for Puerto Vallarta. You bring a few honeys and me and my boys are gonna have one wonderful five day vacation. I intend to destroy that yacht partying. Drink margaritas all day, and fuck all night. What do you all say?" Bing didn't to say anything except, "When are we leaving?"

Besides partying, the men discussed investing in marijuana ventures with Bing. Bing promised outsized impossible returns to potential investors — on account of he didn't know how to read a spreadsheet from a linen bed sheet. Additionally, he vowed to a different blond floozy every month that he would soon marry her. Bing dated blonds exclusively; truly desirous of eventually getting married and convinced his Amerasian child would be beautiful.

Let's consider the reasonableness of Bing having a beautiful child. At most, Bing was possibly 5'1"—wearing boots or shoes with heels. He had almost as many moles on his face and over his body as there were Filipino Islands. His flat face with protuberant cheeks resembled a diseased turtle. He constantly wore a hat perched towards the back of his head to conceal his early balding pattern.

He had two operations from an excellent plastic surgeon located in the high rent district on Bedford Drive in Beverly Hills. The first was to secure his Mickey Mouse style ears closer to his scalp. The second procedure was to separate his webbed toes that caused him constant embarrassment at the beach, in his pool, or surrounded by friends during his drunken hot tub parties. He was truly a Disney character with Mickey's ears, and Donald Duck toes. So much for a beautiful child.

The location in Nichols Canyon was strategic as it was extremely convenient for network executives who partied with Bing and his roommates. The parties should have been called orgies as any women acceded entrance had to acquiesce to what Bing expected of her. And Bing told every athlete, recording artist or movie executive what to anticipate. He collected business cards to notify every guest of future parties. Goldman Sachs would have envied his notebook of Hollyweird heavyweights, and the Marquis de Sade would have pilfered de Asis' catalogue of licentious women.

Bing and friends were playing handball against the living room wall when an unusual event occurred—the doorbell rang. Klutz opened the door and a young man said, "Pacifico Bing de Asis, please. I have a delivery and need his signature."

"Bing," Klutz said. "It's for you."

Bing walked over, signed the receipt pad, and the fellow handed him an oversized envelope. Bing tossed the envelope on the couch and said, "Let's play ball."

Before resuming their indoor handball game, Morrison looked at the return address on the envelope: Diablo Capital. "Can I open this for you?" M asked.

"Sure," Bing laughed. "It's probably just another collection agency letter."

Generally, Morrison read slowly. When he did read, he found it helpful to read out loud. He tried to stand straight but found himself moving nervously from side to side. He read and re-read the letter very slowly to grasp the full meaning. Finally, in a numb tone, he said, "Bing, you'd better read this. And what's this Pacific stuff?"

He handed Bing the letter. The letter was on Diablo Capital letterhead. Bing read it to the group.

==

June 21, 2013
Mr. Pacifico Bing de Asis
Mr. Morrison Guzman
2626 Nichols Canyon Circle
Los Angeles, CA 90046
Re: Loan Document
　　　Deposit and Lease Agreement

Gentlemen,

I was surprised and disappointed that Pacifico Bing de Asis and Morrison Guzman were unwilling to sign the above-referenced documents and furnish the deposit in a timely manner.

It appears you misunderstand the nature of this undertaking to lease the Pacoima building, and separately, the loan documentation required for Mr. de Asis. There is no agreement to arbitrarily hold the building until you are prepared to sign the lease.

Based upon the knowledge of the facts, and your refusal to sign the documents expeditiously, please be apprised that the $3,000,000.00 Loan Agreement offer and the Lease Agreement are hereby rescinded.

The delay is strictly due to your procrastination, which was unprofessional, and I am unwilling to proceed with these two transactions. In fact, I have another Lessee prepared to sign the lease for Pacoima.

Very truly yours,

Adam Copland
Chief Executive Officer
AC/ov

=======================================

Bing yelled, "That fucking bastard. He can't do this to me."

Cary said, "That's a shady thing to do. I don't like this dude at all. I mean that's not right, man." Klutz just stared.

Bing bit his lower lip, impetuously plotting revenge. Morrison didn't know what to do; he felt like an in-betweener. Bing was his dear old friend. But without question, no doubt about it, he believed Adam was the future of Los Angeles MMJ. He held his right hand in his left, squeezing it, thinking where his future was best served.

The bad blood between Bing and Adam had now entered a new phase and there was no going back. Adam felt he had wasted weeks, incurred lawyer fees, only to be 'spat upon' by that little putz Bing.

In Bing's past dealings, an odd combination of double-crossing someone and good luck usually helped him prevail. Like any gambler, notably Cary Sweetzer, one's lucky streak eventually peters out. Bing's luck had gone kaput. And Bing's hatred for Adam was smoldering like Mt. Vesuvius. Bing now hated the Air-Conditioning Man like he'd never hated anyone else. And the Nichols Canyon version of Attila the Hun thought revenge needed to be swift and sweet.

* * *

Tommy Hayes waited as the mini-mart cashier placed two hot dogs smothered with mustard and onions into a bag for a young man. After the customer paid for his dogs, Tommy placed a frozen pepperoni pizza, a carton of vanilla ice cream, and 2-six packs of Miller Lite on the counter. He paid the bill and the cashier placed his purchase into a double-lined bag. Tonight's dinner was the same as last night's meal for Tommy and his co-worker, Roberto Alvarez.

Under the charcoal clouds that blocked the moonlight, Tommy angrily walked back to the metal industrial building. He and Alvarez were unhinged that the marijuana grower once more failed to pay their salaries on time. Tommy was tired of the grower saying, "I don't need to 'splain nothin' to you numbnuts." The two men needed their money, and not in minuscule $25.00 daily dribbles. Tommy and Roberto lived rent-free in the building, and received a reduced salary of $7.00 per hour to compensate the MMJ cultivator for allowing them to live in his grow building. All the other employees earned the going rate in the industry of $15.00 per hour.

The marijuana grow building was ideally located on a cul-de-sac, sandwiched between a Los Angeles County Waste facility, and Valley King Towing Company. Without exception, only a marijuana growing facility would consider being adjacent to a garbage dump as a picture-perfect location. Benefiting from the horrendous smell that wafted south over the metal building, the rotting garbage concealed whatever marijuana aroma seeped from the well-insulated construction.

Paranoia was ubiquitous in the illegal marijuana industry, and for good reason since robbing cultivation sites was the primary occupation of nocturnal tweekers. Constantly looking over his shoulder for an ambush, or anyone following him as he returned to the grow site, Tommy recognized the sound of a car engine starting. Looking across the street, he saw fumes emanate from the exhaust pipe of a beat-up van. As he approached the building, he pushed the button on the automatic gate opener.

The next sound he heard was a mysterious voice with a strong accent, say, "Listen, and listen good, amigo. I have a gun pointed at your back. One false move and your life is over. Understand?"

Tommy felt a gun pressed against his spine, and said, "I'm just an f-ing worker here, man. I don't want no trouble. None at all."

The gunman waved the go-ahead gesture to the driver of the van. The van together with a 16-foot truck drove across the street, and backed into the small parking lot to the right of the industrial building--all set for a swift exit, if necessary. Tommy stared at the van's driver. The gunman said, "Stop looking at us. Look straight ahead." The man then placed a dark hood over Tommy's head and said, "Put your groceries on the ground. Is the door locked?"

Forgetting he had a hood covering his head, Tommy nodded affirmatively. The gunman said, "Drop the keys on the ground. And if I ask you a question, speak up instead of nodding asshole. Do you understand me?"

Tommy started to nod, instead mumbled, "Yeah," and dropped the keys as commanded.

"Place your hands behind your back." He clipped a plastic fastener to Tommy's hands. Tommy passively prayed this would end soon, and more importantly, without harm.

The gunman placed his two hot dogs into Tommy's bag, and tossed the keys to another man. The second man walked 10 yards, unlocked the door, and Tommy and six armed men entered the warehouse.

His legs propped up on a table; his back to the door, Roberto placed his joint in an ashtray, and yelled, "Tommy. Where's my food, dude?"

One of the members of the 'Winnetka 13' gang, a stocky man said, "Don't move asshole."

Roberto turned slightly, peripherally glimpsed a figure approaching, and sprinted towards the grow rooms. He ran as fast as a man that had just smoked a joint could run. Roberto managed to get out of the lobby, through the kitchen, attempted to open the door from the kitchen to the cultivation area when a bullet grazed his right arm. As he let go of the door, a second, third and fourth bullet entered his back. Either through strength, or frozen in what little life remained, he slumped to the ground, positioned in front of his assailant. Looking down at Roberto's limp body, the anonymous man placed the gun on Roberto's forehead. He said, "Should've listened to me instead of running," and he fired the fifth shot through Roberto's skull; blood detonated over the heretofore spotlessly clean floor and walls.

Screaming in terror, Tommy fell to the ground begging for his life. A third man tired of his groveling, grabbed Tommy's baseball bat leaning against the wall, and without pausing whacked Tommy's head as though he was playing softball at nearby Parthenia Park.

The 13 in the Winnetka 13 gang tag stands for the letter 'M', signifying Winnetka 13 is connected to the Mexican Mafia. Although the cartel was slashing its marijuana cultivation sites, while switching to the more profitable distribution of cocaine and heroin, it still received 'compensation' from related alliances.

In short order, five men avoided the room with the baby plants, and focused on the mature plants in the cultivation rooms. They slashed all the marijuana plants that were ready to be harvested. Hurriedly they placed the plants on the ground, grabbed a twist tie dispenser, ripped off three feet of green plastic, and tied the plants tightly. They then lugged the secured bundles to the trucks.

In the large entrance hall, the gunman kicked Tommy in the ribs. He moaned, moved his sore head a little, and prudently lay silently on the cold floor. Intermittently the gunman walked to the glass front door, checked that all was quiet outside, and returned to guard the only remaining employee. One of the most violent Winnetka bangers returned to the lobby, and asked, "Any trouble?"

The gunman said, "Nada." He then watched his older brother savagely kick Tommy over and over. The jolting blows were primarily perpetrated because his depraved mind was thrilled inflicting pain.

He returned to the grow rooms where the men were carelessly snipping electric cords attached to grow lights. He yelled, "If you unplug the lights they'll sell for more money," and he started carrying their booty to the waiting truck, where he stationed one man to load and arrange their newly acquired valuables.

After the robbery and back home, the marijuana plants would be stripped of their 'nugs'. The nugs would be dried for about a week, and then Winnetka 13 members would smoke a portion of the weed, and the bulk of the grass would be sealed in Zip Lock Baggies, and sold to unlicensed dispensary owners. An ad would be placed on Craig's List to sell the grow lights and ancillary hydro supplies at a significantly reduced price. The gang bangers had palpably accomplished this feat hundreds of times, and had eager buyers waiting for the stolen grass and discounted supplies.

After placing supplies in the truck, the older brother, Alphonse, returned to the lobby, and ripped the hood off Tommy. Tommy's face was covered with blood from the earlier blow that cracked open his skull. The wild man placed a gun against Tommy's heart, and said, "Every grower keeps a safe in a grow. If you don't want to end up like your compadre, tell me where the safe is, amigo."

Paralyzed with fear, coughing up blood, Tommy could barely eke out, "There ain't no damn safe here." Tommy's body was shaking.

"Well then," said Alphonse, "I have no use for you." He leaned over and fired one bullet from the gun that was placed on Tommy's heart. Placed that close to Tommy's body, Alphonse only needed to expend one bullet to end Tommy's life. A bullet that cost $.21 lodged into whatever remained of Tommy's heart.

Laughing as he got to his feet, he looked at his younger brother and said, "Now you can help us carry out the supplies. Any problems?"

The first gunman stepped over the pool of blood, and said, "No problemo, Alphonse." He thought his brother was unnecessarily heartless but that wasn't surprising.

The trucks were now brimming with wonderfully aromatic marijuana strains of OG Kush, Skywalker, and Afghan Skunk. There were four unopened boxes containing sizable 5-ton air conditioners on the side of the building. After placing the AC units in the truck, the gang could only manage to fit 60 of the 130 lights into the two vehicles. The less expensive items –- fans, fertilizer, and buckets were left in the building.

Still, it was an incredibly profitable haul. No Winnetka 13 members were injured. All work was accomplished in less than 45 minutes. And with the cold contempt of how they valued human existence, the 2 dead men were inconsequential.

* * *

The following morning, the grower arrived at the building with 4 no-nonsense trimmers originally from Honduras. Shocked and unhappy that the front door was left open, he yelled for Tommy and Roberto.

He heard one of the trimmers scream, "Roberto muerte!"

After inspecting the two dead men, he sent the four trimmers in to check every aspect of the building to make certain the thieves were gone. Despite the difficulty in obtaining landlords amenable to leasing buildings for unlawful marijuana cultivation, he knew it was time to locate another building.

He pondered the most pressing issue--that this building was on turf belonging to Winnetka 13. In spite of the 2 deaths, there was no way on earth he would consider winding down his business of growing marijuana. Growing illegal grass created a great lifestyle of nonstop partying with his buddies. The income from just this building generated slightly less than $1 million a year for him, all tax-free. Cultivation was simple if his crew diligently adhered to his guidelines, and he vigorously made certain that they were implemented. Besides, of all the immediate problems, he could always payoff the Devonshire detectives.

Where else could he make this much money? Furthermore, the man who prided himself as a compassionate grower could replace the two dead men in a flash.

CHAPTER 15

Beverly Hills, CA
Monday morning, June 24, 2013

E very morning was a mighty struggle for Gabriela. She didn't want to rise from the comfort of her bed when it was dark and dreary outside. She didn't want to bother applying make-up or fixing her hair. She wasn't prepared to face the world. Life was untroubled in bed.

The routine of hot coffee and reading the morning paper was like cold water splashed on her face; preparing her to face the days challenges. Yet this morning was different. No paper. No coffee sitting on the mug warmer. Nothing was waiting for her on her bedside. Curious, she wondered, 'What's up with Adam?'

Without her shot of caffeine, she struggled like an old bitty just to walk down the hallway. Reaching the dining room, looking out to the patio, she noticed Adam wedged between the two dogs. His feet were pulled up close, allowing his elbows to rest on his knees. His head was face down into the palms of his hands. Sensing his depression, the boys, as they preferred calling the dogs—and they were more loyal than any spoiled child—were licking him, aware something was dramatically off.

Gabriela was blind to the mornings blazing red sky, and didn't take notice of the birds vitally singing to acquire a mate. She could only focus on the man she loved, whose preposterous energy level every morning drove her wacky. But not this morning. She freaked out. Walking outside, unnerved, she slammed the door behind her. Adam didn't move. He had acute hearing, and 20-20 vision. Adam always noticed the location of birds camouflaged in trees whereas she was almost blind in her left eye. But this morning he was motionless. His normally keen functioning was turned off.

Moving one dog, Ricotta, aside, she sat down and stroked her husband. He didn't move, or couldn't. "Adam," she said. "Talk to me. What in the world is wrong?" No answer. "Did you get a call this morning?" No response. "Is it your parents? Are they okay?" She struggled to get him to talk. Still nothing.

Minutes—that seemed like hours to Gabriela—went by, and he finally raised his head. His look bore straight past her; his eyes were bloodshot as though he had been awake all night. His ever-present smile was upside down. She stroked his arm with her long purple fingernails. Adam's parasympathetic nervous system clicked in, and goose bumps appeared automatically.

"Talk to me," she said. "You're worrying me. Please. C'mon baby."

As bad as Adam felt, he gazed at the woman that gave his life meaning. His face appeared to shoulder the burdens and depredations of all the ills of civilization.

Finally he spoke, "I've done," he paused. Then continued, "Some things in life that I'm not proud of." His normal rapid speech pattern, almost as fast as futurist Herman Kahn spoke, now seemed deliberately slow as though he was absorbed in thought. He scratched his right temple, and stroked his chin with a two-day stubble of growth. "And I'm concerned about ...". And he stopped speaking. He pondered if Blaise Pascal's quote applied to him, 'All of humanity's problems stem from man's inability to sit quietly in a room alone'. Was he taking on too much? Did he already have all he could ever want? Freud would have said, "Lieben und arbieten makes a man happy." He had both.

He said, "Look. I've got some problems. I simply need to think things over. I'm not avoiding this conversation. I'm not proud of certain things I've done. I just need some time to think things out. That's all. Sorry."

But that wasn't all there was. He went to the kitchen to get them both coffee. Adam began to wonder just what had happened. He thought, 'My position in life is to take care of my family, properly. Get over these feelings of guilt. Move forward. As always be your curious self and question everything in life, except Gabriela's devotion. As a child and now as an adult, I was the fastest at every thing I ever did.' His worst fears were now over, nothing to do but move forward. Now let's be the fastest and get over this unnerving Weltschmerz.

After returning with two coffees, he plopped on the chaise, a new man. Gabriela didn't buy his routine. "I know your poker face," she said. "Remember, you can always discuss anything with me. You're a businessman, and there's always a headache with employees or the government. But every time you fall down, you get back up. In fact, you seem to do better cornered than cruising through life. I can think of times you had a business dilemma and you would walk around the room talking to me about the problem, hoping I might help. Needless to say, I didn't understand one iota of your business dealings. It was all gobbledygook, or the same as quantum physics to me. But just talking out loud helped you solve the issue. Just remember, I'm here to help." Nothing more was said, although she worried it was related to the woman's death who had worked at Devil's Playground, Isabella Rojas.

He picked up his laptop, and typed out numerous thoughts that either needed his attention or research accomplished. He finished his 'to do list' for Monday.

* * *

It was 6AM, Bing had just successfully concluded his latest nightclub promotion, and was exhausted.

Bing and T-Rex, parked the car in the garage, and headed into the kitchen. They were stoner high, and their mouths felt like they were stuffed with cotton balls from the excessive drinking. Bing opened the refrigerator and handed Rex a $100 bottle of Svalbardi Norwegian iceberg water. The bottle had a hi-tech seal denoting it was authentic. Last night Bing filled up on Spam sushi, dope, and mermaid cocktails, and now he was drinking water that cost $25 per glass.

Bing couldn't drop his AC obsession. "I don't need that cock-sucking Air-Conditioning Man. He was going to rip me off anyway. I'll take care of him soon enough. How do I know he could even deliver on his $3 million loan? He's a big rip-off artist. What a bullshitter! Maybe the biggest con man in LA." He was certain revenge against the air conditioning man was going to be sweet. He never planned non-promotional events, and distinctively had no plan of attack against the man he despised, yet.

Bing was Lawrence Peter's Principle in action, again, like Morrison attempt to grow grass instead of simply selling it. Bing was unquestionably the best club promoter in LA. He and his friends straightaway believed the success in one field would lead to success in another; his dream was to pursue marijuana cultivation in an unprecedented fashion without a game plan. Undoubtedly one sizable dilemma for Bing was MMJ was agriculture, and demanded attention to detail. Bing was a nocturnal provocateur par excellence. But he didn't have the mental discipline and systemization required to be a farmer, or the love of the land rather than being a city boy.

Before going upstairs to bed, T-Rex whose upbringing was in a permissive TV-addled idiot milieu, addictively, turned on the television to a local news station, Channel 11. A newsman was describing a CHP chase. The fourteen year old driver of a stolen car was going south on the Long Beach Freeway, and then a photo of the 'Fire & Brimstone Bar' was on the screen with the scroll below the Bar photo, stating: *"Next on Channel 11. The Hottest new bar scene in Los Angeles. See it next on Channel 11."*

T-Rex screamed, "Bing. Quick. Get your De Ass over here. NOW!"

The two men impatiently waited. Ads aired. First, an advertisement showed a younger woman with a gray-haired man in a hotel room. Then a local gym ad boasting muscular men and tempting women, who didn't need a gym. Finally the identical erectile dysfunction ad aired a second time. They were too tired for any of their customary snide comments.

Mueller concealed the reason he screamed for de Asis, preferring Bing to see the event they had successfully feted. He was incredibly proud of his roommate and best friend. "Wait," said T-Rex. "It's almost on."

Bing yawned, and said, "You know something? I'm going to miss air conditioning man. I really loved to needle that bastard."

T-Rex wasn't bright, but even a child could recognize the empty words Bing spoke. Mueller said, "Quiet. Here we are."

A woman whose physical attributes qualified her to be a newscaster or a dancer at one of Copland's clubs, announced, "And now. Direct from the grand opening of the 'Fire & Brimstone Bar', located just north of the Capitol Records building on Vine Street, is the hottest new trend in the world. And I mean the world!"

The cameraman moved his camera slowly to show a panorama of the jam-packed 'Fire & Brimstone Bar'. All the women in the video appeared to be exceptionally tall.

She continued, "The bar is offering female customers a discount on their drink orders based on the height of their high heels."

The cameraman now pivoted to Bing de Asis holding a sign announcing:

FIRE & BRIMSTONE BAR OFFERS
ALL-YOU-CAN-DRINK ALCOHOL
FOR ONLY $1.00!

Missy Chesterton, the attractive newscaster, asked, "This is Mr. Bing. Is Bing your real name? Just Kidding. Tell me all about your promotion."

Bing grabbed one of the fifteen girls he delivered as promised to Brimstone's owner, and said, "To qualify for the promotion, a woman's high heels must be at least two inches tall. But the higher the heel, the greater the discount on the bar's well drinks, craft beer, and great California wines."

A voice from the crowd, yelled, "Missy. Show me your come-fuck-me pumps."

Playing along, Missy lifted her leg for a few seconds. She then hiked her dress with her left hand, and poked her right thumb out as though hitchhiking.

Satisfied with all the attention, Bing continued, "Discounts start at 10 percent off your order for wearing high heels. With each additional one-half inch of heel height you'll receive a better deal.

Anyone wearing heels above six inches will receive 75% percent off their bill."

T-Rex stepped in front of Bing, and said, "We're equal opportunity drinkers here. Men, make fools of yourself in heels, and you get the same discount."

Closing the interview, Missy said, "Women. Are you looking for an excuse to buy new shoes? Turns out, wearing high heels can actually save you money... on your bar tab, that is. Fire & Brimstone Bar is running its "High Heels Ladies Night Discount" again on, and every, Thursday night, starting June 27. The special discounts starts at 6 p.m. and runs to midnight. Good night, Los Angeles." This was not exactly a news alert that would make the cover of Foreign Policy magazine or The Economist.

* * *

Copland's first appointment of the day was with Colin Cooper, Jr., at the Peninsula Hotel. Copland had requested Donald Brandt, his computer maven and math whiz, prepare a dossier on the prosperous banker. The first few pages were newspaper articles.

An article from the *Stockton Post* read:

The other side of Eden: Commercial marijuana takes root in Steinbeck country

BY PETER HECHT
THE SALINAS VALLEY

John Steinbeck's quintessential California novel *East of Eden*, about pain and poverty in an agricultural paradise, cast this setting in near biblical tones, depicting it as a place of mystical breeze and light, "full of sun and loveliness" and warm like "the lap of a beloved mother."

Steinbeck called the fields of lettuce "green gold," and to this day, the productive valley—between the Gabilan Mountains to the east and the Santa Lucias to the west—is known as "the Salad Bowl of the World."

But it has seen challenging times. In the 1980s, producers of cut flowers erected cavernous greenhouses south of Salinas. Heated and cooled by abundant sunshine and ocean breezes, these buildings created the perfect micro-climate for growing lilies, tulips, delphiniums and orchids. Then global competition, particularly from Latin America, decimated the market. The downturn, occurring over the past two decades, left tracts of vacant, collapsing structures and helped to push the recent unemployment rate to more than 11 percent, well above the state's 5.1 percent average.

Now, however, many of those valley greenhouses are blooming again with a new flower, as cannabis production moves into one of the world's most fabled agricultural areas.

Even before a large majority of voters in November approved a local initiative to tax commercial marijuana cultivation at a rate starting at $15 per square foot of plants, marijuana entrepreneurs already had begun snapping up aging or retrofitted greenhouses, causing real estate prices for these structures to spike. Currently, more than 20 ventures are seeking large-scale commercial growing permits, and officials predict pot agriculture could bring in $20 million to $30 million annually in new tax revenues, with the county able to step up the tax rate after 2020 to a maximum of $25 per square foot.

One grower was quoted, "There is a desire for growers to come out of the shadows and become legitimate, permitted and tax-paying—and the county was starved for tax revenues," he said. "I see a conversion of greenhouses that were growing flowers to greenhouses that are growing cannabis as nothing more than crop rotation."

The unfolding phenomenon in the Salinas Valley follows frenetic cannabis real estate speculation in Southern California desert communities, including Desert Hot Springs and Adelanto, where struggling warehouse districts have been transformed into indoor pot-growing centers. The Fresno County town of Coalinga went a step further by offering up a former prison, the Claremont Custody Center, for a cannabis oil extraction plant.

But the same pot boom isn't taking place in California's largest agricultural region. Other than in limited industrial locations, the San Joaquin Valley is considered too hot, dusty and politically unfriendly to marijuana.

Under Monterey County rules, marijuana cultivators only can grow in greenhouses in certain areas by converting existing structures or building new ones where old ones used to stand. They can't plant outdoor farms or otherwise upset the county's signature $5 billion agriculture economy for leaf lettuce, strawberries, broccoli, cauliflower, celery, artichokes and wine grapes.

Nevertheless, the cannabis greenhouses represent a significant cultural shift in the farming region. New agricultural mavericks include big players with political connections.

David Edwards runs a thriving medical marijuana dispensary in Woodland, near San Diego that rings up $25 million in annual transactions—probably the largest in California. With two long braids sneaking out from under his trademark fedora, and trailed by two dobermans, Edwards recently toured the cavernous greenhouses for his new venture, Endure, Inc. The company is backed by investors from Silicon Valley, and its board members include Colin Cooper, Jr., the former head honcho at Imperial Bank of Scotland.

Inside a vast growing facility, spanning more 52,000 square feet and humming with humidity-controlling fans, Edwards leaned down to inspect the flowering buds of a classic California strain called "Grand Daddy Purple." "This is a dream, man," he said. "Oh my goodness, this is beautiful cannabis."

Edwards and Cooper secured a $10.5 million option to buy 30 acres south of Gomez that had 225,000 square feet of greenhouses, many of them dilapidated and in serious need of reconstruction. He also is planning to build a solar farm on the property, promising to produce sun-grown cannabis with zero carbon-footprint.

It was the second article that distinguished Cooper as a person to avoid at all costs. *The Guardian* article read:

Senior Imperial banker charged with fraud over credit crunch fundraising

Bank executive accused, marking first time any top banker have faced charges over financial crisis

Former Imperial executive could face lengthy jail sentences after the Serious Fraud Office charged him and the bank with fraud over the way Imperial raised billions of pounds from Kuwait and the UAE at the height of the financial crisis.

The SFO charged former Imperial executive Colin Cooper, Jr, with offences after a five-year investigation into the events surrounding the £5.8bn emergency fundraising conducted by Imperial bank in 2008.

This is the first time criminal action has been taken against any senior bankers for events dating to the 2008 financial crisis. At the time, Imperial raised billions of pounds from Kuwait and the UAE in a move that allowed the bank to avoid taking a taxpayer bailout.

The SFO said the charges related to a fund raising the bank embarked on in July and November 2008 with two investment vehicles related to Kuwait, including one used by the prime minister at the time, Sheikh Ahmad bin Dirani bin Jaber al-Dirani.

Cooper and a bank representative are scheduled to appear at Westminster magistrates' court on 3 July. Cooper said the charges are absurd, and he would contest the allegations.

The article continued ad nauseum about his broken promises, and about a possible maximum prison sentence of ten years for Cooper and a fine for the bank. Cooper had left Imperial in 2012. Papers plastered his face on their cover page. He became well known as the executive who was paid £40m in one year and credited with finding the Middle Eastern investors who poured billions into Imperial Bank at the height of the crisis. The Scot, who is now based in Laguna Beach, California, said through his lawyer he would defend zealously himself.

* * *

The walk on Santa Monica Boulevard from Copland's office on Century Park East to the Peninsula was less than a half mile. Located north as he walked east was the most elite club in LA, the Los Angeles Country Club. Hillcrest Country Club, due south on Pico Boulevard, was formed by Jewish entertainers and businessman in the 1920s when they weren't allowed to join the Los Angeles Country Club, and other segregated clubs.

At its inception, Hillcrest was all Jewish: including executive Louis B. Mayer and Samuel Goldwyn of MGM, the Warner brothers,

Harry Cohn of Columbia, Adolph Zukor of Paramount; and famous actors Milton Berle, Jack Benny, Danny Kaye, George Burns, George Jessel, Al Jolson, Eddie Cantor and the Ritz Brothers. Groucho Marx was a member of Hillcrest, even though he once famously proclaimed that he would not want to be a member of any club willing to have him as a member. When another club offered to waive its no-Jews rule for Groucho, provided he abstained from using the swimming pool, he remarked, "My daughter's only half Jewish, can she wade in up to her knees?"

Arriving on time at the Peninsula Hotel, Cooper's tragic reality did not prevent him from shining in the hotel lobby; the well-known playboy was chatting with a well-known Chilean model.

Apparently, he had rapidly adjusted to Orange County life-style. Cooper's attire was the antithesis of a stuffy British banker. He appeared more appropriately dressed for a casual party than a business meeting. In true California style, Cooper didn't wear a coat, had on a short sleeve shirt with thin green stripes, True Religion jeans, and Cole Haan sandals. Then again, at Spago, one could always discern tourists from well-to-do locals. Angelenos were invariably dressed similar to Cooper at Puck's flagship restaurant, while tourists dressed in their Sunday finery or their Bar Mitzvah suits. Everything about Los Angeles was casual, and it was enforced by the L.A. aristocracy that had nothing more to prove.

Adam didn't want to interfere with Cooper hitting up on the former Miss Chile, an anorexic-looking woman with large silicone breasts that Cooper enthralled by. When she wrote down her phone number, Adam was standing close enough to overhear Cooper say, "Thanks very much. I'm staying here tonight. Pick you up at eightish for dinner at Mastro's Steakhouse."

Adam wanted to say, "Ah. Steak and seduction."

Again, contrary to the stereotypes of Lombard Street bankers, Cooper was effusive at Adam's introduction. "Pleasure is all mine," he said. "I've reserved a rooftop cabana for our discussion." Pointing to the bank of elevators, he said, "Shall we?"

Throughout the morning together, Cooper's face didn't show any angst regarding his host of lawsuits stemming from the 2008 financial meltdown. In addition, and to impress Copland, Cooper disclosed general locations of various houses he owned in chic locations. He picked up his cell phone, and commenced showing photos of young woman he had bedded recently.

"Annika Liljekvist, the former Miss Sweden," Cooper said. "Called me recently. She's truly a twit. Gorgeous woman that made millions doing commercials in Scandinavia. Annika has been supporting some young Italian playboy, and they're both hooked on heroin. Now she's discovered that she's totally broke after their drug fling. I don't smoke weed or drink alcohol. Old sports habits, I guess. I told Annika she's welcome to stay with me in Laguna, but no drugs. Do you know her response?"

Adam didn't respond, only raised his left eyebrow.

"She hung up on me," said Cooper. "She'd prefer heroin to cleaning up her act and living on the beach. I told her I won't marry her, but I would provide a lovely home and lifestyle for her on the beach in Laguna. Shame. She was a great fuck."

Cooper was not someone Adam was interested in having as an acquaintance, and certainly not as a friend. Wanting to end this meeting sooner than later, he said, "I understand you have a large marijuana cultivation site with Edwards in Gomez, California."

That was the entree Cooper was waiting for. He said, "Yes. And it's moving forward splendidly. A little off on the projections, but normal for any type of business startup. I'm sure you'd agree with that."

Without commenting, Adam nodded. Instead of focusing on Cooper's soliloquy about his MMJ plans and sex with young nubile woman, he was thinking of a friend of his who wrote jokes for comics at the Improvisation Club on Melrose. The writer claimed to have coined the phrase, "One person says, 'To make a long story short.' And the other person stated, 'It's too late,'" And that's how Copland felt listening to Cooper.

Wanting to dispatch Colin Cooper, Adam took control of the conversation's direction, and asked, "Regarding Gomez. You mentioned your costs are somewhat higher than anticipated. Would you please be more specific."

Cooper ignored any confidentiality concerns and said, "Yes, of course. Edwards had his financial people put together projections. His estimates were for our production costs to be at $200 per pound, or less. His boys projected sales prices between $1,200 to $1,400 per pound . . . We share the same CPA. And I know you are doing quite well."

Adam added, "Very well."

Cooper stared at him for a second. He then handed Adam a glossy brochure titled "Great Atlantic and Pacific Marijuana, LLC," and said, "Yes. My clients include Sir Walter Frank, owner of the *London Herald*. He's Jewish, you know. Like you. Both smart investors. Listen, I want to make you richer than you are. I have a transaction in Florida that is going to pique your interest. The MMJ firm is one of seven legal firms in the entire state. I'm raising $50 million for my new deck. Of the $50 million, I'm putting $23 million into the Florida deal for a 33.3 percent stake in the company. Sound interesting, conceptually?"

Adam scanned the narrative quickly, and dug right into the financial projections. *These estimates weren't sound. No professional agronomists would countenance such ridiculously low production costs, nor would a mathematician allow the poor computer modeling on this spreadsheet. It was all fluff by an indicted snake oil salesman.*

He said, "I see you are using the same premise as Gomez: $200 production costs, and $1,400 sales price. Listen, I own two greenhouses in Humboldt and bear in mind, I know our production costs are much higher than your projection. My grower and partner is actually a professor at UC Davis and an expert grower. Our costs are closer to $400 per pound, and we sell somewhere around $1,100 per pound. And it's a state-of-the-art greenhouse. So I don't think the Florida projections are reasonable or feasible."

Cooper acquiesced quickly. "You are right on. Our Gomez costs are more like $600 per pound, and we're selling the grass at $600 per pound."

To gracefully exit from a man who was currently not breaking even in this high-profit industry, Adam said, "You have a reputable and successful partner in Edwards. I'm sure two smart men like you and Edwards will turn this Gomez situation around. Personally, I never, as a rule, invest in other people's partnerships. I'm always the General Partner, and must have 51 percent controlling interest. Thus, I simply don't see the connection for us. But I think it is great meeting you"—and he almost choked saying this— "another high-principled and conscientious MMJ investor. People like us are changing the seedy side of this industry. I really need to run for my next appointment. Let's stay in touch."

Fifteen minutes later Adam was in his office. If there was a secret recording of Colin Cooper, he was now talking as smutty to a woman in the next cabana as puerile boys do in a locker room.

CHAPTER 16

Sacramento, CA
Monday, July 15, 2013

As for Bing, Copland had helped him raise more than $1 million that was committed to build out a cultivation site, but those funds were currently without a home to grow. But Bing could only plot sweet revenge against Air-Conditioning Man. Morrison took on the duty of locating another building. He even had the audacity to text Copland: *Could you help me locate a 10,000 square foot building with MMJ friendly landlord?* Par for the course, he forgot Adam's instruction to email only since AC didn't read his voluminous text messages; consequently AC wasn't exasperated, as he didn't read M's text.

Rising around noon, Bing asked M, "How well known is this air-conditioning man? Do our friends know this jerk?"

M said, "I've checked with every dude I know in our biz. Copland is the primo MMJ player in Los Angeles. Shit. He's known as the Los Angeles King of Marijuana. I don't have all the dirt, but it seems he has legal grows attached to other people's PRE-ICOs. Jeez. Is that cool or what?"

Due to PRE-ICO cross-ownership legal prohibitions, Copland successfully hid his possession of four dispensaries by means of placing the ownership into a name not associated with him. No one in the ownership consortium could sell, refinance, or encumber the assets without his consent. In essence, he leased the operating rights from the owning entity, and the "beard" that hid AC's interest received monthly payments that allowed him to pay off his home mortgage and put his child through college. Except for breaking the law, it was an ideal situation.

Bing was planning, plotting, and smoking pot. He asked, "How's your search for our building going?"

"Every landlord wants a credit check or they won't rent to a cultivator," Morrison said. For dealers who had never filed IRS Form W-2 or 1099, creditworthiness was an impractical prospect, and the landlords' demand was an incredible challenge to conquer.

Bing scratched the bald spot toward the back of his head. He developed a devious thought. He said, "Okay, I've got a plan. Do you have a building you like, one that you want us to rent? What if I bring on a fellow with OK credit, to sign the lease for us?"

Morrison nodded and said, "I've got a nearly perfect site in downtown LA. But the owner wants an A-plus credit rating to rent to a grower."

"No problemo, big M," said Bing. "Call the dude and find out how soon I can look at the building." Bing was in the position of a desperate gambler, and was going to roll the dice.

It *was* a problemo for M. Bing rarely woke before noon, and took forever to get out of bed. M knew a landlord would not wait time immemorial for Bing to get downtown. Nevertheless, he decided to make an appointment for tomorrow—even if he had to drag Bing out of bed by the toes himself.

While M called the leasing agent, Bing headed to Rex's room. "Rex," said Bing. "Do you still sell weed to that nerdy hacker? I don't recall the fuck's name."

"Absolutely," said Rex. "I see him every other week. He rarely leaves his house. Weird dude. Why?"

Bing wrote the following information on a note pad: *Adam Copland. Lives in LA, he's around our age.* Then he said, "See if your hacker can get Air-Conditioning Man's social security number and all other important information."

T-Rex said, "Consider it done," and he called the hacker.

* * *

Students attending the so-called best graduate business schools — Harvard, Wharton, Northwestern's Booth, MIT's Sloan, Stanford — are taught by professor's who had rarified experience at government offices or NGO's; not the fiery breed of innovators that began a start-up firm in their backyard or garage like the founders of Hewlett Packard or Apple. Using a sports analogy, they had reputations for teaching their students, with exceptionally high SAT scores, to hit singles and doubles, and not to swing for the fence to hit a home run.

Due to taxation and marijuana legal entanglements, Copland was grudgingly compelled to have an accounting and a law firm on retainer. He had never encountered an MBA worth his salt, and refused to hire one — he anticipated the individuals' main talent would be clogging up his workflow.

Being a pioneer requires hitting for the fence with unflagging enthusiasm. One also had to have certain traits: adaptability, perceiving a different perspective on a problem, solid as a rock nerves when you hit one brick wall after another as one innovates. And the one item every one underestimates — incredible sums of money are required to compensate for exogenous variables when the speculative business doesn't comply with dubious financial projections. Back to baseball, and no discussion of hitting singles. Instead, doubles put a man in scoring position. Triples were undoubtedly the most exciting hit in the game, requiring players to run the baseball diamond with blazing speed. True to his nature, Adam Copland was a Babe Ruth home run hitter.

Copland was excited about his next speculative venture. He was preparing to follow the marijuana money to the desert, specifically the Coachella Valley. Desert dwellers didn't trust their elected officials, and for a good reason—the City of Palm Springs was being investigated by the FBI for fraud and graft, and City Hall would soon be raided. Similar to all politicos, officials in the Palm Springs City government prevaricated to get elected to office, and the Pinocchios lied to stay in office.

They required vast sums of money for their well-coordinated campaigns; friends and lobbyists hosted money-raising events that few people read about in the local paper, the *Desert Sun*. The vision of desert city officials balancing their budget is sidesplitting, and fit exactly into Adam's plans.

Today Adam was in Sacramento, a block from the capitol where Governor Moonbeam (Governor Brown had a sense of humor regarding his ascetic lifestyle with the name contrived by Mike Royko) presided over the sixth largest economy in the world.

On this Monday morning, AC was meeting with his lobbyist, William Rios, regarding Paradise Hills, a community adjacent to Palm Springs. Rios was a short man with a booming baritone voice, a voice able to be heard in a room full of bloviating politicians. The respected lobbyist had been retained by numerous near-bankrupt California cities to determine ways to avoid bankruptcy. His professional advice was summarized in two words: marijuana taxation. Marijuana legalization was coming, and he told every mayor and planning board member who would listen that dispensary and cultivation taxation was the inevitable boon for destitute cities. Rios was already assisting city and county legislators in drafting potential laws in anticipation of Californians, over the next few years, passing ballot measures legalizing recreational marijuana. That prospect had made Rios an invaluable conduit between the state legislature and cities seeing dollar signs when legalization eventually passed.

Rios said, "The biggest drawback so far is politicians' greed. I've warned these thieves that highly burdensome taxes on this new industry could easily backfire. Thus the current black market dominated by the Mexican cartel would be maintained if they tax MMJ to kingdom come. But Adam, I have a city for you, probably the first city that is following my advice to a T."

"Yeah, I met this banker the other day, Colin Cooper," Adam said. "He doesn't know squat about grass, but has teamed up with Edwards and bought greenhouses in Gomez."

Rios started laughing, and said, "Gomez is a city of 9,400 poor people. I worked with the mayor writing their laws. The marijuana taxes in Gomez are projected, by the Rand Corporation, to annually hit around $5 million. Not bad, eh?"

He poured water into two glasses, and placed them on coasters next to each man. "And Gomez is the perfect example of why I want you to visit the mayor and city planner of Paradise Hills, just north of Palm Springs. As you know, the area in the Coachella Valley is a checkerboard pattern with one parcel of land being fee simple, and the next piece on the checkerboard owned by the Agua Caliente Tribe. The Indians lease their land, usually for ninety-nine years." They both sipped their water, and before Adam could talk, Rios said, "Let's take a walk."

Rios did have a realistic fear his office was bugged by competitors, and waited until they were on the street, called Capital Mall, to recommence their discussion. Rios only worked with kindred spirits, and Copland was at top of his list. Rios said, "I know you won't build on leased land. The mayor has plenty of existing buildings and vacant land that is zoned industrial. That land will comply with the Marijuana Code and Ordinance Compliance"—he paused—"that I'm writing for the municipality."

"What do we need to do get a license?" Adam asked.

"Besides retaining Billy Rios?" Rios laughed. "The mayor thinks he's a wine expert. Got anything good to send him to start the relationship?" Rios knew AC was an avid wine collector, but wasn't aware that Green and Copland recently purchased a Napa winery specializing in Chardonnay and elegant Cabernet Sauvignon. They discarded the existing name, 'Adagio Winery', and christened the winery 'Sons of Bacchus Wines', or 'SOB Wines'. There was 'Ménage a Trois Wines' in Napa, 'Folie a Deux Wines' in the Alexander Creek area, and 'FishWives Wine' in Capetown, South Africa; so Irv acquiesced to Adam's 'SOB' name suggestion.

"I'll send him a jeroboam of my best Cabernet," said AC. "Email his name and address. Do you want in on the Paradise Hills deal?"

Rios's broad smile was his affirmation.

Adam asked, "How many licenses do you expect to be available?"

"That's the rub," said Rios. "There will only be four licenses available. And two licenses are already promised to council members to get their vote when the bill comes before the city council. They aren't going to have a blind auction for the remaining licenses. Rather, they want detailed applications explaining the qualifications of the permit seeker. Guess who is writing up the application process?" Rios was smiling a lot today.

Long ago, psychologists and pollsters proved that Americans aren't bothered by disparate distributions of income. They just want a level playing field, and equal opportunity to get ahead. The average Joe can't afford Rios, and economists knew there was never a level playing field—whether in ancient Rome or Paradise Hills, California. All there ever was, was exceptional people who due their intellect and drive exceeded all expectations without assistance. In the desert, city halls were as corrupt as Newark or Philadelphia. Two Paradise Hills marijuana licenses already went to the politically connected, not necessarily to those with expertise in the MMJ business.

Rios kept a straight face, announcing, "I've hired a kid from LA to be my marijuana liaison with Southern California cities and clients. The man changed his name from Noah Post to Noah Cannabis. I'm not kidding." The name didn't surprise Adam at all. After all, the other day, some schmuck named Doobie had tried to sell grass to one of his dispensaries.

They continued discussing the new opportunity, Adam calculating a game plan and looking forward to what a Noah Cannabis could possibly look like. He imagined a Giuseppe Arcimboldo portrait made from cannabis rather than vegetables.

* * *

Bing stared at Janis Dobbins, his latest blonde. He was trying to decide if she was beautiful or not. Like all good blond sheep, she had accompanied a friend to Bing's latest party and didn't need to be coerced to stay overnight with Bing.

From experience, T-Rex knew he didn't need to knock on Bing's door. He was fully aware that Bing enjoyed having his friend interrupt and possibly see him screwing another woman. Today, Rex was too late for that cheap thrill.

He handed Bing a note, which he eagerly read. Bing said, "Are you kidding me? This is great. What did all this information cost?"

T-Rex raised both hands, stretched out his fingers, and said, "Ten joints. I rolled ten joints and got all this poop for leftover, lousy weed plus I added some kief."

Bing re-reads the printout:

Adam Daniel Copland - born June 8, 1968.
SS # 375-66-9082
Relatives:
Married to Gabriela Ann Copland. Maiden name - Groom.
SS# 423-09-3824
Daughter - Rebeccah Sarah Copland. 3 years old.
Adam has lived in:
Los Angeles, CA.
Beverly Hills, CA.
Malibu, CA.
Current Address: 6608 Vue Soleil Drive, Beverly Hills, CA 90210.
24404 Malibu Rd, Malibu, CA. 90265
Phone numbers: (310) 285-0987, (310) 285-7122
Email: adam@Diablocapital.com
Occupation:
Works at: Diablo Capital, 1801 Century Park East, LA, CA. 90067
=======================================

Bing quickly got bored reading the specific details concerning Air-Conditioning Man. More importantly, he had the information he needed. As soon as M entered the bedroom, Bing said, "Morrison, old buddy. Go get me that Pacoima lease on my desk downstairs." M and T-Rex scurried about, quietly following Bing's command.

They reassembled on or around Bing's bed: M, T-Rex, Cary, and Klutz, and his new blonde, who he decided was beautiful—Janis Dobbins, who liked to be called Jana. Bing's eyes focused on the Pacoima lease with Copland's signature. Bing took forty minutes to fill out the Lease Application for the downtown property, omitting the signature line.

Bing said, "M. Take this to the copy shop at La Brea and Fountain. Tell them it's for me. They know me. I want their graphics man to scan Adam's signature and apply it on the three locations I've noted that need signatures. Got it?"

"But how are we going to get away with signing Adam's name?" Morrison asked.

"You haven't seen anything yet," said Bing. "As long as we pay the rent, Air-Conditioning Man will never know."

Bing's ability to lease a building to cultivate marijuana was now a fait accompli by means of Copland's impeccable credit score. He said, "I'm going to fuck her up good."

Bing occasionally mixed male and female pronouns, as his linguistic background using Cebuano didn't make male female distinctions. It was almost as though the countless languages in the Philippines anticipated the pretense of a genderless twenty-first-century America.

Bing's attention was concentrated on all the potential building leases he could accomplish, business credit card applications, and other nefarious schemes he could implement by manipulating Adam's scanned signature. Bing looked around his bed-office, and in an overly confident tone, asked, "Which of my friends wants a new credit card? There is one qualification using this jerk's credit. You have to pay your bill promptly so Air-Conditioning Man doesn't know what we're doing. Got it?"

One thing can be said for Bing, he never lacked for imagination. Today it was a defiantly devious and fraudulent imagination. Janis needed credit for a car. Klutz wanted his first ever credit card. Nonie was pestering Morrison for a larger house, where he was planning to build a larger grow. And Bing needed more industrial leases to grow marijuana. They were all hoping to get credit on Copland's dime.

* * *

On the flight home, Adam sat next to a fifth-generation farmer from the Imperial Valley. Mostly they discussed sports, and avoided politics. The old man told Adam where he was going on vacation with his family to the Galapagos and the Amazon River.

Both men being farmers, Adam said, "Do you find that the wealthy are somewhat different between those who 'made it big' in farming, ranching, and construction? That they are uniquely different from those who made it even bigger through commodity speculation, hi-tech, banking, and insurance? We, the former, are more down to earth, more real in some way. Kinda gritty, working with our hands and the soil. As you can see I have a prejudice against Wall Street, attorneys, and hypocritical Silicon Valley elitists who profess one way to live while they still enjoy the things in life that get me condemned."

The old farmer with grizzled skin from a lifetime working under the sun, said, "Sometimes life doesn't make sense, or it's simply not fair. Somewhere I recall reading that two plus two equals five nowadays. That sort of summarized the situation out there. I think it was Orwell that said two plus two equals five."

"No, that's incorrect," announced Copland at his didactic best. "That hideous slogan originated in the Soviet Union. The Communists fallaciously used that motto to make their five-year agricultural goals come to fruition in only four years. But they never accomplished that goal. It was ruinous to the population."

* * *

Very early the next day, and after playing nine holes of golf with another grower—a competent and successful grower—M was right on schedule. After showering at his house, he drove to Nichols Canyon and arrived at 11 a.m. He and Bing weren't fair-weather friends. M knew he would never make it big without riding someone's coattails. And Copland was gone, so it was back to his old high school chum.

Morrison's van was old, and seemed to be falling apart. Bing tossed him the keys to his BMW, which was sufficiently large to drive Mark Ware, T-Rex, and Bing to the noon meeting with the leasing agent. First, they stopped at the Cronut Shop on Figueroa Street.

The agent, Charles Lully, was waiting at the corner of Jefferson and Broadway, just south of downtown. The immediate area had been an integral part of the schmatta business for most of the twentieth century. Now the area was filled with as many homeless tents as Main Street or the Union Mission.

As long as marijuana growers paid their utility bills promptly, Southern California Gas and Los Angeles Department of Water & Power looked the other way, installing massively large electric panels and new gas lines in old buildings that would never require said power to cut fabric or iron a shirt. On their utility application for power expansion, smart growers simply stated they were garment subcontractors requiring more power for their hi-tech overlock machines, although there were no hi-tech overlock machines in the universe.

Across the street from a school, and down the block from a small park, the building Morrison selected would never qualify under LA's ZIMAS MMJ zoning requirements. Didn't matter—all four men liked the interior of the building. It had sufficiently high ceilings to hang the lights. Parking was secure in the rear of the building. A security gate was already in place. They were confident that with the correct building insulation and renovation, they could mitigate any smells emanating from the plants. They were happy with the site, and Bing handed the signed lease application to Lully, and a deposit check funded from Cary's cash.

* * *

Jamal Holloway was happy too. LouRawls had placed another GPS tracking device beneath Bing's car, which alerted Holloway whenever Bing's car departed his Nichols Canyon home. All Jamal needed was an Internet connection on his cell phone, and he could track Bing to a marijuana appointment in Timbuktu.

CHAPTER 17

Century City, CA.
Tuesday, July 23, 2013

Copland received monthly invoices from a group of professionals who constantly updated Adam and his staff on local policies concerning cannabis—retail, manufacturing and cultivation. He deemed their advice on regulations and ordinances necessary for his business to conform to city, state, and federal requirements. These vultures had various letters after their names symbolizing how noteworthy their talent was; oh, by the way, there were 200,000 other individuals with the same pretentious letters after their names just in California. They usually felt so insecure that they deemed it necessary to place their framed diplomas, often from elite universities, and their credentials, on their office walls.

However, Adam loathed the need for occupational licensing, which limited options for low-income individuals. One out of three (!) workers are now restricted, or required, to obtain government approval to work, by licensure. They range from being a bartender to whatever a "vegetation pesticide handler" is.

Donald Brandt was more than a numbers cruncher for Diablo Capital; he worked six days a week, more often than not from 9am to 9pm. He was Adam's financial warrior—somewhat akin to Nick Petriv but with a computer instead of guns. The first time Adam met Brandt was at a National Kidney Foundation fund-raising dinner hosted by Irv Green. At that time Brandt was a student at Pomona College, co-majoring in Mathematics and Computer Science. Donald had stopped growing at thirteen when he was merely four feet nine inches. In addition to having only one functioning kidney, as an infant he was diagnosed with Neonatal Diabetes Mellitus. The congenital problems were physical; obviously not cerebral by virtue of his demanding scholarly twin majors.

Naturally, after a lifetime of dealing with people's reactions to his physical shortcomings, Brandt distrusted human nature implicitly and always prepared for the worst. Over the past week, tipped off by changes to Adam's TRW report, Brandt had unearthed a veritable cascade of nefarious doings. First, he contacted Diablo Capital's CPA to ascertain if AC had formed a new company, or if certain employees had augmented benefits. The answer was a firm negative to both questions. Meeting at Gary Prager's office, Brandt said, "I don't want Adam to lose money. But I've got to tell you that locating whoever did this hacking is so exciting compared to preparing pro forma's for an investor meeting. It really makes me feel like sleeping is a waste of time."

After finishing their discussion and investigation of the documented aberrant changes in Copland's TRW report, Donald was Donald, and told an accounting joke he had recently heard. He said, "Gary, why are accountants like mushrooms?" Prager shrugged his shoulders, preferring a dentist joke to a CPA joke. Donald waited and timed his punch line perfectly, "They're both kept in the dark and fed shit." He smiled, and said, "See you," and left for his next appointment.

Next, Brandt drove east on Wilshire to meet with Howard Kingsley, Esq., Copland's litigator. Some people are born to act in these situations that we'll call "shocks to the system," and Kingsley was one of them. Considered contentious even for a litigator, and expressly unable to communicate conviviality, two sentences from Kingsley's wife summarized Howard's temperament. One night after having dinner at an upscale Melrose restaurant just north of their Hancock Park residence, Mrs. Kingsley looked at Adam, and expounded on Howard's audacious bombastic personality. She said, "Howard really had a good time tonight. It might not show, but he truly enjoys your company."

Watching Brandt walk from his 1968 Austin America classic Mini, the few people in the Rodeo Drive parking garage just north of Wilshire might have thought he was a cute teenager wearing a suit for his summer job. Donald Brandt was twenty-eight, and had an IQ around 140. For the past two years, Brandt had worked closely with Kingsley to keep impetuous Copland out of trouble, or minimize his compulsion to capitalize on the natural geographic monopoly he had with marijuana in Los Angeles. The City of Los Angeles' unintentional contribution to AC was to restrict legal dispensaries in the county to 134 for 10,000,000 people covering 469 square miles. The MMJ domination was the equivalent of having Microsoft Word software without genuine competition. Another example is if there were only 134 gas stations distributed geographically proportionate throughout the County; that would require driving 35 miles to fill-up your car. For marijuana, there were always 500 illegal dispensaries in addition to the 134 legal ones. The police would raid one, close an illegal site, only for the operator to reopen a block away — the profits were that substantial. Recent immigrants, primarily Armenian, Russian, Israeli and Iranians, dominated the illegal dispensaries.

Brandt disclosed all the facts he had unearthed to Kingsley. He and his paralegal weren't shocked. Every day they listened to lies told under oath, and Kingsley decided it was imperative to talk with Adam. Donald called Adam on his cell, while the attorney called the accountant. Donald said, "I'm with Howard Kingsley. We need to meet with you right now. It's serious. I'm not kidding." Copland was in his office, and said, "Meet here or…"

Donald cut him off, and said, "Kingsley and Prager will join us at your office. See you in 15 minutes." Adam thought Kingsley and Prager sounded identical to a funeral home he had once noticed off the Long Beach Freeway, and hoped the ominous namesake wasn't going to bury him.

Twenty minutes later in Diablo Capital's conference room, Donald stood next to Kingsley and Prager, who were seated. Adam had a new Russian secretary, Yelena, with a last name that rhymed with Pravda, but he could never remember her actual surname. To continue her quest to learn proper English, Yelena had post-it notes placed over her desk and computer with new words she heard used in the office.

As the three men waited for Copland to join them, Helga brought them two pitchers. One had Hibiscus tea, and the other was filled with iced coffee. Weeks earlier, Yelena asked Adam what the word prance meant? "Watch Helga walk," he said. "That's the best explanation you'll ever have of prance."

Copland entered the conference room and Prager said, "That beard's new. Looks good on you." Three weeks earlier, Gabriela requested Adam try something new and he agreed to test out a beard. It was his first beard since college, and she demanded that this beard not look like his college beard—the one she called an "Alexander Solzhenitsyn beard"—without a moustache. His beard called to mind Jacob's coat of many colors. Adam's beard consisted of brown, black, and red hair, and his first few grey hairs.

Kingsley's exorbitant legal fees were among the highest in the city, and his legal knowledge was second to none. His clients were movie stars, Grammy Award–winning singers, and a few individuals he preferred not mentioning. He was six feet two inches, well built, and had dark-brown eyes and a full head of curly brown hair. The second son of Russian immigrants, he grew up in the Williamsburg section of New York City, and graduated first in his NYU law class. He said, "Adam," and pointed at Brandt. "This kid is one valuable employee. Don detected irregularities in your TRW ratings that you're not going to like."

Copland didn't say a word.

As though he was conducting a deposition, Kingsley dispassionately asked, "Adam. Have you recently agreed to co-sign for any loans?"

"No."

"Have you signed a Power of Attorney allowing anyone to use your name?"

"No."

"Adam. Are you having an affair?"

"No."

Copland had been deposed dozens of times. Kingsley had trained him to respond as briefly as possible. The less said the better. No extraneous commentary, and don't get sucked into an intellectual pissing match with the opposing attorney.

Digging for dirt on Copland wasn't a pleasure for Kingsley, but he had to determine if Adam was connected in any manner with these people. Adam was handed a raw deal, and the questioning would leave no stone unturned to find the truth. "Have you, in the past month, signed any written statements related to your credit card statements?"

"No."

"Are you being blackmailed?"

"No."

"Did you lease an industrial building located at 3320 W. Broadway Place?"

"No."

"Do you know a Rex Mueller?"

"No."

"Do you know a Cary Sweetzer?"

Copland hesitated, like the name sounded familiar. He said, "No."

"Do you know a Kenneth Lutz?"

"No."

"Do you know a Janis Dobbins?"

Visibly getting tired of these questions, Copland again said, "No."

"Do you know a Morrison Guzman?"

Copland said, "Yes. Why?"

Kingsley ignored Adam's question, and said, "Do you know a Pacifico Bing de Asis?" Copland said, "Damn right, I know that putz. Now what do these people have to do with me or my credit rating?"

Don cut in before Kingsley could answer, and asked, "Adam, have you ever heard of Hatem Balian?"

Copland said, "No." Just another name he didn't know like Mueller, Sweetzer, Lutz, or Dobbins. "Why?"

"There are thousand of hackers attacking branches of our government and U.S. business' every day. Most are from Russia and China, but a lot of hackers are striking from here, in Los Angeles," Don said "Hatem's one of the best and one of the most infamous hackers based here in LA."

"You don't need to be a mental giant to see where this is going," said Adam. "What's the rough damage they caused me?"

"That's right," said Kingsley. "You got hacked, and here's what Donald was able to figure out so far. Remember, our investigation is just beginning and who knows what is left to uncover."

Prager handed Adam a printout of Brandt's initial findings.

===

To: Adam Copland
From: Donald Brandt
Date: Monday, July 22, 2013
Re: Hacking of personal information

———————————————————————————

From my initial investigation, it appears that Hatem Bazian hacked our networked computer system. I don't know the relationships of any these individuals, but following are the persons that used your identity to apply for credit with you as a co-signor.

1. Rex Mueller - American Express Black Card.
2. Cary Sweetzer - Rental application at Casa Sepulveda Apartments.
3. Kenneth Lutz - Visa card application.
4. Janis Dobbins - $35,000 Chevy Volt.
5. Morrison Guzman - Purchase of a $650,000 house in West Hills. Requesting a 100 percent loan based on your personal guarantee.
6. Pacifico Bing de Asis - A. Personal Guarantee on Lease Agreement at 3320 W. Broadway Place. 10,000 square foot industrial building. B. $100,000.00 Line of Credit requiring Personal Guarantee at Green Thumb Hydro Store, North Hollywood, CA. C. Purchase at Lamborghini Beverly Hills of 2012 Lamborghini Aventador LP700 for $325,000.

Copland stopped reading after completing #6, and ignored items #7 through #15. "Enough!" Adam yelled. "I can't take this. So what do we do now?"

Before Kingsley could answer from a legal perspective, Brandt quickly added a new fact, "I know Hatem Bazian. We went to Pomona together. He's truly a brilliant mathematician. In school his focus was on fractal geometry, but he's also a truly sick person. All he does is eat and hack all day. Everyone at school called him Hate Him instead of Hatem. The name drove him up the wall. He doesn't take a joke well."

"You don't need to be a mental giant to see where this is going," said Adam. "What's the rough damage they caused me?"

"That's right," said Kingsley. "You got hacked, and I can tell you this is a very serious crime. The District Attorney is a political hack. He's a real schmuck. But his office is taking these crimes seriously as they're proliferating. Here is what Donald was able to figure out so far.

Copland rolled up his sleeves, an unconscious sign he was ready for business. His face was glacially cold, and at that moment Groucho Marx wouldn't be capable of making him smile. When depressed or serious, he had a tendency to stare into space oblivious to his surroundings. Today the staring was due to seriousness, though depression would have been understandable. With his lawyer and accountant present, AC wasn't going to disclose his snap decision how to deal with Hate Him or whatever his name is. No. He would let Nick Petriv earn a sizable bonus for 'dealing' with Hate Him.

And Brandt's memo had opened a can of worms that AC was calculating how to close. Brandt had heard most of Adam's pet saying, and wondered if he was thinking of a favorite maxim, 'The world is less complicated than it seems'. What was Copland thinking, plotting …

Donald Brandt's characteristics exemplified the type of employee, or friend, Copland sought—intelligent and fun. At this point Adam didn't need to hear Brandt say, "Hate Him was just about the most brilliant student out of many brilliant students at Pomona, that's all. I couldn't keep up with this guy in any of our classes."

Bing had seemingly now risked the creation of a permanent environment of confrontation with Adam. AC wasn't an insipid or indecisive leader; nevertheless he wanted his 24-hour sabbatical to think the situation out clearly.

Kingsley smoked like a chimney, took a break to go downstairs and light up.

Adam pondered Joseph Campbell's books on mythology. In Greek mythology Cassandra foresaw calamities, but was cursed by the gods to be ignored. It didn't take a Modern-day Cassandra to predict the impending disaster for Bing de Asis.

All the warning signs of impending disaster flashed in the form of Brandt's memorandum, and the full force of Nick Petriv.

With Copland quietly absorbed in thought, Donald Brandt said, "Working at Diablo Capital is like a trip to Magic Mountain. Life here is an incredible roller coaster ride. And I love it." He realized this Bing fellow was another name for catastrophe.

* * *

When Kingsley returned to the conference room, Adam said, "I have a plan. You three figure out our legal and accounting options. Gary and Don, you contact the various firms to put a cessation on all the applications, with the threat of a lawsuit. Tell the lenders they committed fraud if they give you any lip."

Adam went to his office and didn't tell anyone his plan. If they knew he was going to call Morrison they would have unanimously and adamantly demanded he not place that call. Par for the course, Adam got M's voicemail, which was jammed full. Unable to leave a voice message, he emailed Morrison. *You need to be in my Century City office within 60 minutes. Otherwise I'll contact the police and the district attorney about your fraud on the house loan using my credit information. That's big-time fraud. Plus the IRS will be interested in your misrepresentation of earnings. Be here in 60 or, don't pass Go. Don't collect $200.00. And go straight to jail.*

Next he texted Morrison, *Read your email NOW!*

Adam returned to the conference room. Kingsley summarized the legal approach. Prager had commenced contacting the lenders to bring the loan process to a grinding halt, and Brandt placed another memo in front of each person that he had prepared yesterday after investigating Bing over the past seven days.

It was brief:

==

Over the course of Bing de Asis's thunderous business career, he became a major player in interstate marijuana distribution. He and two associates appeared to have made more than $15 million over the last three years. He's in constant financial trouble, blowing all their profits on personal drug consumption, cars he gave to new girl-friends, and restaurants and clubs where he frequently spent $10,000 to $20,000 per evening.

As the cliché goes, Bing's primary nemesis was de Ass (that's what his employees call him), himself. The 3 men are addicted to cocaine. He spends money recklessly, which he keeps all over his house, not trusting banks in case the DEA or IRS investigates him. His personal hygiene is questionable according to ex-girlfriends.

In summary, he's preposterously irresponsible, he's hopelessly simple-minded, and he's an inveterate liar. Whatever the case, he's not an ethical businessman, and is not trusted by any of his associates. He is known to violently retaliate against people who cross him.

==

The meeting continued for another thirty minutes until Adam's assistant Yelena knocked on the conference room door. She didn't wait for an answer, just entered the room to deliver Adam a note: *Morrison Guzman is waiting in the second conference room.*

"Thank you both," Adam said. "Let me digest everything. I'll get back to you tomorrow." Adam followed Yelena and said, "Tell the receptionist not to validate Guzman's parking. Did you turn up the heat in the room?" She smiled mischievously.

Adam watched Morrison pace a bit, looking more like the sky had fallen on the marijuana version of Chicken Little. Adam cleared his throat and entered the room. Before Morrison could say a word, Adam said, "Sit down and shut up. Listen to my words very carefully. Don't bullshit me. It's too late for anything except for you to talk truthfully, or head to prison for fraud and embezzlement. Do you understand my simple words?"

He nodded and looked down. Morrison was unaware and too dim to appreciate the rare hundred-year old Biedermeier table in front of him. The walnut wood was highly polished and he could clearly glimpse his reflection if he wasn't scared to death about going to prison where his younger brother had been for the past five years.

Adam's voice grew louder. "This is what is going to happen." He placed a tape recorder on the table, turned it on, and said, "My name is Adam Copland. I'm sitting with Morrison Guzman on Tuesday, July 23, 2013. Mr. Guzman has joined me of his own free will. Is that correct, Mr. Guzman?" Adam knew that the taped conversation was legally inadmissible, but he also knew it was always desirable to put the fear of Copland into an opponent.

Morrison mumbled, "Yes."

"Please speak louder so that the tape recorder captures your every word."

"Yes," he reluctantly said.

"Please state your name and relationship to Pacifico Bing de Asis?" Adam said.

"Bing and I have been friends since Manchester High School. He was best man at my wedding. We had a grass business together as teenagers. We went our own way, but we still work together, closely, selling pot . . . Listen. I know I fucked up. But I'll do a three-sixty and not act like this again. Please, I have a wife and two daughters to support. Man, don't send me away."

Adam wanted to tell him a three-sixty would put him back where he started. Adam realized regardless of his contrite statement, not to trust him. Morrison would always be loyal to Bing and would always be a reprobate.

"Listen," Copland said. "I gave you very specific instructions on how to respond to my questions. You already showed me you can't follow the simplest order." He intentionally raised his voice, and said, "The unchanging reality is Bing and you fucked me over. At the root of this is Bing. I know this because you're too stupid to dream this up."

Morrison didn't react. His mother had repeatedly called him stupid since he was four. He was accustomed to his wife calling him an *estúpido Mexican*.

"Now let me state this very clearly," Adam said. "Time's running out for these loony ideas of Bing's. The marijuana world is changing. The Mexican cartel is gone, now they're selling harder drugs. People like me are in. Now start talking. I want you to tell me everything Bing has done. And describe his plans for the future."

Morrison slowly recounted Bing's past month of behaving badly. He relied on the calendar in his phone to recall dates and appointments. He persisted with his recollection, and disclosed two salient issues unknown to Copland.

Morrison said, "Remember our meeting at Nate 'n Al's? Later that day Bing and Cary went home and got busted. Seems the idiot put on his security system but didn't lock his door. A client walked into the house, and the silent alarm was tripped. He goes into Rex's room and picks up his one pound of weed. Bing gets tossed into the West Hollywood Sheriff's station for a few hours. Well, the dude is crying and panicky. He can't have a felony record for the dispensary joint venture he's negotiating in the desert."

"What desert cities is he interested in?"

"Poor Bing," M repeated. "The dude is ready to have a heart attack."

"Yes," Adam said. "What desert cities is he considering to buy a dispensary?"

"Shit," Morrison said. "You know Bing never has cash. He's negotiating a joint deal of some sort. He has a dude in LA with an extraction machine that he uses. So he's trying to get a dispensary owner in Palm Springs and Paradise Hills to work with him. Seems he has two guys interested. He's having his lawyer fill out the paperwork right now."

"What happened with his West Hollywood court case?"

Morrison relaxed, and said, "Bing acted like a baby. Begging me to get one of my PRE-ICO owners to write a letter stating he was a co-owner of the dispensary. Was supposed to cost Bing fifty thousand."

"What do you mean it was supposed to cost fifty thousand?" Adam asked. "What happened?"

"Fuckin' Bing pays the dude twenty thousand, and then stiffs him for the balance," said Morrison. "What a bastard."

"Do you have a copy of the letter?"

"Of course," said M. "I had to pick it up at the lawyer's office and run around getting signatures." Morrison conveniently failed to mention that he took his ten thousand finder's fee out of the twenty thousand upfront payment.

"Do you have a copy of the letter with you?" Asked Adam.

"It's in a file on my phone," he said.

"Good." Adam said. "Email it to me right now." Adam waited as Morrison took the phone out of his front left pocket. He quickly punched in Adam's email address, and seconds later Adam confirmed he had the lawyer's letter. Most important, Adam examined the letter, and it had both signatures on the legally binding document—Pacifico Bing de Asis and Viktor Romanovich, President of Sweet Kindness Center, 16290 Saticoy Boulevard, Van Nuys, CA.

It was an understatement to say Adam had found his treasure map. Behind Copland's scowling face, Morrison had no idea what valuable information he had divulged.

Adam looked at Morrison. He was sitting pitifully, like a child waiting in the principal's office. Adam said, "If the information you gave me pans out, you might not be arrested. But. And I mean this. Don't you dare tell Bingo that you talked to me. Got it?"

Morrison eagerly nodded, and Adam dismissed him with a haughty wave of his right hand.

Adam's pesky smile emerged for the first time that day. He said, "Not bad. I got the bastard. No, not bad at all." And a new scheme was hatched.

CHAPTER 18

Century City, CA.
Friday, July 26, 2013

While Adam was dealing with Bing's fraud and lies, he was soon going to encounter a new cannabis foe, Viktor Romanovich. AC could care less about being hated. Until Bing's punk, Morrison, had spoken of Bing's plans, Adam had no idea how he was going to deal with these abominable people. Holding the purse strings, now he was setting a trap for the two fools, and a potential new profit center that would offset any liabilities from Bing's fraud.

Early morning before his minions arrived, Copland enjoyed an iced mocha coffee, reading the morning news, and found Bach's 'Toccata and Fugue' alleviated the drudgery of work. He turned on classical KUSC every morning, and switched to jazz around 2pm — what he called the 'two dead arts'. Listening to the majestic sound and vigorous rhythm of Bach, AC uncontrollably laughed out loud thinking about an otherwise intelligent acquaintance who didn't understand or enjoy classical music. The man once made a maddeningly absurd statement, "I don't listen to it much, but classical music is relaxing." Toccata and Fugue was as relaxing as trying to sleep through a Rolling Stones concert.

Adam had scrupulously thought out his Bingo strategy, and at 10 a.m., called his transactional lawyer. Leonard Penansky, Esq., was pricey, but nowhere close to Kingsley's hourly fee. "Lenny is with a client, Mr. Copland," said the paralegal.

Copland told the paralegal, whom two decades after leaving Stockholm, still spoke with a thick Swedish accent, the terms of a Purchase Agreement he wanted Lenny to draft. In her precise Northern European manner, she repeated every item Adam requested to be written into the document. She said, "I will email you the information you mentioned to make certain it's correct. Please note any changes necessary, and after your approval, I'll give the information to Mr. Penansky to draft your document." She was like a Volvo, efficient and boring.

Adam had wrestled with what price to offer for the business acquisition, and decided $1 million was a fair round number. For a man who all day dealt with managing millions of dollars in investments, he had strikingly grabbed the $1 million figure out of thin air—a pleasant change of pace from deep analytical reasoning. For one of the few times in his life he was being moderately indiscriminate, a rarity to be so devil-may-care with finances. Then again this summary was not truly accurate, he knew the business was worth at least four times his offering price.

Given the size of Los Angeles, both geographically dispersed and including its 10,000,000 people, the city was still provincial within distinct industries. Adam conclusively had an aphorism for every occurrence, and he regularly lectured his staff concerning the reputation of Diablo Capital. He would tell them, "There are only 500 people in the nation I need to know to do deals. I run into the same people all the time. That's one good example why reputation is so essential. We don't manufacture cars or some sort of gadget. Thus our reputation is everything. Lose your reputation, and you're suddenly a pariah in the world of finance." That didn't mean he didn't play street tough.

The document wasn't prepared yet, but Adam had an urge to call and set up the appointment. He dialed Viktor Romanovich at the "Sweet Kindness Center PRE-ICO" dispensary in Van Nuys. Getting past the receptionist, Victor Romanovich answered, "Yes?"

"My name is Adam Copland," said Adam Copland. "I own Adam 'n Eve Healthy Garden PRE-ICO in Woodland Hills. If you have some spare time, I thought it would good to meet another dispensary owner. Get to know each other. We can discuss the rigmarole of how we earn our daily bread."

Romanovich didn't sound excited about the suggestion, but politely agreed to meet. He insisted the meeting place must be outside of the dispensary. Adam agreed to Viktor's suggestion to have coffee next Monday at 1 p.m. Apparently, Viktor didn't like waking up early after an evening of drinking a great deal of vodka, which he did nightly.

It was usually difficult to reach Howard Kingsley before 2 p.m.; he seemed to be eternally in court. Adam waited until 4 p.m., and gave Howard a call.

"What's up, AC?" Howard said.

"Check your mail. I just emailed you the full name of a man who was recently arrested. Would you please check and see if he's up for arraignment, and the court date? Next, if the case was dismissed due to evidence that was sworn by falsely, what's the penalty? Especially if the defendant's attorney knew of the perjury?"

Kingsley methods, outside of court, would be more accurately described as brute force over subtlety. He said, "Shit Adam. Perjury is a damn serious offense. You better not be associated with some schmuck that committed perjury. Under Federal law, perjury is a felony, and you, he, whoever, could be sent to prison for up to five years. What's going on?"

"Don't worry," Adam said. "It's not anything I did. But there is a possibility that the name of the person I emailed you perjured himself. What do we do if he did?"

"Before you spend your nickel getting that information from me," Howard said, "let me check the status of this character, and I'll call you right back." They hung up, and Adam anxiously waited for the update.

* * *

Morrison had a peculiar way of reacting to adversity. He would initially get inordinately depressed. Then he'd drink two six packs and fall asleep for around sixteen hours. Afterward, he'd wake up rejuvenated after the dozen beers. After the therapeutic drinking, he'd worked harder than normal selling his cannabis. Paranoid, Guzman constantly looked in his rear view mirror for a police tail. Once a month he took his car to a friend's body shop, raised it up on a lift, and inspected the entire underbody for any sort of police tracking device. He never found one.

Today, the striking admission was Morrison had a right to feel overly suspicious. He was being stalked as prey as he went from dispensary to dispensary selling his grass, earning his commissions. The predator patiently waited for the right time to strike.

Morrison didn't have a pot to piss in. Still he kept Aquafina in business paying for bottled water, or constantly stopping at a Starbucks for a croissant and an iced tea. His cholesterol was more than 275, as he spread butter over the already rich croissant.

The Starbucks store in the Sherman Oaks Galleria, was jammed with customers doing more talking than buying drinks. Morrison luckily found an empty table on the patio. He was catching up on his text messages when a teenager, around eighteen, asked, "May I share your table? There's nowhere else to sit."

Morrison used his right foot to push the chair out from under the table, and the young woman thanked him. She was too skinny for his tastes. Without asking, she ripped off a small piece of his pastry, smiled, and said, "Thanks."

He looked at her. Decided she had sensual lips, and he liked her short curly pink hair. She was cute but had small breasts—he preferred women like Nonie, who had substantial tits. They talked, flirted, and he gave her a few hits on his vape. Ten minutes after meeting M, she crossed her legs, and started rubbing her foot against his right calf. Her name was Paula Upson, an incoming freshman at Cal State-Northridge, from Bakersfield.

After a period of talking and smoking his vape, she texted him her address so that he could map out the location on his phone. Paula said, "I'll meet you at my place. I have to pick up clothes at the laundry first. So give me about fifteen minutes before you're at my apartment." She smiled and said, "Are you adventurous? You have no idea how dangerous I am in bed." He truly had no idea what risk he was exposing himself to if he left Starbucks.

For fifteen minutes he busily returned text messages. The last text was to Nonie, it read, *having great day. selling lot of product. still working. c u @ dinner.*

In retrospect, Morrison was sorry he let Paula pick him up. He thought what a good fuck Nonie was, but then again, Paula had said she was "dangerous," and he liked the thought of maybe trying something new.

Morrison gathered his belongings, and headed to the parking structure. He was about one hundred yards from his car, when a dog leaped up and started licking him. A few minutes later, a man arrived holding a leash with the collar frazzled from being clawed.

About fifty feet away, the man yelled, "Bad dog. Down, Jekyll." The dog froze at the command, and sat until the man arrived. The man was profusely sweating from running, and said, "Thank you so much for helping with my dog." He held up the leash, and said, "Chows are powerful dogs, and this fellow broke away from me. I parked on the fourth floor and had to chase him down here." Panting, he said, "I'm dead tired chasing this guy."

Morrison thought what a great name the dog had, named after the Heckle and Jeckle cartoon. He said, "Hey, man. That's one cool dog. Jump in the car, and I'll drive you to your car. It's all cool, dude."

The man acted out wiping his brow, attesting that he appreciated the lift and not having to tug the Chow up four flights of stairs. He said, "Thanks mucho. You're way too cool."

Morrison unlocked the driver's door, and reached over to open the passenger door. The Chow jumped in the front seat, and the man said, "Oops. My shoelace is untied. One minute. OK? I'm going to close the door so Dr. Jekyll doesn't escape."

The man bent down, and Morrison petted Dr. Jekyll. The dogs thick tail wagged. The man stood up, motioned in a circular manner, indicating for M to roll down the window. The man said, "Watch this. I'm going to give him a command."

The man displayed a monstrous, evil smile, and simply said, "Mr. Hyde."

At that command, Dr. Jekyll came closer to Morrison's face. He licked him repeatedly like a tame Shih Tzu instead of an aggressive Chow Chow. Morrison could now feel all seventy pounds of Mr. Hyde pressing against his face. He was a bit numbed by the twenty hits on his vape he smoked earlier with Paula. He reached up to feel what he thought was sweat. Unless he was sweating red, it was blood.

He screamed at the man, "Your fucking dog bit me. Get him out of my car, you bastard."

The man calmly said, "Just wait and see what he does now."

Morrison wanted to run. His door was unlocked but the weight of the Chow prevented him from moving. It didn't matter. There are a few dogs with jaws that created more bite force than a Chow, but not many. At that moment, Morrison didn't care about what National Geographic might describe as the most aggressive and dangerous dogs. The Chow didn't need to hunt, it was feeding on Morrison.

Morrison tried to scream but couldn't. The dog was ripping at M's lip. Mr. Hyde had ripped apart M's lower lip, exposing the anterior body of the mandible. Sleazy-handsome Morrison Guzman was no longer recognizable. There was no escape.

After watching his favorite dog tear M's face off, the man gave Mr. Hyde his second command, "Now die."

Mr. Hyde went directly for M's throat, clamped on it so tight it blocked his windpipe. The dog started to twist his head with M's neck in his mouth. Now his windpipe was crushed. His ability to breathe was no more.

* * *

Noticing Morrison was motionless, Nick Petriv said, "Down, Mr. Hyde."

Nick looked around the parking garage, no one was in sight. Pointing to the passenger seat, Mr. Hyde loosened his grip on the disarticulated joints in Morrison's neck. Reluctantly Mr. Hyde let the man's head drop from his bloody canines and obeyed Nick, moving to the other seat.

Nick popped open the trunk. He had a hard time picking up the dead Morrison, and moving him to the trunk. At 6'4" tall, weighing around 230 pounds, Guzman was a big man. Petriv checked the car to make certain no blood was visible on any part of the exterior.

It was clean of any blood drippings, unlike the car's interior, which was drenched in M's blood.

Before sitting in the car, Nick placed three towels on the driver's seat to cover all the blood. He carefully backed out of the parking space, looked over at the now calm Dr. Jekyll, and said, "Good boy. Very good boy." He reached into his pocket and handed him a large cookie, a treat for his skilled handiwork. The treat would do, but it didn't taste nearly as delicious as the man in the trunk.

Nick drove carefully on the 405 Freeway north to the Antelope Valley. His parents had a house on a few acres in the city of Pearblossom. They spent their weekends rehabbing the old dilapidated structure for their occupancy when they retired. At their glacially slow pace, occupancy would be far in the future—maybe ready for their grandchildren's retirement.

Stepping out of Morrison's car, Nick watched as his dog followed him, and jumped down from the car with the engine still running. He walked to the two-story high barn, opened the gate that was falling off its hinge, and placed the dog's big butt in front of the door to stop the door from closing. He drove the car forward into the barn, which was empty except for a few tools his stepfather used for working on the house. He grabbed a shovel, and walked with the dog to an abandoned pear orchard, overrun with weeds. Ducks and feral animals ate the pears that littered the ground.

"Now this is living, Dr. Jekyll," Nick said as he dug a hole in between the pear trees. "We get paid to eliminate a jerk I couldn't stand," he said. "And you get to practice on a live human being rather than attacking a stuffed mitt. What a great day it is."

Paula Upson would be eternally enraged that Morrison had stood her up.

CHAPTER 19

Los Angeles, CA
Sunday, July 28, 2013

Late Sunday morning, Gabriela and Adam were driving north on Pacific Coast Highway to the Malibu Riding and Tennis Club. The club owner was hosting a reception to raise funds for some disease that Copland her never heard of. The club would be stuffed with chamber of commerce types, while journalists noted who attended for the local throwaway newspaper. The couple would schmooze with a few friends, drink too many cocktails, and make a perfunctory donation. Eventually when the self-absorbed attendees were snookered, the Coplands would sneak away from the banal soiree.

After their planned exit, Adam then drove to their beach house, a few miles south of the club. They stripped off their duds, and he licked her nipples—the nipples that always excited him, and reluctantly they put on swimsuits and a t-shirt for a walk on the beach. More licking would come later. A few hours alone, talking, watching the surfers—they were in sandy heaven. Dinner ordered in, watch a lousy movie, and then drive back home. It was wonderful just to be together.

* * *

Meanwhile, Bing was unaware of Adam's maneuvering, and drove his new Lamborghini to a client's house. Steve Stone, a lawyer turned film director, produced movies that went direct from the cutting room to cable television. The only caveat was the film had to play in theaters for one week—even if Strong had to pay the theater to run the disastrous painful-to-watch movie.

Arriving at Stone's house, Bing considered the houses in the Beverly Hills flats—the area north of Santa Monica Boulevard and south of Sunset Boulevard—impractical prospects for his need to relocate after the Nichols Canyon drug bust. He had to break that lease, as the Sheriff was certain to periodically reappear.

The good news for Bing was that Los Angeles was ripe with wealthy individuals ready to invest in cannabis. And Bing knew almost everyone that enjoyed partying with young women.

Strong seemed annoyed that Bing had arrived unannounced, and said, "Bing. What a, umm, pleasant surprise. What's up?"

Bing didn't waste time, presented Stone paperwork that Copland had prepared weeks earlier, and said, "I've got a building in downtown LA that I just leased for a marijuana grow. I make tons of money growing grass. You're a top-notch business dude. I thought you would read that paperwork, and might be interested in putting in a few bucks with me at my new site."

"Look, Bing," Stone said. "Let me tell you how my business works. I put up $1 million to make a piece of crap film. Something kids will like. Show a little titty on a cute bimbo and teenagers get hot. I spend another million promoting the hell out of the schlocky film, and poof, a few months later I make $5 million from cable TV. It's the Roger Corman approach to filmmaking. How can your marijuana beat that? No. I need my money in my business. Sorry. Not interested."

Powerless to respond to Stone's comment, he was lost trying to promote his marijuana deal to a real businessman, rather than studio employee hacks. It was astonishing, but Bing simply gave up. He wasn't impressed by Stone's ideas, but was unable to convince him otherwise. They drank a few glasses of wine, and Bing departed to Santa Monica for two appointments. Considering his life was a mess after the police raid, he met a real estate agent to view houses for lease in Santa Monica Canyon. Satisfied with one house, Bing left a deposit with the agent. A ten-minute drive after the appointment, and Bing was at Keith Emerson's house to drop off grass and other items the founding member of Emerson Lake and Palmer had ordered. Three years later, feeling dissolute, Emerson died in the same Santa Monica house of a gunshot wound self-inflicted to his head.

* * *

Monday, July 29, 2013

Following a wonderful weekend, Adam was invigorated, aware that later today he was scheduled to meet with Viktor Romanovich. Over the weekend, AC read the brief summary Brandt had assembled on the Russian-born Romanovich. Born in St. Petersburg. His father had been imprisoned in the Gulag, and he had been raised by his mother; he had a long record of crime in Russia. His record was clean in the US, though. Reputedly he laundered money for the Russian mob, but Adam distrusted stories about immigrants until proven. Otherwise, every person with the name Giannini or Fortuna would be considered a mobster.

In addition to owning a dispensary, Viktor was a real estate agent and owned a small construction company. He lived modestly in a townhouse in Reseda. Not much more of substance in Brandt's brief summation. The primary item not covered in the memo was where Romanovich got the original money to fund the dispensary acquisition. Brandt couldn't discover that salient fact.

Copland was excited in a way Gabriela hadn't seen him in quite a while. She was busy with Rebeccah and couldn't take the time to inquire why he was upbeat; hoping the intensely amorous weekend was sufficient cause for his joy. Before leaving the house, he always told her his day's scenario so that she could plan dinner. Adam said, "Today I'm in Century City. Have a 1pm meeting in the valley. Will check on my two valley dispensaries as long as I'm in the area. And be home around six. Love you." And just like that he was gone.

Adam's lawyer, Penansky, had prepared the "Offer to Purchase Agreement," and messengered the document to Adam's Beverly Hills home on Sunday when he was in Malibu. Copland read the Purchase Agreement Monday morning, and placed it in a manila folder. He thought a briefcase would be too overbearing for a meeting in a casual bakery. Copland departed his office at 12:15pm, more than enough time to drive on the 405 parking lot to Van Nuys.

Adam met Romanovich at Rasputin's Russian bakery on Roscoe Boulevard, just west of the Van Nuys Airport. Not having a trusting temperament, by experience, Adam had Nick Petriv meet him at Rasputin's, incognito. Petriv was sitting by himself, enjoying a coffee and a ponchik filled with custard. He was reading the obituary column in the *Los Angeles Times*. Nothing about Morrison. So he searched the rest of the paper, still no mention of Morrison.

Apparently Romanovich wasn't the trusting type either. His muscle, Vitaly Andruschenko, was sitting with Viktor, both enjoying a beef-and-potato piroshki. For special customers, the owner put a substantial hit of vodka in their iced coffee.

The tables were spaced closely together so Petriv could hear Adam introduce himself. Viktor acknowledged Adam but didn't introduce Vitaly. Adam decided not to dare look at the man with no neck, a shaved head, and tattoos covering both arms, who made a point not to hide his revolver visible under his blue Nike T-shirt.

The two principals went through the typical greetings formalities. They discussed the tribulations of owning a dispensary, and despite the grief, both agreed that ownership problems were more than offset by the consistent cash flow generated by their legal dispensaries.

Fifteen minutes later, disenchanted with the direction of the conversation, Victor looked into Adam's eyes, and said, "You don't strike me as the type of man for all this small talk. What's the real reason you wanted to meet me? Because if this is all you want to do, to talk like little girls, I have more important things to do."

The time had come to depart the world of verbal semidarkness, and commence plain old-fashioned bare-knuckle negotiating. Adam reached for his folder, and placed a copy of Romanovich's letter validating that "Pacifico Bing de Asis was a 5% owner of the 'Sweet Kindness Center' in Van Nuys" on the table. He said, "Owning a legal dispensary requires being circumspect with your license. This letter indicates you were reckless for a mere $50,000 fee."

Viktor laughed for a moment, and explained to Vitaly, in Russian, what Adam announced. "That little Chinese man, Bing Bing, only paid me $10,000," said Romanovich. "He still owes me $40,000." He pushed the paper back to Copland, and said, "So vat."

Adam pulled another document from the manila folder, and decided it was time to goose the Russian along. Viktor looked at the next document titled Agreement to Purchase. He perused the first page, and said, "Vat's dis? You are offering to buy Sweet Kindness Center, from me? It's not for sale at any price, especially to you."

To further prod Viktor, Adam said, "It's insanely stupid to jeopardize your license. And that's exactly what you did when you fabricated that Bing owns 5 percent of Sweet Kindness Center. I checked with the California Secretary of State. You own 100 percent of the nonprofit corporation that owns Sweet Kindness Center. If the City of Los Angeles finds out about your lie, your 'lie—cense' goes down the drain. Kaput. Say dasvidaniya to your license." Dasvidaniya was one of numerous Russian words Marina del Rey and Yelena had taught Adam. Licentious words from Marina, and Yelena corrected Marina's misuse of certain words.

Still in denial, Viktor acted holier than thou and said, "No. You are very wrong. This is all wrong. And I'm not listening anymore to your rubbish. It's like your mind was affected years ago by the Chernobyl nuclear accident. In Russia, we call people like you *Bbinepabiw*. You understand me? It means you think you are important. But you came out when your mother farted."

"No," Adam calmly responded. "You did this to yourself by fabricating a story that Bing was a minority owner in your dispensary. I'm willing to give you $1 million for your dispensary and a graceful exit. The alternative is to meet with Detective Lopez of the LAPD Medical Marijuana licensing division, and the district attorney. It's your choice Viktor. Hell. This is not the worst problem to have. With $1 million you could buy a clean PRE-ICO license and start fresh. Like I said. It's your choice." Or put colloquially, Adam had him by the balls.

Almost shouting, Viktor said, "No. I don't like this at all. You're trying to take advantage of me. That's not right. Not at all. I'll show you how I deal with scum like you." He nodded to Vitaly, who started for his gun.

Before Vitaly could move, Nick was behind him with his gun pushed into Vitaly's back—hidden by a lightweight wind breaker. Nick said in a mocking tone, "Checkmate."

Adam said, "In any situation it's wise to consider all the alternatives. Just so you understand something about me, I usually get paid a $1,000 an hour consulting fee, if I even consider taking the consulting position. So since I'm feeling beneficent, let's consider your situation, gratis on my part. First, you can leave right now and soon be asked to meet the DA downtown. Second, you can try to hurt me. Not wise since I know where your wife, mother, sister, and other relatives live." Adam reached into his coat pocket, and slid on the table a check in the amount of $1 million , payable to Viktor Romanovich. "Third, you can sign the agreement and cash the million-dollar check."

He paused a short time to give Viktor time to think, but not too long. Like a magician pulling rabbits from a hat, Adam kept pulling papers from the manila folder.

AC said, "This next paper describes a PRE-ICO license I know is for sale. As you can see by the letterhead, an attorney wrote up this narrative and has vetted the license as legitimate. It meets the sixteen points the City of Los Angeles looks for to determine if a license is valid. The owner closed his shop back in 2008 when the FBI was raiding Los Angeles dispensaries. The owner, David Johnson, is a wimp. He got frightened even though he was legal and clean. Every year Johnson has paid his fees and taxes. He rents a small space in a strip mall to show he's open, and the license is available for sale at $1 million, firm. No negotiating. My advice is sign the Agreement to sell me Sweet Kindness Center. With the check in your hands, you can purchase the license and open another legal dispensary. Let me know what you think—very soon. You've got twenty-four hours to respond to my"—he paused and emphasized the next words—"generous offer. After twenty-four hours, every hour you wait, the price drops by $100,000. Don't play games, Viktor. Sign the damn agreement. You're getting a sweet deal."

Adam let Romanovich sweat it out for only a minute. Then he lied and said, "Don't be mad at me. Bing told me the details of your deal. Bing screws everyone he deals with. Hell, Viktor, Bing told me to do this." This was the personification of Adam, given an opportunity he found a roundabout way to get back at double-crossing Bing de Asis.

Viktor's glare inverted to a slender smile. He knew he was beaten. "What the hell," he said. "I like your methods even though I don't like you, Adam Copland. I will sign the agreement if you promise to contact the lawyer and handle the license purchase for me. I know you already. We shake hands and that is good for both us. Da?"

They shook hands. Viktor signed the document in every location that Adam pointed to, and Viktor said, "You are like Russian, not a weak pussy American."

Adam acknowledged the comment, and put the papers in the folder. He stood up and shook Viktor's hand again. And Viktor ended the meeting with these ominous words, "I will take care of Mr. Bing Bing in my own way."

CHAPTER 20

Los Angeles, CA
Monday, July 29, 2013

As long as certain businesses are, or appear, profitable, asser-tive tough characters will forever attempt to steal what oth-ers created; what those ambitious entrepreneurs worked day and night to create. Since Jamal Holloway's systematic planning was proceeding exactly as he intended, with added confidence, he increased the ambitions for BDS by way of a new cannabis target.

One morning as Jamal and his cousin clan ate breakfast at his mom's house, he said to his BDS gang members, "Listen up. All legal dispensaries have to close at 10 p.m. It's some City of LA law or something. It's like a curfew for selling weed. So now we got all this grass and money sitting in a safe in a storeroom. Some stores have night guards even when they're closed. But listen here. Most shops don't have night guards. Hear me? No guards. Money and weed just sitting there."

"What's your plan?" asked Jam, beaming at the thought of putting more money into shoeboxes, stashed far in the back of his closet. He didn't need to worry that his mom would inspect boxes with supposedly smelly basketball shoes in them.

Jamal had a markedly different approach for breaking into MMJ dispensaries in comparison to his robberies of Bing's delivery trucks or cultivation sites. "I didn't tell y'all," Jamal said, "but I bought a flatbed trailer to hook up to my SUV. No messing around here. I found a bro who's a welder. This guy reinforced the trailer with a steel panel under the wood bed. Then I had him put wood sides on the trailer to hide what we all is going to haul in it. Follow me so far?" His tweaker cousin, DeTracy Holloway, mumbled to himself. He learned not to say much of anything. Don't challenge Jamal was his new watchword, it was less dangerous and he remained impassive.

"This dispensary I'm planning to hit isn't legal. It's owned by some Iranian dude. Treats his people terrible. His name is Ashot Bozorgmanesh. Lives in some big house out in Whittier. Try saying Ashot Bozorgmanesh three times without fucking it up." No one took him up on saying Ashot Bozorgmanesh even once.

"I got to be honest," Jamal continued. "The more we hit warehouse trucks, I'm learning more all the time how to deal with these marijuana growers."

Excitedly, Jamarqua said, "Tell them what we did at the El Monte shop."

Jamal knew Jam respected him, and overlooked his remark "we." Jamal announced, "One of the things I've learned is it's essential to have an inside player. That way we get the true layout of the building, and how the place is run." Jamal noticed Jam was extremely excited, barely able to sit still in his chair. He motioned, and said, "Jam. Tell the boys what we did."

"We had cousin Shanice apply for work there," said Jamarqua. "Let's face the facts, our little cousin is one fucking hot bitch. They used to hot big-titty Latin girls over there. But Shanice rolled out her tits in the interview, and the interview was over. That was it. This Iranian dude Ashot likes big tits on little girls."

Jam jammed his mouth full of cereal, chewed fast, swallowed, and said, "You dudes ever watch Superman?" Everyone nodded, even DeTracy. Jam continued, "Seems this little dude Ashot was a general back in Iran. Likes to be called General Ashot by his workers since no one but Jamal can say his last name. When he's not around, everyone calls him General Zod like the villain in Superman. Anyway, so in the interview, Shanice can't say his damn name. Can't even say Ashot. She calls him Ash. Knowing how much we need her to work there, and knowing he likes to be called General, Shanice starts calling him, something like General Ash. Fucking Shanice pulled down her pants and say to him, 'Here's my furry nest, General.' Anyway, little cousin Shanice is now working there eight hours a day."

With an air of being impressed with himself, Jamal said, "Shanice gave me the full board layout of the dispensary. Plus how the General runs the joint. I know the names of the staff. She gave me their work schedule. Seems every damn security guard in every dispensary is some whacko. This guard likes to think he's some military man. Always telling General Ashot what he should do to secure the place, and the fucking General is too damn cheap to put in any of the things the guard suggested. Just more good luck for us."

All the talking made Jamal's mouth dry. He downed a huge amount of coffee, and continued, "Now listen up, just in case we all ever run a business. Don't be cheap. Now Shanice says Ashot is absorbed with this one girl that works as a bud tender there. Takes her out shopping all the time. She has him gambling with her in Gardena at Larry Flynt's Casino. It's called Lucky Lady or something like that. This girl is spending his money big-time. Jesus. All for a little brown booty call."

Jamal was sharp. He noticed everyone but Jam's attention flagging, and decided to wrap up the talk with fewer details. "Tonight's the night, boys. We going to hit our first fucking marijuana dispensary. I'm driving the SUV hookup up with our new flatbed trailer.

Now here's what I need from each of y'all." Holloway explained his plan in specific detail, with a task for each BDS member. "We got a few twists and turns," he said. "If the po-lice shows up." Then he stopped to ponder his last statement, and said, "But this is a poor area. All the po-lice in the area gonna be in San Marino and South Pasadena. They be protecting nice areas where the homes already safe." They laughed ensemble, and closed this meeting—as they decided to quit every meeting—with Grandma Holloway's favorite saying, adopted for their BDS mockery, "Lawdy me!" They shouted a second time, "Lawdy me!"

In the living room, even though Jamal's mom was hard of hearing, she heard their tumultuous shouting. She said, "Those are some good boys we raised, Grandma. I hear them in the kitchen praying together. We got some good boys."

* * *

Marissa, the Copland's vivacious energetic Italian housekeeper, assisted with Rebeccah as Gabriela packed suitcases to accompany Adam for a brief trip to the desert. August 1st in the Coachella Valley; the weather at 10pm normally cooled down, if they were lucky, in the vicinity of 100 degrees. Plus the Weather Channel, that Gabriela was addicted to, had a newscaster in Palm Springs discussing a bug infestation that had hit several desert neighborhoods. He said, "Residents in Paradise Hills and Palm Springs are at a loss for what to do about it. The tiny bugs are showing up in big numbers. Thousands and thousands. Interviewing a local resident, Jeff Marcus said, "Our garage is full of bugs. It's like a biblical plague."

Another interviewer said, "They have become such a nuisance. And we have cleaned up, and cleaned up after them, and there have been thousands, said Palm Springs resident Sherri Sinay.

The script at the bottom of the screen read, *"The insects are scientifically known as Metacorpus Lateralis but more commonly known as "Red Seed" or "Charcoal Seed Bugs" and they are being accompanied in some areas by their cousins, the Boxelder Bug. Experts say they are attracted to light and heat. Although they're a pain to clean up, the bugs are not harmful to humans."*

The last resident interviewed, said, "There was probably an inch thick of them all over the floor in the furnace room. In past years, a visit from the exterminator solved the problem. But this year the first treatment took care of them, for the most part, and then all of a sudden they came back even worse. We have two white globes in the front of our yard and every morning it's covered solidly with bugs."

Gabriela was beginning to act distressed; having serious second thoughts about going to a land resembling Egypt, afflicted with the Pharaoh's third plague.

You didn't need to be Sigmund Freud to observe Gabriela's altered outlook. To change the subject, Adam wrongly said, "Maybe we'll spend an extra day in the desert. Take some time and look at buying another house since I'll be spending more time out there if we win the dispensary bidding. The mortgage would be a good write-off. Plus we could meet friends out there and play lots of tennis."

Gabriela said, "Do you recall what a headache building this house was. No more construction. If you want another house, buy an existing one." 'It worked', Adam thought. She stopped thinking about those cursed bugs.

Adam didn't worry about such things, but he knew she was correct about construction. Besides, he reasoned it would probably be less expensive to locate a distressed owner selling a house that they didn't use anymore, then to build a new house.

A little more than a year after they married, the couple located a $3,500,000.00 house euphemistically termed a tear down. The house was located about two miles north of the Beverly Hills Hotel, just west of Benedict Canyon. The elderly lady who had been the sole occupant for the past thirty years, closed off most of the dilapidated house unable to pay a maid to clean the entire home. AC valued the property solely for its prime location and the unique four acres it occupied atop Beverly Hills. Gabriela simply wanted a home having always lived in apartments, although she dreaded the unknown vagaries of construction.

The acreage was primarily unusable hillside except for about one-half of an acre that was flat as Kansas. The real estate afforded the newlyweds the privacy they insisted was a requisite. Undeterred, their tacky real estate agent attempted to steer them to properties she had listed to earn a double fee. To agree on a price to offer the anxious seller, the agent suggested meeting at a notoriously overpriced restaurant where ostentatious ladies 'do lunch' to be conspicuous.

Adam sat between the two women with Gabriela directly across the table from the agent who was writing up an 'Offer to Purchase'. Gabriela was certain the agent wanted to replace her as Ms. Copland. Despite Adam's blatant infatuation and attachment, despite Gabriela's dazzling good-looks, despite their agreement not to have a Pre-Nuptial Agreement, despite just about every and anything imaginable under the sun, Gabriela was habitually insecure and intensely jealous of any woman under the age of 30.

Picking up her water glass in her right hand, Ms. C swirled her water as though it was the Riedel Bordeaux glass for the Cabernet Sauvignon Adam was savoring. She dearly loved her husband but found his habit of swishing wine in his mouth like it was Listerine mouthwash tiresome. Next she sipped a teensy amount of water, and ever so innocently emitted a stream of the ice-cold water through the small gap between her front teeth, directly hitting the agent with the accuracy of a Cy Young award-winning pitcher. The agent, who had dollar signs for eyes, was too busy to notice the spittle. Eventually the redhead with too much silicone in her lips, looked down at her blouse and was exasperated that she could be perspiring.

Of course, AC coordinated all facets of construction after the couple had approved the third and final revised plans from their architect. The tall architect constantly scratched his scalp, annoyed with the numbness in the areas of his hair transplantation. When he wasn't scratching, he nervously adjusted his wire-rimmed glasses. He had been a friend and tennis partner since Adam's college days. Unfortunately the relationship would soon be terminated when he refused to adhere to Gabriela's design requirements believing his old friendship would override what he deemed her lack of aesthetic taste. The architect wanted an Architectural Digest showpiece of his composition with a plinth supporting bare whitewashed walls and he insisted on an impractical gravel driveway. All the while the couple knew exactly what they wanted, and adhered to the Golden Gelt Rule—he who had the gelt made the rules.

In spite of its completion within budget, par for an industry plagued with sleazy sub-contractors who failed to materialize on site as promised, the date for completion of the house far exceeded the architect's estimation—charitably, it must be pointed that this was out of his control.

The contemporary house was one-story containing slightly more than 8,000 square feet of exquisite luxury. Surrounded by transported groves of mature Palm and Eucalyptus, the shimmering sanctuary's facade was a combination of 14-foot glass walls, expansive use of stone with wood-framed windows, which provided an unparalleled view whenever the smog cover lifted. Utilizing a telescope gifted by the property agent who earned a cool $90,000.00 commission on the sale, the Copland's could look east to the down-and-out hovels abutting the downtown skyline, south to the Palos Verdes peninsula, and west to Will Rogers beach and the Pacific

Ocean. Their northern vision was abbreviated by the estate's verdant mountainside.

That morning, all the suitcases were packed for tomorrows drive to Paradise Hills. Adam spent the day working in his home office, reviewing Rios' comprehensive 126-page 'City of Paradise Hills Application for Medical Marijuana Dispensary'.

＊ ＊ ＊

"I'm damn serious," Jamal said to DeTracy. "One more fuck-up, and you're out of BDS. And don't get your momma to cry to her sister. I'm sick of your momma whining to my momma saying, 'But they is cousins.' My momma ain't gonna listen to your momma's shit no more. Got me? You need to layoff meth and learn to focus. Shit. You know all the money we makin'? Don't be a fool. Layoff the crystal meth. Stop playing the fool, fool."

It had been all hands on deck for Jamal's latest scheme. In preparation for the night's activities, Jamal had Lamond's girlfriend rent a 2012 Chevrolet Silverado Duramax. She'd donned a wig, wore sunglasses, and used a very good fake driver's license that fooled everyone at Hertz.

To start up the robbery in the San Gabriel Valley area of Los Angeles, Lamond's important job was to drive the Silverado to El Monte. Every BDS member was to rendezvous at midnight, at the corner of Valley Boulevard and Ramona—the location of the old El Monte Legion Stadium. The stadium was torn down forty years ago, and had remained a vacant lot for forty years. Now a good place for bad kids to hang out.

Every single BDS member, even DeTracy, was on time. They boasted about the job Jamal entrusted to them, and of their bright future. Not deluding themselves, they were well aware of the potential difficulty in implementing Jamal's strategy.

At 12:30 a.m., they drove south on Valley Boulevard, past City Hall, to the illegal marijuana dispensary. For whatever unknown reason, the El Monte Police Department ignored the site as long as it paid its city sales tax. Every BDS member was serious and quiet, ready for their next heist.

Following Jamal's directions, they all drove to the alley, directly behind the dispensary. The only person in sight was a dumpster diver looking in the trash behind a Chinese buffet. Pulling up last, Lamond was directed to back his rental truck against a fence by Jam, with the front of the truck facing the dispensary. The truck was strategically angled diagonally to the dispensary. Adjacent to the Silverado, was Jamal's SUV pointed in the opposite direction with the trailer bed obliquely lined up towards the dispensary. Jam spray-painted a large 'X' on the wall where, according to Shanice's recon, the storeroom was located.

Everyone except Jamal and Lamond were out of their cars, standing about twenty-five feet from the building, wearing gloves, shovels in hand, ready to rock and roll. To the left of the rear door, and a foot higher than the door, was a closed-circuit security camera. Staring at the camera, Jam grabbed his crotch, and said, "It's me, Jam Holloway and the BDS. What you going to do me, General. You're as illegal as me. Why don't you call the El Monte Po-lice?" He turned to his men, and said, "This camera is a joke. Who's this dude going to call?"

"Ghostbusters," DeTracy said.

Jamal looked from his car, across to Lamond, and asked, "Ready, my man?" Lamond raised his right hand, signaling yes.

Jamal looked at his watch, then up and down the alley. The alley was still lonely except for the dumpster diver who had switched from Chinese buffet trash cans to La Pizza Loca trashcans.

Imitating the flagman at the Indy 500, Jamal loudly said, "Lamond, gun that engine. Remember my man, X marks the spot to hit." Lamond pressed the brake firmly. He kept the car in drive, and gunned the engine. Jamal screamed, "Go! Get that marauder moving. Move it."

Aware that Hertz would never rent this truck again, Lamond used the truck as the Holloway version of an unstoppable seven thousand pound exploding death machine. Blasting off like a ballistic missile, tires burning rubber, Lamond smashed the Silverado directly on the X marked on the building. An area about eight feet high by six feet wide of the frame-and-stucco building crumbled. Lamond pushed the gearbox into overdrive. He pushed the truck to its limit. Grinding up and back, forward and reverse, knocking down plasterboard, and running over everything in his way.

One aspect of crashing into the building Jamal didn't anticipate was the broken windshield, which he didn't care about. He did care about, and felt a terrible responsibility for, the shards of glass that pierced Lamond's face and arms.

The Silverado had opened up a huge area in the back of the dispensary exposing their target, the dispensary safe. The Holloway clan had intentionally remodeled the marijuana store, turning it into the first Los Angeles drive-in dispensary.

Lamond backed the truck out of the demolished storeroom. He pulled it over to a spot thirty yards from where Jam and the other BDS members had commenced working—at least ten times faster than any city work crew ever worked, shoveling debris onto either side of the newly constructed Holloway tunnel that led directly into the dispensary store room that housed the dispensary's safe.

Due to federal banking laws, marijuana dispensaries were prohibited from depositing their significant daily cash into FDIC-insured banks. Consequently, dispensary owners were sitting on truckloads of cash—Ashot's cash soon to be placed onto Jamal's trailer.

In addition to cash, the store's marijuana inventory was placed in the safe every night after the manager closed the shop. The safe was the depository of Ashot's total business, except for the daily funds he spent at the Gardena casino with his new squeeze.

Breaking the wall was only the first task that night. Adhering to Jamal's careful planning, Lamond's handiwork was easy as pie. Now the heavy lifting literally would begin. Carefully backing up his SUV, as directed by DeTracy, Jamal stopped the trailer five feet from the safe. The next battle was "relocating" the 2,000-pound safe. An old-fashioned dolly was out of the realm of possibility for this much weight. Perpetually planning ahead, Jamal carefully rolled two M-10 Roll-A-Lifts down from the trailer. Together they're capable of transporting a safe five times the size of Ashot's safe.

Smoothly pushing the Roll-A-Lift under one side of the safe, Jamal strapped the safe securely to the lift. Simultaneously, Zion Holloway replicated Jamal's actions on the opposite side with the second Roll-A-Lift. The safe was sitting snug between the two lifts, and with five Holloways pushing it, it rolled exactly as the Pasadena Safe Relocation Company salesman had promised. With a smidgen of extra muscle, moving the safe up the trailer ramp was accomplished. The last assignment to complete was securing the safe with four metal clamps to the trailer bed.

Now with the safe fully secure, Jamal turned to Lamond, and said, "Listen, cuz, this is my bad. I just didn't think out the broken glass. I'm truly sorry."

Lamond, always concise, said, "No prob."

"It is a prob when I don't think things out right," Jamal answered. "I fuckin' care about my men. You gonna get a double share for your damn pain you suffered tonight. You stay at my house tonight. Remember, my momma is a nurse. She'll fix you up good." Then he reconsidered the double allotment for Lamond, and said to the group, "Don't worry about Lamond's double share. You shits aren't going to lose any money. I'm taking part of my share to donate to my cuz. We all okay with this?"

Satisfied that he had fulfilled his role as paladin of BDS, Jamal leaned on the safe and said, "This is almost as much fun as fuckin' up little de Ass." Smiling at his cousins, he imitated one of those 1950 Westerns that played on the Old Time Movies Channel. He said, "Okay, boys. Move 'em on, head 'em up. Move them doggies back to Altadena."

CHAPTER 21

Paradise Hills, CA
Wednesday, July 31, 2013

((☾ ☽))

Unusual for the desert, the winds in the San Gorgonio pass were barely perceptible. As the Coplands drove past thousands of wind turbines inhabiting the steep pass, maybe half of the windmills were churning out electricity that day. The mountains on either side of the pass were 9,000 feet above sea level, created eons ago by the San Andreas Fault. In the middle of summer, the combination of the scorching desert heat and a well-publicized insect infestation meant the freeway traffic to their destination was virtually nonexistent. Adam's favorite saying when traveling, and Gabriela laughed as usual at his buffoonery, was, "Don't worry. We're going against traffic." Their marriage was due to last forever since she still found him adorable, and he would be "entertained" by her eternally.

Liquor stores, dry cleaners, motels and restaurants are amongst the most common entry-level businesses for an immigrant, with minimal English skills, to operate. To support their family, it's not uncommon for a recent immigrant to work 16-hour days; ecstatic to be free in America, and far away from China, Russia, Iran, Pakistan or other totalitarian countries.

During her modeling years in Manhattan, Gabriela had been accustomed to neighborhood Cantonese Chop Suey joints that delivered to her 63rd Street apartment. The bland food had taken its toll on her receptiveness to highly flavored Chinese food from Hunan or Szechwan province, and as a result she had never tasted authentic quality Chinese cuisine east of the Hudson River — when she lived there.

Although it may have looked like another romantic tryst, Adam and Gabriela were on a real estate mission. Paradise Hills is a newer, less established planned development in the Coachella Valley—compared to La Quinta or Indian Wells. In the hills just west of Palm Canyon Drive were large single-family residences on one-acre lots with wildly fantastic views of the valley floor. East of Palm Canyon was a 1,000-acre industrial park with many buildings planned, and few buildings built. Palm Canyon Drive was zoned retail, and a large Outlet Mall was under construction. In the early hours before they'd left LA, Adam had spent the morning working in his home office, reviewing Rios' comprehensive, 126-page "City of Paradise Hills Application for Medical Marijuana Dispensary."

Just before noon, entering the Ding Ho restaurant on north Palm Canyon Drive, Gabriela asked, "Is it really necessary to eat here? Can't we just order a beer and talk?"

"Relax. Nick is meeting us here, and his desert security contact works here," Adam answered.

"What type of Ninja warrior works in a Chinese restaurant? Seriously, Adam," she said.

The reputation and dominance of Palm Springs area restaurants was evident; the Ding Ho was empty at lunchtime. The restaurant was in a stand-alone building, with only Adam's car in the parking lot. For additional comfort and more luggage space, he'd left the Aston Martin in the garage, and drove his two-door copper-colored Bentley convertible. In the desert heat, though, he kept the convertible top up all day.

Adam pointed Gabriela to a table with four chairs; there weren't any booths. The anticipated hostess never materialized, and Adam said, "I'll look in the back for someone." Gabriela was hoping he wouldn't find a soul, and they would dine elsewhere.

Smelling lots of garlic frying, Adam walked to the kitchen. A young woman with a long ponytail was busy cooking Szechwan green beans. "Excuse me," Adam said. With the radio blasting music from the 60s and two fans blowing hot air away from the stove, Adam had to repeat, "Excuse me."

The young lady turned this time and smiled, which made her plain face appealing. "Please take a seat in the dining room, and I'll be right out. Grab a couple menus if you like," she said.

Adam picked up one menu, aware that Gabriela would request that he select the dishes, if she were forced to eat here. "Is your contact in the back?" asked Gabriela.

"No," Adam said. "Just a young woman cooking." As Adam stared at the menu, Gabriela noticed a tall Asian man enter the restaurant. She was certain he was part of the family that owned the Ding Ho. She had never met Nick Petriv, who walked to their table, stuck out his right hand, and said, "You must be the one and only Ms. Copland that Adam talks about constantly. It's a pleasure to finally meet you. I'm Nick Petriv." Looking at his distinctly Asian face, Nick's last name bewildered her. She didn't respond to his statement, just stared at him.

Adam smiled, and said, "Hi, Nick. Thanks for meeting us."

Of all of Adam's employees, Gabriela knew the most about Nick, as Adam constantly talked about his loyal, but loose cannon, security chief. Nick was born on Okinawa, to a Chinese mother and a Ukrainian father. Both worked for the US government. Nick's father was a lawyer working as a military translator of information snatched from Russian, German, and Polish diplomatic transmissions. Nick's mother cooked, he claimed, the best Shanghainese cuisine east of the Huangpu River. Nick was probably around six foot, but he slumped and appeared shorter. His dark hair was cut in a crew cut, and he didn't look either Chinese or Amerasian—he looked dramatically distinctive from either parent. Growing up, and later in life, he fought constantly with both parents. Then again, he verbally brawled with everyone he encountered, except Adam.

"Have you met Cassandra yet?" Nick asked. Before Adam could respond the young girl from the kitchen arrived at the table with a plate of spring rolls.

Nick said, "Gabriela and Adam Copland, I'd like you to meet my cousin, Cassandra Yu. Cassandra, the Coplands, my bosses."

"My parents are out shopping. I'll cook for us. What would you like to eat?" she asked. She was apparently oblivious to the reason Nick suggested that they join her for a Phantom Security meeting.

Nick took the lead, and ordered more food than fifteen people could possibly eat. "This is the tradition in our Chinese culture," Nick said. "Never talk business when we meet. Socialize over food and see if both sides feel comfortable with one another."

For about twenty minutes, the men's conversation totally bored Gabriela. They primarily discussed the meeting that Adam would soon attend at city hall. Gabriela was about to speak, when William Rios arrived. He ignored everyone but Adam, and said, "I'll be in the mayor's office discussing today's agenda. Let me lead the conversation. I'll tell you when to speak at the council meeting. If at all. Our application explains it all, but council members might want to target a few questions directly at you. Be at city hall around 2 p.m." Finding it painful to listen to more business bombast after earlier business discussions, and to acknowledge her ennui, Gabriela constantly yawned during Rios's soliloquy.

Rios left and an elderly lady appeared with a tray. She eked out a minuscule smile directed at her nephew, said a few words in Chinese to Nick, and placed four bowls of chicken soup with wontons on the table.

Nick said, "These people are vegetarians. I told Cassie no meat. Only vegetarian dishes."

The old lady nodded, looked at Gabriela, and said in Pidgin English, "It's OK. This is free. Eat. No cost. Eat." She reminded Adam of his grandmother, always wanting him to eat more. She would say in Yiddish, regardless of how much Adam ate, "Ess, Ess, Ess." She always pinched his cheek, and said, "Heaven must have sent you."

After the old woman left, both Coplands pushed their soup bowls toward Nick, who would easily finish off his bowl and their chicken soup.

Adam said, "No hugs from your aunt? My relatives would have squeezed me to death."

Nick answered, "You have to understand old-fashioned Chinese etiquette. Hugs are simply not a public option. ABCs are much more open-minded than their parents, still the idea of hugging is almost a taboo among ABCs too. Exhibitions of affection in public would embarrass our parents. A definite no-no. Even a husband and wife hugging in public falls under this cultural prohibition."

"What's an ABC?" asked Adam.

Petriv laughed and said, "ABC stands for American-born Chinese."

"How are you related to Cassandra?" Gabriela asked.

Between slurping his soup, Nick said, "Long story. She's actually my aunt."

Taking a whole wonton in his mouth, Adam said, "Why did you call her your cousin?" The woman was probably ten years younger than Nick.

Nick scratched a blemish irritating him on his forehead, and grimaced. Gabriela noticed some dry skin flake off and fall onto the table from the chafing. Nick said, "You gotta realize how different every culture is. And this is gonna sound weird to you twenty-first-century white European people. In Chinese culture, family is everything. Filial piety means a child subordinates all his dreams to the welfare of his immediate family. Well." He paused to finish his second bowl of soup, and continued, "Well. My grandfather's best friend, his next-door neighbor from childhood. You know, this friend, you know, couldn't have a child. I don't know if it was him or his wife that had problems. So one day without telling my grandmother, Grandpa Yu picks up ten-day-old Cassandra and walks her over to his friend's house. He gave her to his best friend so that they would enjoy a 'whole' family since they didn't have kids."

Starting on his third bowl of soup, his brown eyes glowed having a receptive audience for a change. Nick said, "Cassandra is a wonderful, bright person. But you can probably imagine the hidden inner problems she suffers from. As a culture, we are taught to be stoic, and keep problems under glass. Imagine how she feels being given away. Her parents gave her away out of love for a neighbor. Now she lives her life feeling expendable. That her life is, you know, a throwaway. No value. Women in most Asian countries are second-class citizens. I remember walking with my parents in Naha City on Okinawa when I was little. Mom always walked five feet behind dad. And my dad, who was born in Kiev, hated that Chinese tradition."

After hearing the explanation of Cassandra's childhood, Nick couldn't tell which Copland had the worse angina attack. Noticing Cassandra emerging from the kitchen, Nick said, "I'll finish the story later. To this day, it's too depressing and much too emotional for Cassie."

After she had placed ten dishes on the lazy Susan in the middle of the table, Cassandra sat in the fourth chair.

"There's no rice," Gabriela said.

"No," Cassie explained. "You are my guests. You are Nick's boss. My mother is very proud that you're visiting her restaurant, which is like being a guest in our home. In China, rice is for poor people. At a true Chinese celebration, rice is served at the end of a meal to fill people up. We never eat rice during a festive meal."

The Ding Ho restaurant wasn't a chic spot located in the Ritz Carlton Rancho Mirage. It wasn't the type of restaurant described as cool or hip that drew the rich and famous that visited the desert when snow fell north of the 45th parallel. After the spectacular meal, Gabriela now understood Adam's enjoyment of good Chinese restaurants restaurants—though his predilection was for hole-in-the-wall hideaways in Monterey Park rather than the PF Chang national chain types. Adam always said to her, "Why eat in a Chinese restaurant started by a Caucasian instead of a Chinese." The PF stood for Paul Fleming of Fleming Steakhouse..

At the end of the meal, when Cassie's adopted mother placed black sesame soup on the table for dessert, the gelatinous paste was too over the top for Gabriela. She asked, "No fortune cookies?"

Nick said, "Too American for us. Not authentically Chinese."

Adam looked at the soup, and added, "Try it. You'll like it," and dug into the dessert soup as she glared at him.

Standing up as tea was served, Nick went to his car and brought back four 2-by-4 boards that he brought with him from his house in LA. He said, "Everyone, please stand up. Adam, hold your hands outstretched with this board in front of your neck. Gabriela, you do the same but hold the board firmly in front of your heart."

In Chinese, he said, "Auntie, hold the board behind your head."

After Nick double-checked every person was holding the board properly, he motioned for Cassandra to proceed with the challenge. It all began with Cassie stretching, and mentally measuring the strike distance. The three individuals were holding their boards properly. Nick picked up the fourth board and standing, placed it between his knees. Cassandra was ready. She moved so quickly, Gabriela barely knew what happened except that all of a sudden, she was holding the pulverized remains of a 2 by 4. Within seconds, the three other boards were split, and Cassie resumed her former humble pose.

Nick said, "The first blow to Ms. Copland's board would have crushed an opponent's sternum. The blow to Adam's board would have crushed a person's neck. The opponent would have lost consciousness, maybe even died. The blow to Auntie's would have broken the man's neck, probably around the sixth or seventh cervical vertebrae. This is why Cassandra should be your Vice President of Phantom Security Services in the desert. Hell, besides security at your hoped-for dispensary, you could compete with those lazy bastards at Coachella Protective Security for contracts here in the desert. I'll train her on all the administrative crap. I mean paperwork. Cassandra is your man, er, woman." And he started his damn laugh, saying, "Eh, Eh" over and over.

The optics they witnessed was amazing. The Coplands readily admitted that Cassie was one tough cookie. Nick collected the broken wood fragments, and walked out back to throw them in the trash can. As he walked back inside the restaurant, Cassie's mongrel dog, Yangtze, trailed Nick into the dining room.

"Oh, my god," Cassandra said. Pointing at Yangtze's tail, she said, "Look." The woman who just smashed boards, freaked out and starting screaming. The dog was unaware that a scorpion was attached to his tail, stuck as Yangtze wagged his tail back and forth like a metronome. The scorpion bounced back and forth on the excited dog's tail, listening to Cassie's shrieking. Nick rose, found a broom in the storage room, and not too carefully, whacked the scorpion from the dog's tail. He swept the eight-legged arachnid out the front door.

Cassie looked crushed when Nick proudly announced, "Those scary-looking legs and its stinger are now spread all over Palm Canyon Drive."

Gabriela noticed Adam's anxious look, checked her watch—one of his first gifts to her while dating—and said, "You better drop me at the rental house, and take off for your appointment."

Nick suggested, "I'll drive Mrs. C to the house. Adam, that way you're free to head to city hall right now." It was a good suggestion, and Adam didn't argue although Gabriela always viewed Adam as her safety net, and preferred Adam doing every thing under the sun for her.

City hall was walking distance from the restaurant if the temperature outside wasn't 114 degrees—outside of the wonderfully air-conditioned Ding Ho. He drove the short distance to city hall, and found the parking structure overflowing, apparently due to the marijuana licensing session. No shaded locations were available. He parked on a side street under a tall palm tree. Wearing a coat and tie, to at least give the appearance of respectability, he found the Paradise Hills heat unbearable.

Since it had only recently been incorporated as a city, Paradise Hills's city hall was constructed a little over two years ago. Approaching the front entrance, Adam stared at the attractive, three-story, all-glass structure. It was a perfect box without any overhang. He quickly realized some inexperienced architect sold the city council a bill of goods. Who in the world would want a glass structure in the desert without curtains or any protrusion to block the sun?

He thought, *There has to be a lot of uncomfortable, blazing hot, uptight city bureaucrappers in that building.* Copland regularly called functionaries, regardless if employed in private enterprise or government, bureaucrappers rather than bureaucrats. They were the type of workers where words like efficiency was as foreign as courtesy. He knew Albert Einstein nailed it when he described bureaucracy as *'the art of making the possible impossible'.*

When Adam arrived, Rios was in the vestibule talking to another lobbyist. The other man was representing a wealthy grower who lived in Taos, New Mexico. A Silicon Valley founder of an online clothing firm that had recently been purchased by Amazon funded all his marijuana grows. Amazon made the techie entrepreneur, educated at Stanford, another Silicon Valley billionaire.

Rios nodded at Adam, and lightly punched the other lobbyist in the right arm. Moving a few feet, Rios said to Copland, "That fellow will probably get the other license for his client. Are your ready for the meeting? You know that the council will want you to deposit $1 million into an escrow account if we win the bid. It's a level of feel good for the city that you can perform. That money isn't a problem. Is it?"

Adam said, "Billy, you know that money is never a problem. That's why you originally contacted me a few years ago. Just get us the license. I have implicit trust in you. That's why you're getting a percentage of this deal. Just tell me when to talk, if they even request it."

Rios led Adam into the jam-packed council chamber to two seats in the first row that had VIP placards placed on each chair. One side of the room was filled with angry older residents who wanted a permanent marijuana dispensary and cultivation prohibition in their city. The cost of the poorly designed city hall, compounded by the few industrial buildings constructed thus far, portended a city tax revenue shortfall. Newly incorporated Paradise Hills had the very real potential of declaring bankruptcy, duplicating the actions taken by the California cities of San Bernardino, Mammoth Lakes, Vallejo, and Stockton in filing Chapter 9.

The rest of the chamber was packed with nattily dressed men representing diverse marijuana entrepreneurs, or as a marijuana magazine named them—*ganja-preneurs.*

Twenty feet to Adam's left was a surprise he had anticipated and prepped Rios for, but seeing smug Bing in the chamber was still jolting. Cary Sweetzer and Klutz were sitting on one side of Bing, and two men Adam didn't recognize were on Bing's right, Rex Mueller and Mark Ware.

Promptly at 2 p.m., a side door opened and five city officials walked into the chamber. A man, hunched over from the pain of premature rheumatoid arthritis, acknowledged the sheriff to begin the session. The council members followed a pre-planned agenda. They began discussing the request for a zoning variance for the construction of a Scientology Church in their city. The elderly residents appeared to be as opposed to the Scientology proposal as the marijuana legislation that was scheduled to follow the church zoning debate.

Following the negative vote on the church, a city council woman, who connived to receive one of the first marijuana dispensary licenses, stood up. She said, "My name is Joy Wentworth. We've previously discussed the merits, both pro and con, of the marijuana dispensary and cultivation legislation in Paradise Hills. The tax revenue that will be generated has been judged by the Rand Corporation to be substantial." Smiling she tried to get a laugh, and said, "After all, we need to pay our hard-working employees." All she got were frowns and a few sarcastic snickers for her joy-less attempt at humor. She continued, "Consequently, in a private session last night, the council voted five-zero to approve the Marijuana Dispensary and Cultivation proposal known officially as Measure MM108."

A loud chorus of boos, hissing, and stamping of feet by the cadre of elderly dissenters permeated the overflowing room at the announcement. She reached for the gavel. It slipped from her clammy palm. She picked it up and was finally able to pound the gavel on the sound block to demand quiet.

The sheriff moved into the crowd, and said, "Any more outbursts, and you're gone. You'll be tossed out of here. Understand me?"

Though she had located what she deemed to be the perfect retail center on Dorothy Lamour Drive for her planned dispensary, Joy didn't have the money in her savings account to build it. In addition, her partnership requirements were so one-sided and onerous, until now she was unable to raise funds from investors. Her city license required tenant improvements to commence within two years from the issuance of the license. Also, the city didn't announce that the $1 million MMJ license deposit was waived for Joy. Ah, City Hall baloney from bureaucrappers in action to assist political-entrepreneurs.

Wentworth said, "This meeting is to announce the decision of the Paradise Hills City Council," she paused and looked around the standing-room-only convocation. And said, "Now I'll name the two applicants that we decided best fit the requirements determined by your city representatives. We have made our decision. First is Ronald Jaworski representing Taos Sunflower Dispensary."

The Taos lobbyist turned towards Rios, and gave a thumbs-up.

A few days before the city council meeting, Copland's lawyer threw Bing a curveball by sending the Paradise Hills City Attorney a certified copy of the arrest record of Pacifico Bing de Asis, obtained from the West Hollywood Sheriff's Department. In addition, Viktor Romanovich signed a letter acknowledging that he perjured himself with his "Letter of Attestation" that Bing owned a percentage of Sweet Kindness Center dispensary. Kingsley had persuaded Romanovich's lawyer that Viktor had no liability signing the letter since he sold Sweet Kindness Center to Copland, and any and all liability flowed with the nonprofit corporation. Adding to that fact, Kingsley accurately stated that the one judge that handled marijuana related cases was so backed up, if the DA did want to proceed regarding the prevarication, it would take two to three years to get in front of the one judge for all Los Angeles County marijuana cases. More to the point, why would a lawyer allow his client to sign a letter with blatant liability? The solution was the $1 million Letter of Credit Copland posted to reimburse Romanovich if he was convicted and fined.

Wentworth said, "Before I announce the next winning bid, I should say that we do criminal background checks on all individuals that submitted applications. We have to automatically eliminate any person with a felony conviction."

Unaware that Kingsley contacted the Paradise Hills DA, and of the retraction by Romanovich, Bing appeared unconcerned by Wentworth's exculpatory statement. Wentworth continued, "With that said, the second and final marijuana dispensary allocation is awarded to Mr. Adam Copland of 'Adam 'n Eve Healthy Garden PRE-ICO, Inc.'"

The little weasel, Bing, jumped from his seat and yelled, "This isn't fair. I want to lodge a complaint of—"

Wentworth cut him off. "Please calm down. If you want to talk, step up to the microphone and calmly state your name and complaint."

As Bing moved to the microphone, Adam turned to Rios and said, "Get ready for the party. Life in Paradise Hills is about to get exciting. The scum of the earth is about to speak."

Bing said, "I submitted a detailed package prepared by my Palm Springs attorney."

Wentworth interrupted him and said, "I'm sorry, sir. Please state your name."

"My name is Pacifico Bing de Asis," Bing said. "My application was listed under the name Master Doobie, LLC."

He wasn't close to completing his vitriolic complaint, when the City Attorney, Jeffrey Leidy, rose and said, "Excuse me, Mr. de Asis. Please step forward."

The sheriff opened the door of the wooden gate, and pointed Bing toward Leidy, who had walked in front of the council rostrum. Leidy looked down at the diminutive de Asis, and said, "For your sake, I thought this should be a confidential discussion." He handed Bing two pages. First was a copy of Bing's West Hollywood Arrest record, and then Romanovich's retraction letter.

Recall that Bing was a rotten student at Manchester High. Not only did he read slower than average, he often needed to reread a letter to absorb what he had just read.

After taking the time to read the letter a second time, Bing glared at Leidy. He let the two pieces of paper drop from his hands and fall to the floor. Angrily he turned around, saw AC in the front row, walked over to Adam, and leaned on the polished railing. He said, "I don't know how you're involved in this. But I know you skunked me."

The sheriff immediately moved next to Bing, and said, "Sir, you need to move to the other side of the railing."

Bing's infuriation had reached a boiling point. He marched out of the hall, followed by his entourage.

Rios looked at Bing charging through the chamber doors and said, "That mad man is trouble. Seriously. You better be very careful."

"Don't worry," Adam said. "I have my security guard with me. In fact, he's waiting with Gabriela at my rental house right now. Bing's a little punk. I can take care of myself."

Reaching over and placing his hand on Adam's arm, Rios said, "Adam, be careful." Rios gave Copland a large binder containing the finalized Paradise Hills rules and regulations for MMJ and said, "I'm flying to Las Vegas tonight. I'll be back in Sacramento late tomorrow. Let's talk on Friday about how to proceed. Take care."

Adam walked outside. First the excruciating heat assailed him, and then Bing approached him.

Bing reached up and grabbed Adam's coat lapels, and said, "You fucked me. I know you're behind me losing this deal. You're a real fucker."

Adam brushed Bing off and said, "We have nothing to discuss. Get lost."

Mark Ware stepped up. "We haven't met. I'm Mark Ware. I'm a business partner of Bing's. I believe I have a good solution for this situation. Pay Bing $3 million, and he'll leave the desert marijuana business to you. Period. You'll never see him or me in the desert."

Copland stared at Ware the way an elephant stares at an annoying flea. "I just won the desert marijuana bidding. Why in the world would I pay that schmuck $3 million when I already have the Paradise Hills marijuana license? Huh? I'd sooner buy Bing his sarcophagus than give him $3 million. Now get out of my way."

Ware said, "I kinda assumed that would be your answer."

Adam started to leave when four men blocked his way. Sweetzer, Lutz, Mueller, and Bing were standing between Adam and his car. Before Adam could do an about-face to return to city hall, Ware had grabbed Copland by the neck and Sweetzer tasered him. They dragged him to the side of the building. No one could see them begin to pummel Adam.

Bing laughed and said, "I warned you. I told you I'd get you. He raised his foot and viciously smashed it into Adam's face, breaking his nose. Klutz was the strongest of the five men, and lifted AC so that Sweetzer could use his limp body as a punching bag.

Ware looked at Bing and said, "He'll need a lot of plastic surgery when we're done with him. He should have at least negotiated on the $3 million offer."

Ware stopped talking when a man emerged from the parking structure and yelled, "Hey, stop that. I'm calling the police."

Klutz let Adam collapse on the gravel.

As the five men ran to their cars, Bing and Cary took their time to key both sides of Adam's car.

CHAPTER 22

Paradise Hills, CA
Wednesday, July 31, 2013

Tasered and beaten to a pulp, Adam remained unconscious, spread out on the gravel. All the excitement of winning the dispensary bidding now voided into mindless catastrophe. Adam had as many bruises on his body as St. Sebastian had arrow piercings.

The stranger's yelling had ended the beating; Klutz had abruptly dumped Adam on the gravel, prostrate. Bending over Copland, the Good Samaritan put his hands on Adam. There was no response to his touch. The vigilant man rushed inside City Hall to find help. He located two policemen in the building lobby escorting enraged entrenched elderlies, who were still protesting the MMJ legislation out of the council chamber. Appearing quickly at Adam's side, the two cops decided it was safe and faster to carefully lift him, and drive five miles to Desert Regional Medical Center in Palm Springs.

The presence of more than twenty-five people in the Emergency Room didn't bode well for instantaneous attention for AC. Two orderlies took Adam from the two policemen, placed him on a gurney where he remained for more than thirty minutes. Towels were placed on both sides of his face to stem the bleeding, or, more to keep the blood from streaming onto the unblemished floor.

Copland ended up on the gurney for what seemed sufficient time to complete the entirety of Wagner's Ring Cycle. Adam awoke on a gurney feeling more drunk than when he'd had too many bottles of Bordeaux with his wine-drinking buddies. Looking around the crowded ER, too groggy to stand, he reached for a passing nurse and asked, "Where am I?"

"Honey," she said. "You're in the Emergency Room at Desert Medical Center. Your cute little face is a mess. Be patient. Someone will be with you shortly."

Copland had triumphed in Paradise Hills, but now he was paying the price for winning the marijuana licensure. Bing and his swinish worker ants pretended to disappear when their five-against-one one-sided brawl was interrupted. Surreptitiously they had stationed Klutz, sweating profusely, in the hospital parking lot to keep an eye on Adam's movements when he was discharged. They weren't through shedding his blood.

In a hospital, Adam's expectation was to be cared for. Thirty more minutes lapsed. Feeling groggy, but sufficiently stable to walk, Adam approached the woman behind a glass-shielded counter. Adam waited for her to end a conversation, but after being neglected for a few minutes, he interrupted, and said, "I'm really hurt and need a doctor now."

"I've got your paperwork here describing your wounds," she answered. Without looking at the narrative, she said, "Says right here you'll live. Just a broken nose. That's all. You wait your turn like everyone else." She immediately looked away and starting talking to another staffer. Bureaucrappers in inaction.

Adam's attention and anger rose until severe agony arrived again, sapping his strength and causing him to walk back and momentarily lie down on the gurney.

Several minutes passed. Not accustomed to, and tired of waiting, Adam stood up and reached for his cell phone and call Gabriela.

She answered, heard the helplessness in his ebbing voice, and said, "What happened? Where are you?"

He handed his phone to a nearby nursing aide, and said, "Please tell my wife where I am." Panic-stricken, Gabriela put the phone on speaker mode for Nick to be able to listen to the CNA explain Adam's condition, and the location of the medical center.

Gabriela looked at Nick; he grabbed her hand and led her to his car. Driving as fast as Adam, Nick had them at the ER in less than ten minutes. Neither person was aware of Kenny Lutz sitting in Cary's 'I am curious' yellow corvette parked four spaces from Nick's car. Kenny was not happy waiting for Copland, but Klutz was staggeringly stupid, and he would remain the lowest person on the Bing marijuana totem pole. Several minutes passed, and Adam ebbed in and out of consciousness.

When he awoke again, Gabriela and Nick were looking down at him, along with a man in a doctor's coat. He had a full beard, short blond hair, and blue eyes, and softly informed Adam that he needed x-rays. Gabriela moaned Adam's name. And then everything went dark.

* * *

Gabriela tried to focus as Dr. Ragsdale explained Adam's injuries. "Your husband was severely beaten. His nose was broken. He may have damaged his right eye. I'll only know once he's cleaned up. X-rays will most definitely indicate specific injuries. When I touched his backbone, it appeared that he most likely has a few broken ribs. Listen. This looks worse than it is. I checked all his vitals. He's one extremely healthy man. He'll need lots of bed rest. But he'll be fine. Now sit down. Have some coffee and try your best to relax for a few hours while I operate on him."

There weren't any seats available. Nick stared angrily into space. After seeing Adam's bloody and bruised body, Gabriela's secure life seemed to vanish completely. She didn't know any of the facts, except they were in Paradise Hills for marijuana. Although she loved to smoke grass, she was inwardly cussing that Adam was in this cursed business.

Outside the operating room, Ragsdale described his surgical task to Adam as a nurse placed an IV drip next to his gurney. Ragsdale informed Adam what to expect as the RN patted his hand and pierced the skin inserting the peripheral IV into his vein. Minutes after the doctor had left, Adam turned his head to the nurse, and said, "Wow. This anesthesia is really affecting me. I'm feeling groggy already."

The nurse picked up his chart, found his name at the top, and said, "Mr. Copland, I haven't connected the needle to the IV line to the IV bag yet." She smiled, and said, "But I'm glad you're drowsy," and left.

The time protracted for three long hours. Half that time Adam had spent monotonously waiting on the gurney in the prep room. He perused the medical library, and leafed through a medical dictionary to pass the time. Three hours later, an RN escorted Adam, in a mandatory wheelchair, to the lobby. Gabriela gasped at the condition of his face. His severely broken nose had been realigned, and he wore a metal protective nose guard taped over his nose. The area below both his eyes was swollen, and black and blue. He had a temporary patch over his right eye primarily to keep blowing sand and dust from irritating it.

The kindly nurse slipped Adam some samples of Tramadol into the outpatient bag he had on his lap, and said, "These will help the pain. You're numb now, but you're going to feel terrible pain once the topical wears off. Take two every six hours. Good luck."

The first thing Adam said, "Can you believe this? The doctor asked if I had been playing touch football." Laughing more than Gabriela did at his statement; his cheerfulness hurt his taped ribs. "Let's go home. I want to go to bed, and sleep for a week."

Outside the ER, Nick pulled up his car and helped Adam wobble into it. Once all were inside the car, Adam said, "Doc said it would take about two weeks to heal. At that time I can stop wearing this ugly nose guard." Adam pulled a SafeTGard Nose Mask from the bag, and held it up. He said, "Check this out. I'm 5'9" and I'm going to look like Kobe Bryant or some NBA player with my nose mask." Again, no one laughed but him.

Heading north on Indian Canyon Drive, they reached Tennis Club Way in Paradise Hills, and Adam said, "Nick. Stop at City Hall. Let's have Gabriela drive my car so we don't get a parking ticket."

"No way," she said. "You know I hate driving your cars. No way Jose. Just leave the car there."

Despite Gabriela's protests, Adam insisted they stop at city hall so that he could pick up his Bentley.

No one in Nick's car realized that Kenny Lutz had pulled out behind them and was was tailing them through the light evening traffic.

* * *

By this time in their marriage, Gabriela knew not to waste her energy struggling to dissuade Adam when he was either emotionally charged, or his opinion was anchored. She decided he was too emotional at this moment for her to argue with, regardless if it was safe for him to drive. AC got out of Nick's car, and drove his car unusually slowly to their rental home, trailed by two drivers: Nick was within three car lengths and Klutz was a short block away.

The one-story Spanish colonial with a red tile roof was six months old. The house was tucked behind a tall hedge of deciduous trimmed Japanese Holly bushes and under a row of palms. Unable to sell the house, the developer provided high-end furniture from Kriess in Los Angeles, and rented it out on a three-day minimum stay to generate some cash to pay the mortgage.

After the gates closed, Klutz approached and parked a few houses from the rental property. He stepped out of Cary's 'vette, and snapped ten photos of the house from assorted viewpoints as Mark Ware had instructed.

An inveterate entrepreneur, in addition to his skate shop, Ware also owned a camera shop and had recently started a drone business. For the past decade, Ware attended every Burning Man festival in late August located in the Black Rock Desert of Nevada. Anywhere he could sell grass, Ware appeared. While in Indio at the Coachella Valley Music Festival, selling cannabis and other drugs, Ware searched and struggled for what was missing at the Indio festival. Memories of the festival were the lightening bolt that rocked his mind. It wasn't enough to attend Coachella, Ware wanted to give everyone their Kodak moment from above.

Speculating on the future, Ware took a flyer and purchased a few drones. Still not happy, he hired a techie who attached a camera to the drones, and he proceeded to capture the wild crazy antics at both festivals. It worked. The stoner had another thriving business. Marketing his drone firm to every outdoor spectacle north of the Rio Grande. Ware was soon retained as the premier drone camera firm recording festivals, geographically ranging from the contests at the Pomona Fairgrounds where new artisanal marijuana strains competed at the 'High Times Magazine' Cannabis Cup, to Miami Music Week. And despite his pro-Occupy Wall Street sympathies, he was getting richer with every new business concept.

Behind the Southwestern-style iron gates, parked on a circular driveway, Nick ran from his car to the Bentley. Adam was leaning on the steering wheel. Nick opened the car door, and held Adam's arm as he edged out of the car. Gabriela directed Nick to conduct Adam through the house to the master bedroom. Gabriela said, "I'll be right back. I'm going to get three glasses of iced tea."

Nick was sitting in an oversized creamy chair when Gabriela quickly returned with the drinks. She placed the tray on a side table next to Nick, and handed a glass to both men. "Okay," she said. "Time to let the cat out of the bag. What happened? Did you resist someone trying to rob you or what in the world happened?"

Sitting up in bed to take two more pain pills, Adam said, "No robbers, baby. That bastard leprechaun, Bing, was at the marijuana-licensing meeting. When he was eliminated from the bidding process, he exploded in the council meeting. He and his homeboys did this reworking on my face. One of his partners walked up to me, and starts acting all palsy-walsy. He stated he had a solution for the dispute with Bing. He proceeded to ask me for $3 million and said, 'They'd keep their distance from the desert if I paid up.' Can you imagine the audacity? That's when I laughed in his face."

Adam pointed to his own face, and said, "Well, that's when this happened. I'm not sufficiently vain for a nose job, but I inadvertently got one anyway."

Nick was not happy. He stood up, shouted, "Goddam," and left the room.

Gabriela's anxiety dissipated quickly. Unencumbered outrage altered Gabriela's normal frenzied predilection to anxiety-plagued inertia in a situation like this. Instead of her common panic attack and inability to speak, she passionately wanted revenge against Bing and his boy's beastly actions against the most important person in her life. She stroked Adam's leg, uncertain where it was safe to touch him without exacerbating his pain.

"I thought Bing was nothing but hot air," Adam said. "Wow. Was I wrong."

Gabriel asked, "Now what happens? Where does it end?"

Before Adam could respond to a question he couldn't answer, Nick reappeared. "I want us to return to LA tomorrow where you'll be much safer. I can control events better in our hometown. In the meantime, Cassie and a few of her friends are going to watch the house. Just an additional measure of safety."

"What does this jerk want from you?" Gabriela asked.

"It's a very long story," Adam said. "Briefly, Bing owes the Peckerwoods and the Krazy Ass Mexican gangs in LA a few million dollars. They are as dangerous a group of reprobates as there possibly can be in LA. I was going to lend him the money, but the putz never signed the loan docs. Best deal that I never made. Green and I would be out $3 million if that moron simply signed the paperwork on time. Next, he stole my ID and used my credit." Gabriela's jaw dropped, but Adam wasn't done.

Adam said, "Then the mental midget got arrested. You've met Howard Kingsley. Howie sent the arrest records to the Paradise Hills DA, which precluded Bing from bidding on the dispensary. Man was

Bingo pissed off when the City Attorney told him a felony record eliminated his application." Adam formed a feeble smile, and said, "You know, or see, the rest."

Nick left a second time, called Cassandra again, and said, "Bring all my supplies I left in your storage shed. Pronto. I left the key under the trashcan. This Bingo jerk has taken his dispute with Adam to a new level of unreality. If available, bring some muscle from your mixed martial class. We're going to need protection for Adam. We're gonna need a lot of bodyguards for the boss."

When Nick returned to the bedroom, Adam was describing Bing, "Think of the marijuana business as a living body. Bing is like marijuana cholesterol. Bing's the equivalent of too much LDL bad cholesterol in your blood. Lipitor can diminish the danger of cholesterol, but there's no remedy for Bing. He can kill."

Nick interrupted. "We need a safety net in case Bing does something stupid. Scratch that. When he does something stupid. I have Cassie and her MMA boys coming over here."

Adam said, "Let's see if I understand this correctly. Cassandra the Chinese restaurateur plus me a Jew. We join forces to fight Bing and his barbarian horde. Does that make Cassie and me blended as one?" He paused for the right timing. "We must be, why yes, we're Genghis Cohn."

He sounded healthier than he looked. No color in his pallid skin, bandages and gauze covering wounds, and he strained merely breathing due to broken ribs. Despite his attempt at humor, the insidious beating took its toll. Adam tried to fight it. However the pain medications were taking over, and his eyes slowly closed after his wisecrack allusion to the Romain Gary character.

* * *

Within an hour, Cassie and her contemporary equivalent of a Roman legion arrived at the house. With Nick at her side, they inspected the landscaped grounds. Together they made decisions where to strategically place her MMA friends in distinct locations they decided were both ideally defensible against any attack by Bing, and importantly somewhat sheltered from the excessive heat. Cassie then realized they had one glaring deficiency. Ululating as seriously as a funeral lamentation, she said, "We forgot food for the men."

Nick's mouth curled, and he said, "I'd marry you if we weren't cousins."

"Think so?" she asked. "I'll call mom and have her put together a huge care package for tonight's dinner. That will be easier than making sandwiches for everyone here." Realizing Adam was sleeping, and Gabriela was taking a break, they readied to take off to the Ding Ho.

As the gate opened, they noticed a yellow Corvette parked two houses away. Bending over when he noticed the security gate begin opening, Klutz was hiding and a Corvette or any jazzy car in this neighborhood wasn't unusual or suspicious. When Nick's car was out of sight, Klutz gunned the engine, did what Sweetzer called a 'huey', and headed to Ware's Weekend getaway in Palm Desert to update Bing of the situation.

Driving south on Palm Canyon, Cassie said, "Now seeing the problem you described, I still don't know the root cause. You never told me what's behind all this fighting. What's the lowdown here?"

Nick said, "You have to look at these two men as fighting to be the new robber barons of cannabis. Just like Facebook, Google, Apple, Amazon, and Uber dominate the new Internet economy, Adam wants to be a major player in cannabis. Besides his LA operations and now Paradise Hills, he recently offered to buy three existing dispensaries in Arizona. Las Vegas is next."

"So what's the dirt on Bing?"

"I remember having to read a novel by some French author back in school. The man said behind every fortune stands a crime," Nick said. "Well, I admit Adam cuts corners here and there. But Bing is an outright crook. Adam didn't authorize me to do this, but on my own dime, I'm had Big Johnny trail Bing. I know his every routine. From shipping grass out of state, to his illegal vape business. Johnny also noted some black dude is following Bing around. Bing's being two-timed. All my life I've wanted this type of relationship with a boss. Adam trusts me and that's why I want you involved in the desert. Adam has plans to market edibles to all the senior communities in the desert to ease their medical problems. Adam is one sharp cookie. Bing is out of control, and dumber than a rat going after AC, since even rats supposedly learn." They ended the discussion of the intricacies of Copland versus Bing, and that Cassie was joining Phantom Security, as they got out of the car at her parent's restaurant.

On the table next to the cashier, the food was boxed and ready to go. She grabbed the bell used by the cook to inform servers when the food was prepared. Due the comments by Nick, Cassandra said, "Let's drop by the house and pick up some clothes. This guard duty could last awhile."

Driving to Cassie's parents house, Nick said, "Patrolling that house is going to last until I get them back to LA. There ain't gonna be no kumbaya moment between Bing and Adam."

Cassandra always dressed modestly. She placed two pairs of jeans, undies and socks, a few blouses, and tennis shoes in a gym bag. "Do you have additional plans, Nicky?" She asked.

"I just want to kick the can down the road," said Nick. "I want to keep them safe here, and get back to LA where I have more resources to protect them. The problem is I'm afraid that runt Bing is going to do something stupid sooner than later."

On the drive back to Adam, instead of thinking about the Copland's security, Nick fantasized about him making major plans of hiking trails in the Sierra Nevada—anything to get out of LA. The conflict for Nick was his desire to leave everything behind and enjoy rootless solitude; the daunting effort was to take that first step in place of mere talk. His dedication to Adam precluded any serious effort to leave; along with the fact his wanderlust for mountain trails was primarily meaningless talk.

To escape the pervasive fear inhabiting Gabriela's psyche, she perused the bookshelf looking for a light read. The only thing that mildly interested her was a James Patterson novel, a writer she avoided, as he seemed to churn out a new book out every other month that was a facsimile, with minor changes, of a previous book.

Entering through the door from the garage to the kitchen, Nick placed his loaded gun on the counter, and carried in boxes brimming with food as Cassie made tea.

Nick noticed Gabriela reading. Not wanting to bother her, he walked to the bedroom to check on Adam who was sleeping soundly. He placed the bell that Cassie had taken from the Ding Ho on the bedside table.

Obsessed with Adam's experience with Bing, Nick went outside, checked the guards and the grounds for any intrusion. Remaining outside, he dismissed half the guards to eat dinner as he walked the property.

Not a rude woman, Gabriela suffered fools about as well as Adam. Which was not at all. The only female among the guards, Nola, noticed Gabriela in the LR and the book she was reading. She said, "Excuse me. Do you like that Patterson book?" Gabriela shrugged nonchalantly. Nola said, "I tried to read one of his books, but I find him too difficult to understand." Gabriela established it best not to respond, fudged a smile, and held back quoting Dorothy Parker, *You can lead a horticulture, but you can't make her think.*

Around 11 p.m., Gabriela sneaked quietly into bed, avoiding Adam's bandaged body. The night remained uneventful. No one was aware that two of Mark Ware's drones were floating above the adjacent houses, cameras directed at Adam's rental, and monitoring every movement made by Nick and his version of the Praetorian Guard.

CHAPTER 23

Paradise Hills, CA
Sunday, August 4, 2013

W ithout embarrassment, Adam slept nineteen hours a day for three days, adhering to the doctor's prescription to take either Percocet or Tramadol, depending on the level of pain; the unmistakable side effect of the pain pills dictated unconstrained drowsiness for those three days.

By Sunday morning, Adam was feeling relatively better, and characteristic for a man who detested pills of any sort, decided to omit the scheduled pain pill. Adam looked at the clock, saw Gabriela in the chair next to the bed, and said, "Good morning, beautiful. What day is this?"

Excited, she forgot to use her bookmark, dropped her novel on the floor, and walked four steps over to the bed. "It's Sunday morning, big boy," she answered and leaned over to delicately kiss him. "Are you feeling better? At all?"

Hampered by the meds, his sharp mind was working at a walking pace instead of its usual lively gallop. "Could I please have a glass of cold water?"

She was excited that he appeared to be regaining his spirit, and she hoped Adam would utter a silly, childish remark—then she would know he was on the mend. Instead, when she returned he was standing at the window, gazing at the people holding guns who were posted around the perimeter of the yard.

"You should be sitting down," she said as she handed him the glass of water.

"Who are all these people outside?" Gabriela explained that they were friends of Cassandra, protection against any potential devious shenanigans from Bing, who was a vicious outlaw in her mind.

As Gabriela sat on the bed close to Adam, Nick didn't bother knocking on the door, and walked in the room. "Morning. Everything is under control. But I still think we should return to LA ASAP. I'm simply not comfortable here."

Adam was about to speak, when to change the subject, and following the doctor's recommendation that Adam wasn't prepared to travel, Gabriela said, "Talking about news, I have news that will cheer you up. First, the news alert of the day is . . . I'm pregnant."

Adam beamed, hugged her as tight as his wounded body allowed, and Nick said, "Mazel tov."

Considering Nick was half Chinese and half Ukrainian, Gabriela wanted to ask how he knew the correct Hebrew words for congratulations. She decided against getting him started. She said, "The second bit of news is actually a story about your daughter. I explained to Rebeccah what pregnancy meant and that she would soon have a baby brother or sister. Our babies face transformed and she looked spectacularly depressed—if a three-year-old can be depressed. Then your adorable little daughter said this juicy tidbit in response to my announcement, quote unquote, 'Is having a baby like going to a department store to buy something?' Then she raised her chin, stared directly at me, and said, 'When can you return it?' That was her response. I don't think she wants to share you."

They chatted some more, and Adam felt sufficiently well to walk into the den. He asked Gabriela for a piece of toast and tea. He sat at the kitchen table with Nick, and watched the Palm Springs tramcar reach the top of the Mt. San Jacinto plateau, about 2,000 feet below the mountains peak.

Adam said, "Years ago, I stayed at a friend's cabin in Idyllwild. For hours the two of us hiked from Devil's Slide trail on the Idyllwild side of the mountain to where that tram is now. I don't think I'll be doing that for quite a while."

Looking in the same direction, Nick frowned and was distracted. He picked up his gun, walked out back, and aimed his gun at the sky. Adam started to say, "What the—" when there was an explosion.

Nick put his gun in his holster, picked up the fallen drone he had blasted out of the sky, and inspected what was left of it. He returned to the kitchen carrying the drone as Cassandra ran from the front yard, through the house to the kitchen.

"I heard a gunshot," Cassie said.

Noticing three extremely anxious people staring at him, Nick said, "Don't give me those awful looks. Check this out." He placed the drone on the table and pointed at the tiny camera. "First of all," he said. "How often have you seen a camera on a drone?" He turned the drone over. Squinting at the small print, he read the brand name. He said, "Says here this is the property of Ware Video Drone Company. Name sound familiar, Adam?"

"Shit," said Adam. "Mark Ware is Bing's partner. He's the bastard that asked me for $3 million."

"Obviously," Nick said. "Bing is watching our every move. For the most part in a battle, you don't want to divulge what you're doing. But let's piss Bing off and make him think were leaving."

Cassandra said, "Cuz, I don't follow you."

Nick said, "Let's cut through all the BS. We need to throw Bing off our tracks. Let's pack up the cars, and pretend we're going home. We'll have a few of Cassie's friends drive our cars back to LA. They'll be armed to the teeth, anticipating trouble. Once the decoy is gone, we wait forty-five minutes to make certain Bing fell for the bait. Then we call Enterprise and rent a car to take the four of us to Los Angeles. We bring Cassie along for added protection. What do you think?"

The three looked at each other, didn't say a word, but nodded in agreement. Adam said, "Good thinking. It's a good plan to avoid Bing, the thousand-headed monster. But you better warn your group driving the cars to be ready for a battle."

Everyone went to their rooms to pack, and prepare to depart. "I'd like to spit in the face of Bing for what he's done to you," Gabriela said.

Adam thought, *You might get your chance very soon.* Trying to deflect her anger, he said, "It's not the end of the world. It will all work out. I've just got some temporary pain. Realize quite simply that we aren't going to capitulate to these sicko pygmies. They picked the wrong fight. No one knows me better than you do, and you know best that I'm a fighter till the end."

Neatly packing their clothes, Gabriela thought, 'No, you're more of a riverboat gambler type than a brawler. You're strong, but you use your brain'. She was betting that Adam's innate requirement for oneupmanship would provide the safety they needed. She knew that there was no worse enemy to have than a furious Adam Copland. Plus, Nick's plan seemed plausible, and the best way to avoid a day-mare of a melee with Bing.

After taking the time to brush his teeth, Adam said, "This is kinda like Muhammad Ali's rope-a-dope strategy against George Foreman. Tire out the opponent and don't get hurt."

* * *

In another house nearby, Bing was trying to figure out if they should follow the two cars heading toward Highway 111, or listen to Klutz, who was watching the house through binoculars on the adjacent hillside. Kenny was stupid, but he had 20-20 vision, and he'd said, "Listen. Sure they piled things in those cars. But after the cars took off, I can still see four people staying in the house. And two are women. They didn't leave. I'm telling you they didn't leave the damn house."

Until now Bing had let Ware maneuver his drones, intimidate Bing with the technical aspects of the unmanned camera drones, and feed Bing the information he requested. The inveterate gambler, Cary Sweetzer, said, "I bet on my boy. If Klutz says they're there, then they're there."

Trading barbs about who to chase and destroy, Ware asserted that his cameras clearly indicated the Coplands had left the house, and Bing should attack the cars.

Noticing the panic in Bing's eyes, Ware said, "Let me suggest that we take out the two cars first. If it's true Copland is still in the house, well, the distraction of the cars will be for a short time." To make Bing happy, Ware used Bing's epithet, and said, "Then we can attack Air-Conditioning man and his friends."

Long ago Morrison Guzman stated the unvarnished truth about Bing; he couldn't deal with being challenged. "This air conditioning man belongs in a." He paused trying to think of the correct word, and Bing finally said, "He belongs in a retirement home playing crossword puzzles. You know why crossword puzzles, Mark?" The question was rhetorical, and Bing said, "Because Copland talks too much. Like you're starting to do." He looked around Ware's Palm Desert house, and said, "Grab your weapons. Tell Kenny to meet us in front of Adam's house in about thirty minutes. Fuck those two cars. We're going to that house right now. My gut tells me Kenny is on top of this, not those damn drones."

Again and again, over and over, Ware thought how wrong Bing's approach was. But there was no changing his mind. Ware and the others piled in two cars and drove to Paradise Hills.

Arriving at the house, Bing bit his lower lip. The hindrance Klutz had failed to mention was the solid hedge obstructing a view of the house from the street. Never one to back off, Bing walked about one hundred yards to where gardeners where pruning trees and cutting the grass. The sign on the truck read "Humberto's Lawn and Tree Service."

There was too much noise to talk over the buzzing tree saws, and Bing waved to the closest man who appeared to be directing the four workers. Bing yelled, "Which one of you is Humberto?"

"I'm Humberto, señor," Humberto said. "How may I help you?" He seemed more like a gardener than a Riverside homeboy, but Bing noticed Humberto and his men had as many gang tattoos as those damn Peckerwoods and 'Krazy Ass Mexicans.'

"Yo, hombre," Bing said. "I own that house a few doors down. I need the trees in the front yard cut down pronto. My wife says she can't see the street. Can you do that for me right now?"

About seven years ago shortly after Humberto's older brother had been cut down, shot five times in the back, Humberto decided to change his life, and joined Homeboy Industries in downtown Los Angeles. They were famous for helping ex-gang members and recently released incarcerated gang members obtain job skills. Humberto and his Riverside Home Boys turned over a new leaf as gardeners.

"I'm busy now," said Humberto. "How about next Thursday around 6 p.m.?"

"It's very important to keep my wife happy," said Bing. Bing considered his two options for faster service, pay the man extra money as an incentive or put a gun to his head. Bing pulled ten one hundred dollar bills from his wallet, and said, "Yo, dude. Here's $1,000. Do the work right now. Simply chop down the trees and come back Thursday to pick up the crap. How about it?"

Aware he had a sucker, Humberto snatched the ten big ones, and yelled for his men to stop their work. They followed Bing down the street, and Bing pointed to the trees he wanted chopped down. A hedge of symmetrically perfect Japanese Holly bushes wasn't about to impede Bing's thirst for revenge.

In light that Humberto had become an avid horticulturist, he thought it cruel to cut down the healthy hedge. $1,000.00 superseded any landscape sensitivity, and he arranged for his men to mow down the tree-like hedge, about two feet from the ground.

* * *

Over Nick's shoulder, Cassandra saw trees dropping as though gophers and beavers had joined forces. "What are those gardeners doing?" she asked.

Wondering why in the world perfectly healthy shrubbery was being chopped down, the foursome moved to the large bay window in the living room. This wasn't what Adam anticipated. Directly behind the gardeners was Bing de Asis and his cold-blooded minions. Klutz and Cary were lifting guns and ammo out of two cars. Each man now laden with sufficient arms to resemble a prepossessed Pancho Villa caricature.

"There's a lot of firepower out there." Nick shook his head. "Let's go. We need to get out of here like right now."

In unison they raced toward the back door, when Cassie abruptly stopped. She said, "The weapons. Quick. I packed them up. They're in my bedroom." Urgently running to her bedroom, Nick grabbed the gym bag filled with guns, distributed a gun to each person, and the group charged through the house to the backyard.

Unseen were the additional drones. Ware constantly kept his cell phone in his hand. The images streaming from the camera were integrated with software that allowed Ware to redirect the drones to any location. Bing snatched the car keys from Ware to grab his water bottle left in the car.

Ware yelled, "Bing! Adam just came out of the house. He's leaving through the back yard. Come on, man." Ware thought, 'Bing is such a fuck-up'. Their reciprocal mutual bitterness and tension was bursting forth.

Humberto and his workers watched as the armed men hopped over the two holly bushes that were already chopped down, out of the fifteen bushes that comprised the hedge, and raced around the side of the house.

"We need to head toward the mountains," said Nick. "Get to higher ground."

Verifiably, exercise for Gabriela consisted of raising a glass of wine. Running as fast as she could, she was already lagging behind. At her acrobatic best, Cassie easily and quickly climbed over the eight-foot-high block wall, and leaped into the yard of the adjoining vacant property. Adam and Nick formed a human ladder, and lifted Gabriela to top of the wall. She momentarily hesitated, sitting on the top of wall, when Cassie shouted, "Jump, Gabriela!"

A bullet hit the wall. It was the supercharger she needed. Prompted by the bullet, she jumped, hit ground, rolled over, bound up, and ran with Cassie through the yard. Cassie opened a gate that led to the parallel street. Nick turned, pulled out of his holster a Walther P99, and unloaded his semiautomatic pistol in the direction of Bing's men.

None of Bing's men had been in the military. Nor were they accustomed to using a gun, except for Cary keeping a gun handy but never actually firing it. All of Bing's men took cover on one side of the garage, allowing Nick and Adam more than enough time to vault the wall. Adam jumped down while Nick stayed on top of the wall to fire a few more rounds to keep Bing at bay. Nick was a dedicated gun enthusiast, hitting the gun range weekly. He constantly won shooting contests held at valley gun ranges, regularly putting to shame inferior opponents. Adam needed his expertise more than ever as Adam had never fired a gun, nor had even held one.

Jumping down and bursting through the neighboring yard, Nick stopped. He turned, pointed his gun to the sky, and dropped another drone. "How many of those darn drones do they have?" He asked rhetorically.

Nick glanced back, no one in sight—yet. Out on the street, Adam motioned ahead to a perpendicular road; he knew they must avoid climbing walls because of Gabriela's below par athleticism. In addition, Adam was woozy from the medications, and stiff from the broken ribs. Everywhere there were cactus gardens, not the type of surroundings that provided a hiding place or good cover if you wanted to be invisible rather than dead.

They were in the open, without a strategy, with two lousy shooters out of four. Logic dictated that Adam's group should run, hide, avoid a direct confrontation, and perhaps it was time to cry for help.

Nick threw logic out the window. "Here's what we do," Nick said. "Any second those bastards are gonna be down our necks. Cassie, you position yourself behind that wall." Pointing down the street, he looked at the Coplands, and said, "You two run down the street. Stay in the open. Don't hide until shots are fired. Don't be worried. The shots will be me firing at Bingo."

Adam assumed he grasped Nick's intention, grabbed Gabriela's sweaty palm, and they sprinted in the direction Nick stated as Cassie moved behind a wall.

* * *

Not known for his athletic prowess, Bing waited as his monsters climbed the wall. Bing turned and headed for the front yard. Rather than going through the gate, Cary shot holes in a glass door, and they all ran through the vacant house. Their delayed appearance allowed Nick sufficient time to position himself, locate the remaining drone, and blast it from the sky. Their odds were vastly improving without big brother watching.

Nick was prepared to spend day and night, night and day, fighting to protect his boss. During initial job interviews, Adam always attempted to ferret out applicants that displayed a personality type that he anticipated would learn skills from him and eventually start a competing business. His forte was determining those applicants that displayed traits of loyalty. Those traits included openness, willingness to look directly at another person, and perhaps a military background. Nothing about Nick Petriv was normal, but his loyalty to Adam was eye-opening, and once again was paying off.

Minutes later, Bing's troops arrived, and didn't notice the hidden positions of Nick and Cassie. Sweetzer saw Adam up ahead about 125 yards, directly in his sights. He dropped to a kneeling shooting position. But before he could cock the shotgun Ware had given him, a blast from Nick's semiautomatic laid Cary out, permanently.

* * *

Adam and Gabriela didn't look back at the thunderous noise, because the road started to ascend and twist as they approached the Palm Springs Tramway. Running through the gravel parking lot, they reached the ticket office, and although it seemed like participating in the theater of the absurd, bought two round-trip tickets. "The next tramcar is coming down the hill and will be here in about five minutes," said the elderly man in the ticket booth.

Signs pointed up the ramp leading to a platform. They stopped at the tram gateway, and Gabriela said, "I haven't been this tired since . . ." Inasmuch that savages were chasing them, she decided to leave sexual innuendo to her husband, who for once was too scared to tease her.

Adam breathlessly said, "If we can get on this tram before Bing arrives, we've got at least a thirty-minute head start once we reach the top."

* * *

In the front of Adam's rental house, Bing reached Humberto as his workers were picking up their tools to walk back to their other job. He asked, "Do you and your men want to earn a quick $2,000 each?"

Humberto's eyes narrowed. He knew a sleazeball when he saw one because he had seen so many. But that didn't stop him from asking, "What illegal thing do you want done?"

Bing didn't hesitate to lie, and said, "That bastard in my house stole a lot of marijuana from me. I'm out hundreds of thousands of dollars. My boys are chasing him, but we could use your help. Do you know how to use a gun?"

Clearly Humberto's laugh furnished Bing with the answer. Humberto knew how use a gun, a rifle, or a grenade if necessary and available. "You want me to shoot that man?" he asked.

A lizard ran by, Bing stepped on it, and said, "I want four people dead."

It took Humberto about thirty seconds to understand it was more profitable to temporarily be a homeboy again than a gardener. He stretched out his hand, and he said, "Ten thousand for me, and $5,000 for each of my men and you have a deal."

Bing said, "You know I don't have that much money with me." He tossed Humberto the keys to Ware's BMW and said, "This is a deposit until the killing is done."

Humberto explained to his men, in Spanish, the death-dealing agreement and what was required. Bing sat in Humberto's beaten-up pickup truck; without hesitation, the three workers piled in the truck bed.

"Which direction?" Humberto asked.

Bing said, "Hang a huey and make a right on the first street." Bing's new killer followed the directions, but at the end of the second street, he could only turn left. Humberto gestured toward Cary who was lying in the middle of the street in a pond of his own blood.

Now crouching behind a car, Cassie signaled Nick to leave the scene. Even Nick knew they were outgunned, and besides, Adam should be safe momentarily. Now their survival was paramount. The cousins retreated, climbed over fences, met on the next street, and Cassie said, "Adam was running toward the tram. I don't know if they made it there, or if they're hiding in one of these vacant houses."

The cousins proceeded to move along the sides of each house, slowly moving forward, prepared to duck behind a wall.

Humberto and Bing stepped out of the cabin of the pick-up. Bing looked every which way. He didn't see a person or a weapon, and screamed, "Where the fuck is everybody?"

Klutz let out an ever so muted response, "Here."

"Where the fuck is here?" asked Bing. "Come out you chickenshits." He stared as three men approached him, shoulders slumped and embarrassed they weren't there to protect or assist the now dead

Cary Sweetzer. Klutz's jeans were torn from when he decided to leap for safety at the sound of bullets, not from fighting.

"I have a simple question for you assholes," Bing said. "Which way did Adam go?"

Mark Ware said, "Adam was running down the street, and turned right at the next street." Pointing to a house behind Bing, Ware said, "That security guard was hiding behind that house."

Bing cut him off, and said, "I asked you where Adam was. I don't give a damn about anyone else. You cocksuckers are worthless." Bing pointed to Humberto. "This man is Humberto. He and his men are going to help us to in air-con man. Something that you worthless pieces of shit couldn't do."

Turning to Humberto, Bing said, "Follow me." He forgot there were no cars, only the gardener's truck. "Shit," Bing said. "Come on. Jump in. Let's get him." Six men crouched in the back while Bing was in the cab with the driver.

The neighborhood consisted of a few vacant houses built by developers on speculation, a smattering of occupied houses, and predominantly vacant lots. Adam was nowhere in sight, but adjacent to the housing development was the Palm Springs Tramway parking lot.

Bing looked at Humberto, deviously smiled, and said, "We got 'em. He has to have taken the tram to the top, thinking he could hide from me. Let's go. We got the son of a bitch trapped."

Bing avoided the Palm Springs Visitor Center, walked past the old man sleeping in the ticket office, and kicked the gate waiting for the next tramcar. Bing was emotional, granted all this fighting was new to him. Tough as nails and emotionless, Humberto had been a street fighter as a smart-alecky kid, and now he was quieter than pithy Klutz prepping for a battle. Waiting for the tram with Bing, he wanted to earn his $10,000.00 as quick as possible and as painless as possible.

Rex asked, "How are we going to find Adam? And what do we do when we catch him?"

Bing stared at his roommate. He was seriously tired of dealing with idiots, and with a flourish said, "Mark said the drone showed Adam's wife is with him. She has to slow him down. We'll find him. Don't worry. We'll find them."

* * *

At the top of the tramway, Adam exited first and extended a hand to Gabriela. Aware she was pregnant, he said, "How are you holding up. Your energy level okay?"

"I think you should tell Bing to cancel his funeral plans for us," she said. "I know you aren't going to let him hurt us. You need to meet your baby due in six months." She took a deep breath, and said, "I'm ready. Let's go."

High above the desert floor, the temperature was at least thirty degrees cooler. In the refreshing mountain air, the Coplands took off from the tram exit. Sprinting with broken ribs was agony for Adam, and every step he had to take he grimaced with pain. He acted like a superman caught up in the adrenaline.

Adam held Gabriela's hand, leading her toward the rocky mountainside he knew so well from his Idyllwild hikes. She almost fell over as Adam abruptly stopped. He slowly turned and raced to the tram gift store. "Come into the store but keep an eye on the tram for de Ass," Adam said.

Rushing around the store, he got hostile looks from slow-browsing customers. Gabriela thought the store closely resembled the Fred Harvey–type gift stores in the national parks throughout the Southwest. It seemed insane for Adam to be rushing around a store with Agua Caliente Indian artifacts instead of locating a hiding place.

Notwithstanding all the tourist trash, in a flash Adam detected a possible source of crucial assistance. He handed Gabriela four Indian spears. They were made of wood, and were about five feet long with obsidian spear heads. What caught his eye next was a basket filled with molted porcupine quills, each quill covered in protective clear cellophane wrap. But under that wrap, there were backward-facing barbs at the tip of the quills—like fish hooks.

Adam grabbed a handful of wrapped quills, and left five twenty-dollar bills on the counter before the cashier could count the quills and spears. He whistled for Gabriela and went straight to other side of the plateau.

Before them was the children's petting zoo; a safe distance from the petting zoo was the "Mt. San Jacinto Creatures of the Night and Serpentine Safari." Adam purchased two tickets from the dispenser and started to go through the turnstile. Adam saw a reluctant Gabriela hanging back, and he said, "Come on, baby, let's go."

Paying no attention to the reptiles, Adam walked to the shed marked, "Employees Only." Inspecting the interior, he overlooked the dead animals kept in large glass tubs. He didn't need the cooler containers filled with edibles for the reptiles. Then he spotted his objective. One glass jar had latex stretched over the top with a label that read, "Western Diamond Rattlesnake Venom—Do Not Touch."

He grabbed the vial, and they left the shed. The directional signs pointed to varying points for the cross-country ski trail, the guided nature trail, and the wilderness permit trail. The first two easy walks wouldn't do. Adam said, "Let's go," and they walked past the unmanned Long Valley Ranger Station. The trail enlarged as they reached Round Valley Camp.

"This is the end of the easy walk," Adam said. "It's all uphill from here. I can hide you someplace that Bing will never find you, or . . ."

"No way, Jose," Gabriela said. "I'm sticking like glue to you."

Adam took his cell phone from his pocket and texted Nick: *Took tram to top. Heading to reservoir at Drury. HELP!*

"Okay," Adam said. "Let's head out. The plateau is around eight thousand feet here." He pointed straight ahead. "Mt. San Jacinto is around ten thousand feet."

At that moment, Adam's love for Gabriela was beyond anything his pitiful imagination could have ever imagined when they first met. He was proud of her stamina and strength in this horrid situation, and told himself he would never let anything happen to her. Adam's heart was torn to shreds for this snowballing morass that Gabriela was now a participant in. Emphatically precise with the veracious meaning of words spoken, Adam had never told any other woman he had dated that he loved her. Gabriela was his one and only love akin to a fairy tale. They were meant to be together for eternity, and he needed to stop Bing. Over and over, Adam told himself, *I can't let anything happen to Gabriela. I can't let anything happen to my baby.*

Adam checked his watch. The sign at the tramway office pointed out that the trams departed every thirty minutes plus there was a ten-minute ride to the top. He had used up ten minutes in the gift store and the maintenance shed, and still had a thirty-minute advantage over Bing.

"What part of your clothes is easiest to rip off?" he asked. "It needs to appear natural. Or a Kleenex, or anything that denotes our presence. That it's us?"

Never modest, without looking around in case anyone was able to see her, Gabriela pulled her purple T-shirt over her head and handed it to him. Her glorious firm breasts were unveiled. Adam lavishly kissed both nipples, and said, "These are why we're going to make it home."

Unaware of the bush's name, Adam selected a Curl leaf mountain mahogany blooming with tiny flowers to use as an eye-catching marker for Bing. He rubbed her shirt against the red-brown bark, nothing happened except it now needed to go to the laundry on Robertson Boulevard. Pushing harder against the ten-foot high ironwood, pieces of the Armani Express shirt dug into the dense bark. Mission accomplished to encourage Bing's belief that Adam was careless, and the direction of the trail they hiked. Gabriela put the filthy shirt over her head and pulled it into place.

As they trudged uphill, the mist kept Gabriela and Adam cool. A small stream of water began to accumulate, slowly cascading down the side of the trail as pebbles lazily slid down the hillside. For Gabriela, Drury Point seemed as far away as Honolulu.

Right now the grade became steeper, and from their location on the switchback, Adam could see glimpses of the Drury Reservoir. Gabriela had never walked so fast in her life, and her flowing adrenaline kept the momentum building up.

* * *

Reaching the top of the tramway, Bing pushed open the door, and proceeded toward the wide plateau of Mt. San Jacinto.

A light summer rain began to fall, causing the few tourists on the plateau to walk to the gift store or queue up for the next tramcar. Bing took his time, walking about the open meadow, instructing his men to look for any clues of Adam and Gabriela's whereabouts.

Adam would have preferred to race up the hill, but he proceeded patiently to allow Gabriela the feeling of being half-way comfortable. After all, she was three months pregnant, and he was hopeful for another adorable daughter. The difficult walk continued, and inadvertently Gabriela brushed against a bush—another piece of clothing tore as an unintended marker.

A helicopter originating from the Palm Springs Airport flew over the mountaintop, giving the tourists inside the copter a phenomenal alternative view to the tram ride. Besides the pilot, there were two occupants in the helicopter. Although searching the ground for their friends, neither could see the hiking Coplands as they were obscured by the tall subalpine forest trees. At any other time, this was exactly the type of hike and exercise that thrilled Adam.

"Keep pumping, babe," Adam said. "We're almost there." His remark was a blatant lie. Two miles of strenuous uphill hiking remained to get to the reservoir. Besides, he thought *she had been sturdy enough for their annual hike into the Grand Canyon wearing a backpack with 20 pounds, and their campout for a few days at Phantom Ranch, adjacent to the cold water flowing in the Colorado River.*

The next portion of the trail was poorly maintained; overgrown greenery made it extremely difficult to traverse. An hour later, which seemed like forty years in the wilderness to Gabriela, they emerged at just below the summit, and at the entrance to the Drury reservoir. The terrain at Drury was flat and seemed limitless. Religious Adam deemed the safety of the area Zion; nonreligious Gabriela deemed it Shangri-La.

At the higher elevation, rain was becoming torrential, which was a blessing to slow down their young able-bodied pursuers—all strapping men except butterball Bing.

Adam took a few seconds to scan the area; he sent Gabriela to wait under the eaves of the ranger station, which was adjoining the water reclamation building. The weather continued to deteriorate. The valley floor needed the rain but not as much as the Coplands did.

The reservoir was filled with different varieties of trout, although all Gabriela caught were mosquito bites. The earthen dam structure was well-built and sturdy. Adam broke a window, and climbed through the window to enter the water reclamation building. He searched for the controls of the adjustable crest gates. Finally, he found a panel with so many controls, locks, and sliding bars that even perpetually confident Adam felt bewildered. *What the hell am I afraid of? Let's test these.*

Despite all the options in front of him, fortuitously on his third try, he located the locks for the crest gate. Water slowly dripped from the gate, nourishing nearby plants thirsty for its sustenance.

"That's done," he said, and raced from inside the building over to Gabriela. "Keep the cellophane on the porcupine quills as a covering to protect our hands. Let's carefully dip the spears and the quills in the snake venom. Don't think about Bing coming up here. Let's focus on this right now. This is just a backup plan."

* * *

Flummoxed at the myriad trailheads and the fifty miles of trails, Bing became apoplectic because he couldn't determine where to proceed. Humberto told his men to fan out and look for any evidence of their intended prey. The gentle rain was becoming more forceful; nevertheless, the gardeners turned assassins stayed on the prowl.

One of his men, a former gangbanger named Esteban Flores, bent over and inspected a bush. "Here," he screamed. "Humberto. Over here." Running to Esteban's location, Humberto looked at the piece of material. He scratched his head—it seemed too easy, too much of a setup. Almost like the prey was inviting the predator to follow him. But for $10,000, and equipped with a multitude of semiautomatic weapons, the group commenced the hike on the trail to Drury Point.

Walking the Drury Trail commanded great vitality, and the trail had become perilously slippery since the thundershower started. The rain didn't stop Humberto, who wouldn't pause, knowing he had to get the killing done now.

Bing was the caboose on the hike, and he had a strange angst that the attack wasn't going as planned. Blinking at the rain hitting him in the face, the chickenhearted leader intentionally fell further behind.

Mark Ware looked back, and Bing said, "Keep going. Don't worry—I'm just out of breath at this altitude. I'll catch up."

Ware stared at him. In the middle of the hunt, Bing was acting bizarre, as though he may be having second thoughts. Ware thought Bing was acting as though he had end-stage rabies, thoroughly irrational even for unpredictable Bing. Ware continued hiking unaware that Bing had turned around and was quickly walking to the area near the gift store.

The rain pushed strands of Humberto's brown hair into his face that he ignored. He constantly checked both sides of the path for any noticeable signs of the Coplands. He knew the odds of finding someone in this downpour were not good since their tracks were being erased by the water and mud obscuring the trail.

* * *

After dipping the spears and quills in snake venom, Adam focused on his enemy. His strategy was established, and the weapons were ready. Originally educated as a businessman, now the amateur military strategist waited in a strangely hostile reality. Honestly frightened, he anticipated Bing walking into his trap, and the conclusion needed to be as decisive as Waterloo or Dien Bien Phu.

Through the shrouded mist accompanying the rain, a figure emerged on the curves of the switchback about one-quarter mile below the reservoir. "Stay here," he said. "The assholes are nearing."

Adam trudged through the mixture of gravel and mud to the building housing the control panel. Forcefully he twisted the challengingly onerous controls. The controls hadn't been used in years. They were opening only at the minimum, rock bottom of the adjustable crest gates. He needed more force. He stopped. Looked outside. Went walking to where he could pick up a four-foot branch about fifteen feet from the building. Returning inside, Adam placed the branch through an opening in the ball valve.

His attempt to use a wooden lever to turn the wedged valve quickly faded when the branch broke in half against the steel handle. The water flow was minimal; time was wasting.

The immediate area was surging with water, destroying bags of concrete intended to extend the concrete walkway around the reservoir. Imagining she knew Adam's intention, Gabriela moved to the stockpile of construction equipment. Bending down, she selected a steel rebar rod used for anchoring concrete. For a moment the rushing water made her hesitant, then she charged through the newly established Drury rivulet.

"Adam," she screamed. He opened the door, and noticed she had lifted the rebar. She was realistically terrified of the rushing water, and decided it was best to toss the bar. Implementing her best nonathletic manner, she heaved the bar. Plop. It landed in the flowing stream, but didn't budge due to its heft.

The choice between risking injury wading into the rushing water strewn with many baseball-size rocks to retrieve the rebar against inaction was an easy one. Perhaps recklessly, without looking at what was approaching in the flowing water, Adam left the building and walked directly to the rebar location, was hit in the ankle by two rocks, and picked up the prize.

Gabriela sighed. Adam returned to the water reclamation building, and pushed the steel bar into the valve opening, and pulled with all his substantial might. Adam could finally sense a flood of water rush under the crest gate. The more he turned the now lever-aged valve, the more vindicated he felt concerning the worthiness of his plan. As the water poured out of the reservoir, the lower sub-structure of the fabricated trail guided it; subsequently the trail was doused with a three-foot-high flood that soon overflowed down the mountainside.

The water rushed downhill so quickly, and so unexpectedly, faster and faster as gravity pulled it downward like a baseball thrown at ninety miles per hour. The movement of the water carried rocks and sediment that pelted Humberto and his men. Seconds before the flood Humberto felt everything was fine, just heavy rain. Now he wanted to yell, "Turn around." But he slipped. While attempting to stand, he was assailed with rocks and branches that struck him like ten hammers pummeling his slumped body.

Adam and Gabriela discussed what to do next, when a familiar voice asked, "Need any help?"

Walking toward them were Nick and Cassie. Nick said, "Before you ask. That was us in the helicopter. We climbed down a rope ladder. Cassie knows everyone important in the desert. The pilot is waiting for our call. But first there's something I'm looking forward to. Cassie and I need to take care of these bastards. See you shortly," and he tossed a rope around the sturdy ironwood bush as a counterbalance to the water. Adam moved back to the control to turn the valve and close the gate, assuming the damage to Bing was accomplished.

From his prior attempts, Adam knew colossal strength was required to twist the valve. Again Adam pushed the rebar through a hole in the valve opening, and once more it resisted his attempt to turn the valve clockwise. He stopped trying, and caught his breath. The worst of the thunderstorm was over, and the sun was breaking through the clouds. Adam planted his feet, as well as he could in mud-soaked shoes, and twisted. No movement. The cousins were going after Bing's savages, and Adam was at loggerheads with this inanimate metal device.

"One last try," he said.

The water slowed to a trickle, the gate closed, and Gabriela screamed, "Success! Let's go help Nick and Cassie."

They held hands and cautiously started walking from the ranger station to the trail. They stopped when a thundering explosion came out of nowhere. Adam said, "What in the world was that?" He felt foolish, but looked skyward. The clouds were dissipating. Gabriela turned around, and the dam was holding back the water as intended.

Covered in mud, Cassandra and Nick unexpectedly reappeared at the reservoir trailhead. Gabriela asked, "We heard the equivalent of a sonic boom. Do you know what happened?"

Cassandra said, "We were barely able to move downhill. The combination of mud and debris made it virtually impossible to reach Bing's men."

After inhaling deeply, Nick explained. "Mudslide, Adam. When you opened the reservoir's gate, it created a sluice that followed the switchback. Except it didn't neatly adhere to the curves, and all that surplus water ripped up plants, tore out bushes, and knocked down trees. This area has probably never seen that much water in a hundred thousand years. Bing and his boys received an early funeral under six feet of mud courtesy of Mr. Copland. Congratulations, you did them in without our help." He turned his head sideways, scrutinized his boss, and said, "Was it your intention to create a mudslide?"

"No," Adam emphatically said. "I just thought the water would slow them down, and then we would ambush them."

"Too many hombres for an ambush," Nick said. "Your mudslide was definitely better."

Cassandra said, "Now let's call that helicopter pilot and get to safety." A mudslide in this mountainous area was common—the area often has flash flooding and slides. What the ranger found abnormal was the broken window in the water reclamation building. He thought *damage from kids probably.*

CHAPTER 24

Los Angeles, CA
Wednesday, August 21, 2013

《《ℚ ℚ》》

The Monday morning edition of the *Palm Springs Review-Journal* had an article concerning the loss of lives in the Mt. San Jacinto flood and mudslide. The story was located on the front page, written by the paper's ace reporter, who termed the disaster a dire warning to all those naysayers about the dangers of climate change.

To ameliorate all the problems expressly precipitated by Copland, Adam notified Leonard Penansky to make an anonymous donation, regardless of cost, to the rebuilding of the Drury trail and concomitant damage.

Two weeks after the Paradise Hills imbroglio, Adam made a reservation for the Coplands to dine with Nick and Cassandra at the Elysium Terra Restaurant. Elysium is located in a small shopping center on the western side of Beverly Glen Boulevard, just south of Mulholland.

The cousins arrived at the restaurant fifteen minutes early, Cassandra entertained by the celebrity sightings, and Nick being grumpy Nick. Perplexed for two unpretentious individuals when the

Elysium hostess claimed there were no tables available, Nick pointed to empty tables clearly in view; Cassandra ordered two $25.00 glasses of champagne to relax her favorite relative.

Dressed elegantly causal, a quintessential desideratum to be hip in Los Angeles, Gabriela and Adam arrived punctually at 7:30. Original investors with Green in Elysium, the Copland's were greeted by a now gracious hostess, and the group were seated immediately at a table marked 'Reserved'.

"Never heard of this joint," said Nick.

Gabriela looked happy, and said, "No, it's just a nice local 'joint."

Predictably, the pervasive constancy of snobbishness extended to restaurants in the City of Angels. Elysium imitated the senseless snootiness established by Ma Maison in the 1970's, repeating Patrick Terrail's policy of having an unlisted phone number for his restaurant.

Adam ordered a favorite champagne, and not wasting time, Nick searched the menu for items suitable for his newest diet fad, the Paleo Diet. He located appropriate dishes, and the astonished look on Nick's face indicated he also located the 'Diamond Jim Brady' price per item.

To assuage any anxiety Nick felt, Adam piped in, "Tonight we're celebrating life. You're my guests so let's enjoy." Adam raised his glass. "Tonight we're celebrating life. Together we survived a nightmare, and the two of you wouldn't have been participant unless you were so loyal to me. L'Chaim."

They raised their flutes and toasted. Nick perhaps also toasting he didn't have to contribute for a Japanese Wagyu Rib Eye dinner costing the equivalent to 50 cups of his morning coffee at Peets. Drinking a lot, watching Nick eat a lot, the foursome's conversation inevitably turned to Paradise Hills.

Nick asked, "You know I got your text that you were located at the reservoir. I just need to know. What were your plans for Bing up there?"

Adam said, "I was winging it. I searched the gift store for a makeshift weapon, and later located snake venom in the employee's shed. Gabriela and I dipped the spears and porcupine quills in the poison. I thought if we pierced their skin, well, the venom would inflict them and make them sick. We never got the chance to implement the strategy because the rain came down so hard. That stopped us from my hit-and-run guerrilla approach."

"They would have slashed you in half," said Nick. "They had too many people and would have chased you down." It wasn't good news, but probably accurate. Cassandra nodded in agreement. Most importantly, the point was now moot.

Adam said, "I guess the law of unintended consequences worked in my favor for a change."

"Luckily, it's all over," Cassandra said. "Bing is gone, and life goes on."

"Sorry, but I strongly disagree," said Adam.

Looking inordinately perturbed, Gabriela said, "What in the world do you mean by that statement?"

"The problem with Bing was his love of, shall we say, the love of shiny objects," Adam said. "Shiny objects don't shine forever."

Gabriela said, "I have absolutely no idea what you're talking about."

"Look," Adam explained. "The term I used, shiny object, is just a metaphor for greed, avarice, love of money, whatever drives a person for filthy lucre. For me, investing is just making money. It's not personal, and I don't dislike my competitors. They're basically irrelevant to me." He stopped and took a sip of champagne.

Gabriela thought *They wouldn't be there if Adam hadn't started that dubious partnership with that reprobate Bing. In a way, Adam put everyone in harm's way. Gabriela thought about calling him out on the problem that engendered the confrontation. And realized that this public setting was not the right location to challenge his amoral rationalization.*

Adam continued. "There's more to money than simply acquiring more money. More specifically, money allows me to enjoy my wonderfully perfect life. Besides my love for you and Rebeccah, what do we enjoy? We love Tuesday evenings listening to classical music at the Hollywood Bowl combined with a picnic dinner. How about our safari in the Okavango Delta and a side trip to Sabi-Sabi at Krueger Park in South Africa? Your purchases of great painting and antiques require incredible sums of money. And I'm not complaining, I love our museum like treasures. I grew up dirt poor, and I can tell you life is benighted in poverty."

Adam stopped and ordered another bottle of wine, a 1982 Pichon Lalande. He then stated what would worry Gabriela the most. He said, "In history, a battle or war might end, but often what engendered the crisis remains. For example, the inequitable Versailles Treaty ended World War I, and eventually led directly to World War II. The unbelievable amount of money to be made in marijuana over the next decade means another schmuck will replace Bing. It's inevitable. For every ethical professional that decides to make an investment in the MMJ industry, there will be avaricious miscreants like Bing and Morrison. That's simply the way the world and business works. It always has been and always will be that way."

Swirling the '82 Bordeaux, viewing the ruby color of the wine, enjoying the aroma of the ripe rich fruit, Adam enjoyed the third flight of wines for the night. He looked at the three people at the table. He didn't want to belabor the point, and said, "Let's face the facts. I'm relatively young. My talent is selecting and operating a business." He chuckled and said, "Well, maybe running many firms.

But I know what I'm not. I'm not a professor teaching unappreciative students or a politician, or a . . ."

And he could have continued ad infinitum listing vocations that he wasn't interested in, or qualified for. Long ago he made a conscious choice how he wanted to live his life. Unlike the multitudes that grind out a meager living, happy just to subsist, Adam was grateful for the family he loved and the sumptuous existence he venerated.

A psychologist would have analyzed Adam's speech as doubling down on the MMJ business, and that the brush with death didn't chasten his desire to remain the King of MMJ in Los Angeles. Apparently Adam threw his hat in the ring with Honore de Balzac's adage that *Behind every great fortune there is a crime.*

* * *

Three thousand miles south of Los Angeles, a passenger on a Delta Airlines flight from LAX to Quito, Ecuador, was throwing a hissy fit. He wanted more wine as the flight was landing at Mariscal Sucre International Airport. In addition, he wouldn't listen to the stewardess who demanded for the fifth time for him to put away his vape.

The attendant complained to another passenger. "Everything this man does is wrong. He's fat and ugly but constantly flirts. He wants food we don't have on the plane. What in the world should I do?" She stopped, as the problem passenger stood and waved for her. "What am I supposed to do with him?"

While Rex, Ware, Humberto and his men were storming into a mudslide, Bing de Asis was creeping ever farther down the trail. By the time his "friends" were breathing their last breaths, Bing was at the gift store, buying a soda and chips.

Bing smiled smugly as he walked off the Delta flight. The heavy, humid air reminded him of home in the Philippines. Inside the terminal, Bing turned his head, looking for his local contact. Someday in the not so distant future, the little man would reappear in Los Angeles with a new Ecuadorian identity. And Pacifico Bing de Asis would never forget Adam Copland, or forgive him.

THE END OF BOOK 1

ACKNOWLEDGEMENTS:

I want to sincerely thank all of the following individuals:

Chuck Shepard - at Jewish World Review and his column titled 'Weird'

Nassim Nicholas Taleb

An Empire of Their Own, Neal Gabler

John Steele Gordon (Sep–Oct 1990). "The Country Club". American Heritage Magazine.

Peter Hecht at the Sacramento Bee

Numerous thoughts portrayed in daily columns of Victor Davis Hanson.

Bill Gross for the Kafka story

Matt Ridley's 2017 Keith Joseph Memorial Lecture, titled "The Case for Free-Market Anticapitalism."

Ilya Pestov

Burt Prelutsky

KMIR Vince Marino, Video Journalist for the desert bug infestation story.

for chinese culture - Professor Yang Chunmei is a professor of Chinese history and philosophy at Qufu Normal University.

Los Angeles Times articles. Daily Llama article, Reuters,

Montaigne Essays

Dr. Steven Hoefflin